UNTIL MIDNIGHT

OTHER TITLES BY LUANNE RICE

Last Night

If Anything Happens to Me

The Shadow Box

Last Day

Pretend She's Here

The Beautiful Lost

The Secret Language of Sisters

The Night Before

How We Started

The Lemon Orchard

Little Night

The Geometry of Sisters

The Letters (with Joseph Monninger)

The Silver Boat

Secrets of Paris

What Matters Most

Sandcastles

Summer's Child

The Deep Blue Sea for Beginners

Blue Moon

"Luanne Rice is the master of small towns with big secrets. With a deft touch, she draws us into a picture-postcard New England village, behind the closed doors of a well-loved home with its beautiful gardens and perfect family, only to expose the truths within. Surprising, powerful, a total page-turner."

—Lisa Scottoline, *New York Times* bestselling author of
Someone Knows

"In *Last Day*, Luanne Rice shows once again her unique gift for portraying the emotional landscape of a family. By adding a riveting thread of suspense, she proves beyond the shadow of a doubt that love and murder make brilliant bedfellows."

—Tess Gerritsen, *New York Times* bestselling author of
The Shape of Night

"*Last Day*, by Luanne Rice, shines with its brilliant plot about four women friends, their families and loves, and, shockingly, a murder. Rice's writing is flawless and fast, her characters are like the women I have coffee with, and the desire, violence, and betrayals shock me and remind me of Liane Moriarty's *Big Little Lies*."

—Nancy Thayer, *New York Times* bestselling author of *Surfside Sisters*

"A dark family history. A deeply flawed marriage. The complicated tangle of the ties that bind. Luanne Rice writes with authenticity and empathy, unflinchingly exploring her characters and diving into the shadowy spaces where they hide their secrets. Like all great stories, *Last Day* is a compulsive, twisting mystery dwelling inside a searing portrait of what drives us, as riveting as it is human and true."

—Lisa Unger, *New York Times* bestselling author of *The Stranger Inside*

"A brutal murder, a failed marriage, secret lovers, and enough suspects to fill a room. The truth lies somewhere between betrayal and love. A compelling mystery you won't put down or solve until the final pages."
—Robert Dugoni, *New York Times* and Amazon Charts bestselling author of the Tracy Crosswhite series

"I've long loved Luanne Rice for her trademark elegant style and her deep understanding of familial relationships, and she brings these superpowers with her as she delves into suspense. *Last Day* is a true page-turner, peopled by characters I care deeply about, with an ending I never saw coming."
—Joshilyn Jackson, *New York Times* and *USA Today* bestselling author of *Never Have I Ever*

Home Fires

Dance with Me

Stone Heart

The Edge of Winter

Light of the Moon

Last Kiss

Follow the Stars Home

Firefly Beach

Summer Light

True Blue

Safe Harbor

The Perfect Summer

The Secret Hour

Silver Bells

Summer of Roses

Beach Girls

Dream Country

Cloud Nine

Crazy in Love

Angels All Over Town

UNTIL MIDNIGHT

LUANNE RICE

THOMAS & MERCER

Text copyright © 2026 by Luanne Rice
All rights reserved.

Published by Thomas & Mercer, Seattle

www.apub.com

Amazon, the Amazon logo, and Thomas & Mercer are trademarks of Amazon.com, Inc., or its affiliates.

ISBN-13: 9781662526633 (hardcover)
ISBN-13: 9781662526640 (paperback)
ISBN-13: 9781662526664 (digital)

Cover design by Ploy Siripant
Cover image: © Stan Tess / Alamy; © muratart, © underworld / Shutterstock

Printed in the United States of America

First edition

To Deborah Goodrich Royce, with much love and admiration

PROLOGUE

The Day of the Wedding

Saturday, July 3; 6:00 a.m.

It was a perfect day for the wedding. The Ocean House gleamed yellow in the early-morning July sun. The sea sparkled, the blue hydrangeas were in full bloom, the scent of beach roses filled the air, and the large white tent, erected yesterday afternoon for this evening's wedding reception, shaded the grass beside the croquet lawn. This was the quiet hour, when the early-rising hotel guests were having their first coffee. The only sound was the crash of waves, their white-frilled edges spilling onto East Beach.

Most of the wedding guests were staying in the legendary hotel. She was staying there, too, with a man who thought he was her boyfriend. They had gathered for last night's rehearsal dinner in the Harbour Room. She had no doubt that the dinner was seared into their minds; thanks to her, they would remember it forever.

They had checked in to rooms and suites with views of the Atlantic Ocean or Watch Hill's sailboat-studded harbor. A mansard-roofed tower, with pediment-topped porthole windows, crowned the hotel. The American flag flew from a flagpole on the very top. The tower contained a magnificent suite—*theirs*, not hers—but she tried not to think about that.

Maybe if she had taken a different path in life, happiness could be hers. She had known love, she couldn't deny that, but the life she had chosen guaranteed it wouldn't last. Here she was, in a house diagonally across the street from the hotel. She called it the Finishing School, to continue a tradition.

Other Watch Hill houses had names like Bluffside, Seawinds, First Light, and Grey Ledge. The names were sometimes painted above the front door or etched into stone pillars at the ends of private drives. But the Finishing School was the name of this house and others in the network, and it did not appear anywhere on the properties. The Finishing School wasn't a place; it was a state of mind.

The hundred-year-old house was charming. Its white cedar shingles had been silvered by a century of salt air. It had white shutters with anchor cutouts, window boxes full of coral-pink geraniums and deep-blue lobelia. Best of all, there was a view of the Ocean House from the upstairs bedroom.

So much planning had gone into this day, down to the exact detail. The invitations had been printed on Crane medium-weight paper. Her mouth twitched—a tiny smile—at the fact that there was one small typo. Well, not really a typo—she had inserted it. She deserved to claim a little happiness, didn't she?

She read the invitation now:

KATE WOODWARD & CONOR REID
SATURDAY, JULY 3
CEREMONY 6:30 P.M.
WATCH HILL CHAPEL
BELLES WILL RING!
DINNER AND DANCING TO FOLLOW
OCEAN HOUSE

By 6:30 p.m., the sun would have gone around the point, and the summer day would start to cool down a bit. The idea of an evening wedding was to give guests the chance to enjoy the Ocean House for the entire day: go to the beach, take a sail, relax at the spa, stroll past the harbor on Bay Street, or go golfing at Winnapaug with Conor and his brother, Tom.

She drifted toward the bedroom closet to look at the wedding dress. It had been made in Italy by Alexander McQueen, a sleek column of white crepe with a crystal neckline and a trumpet silhouette. She thought of the time-honored traditions: something old, something new, something borrowed, something blue.

Old was the plain silver ring. New was the dress. Borrowed was the veil—a family heirloom, never to be owned by any single person but, rather, passed down through the generations.

She stared at the dress, then took it off the hanger and carried it to the window. She gazed over at the Ocean House. The enormous white sailcloth tent glistened in the morning light, and festive medieval-style banners flew from the peaks. The hotel verandah was starting to fill with guests having their morning coffee and croissants. She stared up at the stately yellow tower and tried not to think about the people inside. She would have given anything to trade places with the bride.

Life was nothing but a series of lessons and choices. She had been the pupil, and then she had accepted the challenge of becoming one of the teachers. She thought of the boat and of all the other places where lessons had been learned and where she had started to pass them on to the new pupils. She thought of the torn canvas—the ruined painting. She wondered whether she might be insane, but she knew she wasn't.

This was their fault, not hers.

They were all in the Ocean House, getting ready for the wedding. She stared out the window at it now.

The tower reminded her of the top of a wedding cake, a symbol of the way life builds upon itself and how love reaches for the sky. There was one single suite in the tower. She pictured the spiral staircase, the warm wood varnished like the interior of a yacht, and the view of three states from those upper windows. She thought of the tower, the wedding cake, and she was filled with overwhelming emotion. Her eyes stung with tears, and her heart burned with hatred.

She wondered what was going on up in the tower. Love wasn't always what it should be. It wasn't always fair. She was trying to right the wrong; she deserved it after all she had been through. This was the day she would make him pay.

She couldn't resist putting on the wedding dress. She let her robe slide to the floor, and then she slipped the dress over her head. The white crepe felt cool to her skin; the weight of the crystal-beaded neckline caressed her chest.

"Beauty," she said out loud, looking at herself in the full-length mirror. "Belle," she said, staring into her own eyes.

Downstairs, the front door swished open and shut. Her heart sped up. She wasn't expecting anyone. For a minute she considered running into the bathroom and hiding so they couldn't see the dress, but then she figured it was meant to be, so she stood right where she was.

She stared into the oval cheval glass next to the bedroom door as she listened to the footsteps on the stairs. She had no idea what they would say. She hoped it was him, not her. If it was him, he would put his arms around her from behind, turn her around, kiss her, and tell her she was his, that she could never leave him, leave *them*. The moment was electric, more frightening than exciting, and she closed her eyes, steeling herself for his embrace.

The touch felt like a caress, like the gentle tickle of a fingertip tracing her throat. It didn't hurt, but it startled her, and she opened her eyes and looked in the mirrored glass. It struck her, how odd it was to see the white wedding dress turning crimson. Red spray pulsed out of her neck in time with her heartbeat, and she lifted her hand to try to stop it.

Her gaze in the mirror met the familiar face, and she gasped because it wasn't him at all. She saw the curved blade. She saw rage in those eyes she knew and loved better than anyone else in the world.

Her hand cupped her throat; the blood felt warm. The dress was scarlet now. She fell to her knees, then toppled over. She lay in a patch of sunlight streaming through the open window. She stared at the wall. She remembered how they could hear the train whistles and the ferry horns from their street; she remembered holding his hand.

It's true, she thought: At the end, your life flashes before your eyes.

Her voice was garbled, but she said a name out loud anyway. It was a name full of love and protection and devotion. She whispered it through her own blood as she died.

"Conor."

1

The Night Before the Wedding

Friday, July 2; 5:30 p.m.

When it came down to considering venues for Kate Woodward's wedding to Conor Reid, there had been only one choice: the Ocean House. Conor had proposed to Kate the winter before last, right here on a snowy terrace overlooking East Beach, during a record-breaking blizzard. As if to balance the meteorological scales, this weekend's weather was as perfect as summer in Watch Hill could deliver.

Kate hadn't seen Conor since right after breakfast, when he had left to go golfing with Tom and a few friends. The rehearsal dinner was at 7:00 p.m., just an hour and a half from now. She had thought he would be back hours ago, but there was no sign of him.

Friends and family who hadn't checked in yet had started to arrive, so she thought maybe he had run into one of them. She changed into the pale-blue shift she would wear to dinner, and she walked through the hotel, looking for him, starting in the Club Room.

This room embraced guests with its warmth, its wooden walls lacquered to resemble a yacht's interior, banquettes flanked with red leather chairs, a welcoming fireplace, and museum-quality art in gilded frames. The French doors opened onto a wide terrace, and Kate felt the cool sea breeze wafting in. Brian Goldrick—tall, with close-cropped white hair and a warm glint in his blue eyes—stood behind the bar. He greeted her.

"It's starting," he said, smiling. "The wedding weekend."

"I can't believe it's finally here," she said.

"We're all set for tonight," he said.

"Thank you so much, Brian," she said. She and Conor had chosen the Harbour Room, just across the hall, for their rehearsal dinner. They had gotten to know Brian over the years, and they always loved seeing him. He had told her that he was creating a signature cocktail just for them, as a wedding gift.

"I hope Conor gets back soon," she said. "He has to change for dinner."

"He came in with his brother a little while ago," Brian said.

"He did?" she asked, taken aback that Conor had returned from golf and come here instead of finding her upstairs.

"They tried out my concoction. Would you like me to make you one?"

"No, I want to be surprised. Do you have a name for it?" she asked, unsettled about Conor.

"That's going to be the *real* surprise," he said with a wicked smile. "I'll tell you at the dinner."

"I can't wait," Kate said, and she walked across the room and stood in front of a painting. "You still have it up?"

"Yes," he said. "But don't worry, it will be all wrapped and ready in time for the party."

As the owner of the Woodward-Lathrop Gallery in Black Hall, Connecticut, Kate always studied the art wherever she went. The Ocean House had a first-rate permanent collection; there were also temporary exhibitions of works on loan from an excellent gallery in town.

She gazed at a stunning luminist painting by James Suydam, done in 1860. It was a night scene of East Beach and the Watch Hill lighthouse. The moon glowed eerily through white fog, casting a silver web on the dark sea, barely illuminating the shadowed beach path.

"Did you notice if Conor looked at it when he came in?" Kate asked.

"I didn't," Brian said.

Kate glanced at him. "I thought he might have guessed."

"No," Brian said. "And I didn't say a word. I know how to keep a secret."

"You do," Kate said, and Brian chuckled. Every time she and Conor walked past the Suydam in its intricately carved gold frame, Conor paused to stare at it. He liked art well enough, and Kate knew he indulged her passion for it. So it intrigued her to see him so entranced by this painting. She knew what East Beach meant to him.

It was the site of a crime that had become his most important case. He had solved the murder and brought justice to the family—people both he and Kate had come to love. Because of that connection, Kate had spoken to the Ocean House's curator so she could buy the painting of East Beach for Conor, as her wedding gift to him.

"Did he say where he was going?" she asked.

"No," Brian said. "I didn't see them leave."

"Thanks, Brian," she said, and continued her search.

Out on the verandah, she spotted several of their guests at tables overlooking the sea. Judge Michael Reid—Conor's uncle—was sitting with his wife, Anne. Several pals of Kate's from the New York art world were sharing a platter of Ninigret oysters and a bottle of Veuve Clicquot champagne. They beckoned her over, but she just waved. There was a large table of three Coast Guard officers that she recognized as Tom's colleagues. Also at the table were Rhode Island State Police detectives Joe Harrigan and Garrett Milne.

Conor was a detective on the Major Crime Squad of the Connecticut State Police, and Joe was his Rhode Island counterpart. Garrett was Joe's partner. Whenever a case concerned boats or coastal waters, they coordinated with the USCG enforcement division, escalating up to CGIS—Tom's Coast Guard Investigative Service team. Two

Decembers ago they had all worked together on the Maddie Morrison case, the murder of a young mother on the path to East Beach.

The investigation had been intense, and Conor and Joe had become very good friends. Garrett less so. But when Kate and Conor were making up the guest list, Conor had said that Garrett kept hinting he wanted to be invited. He said that he had never stayed at the Ocean House before and that his new girlfriend was really pushing for it.

But Kate thought it was something else: Conor and Joe were tight senior detectives, and Garrett wanted to be part of their inner circle. She felt gratitude toward him for helping Conor in that important case. She didn't want him to feel left out, so he was on the list. Joe, long divorced, had decided to come alone. Both Kate and Conor had the feeling he was hoping to meet someone at the wedding. Garrett's date was nowhere in sight.

The white tent, where they would have their reception tomorrow, had been installed that afternoon; it rose beside the croquet lawn like a fairy-tale castle. Directly across the street was Watch Hill Chapel, where they would say their vows. Kate's heart skipped so hard she had to catch her breath. Was she having wedding nerves? She was forty-two, and she had never been married before. Conor was six years older, and this was his first marriage too. They had each had their own reasons for staying single, but over the last few years, they had managed to break through to each other.

She looked at her cell phone—nothing. He hadn't replied to her last three texts. Even when he was on a case, he would text or call to let her know what was going on. She texted him again.

Where are you? I'm looking for you.

No reply. She texted her assistant, Maeve Longacre. She'd brought Maeve and her boyfriend along to help with last-minute wedding details.

Have you seen Conor?

No, I'm with Suzanne, just finishing up the table assignments.

Suzanne? Kate texted back, wondering who that was.

Calligrapher, helping out.

OK, Kate wrote, surprised by the name Suzanne because she could have sworn she'd seen a contract with someone else.

"Hey, Auntie," her niece Samantha Lathrop said, coming up from behind and giving Kate a hug. Sam was the daughter of Kate's late sister, Beth. She was twenty-one, tall, with long strawberry-blond hair. Kate had been like a mother to her after Beth died. Although Sam had been a wild child in her teens, she had just graduated from college.

"Aunts and nieces," Kate said, seeing that Sam was with their friend Hadley Cooke and her seven-year-old niece CeCe, all dressed for dinner. Kate, Sam, Hadley, and CeCe were members of a club no one would ever want to belong to—sisters and daughters of murdered women. It had made the four of them very close.

"What are you up to?" Sam asked.

"Looking for your uncle-to-be," Kate said.

"CeCe and I are going to walk down to the harbor and back before dinner," Sam said. "Maybe there's just enough time for a ride on the merry-go-round."

"Is that okay, Aunt Hadley?" CeCe asked.

"You bet," Hadley said.

"Let's all go," Kate said, thinking they might find Conor and Tom—a Coast Guard commander who could never stay far away from boats, and the harbor was full of them.

The four of them set off from the hotel. They walked along Bluff Avenue, passing the path to East Beach, where CeCe's mother had been killed. Both Kate and Hadley watched for the little girl's reaction; CeCe didn't say anything, but she resolutely turned her head away, picking up her pace and walking straight ahead.

They turned downhill on Larkin Road. CeCe grabbed Sam's hand and began to run toward the merry-go-round. Every mooring in the bright-blue harbor was occupied. Bay Street was crowded with visitors browsing in shops, getting ice cream at St. Clair Annex, waiting for a table at the Olympia Tearoom, or strolling along the seawall.

Kate scanned the waterfront for Conor but was distracted by *Aphrodite*. The seventy-four-foot yacht was a treasure—built in 1937. She had a gleaming black hull, topsides of mahogany brightwork, and—to Kate's mind, the sleekest design of any boat on the East Coast or beyond. It was a floating work of art.

Sam paid for CeCe to ride her favorite painted horse at the merry-go-round as the organ music began. Watch Hill proudly claimed the carousel as the oldest in the country; it had been built in 1867, and Kate thought CeCe and Sam looked appropriately old fashioned in their flowing yellow dresses.

As Kate walked toward *Aphrodite*, she spotted Conor near the dock at the far end of the Bay Street's curving bulkhead. He was sitting beside a woman on a bench by the seawall. Kate saw the way they were leaning into each other with intimate familiarity. Their shoulders were touching, their heads bent together, as they looked at something on a cell phone. Kate felt taken aback by the emotional intensity between them.

"Hello," Kate said when they got closer.

"Kate!" Conor said, sounding startled. The woman smiled and stood. She had straight blond hair with long bangs that framed her oval face. Freckles dusted her nose, and lines creased her forehead and bracketed her cheeks. Her white sundress fluttered in the breeze. Kate guessed that she was about the same age as Conor or a little older.

"Hello, Kate," the woman said. "I've heard so much about you."

"This is Belinda, Garrett's girlfriend," Conor said.

"Nice to meet you," Kate said. She introduced Hadley.

"Belinda and I grew up next door to each other," Conor said.

"That's amazing!" Kate said. "Wow, how cool to reconnect."

"That's what we were just saying," Belinda said. "And now it's memory lane. Good old New London. Every so often, I drive down our old street. His house looks the same as it always did—I was just showing him pictures." She scrolled through her phone and started to hand it to Kate. Kate noticed that she wore glittery turquoise nail polish and had a thin silver ring on her pinkie finger.

Kate reached for the phone, but then it buzzed with a text, and Belinda drew it back.

"Oh, it's Garrett," Belinda said. "Wondering where I am. I'd better go meet him. The Ocean House is so beautiful! Thank you for having us!"

"We're glad you could come," Kate said.

"See you at dinner!" Belinda said. "Kate, we can talk more later. I have so many childhood stories about Conor and Tom."

"I'd love to hear them," Kate said.

Belinda gave her and Conor quick hugs, then turned and headed up the hill toward the Ocean House.

"I'm going to get CeCe and head back to the hotel," Hadley said, glancing in the opposite direction at the merry-go-round. "I think she has gone around enough times. I'll get her and Sam, and we'll meet you at dinner. Are you excited?"

"Just a little," Kate said.

Kate looked at Conor when Hadley left, waiting for him to say something. She tried to read his expression, but he was gazing past her, at all the boats in the harbor. Was he deep in thought or just avoiding her eyes?

"What was that about?" Kate asked.

He didn't reply, and she saw that he was staring past *Aphrodite*. Sunlight danced on the water's surface, glancing off the vessel's polished black hull and bronze fittings. A gray inflatable dinghy was heading toward shore from out in the mooring field.

"Here comes Tom," Conor said, gesturing. "He can't stay off the water, even when he's off duty."

"What was Belinda saying?" Kate asked. "It looked intense."

"She's nostalgic about the old days," Conor said. "I was completely surprised to see her."

"Why didn't you mention that Garrett was bringing her to the wedding?"

Conor put his arm around Kate. "Because I didn't put it together."

"What about her last name?" Kate asked, feeling unsettled. She tried to remember what Garrett had told them for the calligraphed place cards. Then she had it. "Tyler. Belinda Tyler?"

"She was Belinda Quinn back when we were kids," he said. "She married a guy named Tyler."

"They must have gotten divorced," Kate said. "Since now she's dating Garrett."

"She told me she's a widow. Her husband died years ago."

"Oh no," Kate said. Maybe that explained the feeling she had gotten, seeing Conor and Belinda deep in conversation. "That's so sad. How did he die?"

But before Conor could answer, they saw Tom draw even with the dinghy dock. He threw the line around a cleat and walked up the weathered wooden ramp toward them.

"Nice," Conor said. "Half an hour to our rehearsal dinner, and you're covered with salt spray."

"I'll take the quickest shower in history," Tom said. "I'm used to it, from being at sea."

"Coastie," Conor said.

"Cop," Tom said.

Kate loved the way the brothers teased each other. They were both in different arms of law enforcement, but they often shared cases. They could be merciless about whose work was more important. Tom was one year older. They both had brown hair and bright-blue eyes. Conor's wavy hair was longer than Tom's military cut, a fact Tom gave him grief about.

The three of them started up the hill. A navy-blue pickup sped past them, and Conor put out his arm to keep Kate from being hit.

"Whoa," he said, staring as the truck turned into a driveway across the street from the hotel.

"Someone's in a hurry," Tom said.

Kate saw Conor watching to see who the driver was, but she tugged on his arm, and they kept walking. When they got to the hotel, the valets greeted them, and so did the entire lobby staff. Kate and Conor had become regulars here, often visiting Hadley and CeCe, who had moved permanently into the Sea Garden Suite. Everyone was excited about the wedding. Kate knew how much the Ocean House staff loved CeCe. She had become one of their own after her mother's murder, and many of them had told Kate how much it meant to them, how touched they were that Kate had asked CeCe to be her flower girl.

Tom took the elevator up to his room, to shower before he and his wife, Jackie, joined them. Conor and Kate walked down the lobby staircase to the Bemelmans Gallery, a serene spot where they could have a minute alone. The gallery walls were painted Buxton blue, to echo the ocean, and they were covered with the largest private collection of works by Ludwig Bemelmans in the world. The owners displayed them so everyone could enjoy the charming and playful art.

Kate gazed at the illustrations of Madeline—the heroine of a favorite childhood book—and at the *Farewell to the Ritz* series of drawings, made from the artist's experience at the Ritz in New York. They brought back memories of dates she had had at Bemelmans Bar at the Carlyle, with a series of mostly forgettable boyfriends. No one had really mattered to her until Conor.

"Okay," she said, looking into Conor's blue eyes. She knew him so well, and she could tell he was shaken about something. "Tell me what's going on."

"Nothing. It was just strange to see Belinda after all this time."

"What was she showing you? You looked very serious."

"You sound jealous," he said as if it were a joke, but he wasn't smiling.

"Should I be?" Kate asked.

"Of course not," he said. "We were neighbors. She was the girl next door, and she moved away when we were just kids."

"You looked awfully close, there on the bench."

Conor put his arms around her and held her very tight. Then he gave her that devilish Irish grin that always turned her inside out. "That wasn't close," he said. "*This* is close." He kissed her, softly at first, then as if he wanted to take her upstairs to their suite.

"Excuse me," a voice said.

Kate and Conor broke apart, and she saw a young woman standing there. She looked about Sam's age—twenty-one or so—and she had dark-blond hair, a golden tan, and startling blue eyes. She wore a maxi dress with white and indigo flowers that complemented her eyes. Kate noticed that her fingernail polish was turquoise, the same color as Belinda's.

"I'm Suzanne," she said.

"Hi," Kate said. Then, with a slight question in her voice, "The calligrapher?"

"Yes. I'm so sorry to interrupt," Suzanne said, sounding anxious. Her eyes lingered on Conor, then looked away. "All your guests have arrived. Maeve asked me to find you."

"Thanks," Kate said. Suzanne nodded and ran upstairs ahead of them.

Kate's chest tightened; something about the girl—not just her nail polish—had unsettled her, and the feelings that had swept over when she'd seen Conor with Belinda rushed back. She grabbed Conor's hand.

In that moment, she had a powerful urge to skip the party, to be alone with him. She had a bizarre premonition that if they went to the dinner, everything would change.

"Conor," she said. "Do you . . ."

He waited for her to finish the question, but she couldn't, because the confusion she'd felt down at the harbor was still with her; she didn't know exactly what she wanted to ask. She looked into his eyes and steadied herself.

"Never mind. Everything's fine," she said.

"Better than fine," he said.

She and Conor walked upstairs. Faith, the harpist who played in the lobby, was strumming "Love Story" by Taylor Swift. It made Kate feel better as she and Conor approached the Harbour Room. And as soon as she and Conor walked through the door, and she saw the beaming faces of so many people she loved, she forgot all about the weirdness she felt, and she smiled back—at the crowd and then at Conor. And she and Conor took their seats, and tomorrow they would be married, and everything was fine, better than fine.

2

Kate sat between Conor and Tom at the rehearsal dinner. Friends and family filled the long table. The chef had outdone himself, sending out hot buttered lobster dumplings, pan-seared day boat scallops, wild mushroom ravioli, a roasted rack of Australian lamb, and, fresh off the grill, harpooned Block Island swordfish.

At the very start of dinner, Brian had served his cocktail creation, with a mocktail version to those who preferred it without gin and champagne: St-Germain elderflower, lemon, clear honey, and one long, paper-thin twist of cucumber. He presented a glass to Kate first. The ingredients were local and fresh; the slice of cucumber, twisted around the inside of the glass, gave the drink an alluring pearlescence, a white opacity—like coastal fog.

"It's delicious," she said. "And now you have to tell me what it's called. You said the name was part of the surprise."

"That's right," Brian said. "Can't you guess?"

She sipped again, thinking of the possibilities. But then he gestured toward the back of the room, where he had placed a large package wrapped in white paper and tied with a black grosgrain ribbon.

"The same as the title of the painting?" she asked in a low voice, so Conor wouldn't hear.

He nodded, beaming.

She felt delighted. The painting that would be her wedding gift to Conor—James Suydam's depiction of moonlight and the lighthouse through fog. It hinted at anticipation, of waiting, of the evening's romantic mystery, and it had the most perfect title: *Foggy Night*. And now, looking at the cocktail, she saw exactly what Brian had been going for; he had absolutely captured the essence of the painting. It was so thoughtful, she grabbed his hand and squeezed.

"Foggy Night," he said. "In honor of your wedding."

Then he filled glasses for the entire table, and he and the wait-staff served them. Kate sat back, surveilling the table, feeling so happy. Conor and Tom's aunt and uncle—Anne and Mike Reid—were speaking with Joe, Garrett, and Belinda. Mike was a retired Rhode Island Superior Court judge, and both Joe and Garrett had testified in cases before him.

"That's a sight you don't see every day," Conor said, leaning close to Kate. "Cops socializing with the judiciary."

"Looks as if they're all enjoying themselves," Kate said before sipping her drink.

"Uncle Mike loves holding forth," Conor said. "He's competing with Bernard for the most booming voice."

Kate smiled. Bernard Lafond, CeCe's father, had flown in from Los Angeles and was lamenting how hard it had been to take time off from shooting his hit series, *Border Saints*. The director had been furious, but as the star, Bernard got what he wanted. Bernard had brought a new girlfriend, Miranda, and she was leaning into him and laughing in all the right places.

Kate noticed Suzanne bustling around. She seemed to be making sure the guests had everything they needed. She spoke to the judge and his wife, then Belinda, Sam, and Hadley. Then Kate felt perplexed at this "hostess" she'd never met before. She'd have to ask Maeve exactly how Suzanne had come to work at her rehearsal dinner.

Toasts were made. Some were romantic, some were funny.

Bernard, with his shaggy white mane and actor's theatricality, slugged down his cocktail and asked Brian to bring him a glass of his favorite burgundy. Brian obliged, and Bernard stood, cleared his throat, raised his glass of Gevrey-Chambertin, and said in his thick French accent, his deep actor's voice:

"To our fine couple, Kate and Conor. Nothing less than this poem by William Butler Yeats will do to celebrate them:

> Wine comes in at the mouth
> And love comes in at the eye . . ."

He finished reciting the poem, bowed his head, and nodded in showy humility at the applause. Kate saw Conor looking not at Bernard, but at CeCe. Bernard was a mostly absent father. She knew that Conor disliked him for that reason—because he loved CeCe so much. CeCe was beaming, proud of her father.

Tom and Jackie stood together. Kate had expected a bantering, teasing toast from Tom, but instead she watched Conor's brother's eyes well up.

"Ah, Con," he said. "I've watched you all through life, seen you solve the hardest cases, win medals and awards, rise through the ranks. You're tops in all you do, but one thing has been missing." He paused, put his arm around Jackie. "Love. Like what I have for Jackie. And now you've found Kate." He looked at Kate. "Kate, we've loved you from the moment we met you. You're our family, and we're yours."

"Thanks, Tom," Conor said. "What you said means a lot."

"It should," Tom said. "I was up all night writing it."

"No wonder you look like hell today, you didn't get any sleep . . ."

The brothers kept at it until dessert and coffee were served: strawberry shortcake, pignoli olive oil cake with dark chocolate and brown butter, chocolate profiteroles, and macarons. Kate walked toward the door, where Brian had placed the painting. He had arranged to have someone from the boutique wrap it, and she planned to give it to Conor right here, at the dinner, in front of the people they loved most. Suzanne stood beside the painting as if guarding it.

"I am so excited," Maeve said, coming to stand beside Kate. Her boyfriend, Lincoln Adams, was with her. He had met Maeve at the gallery—his father, Crispin, was one of Kate's biggest collectors and had become a friend.

"He's going to love it," Lincoln said.

"He is," Kate said.

"It's so romantic," Maeve said, giving Kate a hug.

Kate couldn't have a better assistant or protégé. Maeve had started working at the gallery straight out of college a year ago; she had caught on fast, learning both the business and Kate's taste.

"Would you like Maeve and me to carry it, so you can give it to him now?" Lincoln asked.

"A grand presentation!" Maeve said.

Kate glanced at the table and saw that Conor was still talking to Tom.

"I'll do it," Kate said. "As soon as he sits down."

She saw Conor glance over and smile at her. She took that as a sign and began to lift the painting. It was large and heavy, but she was used to moving art around at the gallery. As she leaned down to pick it up, she saw Conor's eyes widen at the sight of Belinda, who was walking toward Kate.

"Kate?" Belinda asked.

She was wearing the same white sundress she'd had on when she'd been down at the seawall with Conor. It suddenly struck Kate as odd, thoughtless—to wear white to another woman's wedding weekend.

"Hi, Belinda," Kate said.

"I'd love to talk to you," Belinda said.

"Me too," Kate said. "That would be great. A little later?"

"No, now."

Kate was alarmed by Belinda's sharp tone.

"Is everything okay?" Kate asked.

"Conor probably told you I'm called 'Belle,'" Belinda said, her voice a strange, disturbing singsong.

"No, he didn't," Kate said.

"*Beauty and the Beast*," Belinda said.

"What?" Kate asked.

"They were lovers," Belinda said. "Beast and Belle. Belle was Beauty's name, you know. And my name for my lover is 'Beast'—he is one, you know. A beast." She laughed. "Though I doubt he's let you see that. He saves that for me." She gazed at Kate, watching for a reaction, but Kate was frozen. Was she actually hearing this?

"Excuse me, Belinda," Kate said. "I have to give this to Conor."

"No! You're going to listen," Belinda said. "Beast and Belle couldn't stop. The only word for it is *passion*—passion beyond your wildest dreams. Well, and love, of course. Love to the death. They have eternal love—nothing can ever kill it. Do you believe in fairy tales? Ones that start in childhood?"

Kate took a step back. There had to be something wrong with Belinda. Was she drunk or high? She couldn't believe that this was actually happening, that this person she had never heard of until a few hours ago was standing in front of her, talking about passion and fairy tales. She noticed how the deep lines in Belinda's face pulled her mouth down, as if a frown were her natural expression, as if she had spent her life unhappy.

Belinda blinked and looked away. She seemed to lose her train of thought, then returned her gaze to Kate. Her expression intensified.

"I have a great memory," Belinda said. "It's one of my superpowers. When we were little, in first grade, Conor said he wanted to marry me. It was after he broke his arm. I was the first person to sign his cast, you know. Our parents took us to Ocean Beach, and when we went on the little train, he proposed. I still wear the ring." She held out her hand, and Kate saw the glittery turquoise nail polish that she had noticed earlier, the tiny silver ring on her pinkie finger.

"Lots of little boys want to marry little girls," Kate said, trying to keep her voice steady. "They grow out of it."

"Some don't," Belinda said. She stared hard at Kate, smiling with wild eyes.

Kate stood still, without expression, breathing calmly, knowing Belinda was unhinged—that was clear. She and Conor would laugh about it later—he would reassure her that there was nothing to worry about. She wondered how Garrett could have wound up dating this crazy person, how he could have brought her to the rehearsal dinner. One thing was for sure: There was no way she was coming to the wedding.

"There's something I have to show you," Belinda said, holding her phone out.

Kate turned away. She told herself that nothing on earth could make her look at that phone, but Belinda grabbed her arm with one hand and shoved the phone into Kate's face with the other.

"Look!" Belinda said, her voice rising, her tone aggressive. "Look at this, now!"

"Kate, is everything okay?" Maeve asked, stepping forward. "Should I get Conor?"

"Yes, get Conor," Belinda said.

Kate didn't want to give Belinda the satisfaction of looking at her phone—she had told herself she wouldn't—but suddenly she couldn't stop herself. Her gaze was pulled to the screen, where she saw a photo of Belinda holding an infant.

"Our baby," Belinda said.

"What?" Kate asked, her head buzzing, making her feel as if she might pass out.

"Our daughter. Conor's and mine," Belinda said. "Look at her eyes."

Kate stared at the phone. The photo was a selfie; Belinda had been balancing the baby while holding her camera, and the picture had blurred. Kate couldn't tell how long ago it had been taken, although she had a fleeting impression of Belinda looking very young. But every detail fell away except for one: The baby had blue eyes.

"Conor's blue eyes," Belinda said firmly, loud enough for everyone in the room to hear. "And he knows all about her. Even if he tries to tell you he doesn't—believe me, he knows."

Conor bolted around the table. Garrett was right behind him.

"Belinda," Garrett said. "What the hell?"

Conor didn't bother with words. He was very quiet. He stepped between Kate and Belinda. He reached for the phone, but Belinda yanked it away so violently that she lost her balance and stumbled backward into the wrapped package. Kate heard the antique gold frame crack and the painting's canvas tear.

Garrett crouched beside Belinda, who had struck her head when she fell. He seemed to be checking her over, making sure she wasn't badly hurt. Kate heard her whimpering, but she could only look at Conor.

"Is it true?" she asked.

"Kate," Conor said.

"It is true, isn't it?" she asked. The look on his face, and the fact that he didn't answer, told her what she had known the minute she saw those blue eyes.

Then she turned and walked away, out of the room, away from the life she had thought was hers.

3

Friday, July 2; 10:00 p.m.

Conor stood still, his heart thudding out of his chest. He stared at Belinda crumpled on the floor. What had she just done? He had only heard part of it, but he had seen the devastation in Kate's eyes. He started to run after Kate—he would catch up to her, hold her, make everything go back to the way it was supposed to be. But Tom grabbed his arm and held him back.

"Conor, hold on," Tom said. "Take a minute."

"I have to get to her," Conor said. His face felt hot.

"Not yet," Tom said sternly.

Conor saw shock in Tom's eyes, and he knew how he must look. Throughout his police career, Conor had broken up many fights. He had been called to the sites of countless domestic disturbances, and he had always done what Tom was doing right now: separating the couple until they could cool down.

Their uncle Mike was right behind them, and he took Conor's arm. As a judge, he was no stranger to altercations.

"Let's take a walk," Mike said.

They crossed the lobby and stepped onto the verandah. It was bustling with people enjoying the summer evening, but Conor barely saw them as Tom and Mike led him down the steps. The breeze was cool, the sky perfectly clear. Stars blazed in the cloudless sky. He looked over his shoulder, up at the top of the hotel, at the tower, where he and Kate were staying. The round windows glowed from the lights inside the suite.

Tom tried to steer him along the walkway toward the beach, but Conor pulled back. "I'm fine," Conor said. "You don't have to worry."

"You're the calmest one in the family," Mike said. "Unflappable. So when you lose your cool, we're going to worry. What's going on?"

Conor stared at his uncle, his father's youngest brother—the last Reid of that generation. The Honorable Michael Reid had presided over many high-profile Rhode Island cases; he was often urged to run for political office. He had political and legal clout, and he was well known throughout the state. To Conor and Tom, he was just Uncle Mike.

"I know you're trying to help, but I have to talk to Kate," Conor said.

"First, you're going to talk to us," Mike said. "What was all that back there?"

Conor just stared at him.

"Why was that woman yelling at Kate?" Tom asked, as if Conor needed prompting.

"Didn't you recognize her?" Conor asked.

"No, should I have?" Tom said.

"Tom, that's Belinda Quinn," Conor said.

"From next door? Montauk Avenue?" Tom asked.

"Yeah," Conor said.

"Wow, *that* girl?" Tom asked. "Everyone at school thought she died."

"There were a lot of rumors," Conor said. He thought back, remembering how one day Belinda had been their neighbor, and one day she was gone. Not long after that, the rest of the Quinn family moved away.

"Never mind the past," Mike said. "Let's discuss what just happened—why did you shove her?"

"I didn't," Conor said. "That was all an act—she fell on purpose."

Both Mike and Tom squinted, as if wondering if they should believe him. Conor knew Tom had seen it a hundred times in his law enforcement career and Mike had heard cases where that behavior had played a part—someone faking for effect. Just then, Anne beckoned to Mike. He looked over at his wife, then gave his nephews an apologetic shrug and walked over to her.

"Belinda went down pretty hard, Conor," Tom said. "Garrett will probably call for a paramedic, and then he'll come looking for you."

"I hope he does," Conor said. "He should know who he's dating. I'll tell him."

"Based on what, knowing her when you were six?" Tom asked.

"Look, forget it. I've got to go to Kate."

"I'm going with you," Tom said.

"I can handle talking to Kate on my own," Conor said, glaring at his brother.

"Maybe so," Tom said. "But I'm still going with you."

They heard a distant siren, and Conor felt a new rush of anger. He figured that Garrett had in fact called the paramedics. Belinda was clearly a good emotional con artist. That tumble had been contrived. Conor knew she had fooled Garrett the way she'd tricked him. She'd invented a damsel-in-distress fiction that had probably worked for her before.

He and Tom walked back through the lobby toward the elevator. It was evening now, and the harp music had given way to piano. Everyone knew about tomorrow's wedding, so when the piano player spotted Conor, he played a few bars of the "Wedding March." Conor tried to smile at him, but he felt sick inside and couldn't.

Conor and Tom got off on the fourth floor and took a left. The door straight ahead was flanked by glowing lanterns and bore a discreet plaque that read *Tower Suite*. Conor used his key card to open it.

"Kate!" he called as he stepped inside.

No answer. He knew how upset she was, and he just wanted to get to her, put his arms around her, tell her how much he loved her. The suite had three levels. He checked the bedroom, then tore upstairs into the living area—their favorite place to sit by the fire while surrounded by windows that overlooked the ocean, the bay, and three states—but she wasn't there.

A polished and gleaming wood spiral staircase went up to a reading nook on the top level—a spot Kate loved, where she could nap and dream. Conor ran up, two steps at a time, but she wasn't there either.

He looked down from the high perch at Tom, standing in the living room. Tom was staring at one of the window seats, where Conor could see there was a pile of shredded white fabric.

"No," Conor said, hurrying down the spiral stairs. "Kate's veil."

Tom started to touch it.

"Don't," Conor said, grabbing his brother's wrist to stop him.

The veil was delicate lace, and it had been torn into small pieces. Conor had never seen Kate's wedding dress—that was a sight to be saved for tomorrow, in the chapel—but he had seen her veil, and this was it. It had belonged to his and Tom's mother. Jackie had worn it at her wedding to Tom, and they had given it to Kate, to wear at her wedding to Conor.

"Kate ripped it up?" Tom asked. "That's how angry she is at you?"

Conor had an internal struggle between his two selves: detective and husband-to-be. In that instant, the detective won out. He crouched by the window seat, undistracted by the view of the dark night ocean, and looked more closely at the fabric. It had been cut, not torn. The edges were smooth with no trailing threads. A sharp blade had been used to slice the veil into fine ribbons.

"Kate didn't do this," Conor said. "She wouldn't."

"Then who?" Tom asked. "Does anyone else have a key?"

"No," Conor said.

That's when his heart began to crash. He had watched Dermot, the valet, hang the garment bag holding Kate's wedding gown inside the bedroom closet. He ran down the stairs to the first level and opened the closet door.

Their regular clothes were still there, his and Kate's. Her blouses, a pale-green linen jacket, a flowered summer dress, and the blue suit he was going to wear to their wedding. But the garment bag was gone.

And so was Kate.

Friday, July 2; 11:00 p.m.

After finding the ripped-up veil, Conor and Tom went through the whole hotel. Conor felt panic building. They spoke to the security manager, who said that he hadn't seen Kate but would keep an eye out for her. Then they took the walkway from the hotel to Dune Cottage, the café by the beach, to see if Kate was there. The light was dim, perfect for candlelight dining, but not great for finding Kate.

Conor stared at the beach, listening to the sound of the steady surf. He heard the bell buoy tolling off Watch Hill Point. His stomach flipped to think of Kate being so upset that she wouldn't even talk to him. The beach was dark other than the edge of the waves catching light, streaming down from the Ocean House, white foam fizzing on the wet sand.

Garrett came charging onto the Dune Cottage deck. "What the fuck, Conor?" he asked. "I've been looking for you all over."

"I figured you would be," Conor said. "Is Belinda okay?"

"No," Garrett said. "She hit her head when you pushed her."

"Is that what she told you?" Conor asked.

"It's what I saw," Garrett said.

"No," Conor said. "You saw me reach for her phone and her faking a fall."

"You lunged at her," Garrett said. "You had the whole table watching you. And what's this bullshit about you proposing to her, her having your kid?"

Conor stiffened up, wanting to shove Garrett away. He could feel Tom's eyes on him. His brother had been sitting across the table and hadn't heard that part.

"It's bullshit," Conor said.

"She showed me the ring you gave her," Garrett said.

"We were six," Conor said. "We lived on the same street. I made her a ring out of some soldering wire I found in the garage."

"And she kept it all this time?" Garrett asked.

"I don't know what to tell you about that," Conor said, burning to get going, to find Kate. He pictured those shreds of his mother's veil—*Kate's* veil—and his thoughts were revving, going to terrible places, wondering what was happening with her.

"Yeah, well, you better tell me *something*," Garrett said. "I told the paramedics to take her to Westerly Hospital, to check her for a concussion. I'm on my way there, but I had to see you first. I'm going to give you a chance to explain . . ."

"Before what?" Conor asked.

"I arrest you for assault."

"You'd better ask *her* to explain before you do that," Conor said. "I have things to say, but you talk to her first. And really listen—I mean, past the words."

"You mean like I'm interrogating a suspect?" Garrett asked.

Yeah, like that, Conor thought. But he held the comment inside.

"Why were you grabbing for her phone?" Garrett asked.

"Ask her," Conor said.

Garrett left, but Conor didn't miss the fact that his hands were balled into fists.

"That was nice," Tom said. "Two friends and colleagues having a civil discussion. What's this about a kid?"

"Belinda's playing a game," Conor said.

"Is it called 'destroying your life'?"

"Seems to be," Conor said, but just then he didn't care what Belinda did. Only Kate mattered, and he had to get to her before Belinda had the chance to do any more damage, to twist the truth and tell Kate her version of the longer story.

He couldn't get that cut-up veil out of his mind. Could Kate have been so angry that she'd done it? In his worst nightmare, he couldn't imagine that she could. It was a question he encountered in many investigations: How well do people know each other?

Even people in love—he had seen it over and over. Secrets sometimes led to unfathomable behavior. Conor had always told himself that he and Kate had been through so much together, they knew everything important about each other.

But that was letting himself off the hook.

He had never told her the worst thing. After what had just happened with Belinda, he could barely confront it himself.

Maybe Kate had just revealed a side of herself he'd never seen—the ability to destroy that veil—a symbol of their love, of the marriage vows they had yet to say. A family heirloom that they could pass on to a daughter.

Then a worse thought hit him: If Kate hadn't done it, who had? If Kate wasn't hiding, had someone taken her?

"Where are you?" he asked out loud, but the only answer he received was the sound of the waves.

4

GIRL #1

Late fall, nine months earlier

The woman had found her, taken her away from a place she'd never wanted to be. The teaching began right away. The woman had a soothing voice and a twinkle in her eye that seemed to promise that everything would be worth it. She brought them gifts, and she assured them that the lessons might seem rigorous at first, but life would get better and better. It would be like a dream. She took them to the spa, treated them to days of beauty and massage, and she gave them a place to live.

That's when the man came.

Sometimes he took the girl to the boat. She always hoped it was the last time, but then he would get mad and tell her it was time to go back. He would blindfold her. Then he would unlock the bedroom door and lead her down the stairs and out of the house. She breathed the fresh air. It smelled like salt, and sometimes she felt tiny drops of water on her skin, and she recognized the feeling of condensation, of fog. He had her on a leather leash, like a dog. They walked a short distance, and grass tickled her bare feet. Then she would feel rough boards under her feet, and they would step onto the boat.

He would take the blindfold off and unclip the leash. The door would be open just long enough for her to walk to the bunk. He didn't touch her, didn't lead her there. He made her lie down by herself, as if it were her idea, and in some secret way, deep inside herself, that made it worse. Then he'd clamp the cuffs around her ankles. At those moments, she wished she had never been found—"rescued"—by the woman.

The boat moved on the wind and tides, and sometimes the movement made her feel sick. The month of October had been cold; her hands were numb. She was so alone here. She twirled the ring on her finger. It began to feel like a friend, a companion, her ring.

She reached out, placed her hand flat on the porthole. Maybe someone outside would see and think she was waving. She tapped her ring, then turned it and dragged the stone across the glass. If she died, she would have left a little clue. A mark that would say she had been there. He would be so surprised. He would deserve it. She tried to press harder, but she felt very weak.

She wished he would come back and take her to the mansion. Even if there was a party, even if all the other men were there in their tuxedos—and the woman directing all the pretty girls in their gowns—even if they demanded she obey, even that would be okay. The cuffs would be off, and she'd have the chance to run away.

The woman had promised her that life would be a dream.

She began to cry, calling for the woman to come and take her back to her old life, to her old dreams, to anything but this.

She cried for anyone, even one of the tuxedoed men, to come and save her life.

5

Saturday, July 3; 3:00 a.m.–7:00 a.m.

Tom tried to get some sleep, but he and Jackie were too stirred up and worried about Kate. Their room was on the second floor, with a terrace that had a view of the Watch Hill lighthouse. They sat outside, watching the light flash every two seconds. There was very little wind, making it possible to hear the clang of the bell buoy marking the south end of the reef at Watch Hill Passage.

The steady pattern of the light's beam, and the toll of the bell, calmed Tom. He and all Coast Guard personnel appreciated lighthouses, buoys, and other navigational aids that kept mariners safe; in spite of that, the USCG was evaluating which buoys to remove, considering that GPS had rendered some of them obsolete. There was huge opposition from boaters. And Tom thought it was a terrible idea.

He wished there were navigational aids for his family. They all looked after each other. That was the best they could do. But Tom was at a loss right now. He would do anything to help his brother and Kate, but he had no idea what to do. He thought of how he had always believed that Kate and Conor were going to keep each other safe throughout life, and he stared at the lighthouse beam and hoped that that was still true.

After a while, he and Jackie went inside. Jackie eventually drifted off, but by 5:30 a.m., Tom had given up. He climbed out of bed, leaving

Jackie deeply asleep; he got dressed and went downstairs. He grabbed a cup of coffee from the high-tech Italian machine in the lobby, stepped onto the verandah, and sat in one of the wicker chairs facing the ocean. With an hour to go until sunrise, there were still faint stars in the sky.

He texted Conor, then Kate, then Conor again.

Maybe they had found each other, he told himself. Maybe they had had a long talk, cleared the air, laughed at that nutjob Belinda, and had gone to bed up there in the Tower Suite. He hoped for that as much as anything he'd ever hoped for in his life.

Conor and Kate had been lost in different ways before they got together, and Tom thought about how they had met. When Kate had been only sixteen, she; her younger sister, Beth; and their mother had been tied up together and locked in the basement of the Woodward-Lathrop Gallery.

Conor had been a town cop back then—he'd joined the force straight out of college. He had discovered and rescued the sisters, but it was too late for their mother. She had died during the night, and it had been a horrific experience for Kate and Beth, unable to help her. The psychological damage was long lasting.

Years later, Conor had been assigned to another case involving Kate—an even worse one: Beth's murder. He had solved it, but he couldn't stop the sorrow that had rocked Kate for the months and years that followed. There were threads that connected to Kate's family and friends, and they had triggered memories of that terrible night in the basement.

Could one family be cursed? Sometimes it seemed that Kate's was. Tom had watched how Conor had loved her through the violence and its aftermath, through the trauma of two brutal crimes. Kate had gone through a period of depression—who wouldn't, after those experiences, those losses?

She had thrown herself into her work at the gallery, steady in the art world but at times unpredictable in her relationship with Conor. She was half owner of the Cessna that she and her best friend, Tallulah

Granville, kept at Westerly State Airport, and she occasionally took off—literally—by herself. Conor saw that tendency as proof of her independence, and he was proud of her for it. But Tom and Jackie sometimes wondered where she went without him. And why she had to.

Was this situation—Conor and Kate driven apart at their rehearsal dinner—due to bad luck? Or bad choices?

Tom still didn't have the whole story about Belinda, but something was off base with Conor, and that made him feel uneasy.

He watched the sun rise. It was 7:00 a.m. when he saw Conor and Joe walking up from the beach. Conor looked unsteady and unshaven. When Conor came up onto the verandah, Tom saw his red-rimmed eyes. He felt jolted to see his brother's pain. Joe waved and went into the lobby to get coffee.

"She's gone," Conor said.

"Come on. Don't think that, Con. She's probably with Hadley or Sam," Tom said. "Sam's her maid of honor, right? Part of that role is holding the bride's hand when she needs it."

"I don't think Kate wants to be a bride anymore," Conor said. "I think she's left me."

"Does she have reason to?" Tom asked sharply, trying to read his brother. But there was no reaction, just a numb look in his eyes. Tom hated seeing him like that. "Go to your suite and clean yourself up. She's coming back, I am sure of it. You want her to see you like this? Let's go."

They were headed across the verandah, into the hotel, when Tom heard a phone buzz with an incoming text. It was Conor's.

"Is it Kate?" Tom asked.

"No," Conor said, staring at the screen. "Unknown number."

"What do they want?"

"It says 'help her.'"

"Her?" Tom asked.

Just then, they saw a marked Westerly police car speed up Bluff Avenue. It was a jarring sight, just past the white tent standing ready for a wedding that looked increasingly unlikely.

The patrol car stopped in front of a gray-shingled house with white shutters diagonally across the street. Tom saw Conor snap out of his numbness; he walked, then began to run toward the officers. Tom recognized them from the Maddie Morrison case—Officers Miles Cutler and George Bouchard waved when they saw him and Conor rushing over.

"Hey, Conor. Hey, Tom," Miles said.

"What's going on?" Conor asked.

"We got a call about blood in the house," George said.

"Seeping under a bedroom door upstairs," Miles said. "The caller didn't want to open it."

"We'll go up with you," Conor said.

"You don't have to," George said with a tight smile. "Word is, you're getting married today. Isn't that your tent?"

"Come on, let's go," Conor said, ignoring the question. "Someone texted me for help. It might be about Kate."

Tom understood; this wasn't Conor's jurisdiction. But his brother had worked with these officers before, and they trusted him. Tom's pulse was pounding as hard as he imagined it was for Conor. A feeling of tragedy was already in the air, and Conor had gotten that text. Tom silently repeated the words *Don't let it be Kate.* They walked around a navy-blue Ford pickup parked in the driveway—Tom was pretty sure it was the same one that had nearly hit them on the way up from the harbor yesterday.

Maeve, Kate's gallery assistant, stood just inside the door. She steadied herself against the wall.

"Did you text me?" Conor asked. "'Help her'? Who, Kate?"

"What? No, I didn't text you," she said, looking bewildered.

"But you're the one who called 911?" George asked.

"Yes," she said. Then, "Oh god, Conor. It's bad." She pointed toward the second floor, and Conor tore up the stairs.

While the Westerly officers rushed up behind Conor, Tom said to her, "Don't leave. They'll need to talk to you."

Maeve nodded, and Tom saw tears glittering in her eyes. He then ran up after his brother and the two officers.

By the time he reached the landing, the others had already entered the room. The two Westerly cops stood back, to avoid stepping in the blood pooling on the parquet floor. But Conor had rushed straight toward the woman lying on her side, her white dress soaked with blood.

Tom let out a groan, even before Conor did. Tom recognized the dress. He had seen it when Kate had come to his and Jackie's house right after her last fitting, when she had stopped by to pick up the veil.

"Kate," Tom said, his voice breaking.

"No," Conor said, turning toward him. And in that moment, Tom saw the woman's lifeless eyes were wide open, and he saw that her throat had been slit.

And he saw that the victim wasn't Kate at all.

It was that woman from last night, the one he and Conor had known as children, the one who had ruined the rehearsal dinner and started this family heartbreak.

It was Belinda.

6

Saturday, July 3; 8:00 a.m.

Conor was used to securing crime scenes, not messing them up. He stood in the hallway, just outside the bedroom where he'd found Belinda's body thirty minutes earlier. He knew that the fact that he was allowed to stay here was just a courtesy. If he hadn't had a long and respected career as a Connecticut State Police detective and hadn't worked closely with Rhode Island law enforcement on a high-profile murder case, they would be treating him differently. Even so, he understood that he would have to be questioned.

He felt sick. His shoes were covered with blood. He had stepped in it, and he had it on his hands and on his face, and on his sleeves and the front of his shirt, from when he had lunged forward, leaned down, turning the victim's face toward him—from when he had been convinced it was Kate, when he had crouched beside her, wanting to take her in his arms.

The responding officers cleared the room where Belinda's body had been found, and Conor moved downstairs. The crime scene team arrived and took numerous photos of Belinda's body and the bedroom. They had him remove his shoes and bagged them, giving him a pair of paper booties to put on over his bare feet. Conor was directed to take off his shirt so they could examine his body for cuts or scratches, potentially defensive wounds made by the victim during the attack. They took photographs, paying special attention to his hands.

The murder scene was horrific. Belinda's throat had been slashed. The carotid artery had been severed. With her heart still pumping, the arterial spray had been violent, pulsing onto the wall and ceiling, dripping down and pooling on the wooden floor. Conor knew with that type of wound, death would have happened very fast.

The responding officers had called in the detectives. Conor looked for Joe, but Garrett was first to arrive. He walked straight to Conor.

"Where were you earlier this morning?" Garrett asked. It was a simple enough question, but Garrett delivered it with high velocity, as an accusation.

"Looking for Kate," Conor said.

"And did you find her?"

"No," Conor said.

"So you were looking for your fiancée, and you just happened to stumble into this house, to find a body? To find *Belinda*?"

"I wouldn't put it that way, Garrett," Conor said. "And I am sorry about Belinda. I know you were—"

"You don't know anything," Garrett said harshly.

Conor stared at him, kept his cool. Despite everything, the shock of Belinda's death and his worry about Kate, he managed to note that Garrett was acting more in anger than in grief.

"Why did you come here? To this house?" Garrett said.

"Someone texted me, then I saw the police car."

"How do those two things go together?"

"The text said 'help her,'" Conor said.

"Was that about Belinda?" Garrett asked.

"I have no idea—I don't even know who it was from," Conor said. "I thought it was about Kate." In the back of his mind were other texts and calls he had gotten over the last year—anonymous ones—that he was sure had been sent by Belinda.

"That's convenient," Garrett said. "Let me see the text."

Conor felt rage spilling out of Garrett, and he took a step back. "Maybe you shouldn't be investigating this. You're too close to it. Belinda was your girlfriend—"

"Don't you say her name," Garrett said. "And I am investigating this. I have questions for you."

That could be challenging, if you don't want me to say the name of the victim, Conor thought. In spite of how upset he had been at Belinda last night, he felt shaken to see her murdered so brutally—the girl next door, whom he had cared about when they were children.

"What questions?" Conor asked.

"What do you think?" Garrett asked. "Can we start with the murder?"

"I had nothing to do with that." Conor felt as if his head were going to explode.

"You assaulted her last night," Garrett said. "She's got a big, long story about you. About your *history*."

Conor shook his head. "Listen, Garrett, everything about this is messed up. But you know me. You're my friend, it's why Kate and I invited you to our wedding . . ."

"Back to the point," Garrett said. "You came flying into this house—why?"

"Because I got that text, and I can't find Kate. That's all that matters to me."

"You said you were out looking for her all night, that's your alibi," Garrett said.

"First, I was with my brother, then Joe. We were all searching. And that's what we should be doing now!"

"You're covered with blood," Garrett said. "Want to explain why you were touching the body?"

"I told you, I thought it was Kate," Conor said. "She's wearing Kate's wedding gown."

"What?" Garrett asked.

"Yeah," Conor said, pointing into the bedroom. "Belinda is wearing Kate's dress. So when I saw her lying there, what did you expect me to do?"

And the thought hit him like a brick: Was Belinda the intended victim? Or had the murderer seen her in Kate's wedding dress and thought—exactly like Conor—she was Kate? Did he think he was killing Kate?

"But it wasn't Kate, was it?" Garrett asked.

"Listen," Conor said, "someone wanted me here, maybe so I'd get blamed. It's crazy . . . But, Garrett, I need to find Kate. Come on, let's work together. We can't lose more time."

"It's obvious there is a connection, considering that Belinda was murdered in Kate's dress," Garrett said. "What kind of history does Kate have with her?"

"You saw," Conor said. "Last night. That's the history, end of story."

"Except it was pretty obvious that Belinda is—was—in love with you, and that clearly made Kate jealous. Not to mention, dressing up in her wedding gown. What was that about? I can imagine it causing a pretty violent reaction."

Conor knew Garrett was baiting him, hinting that Kate could be a suspect. It took everything he had to not react the way he knew Garrett wanted him to.

"Belinda was your date, Garrett. I hadn't seen her in years, and Kate met her for the first time yesterday."

"I'll tell you, Conor. I think you wanted witnesses. You waited for the officers to show up, and you came with your brother," Garrett said.

"Witnesses to what?"

"You throwing yourself at the body. Your big excuse for contaminating the scene."

"Why would I do that?"

"Hypothetically, if a person committed murder and was afraid that he'd left evidence behind, what better way to explain it than returning to the scene, plowing in, and tampering with everything? Destroying the evidence he had left during the murder?" Garrett asked.

Conor stared at him—it wasn't a bad theory. But the way Garrett was accusing him, with such intensity, made Conor feel this had everything to do with Garrett's personal feelings. He wished Joe would hurry up and get there.

"Hey, Conor," Tom said in a warning tone as he entered the room. Conor was surprised the local cops had let him back in, but he knew it was hard to say no to USCG Commander Thomas Reid when he got into his command-bearing mode.

"What?" Conor asked.

"I called Uncle Mike, and he's outside. He wants to speak to you before you answer any questions," Tom said.

"You mean your uncle the judge?" Garrett asked.

"Yes," Tom said.

"Oh, so you need a lawyer?" Garrett asked Conor.

"I don't care about that," Conor said to Tom, ignoring Garrett. "I just need to find Kate."

"I'm having George give you a ride to headquarters. You can answer questions there," Garrett said, stepping forward, putting his face in Conor's. Conor jumped back. Why was Garrett being so aggressive? He had the sudden thought that maybe Garrett had something of his own to hide.

"Garrett, shut the fuck up. You're not listening to me. I'm not going anywhere till we find Kate. There's a murderer here, and she's missing, so pull it together, okay?"

Tom tapped Conor's shoulder. "You're right, but calm down," he said. "Come with me *now*."

Conor felt like decking his brother, but he followed him outside. He saw Maeve leaning against a stone wall. Standing beside her was a detective Conor hadn't seen before, taking notes. The detective looked over at Conor, then resumed questioning Maeve. Conor noticed the blue truck in the driveway and flashed to yesterday—it had sped past, and he'd been afraid it would hit Kate.

Conor and Tom's uncle, Michael Reid, stood on the front porch. At seventy-seven, he was still an imposing figure. He was six three, with a head of thick white hair and sharp blue eyes that gave anyone who faced him in court the feeling he could see right through them. Even here in his khakis and polo shirt, he had the bearing of a judge. Conor was used to having his uncle joke around with him and Tom, in the Reid manner, just as his father had done. But at that moment, Mike looked stern.

"What have you said so far?" Mike asked.

"Nothing. Basically, just that I know that the victim—Belinda. And that she's wearing Kate's wedding dress."

"That's not nothing," Mike said. "You know better than anyone not to talk to the police. That's what trips up half the defendants who come to my courtroom. They open their mouths and they pay the price. And the victim is someone you not only *know* but have a troubled history with."

"There was no 'troubled history' until last night," Conor said, but again he thought of those anonymous texts, and a brief period that had preceded them.

"Well, you certainly made up for lost time," Mike said. "The whole room saw the fight. It was spectacular, to say the least."

Conor felt like walking away, but he knew he had to make himself clear, just so they could move on and find Kate. "Garrett's got it in for me. He told me his theory. He's already decided I'm guilty, and he's looking for facts to make them fit."

"What's his theory?" Mike asked.

"That I killed Belinda early this morning and came back when there were witnesses, to make sure they saw me tracking through the blood and touching the body."

"Ah, to explain the evidence you left behind when you murdered her," Mike said. "And does his theory include the fact you wanted to shut Belinda up? From stirring up more trouble with Kate?"

"I think the damage was already done," Conor said.

"Well, thinking like a prosecutor, here's another theory: Maybe you thought you were killing Kate. Considering that Belinda was wearing her dress."

"That's insane," Tom said, and Conor was grateful his brother was speaking up for him. "I want to know about this house. How did Belinda wind up here?"

"Good question," Mike said. "Years ago it was owned by friends of Anne's and mine—the Rancourts. They spent half the year in Watch Hill, the other half in Paris. But when Geoffrey died, the kids began to fight over the estate, and the house was sold. Belinda must have known the current owners. Is that their vehicle? Check the registration."

Conor turned to look at the navy-blue pickup truck in the driveway. For the first time, he noticed the number 1740 discreetly stenciled onto the driver's door, encircled by prickly garland. "That nearly hit Kate yesterday—as if it were aiming for her," he said. "You saw that, right, Tom?"

"The driver was definitely in a hurry," Tom said.

Conor saw George beckon him toward the squad car.

"You have to find Kate for me," he said to his brother and uncle. "Tell her they're going to question me at headquarters."

"Garrett is taking this ridiculously far," Tom said. "Where's Joe?"

"Find him, too, will you?" Conor said.

"I had assumed the questioning was pro forma, but I think you're right. Garrett has it in for you. Give me your phone," Mike said.

"It's evidence," Conor said. "They'll want it."

"As you well know, they will go through every call, every text, every internet search, to use against you. I'm not saying you have anything to hide, but you still don't want the police to have it," Mike said. "Not without a subpoena."

"Give it to me," Tom said sternly, holding out his hand.

Conor hesitated. What if Kate called him and he didn't have his phone? He was a cop, and he believed in the process. He wanted to comply with the investigation. But Garrett's attitude was vicious, personal, and even though Conor would have to give consent—and his password—to have the contents of his phone searched, Conor didn't want Garrett having custody of his phone at all. He sensed that Garrett was using aggression toward him as a distraction, a way of hiding something of his own.

Tom kept his hand out, and Conor eventually slapped his phone into it. Tom quickly put the phone in his back pocket.

"I'm calling a friend of mine," Mike said. "Leo Kennedy is one of the best defense attorneys in Rhode Island, has his own firm in Providence. I'll have him meet you at the state police barracks. Don't talk till he gets there."

"For the record, I have nothing to hide."

"That doesn't enter into the equation," Mike said. He dialed his friend's number. He got voicemail and left a message. Then, to Conor: "Remember. Keep your mouth shut—on the ride to headquarters and when you get there—not a word."

7

Saturday, July 3; 11:00 a.m.

Kate lay in bed in the guest room of the Sea Garden Suite. It was on the third floor of the Ocean House, where Hadley and CeCe lived, and her gaze kept drifting toward the terrace. On this bright summer morning, she squeezed her eyes tight to keep herself from seeing the snow that had been falling that December day Conor had proposed to her. She would do anything to block that memory right now.

She hadn't slept all night, but early that morning she had started to doze. Then, around eight, the sound of sirens woke her up. She couldn't tell where they were coming from, but she knew that someone was having an emergency. Whenever she heard a siren, she remembered her mother's death, her sister's murder, and how police had closed in on the scenes. It was one big PTSD-fest. Her saving grace was that Conor had been there for her. He had stepped into her life at those times of tragedy.

She had wondered why she was still alive, when her mother and sister were dead. Conor had pulled her from those depths of despair, made her feel that she wasn't alone, that life was a gift. He had made her want to be here on earth, with him, looking forward to whatever came next.

And now, all of that had fallen apart. She tossed in bed, wishing she didn't have to think at all. Images flashed in and out of her mind—the little silver ring, the glee in Belinda's face, the blue eyes of that baby.

The blue eyes that reminded her of Conor—the ones she had loved so much, that had promised her they would be together forever.

Eventually she reluctantly got up and went into the dining area of the suite, where Hadley and CeCe were having breakfast. They offered her some, but she wasn't hungry. They left the table, and she heard them talking, moving about, Hadley getting CeCe into her bathing suit, but she'd barely registered any of it.

July sunlight glanced sharply off the ocean and streamed through the tall windows. The French doors were open to the terrace, and the sound of the waves came through, beckoning her outside, but she couldn't bear that idea.

The memories she had blocked while lying in bed came forth so clearly now, she had to let them in. The suite's terrace was where Conor had proposed during that epic blizzard on Christmas Eve. There had been a holiday party here in the Sea Garden Suite, with dancing and champagne and twinkling lights on the tree. Hadley had gathered friends and family together, to create a happy holiday for CeCe—for all of them.

Kate and Conor left everyone by the fire and stepped outside, onto the terrace. The snow and wind had momentarily stopped, and there was a short spell of calm in the heart of the blizzard. They had stood by the rail, thinking of how fierce the storm had been and how clear and still it was at that moment. They could see the five windmills on the far side of Block Island, miles across the water, gently blinking red.

And then Conor started to tell her why he had brought her to the Ocean House. Right in the middle of his proposal, he discovered he'd lost the engagement ring. He started to panic, and Kate laughed. She held out her hand, and in her palm was the sapphire-and-diamond ring she was wearing right now.

"You dropped it," she told him. In the living room, when he had been giving CeCe a gift.

So he took it from her and put it on her finger, and they kissed. That was the moment she had believed that, after everything that had happened to her, life was good and safe. That she and Conor loved each other so much, they would protect each other till the end of time.

It had meant so much to both of them that they had gotten engaged on this seaside terrace, while people they loved were just inside: Tom and Jackie, Hadley and CeCe. When the time came to plan their wedding, they knew it had to be right here, at the Ocean House, the site of that magical evening, just after the blizzard. And they knew that the people who had been there with them, the first to see Kate's ring and hear that they were getting married, would be here for them, be part of the ceremony. There had been no doubt in their minds.

"Are you okay?" Hadley said from across the room. She had barely left Kate alone all day.

"Where's CeCe?" Kate asked. She'd been there just a minute ago.

"I asked Sam to take her to the beach so you and I could talk."

"I don't really have much to say," Kate said.

"I can imagine," Hadley said. "But I know you didn't sleep all night, and you didn't have breakfast, and you look totally shell shocked. I'm worried about you."

Kate's eyes welled up. It was times like this she missed her sister, Beth. Of all the people she knew on the planet, Hadley was the only one who really understood what that was like—to have a sister stolen, to have her life taken away by a murderer. Hadley got it. Like Kate, she knew more than anyone should about loss.

"I guess I *am* shell shocked," Kate said. "I've never trusted anyone the way I trusted Conor. He's the best man I've ever known. He's so good, and he made me feel so loved. But now . . . it all feels like a lie."

"But you don't know for sure that it is a lie," Hadley said.

Kate knew what Hadley was getting at. After Belinda's bombshell last night, Kate had run off, come straight up here, and hadn't given Conor the chance to explain himself. She had spent the night in Hadley and CeCe's guest room. She hadn't seen Conor or returned to the Tower Suite, their home for this wedding weekend; they hadn't talked. He had knocked on the door—or at least she assumed it had been him—and she'd asked Hadley not to answer it.

She kept thinking of that moment after the rehearsal dinner, after Belinda had shown her the photo. Kate knew him so well, she had been able to read his expression, and the way he'd said her name, when she'd asked him, *"Is it true?"* Talking wouldn't change that.

"It just feels unreal," Kate said.

"Kate, everyone has a past. Do you really think you're the only one he's ever been with? Haven't you had boyfriends before Conor?"

"Of course, and I know he had other girlfriends before he met me. But I didn't have their children."

"That woman seemed crazy," Hadley said. "To pull a stunt like that in front of a crowd. At your rehearsal dinner? I wouldn't believe anything she said."

Kate didn't want to, but she pictured the baby's blue eyes. Plenty of people in the population had them, but when she put it together with that silver ring, Belinda's tone of possession, and Conor's reaction, she was tilting in and out of believing her. Her father had cheated on her mother, and it was how her family blew up. She had always believed she had an unwanted talent—accurate radar for betrayal—because she had grown up with it.

"Can you tell how old Belinda is in the photo?" Hadley asked.

"A lot younger than now," Kate said.

"The timing would make a huge difference," Hadley said. "Because if it was before you and Conor were together . . ."

Kate wrapped her arms around herself; she was shaking, and she couldn't stop. She knew what Hadley was saying: It wouldn't be fair of Kate to hold Conor responsible for something that had happened years before he'd met her. But a baby? How could he not have told her? Belinda's revelation had been such a bombshell; she should have talked to him right then, heard him out, but she'd gone straight into shock. Now she was ready.

"You're shivering," Hadley said. "Are you cold?"

Kate nodded. "Isn't that weird? On this beautiful summer day?"

"It's the salt breeze coming through the door," Hadley said, although Kate knew that wasn't true. She watched Hadley cross the room, start the cozy fire. It blazed in the hearth the way it had the Christmas Eve before last.

"What time is it?" Kate asked.

Hadley glanced at the screen of her mobile phone. "Almost noon," she said.

Kate closed her eyes. "Our wedding is supposed to start in five hours."

"It still could, Kate," Hadley said.

Kate knew that Hadley was right—they could still get married. They could wipe the slate clean and start life over right now. She and Conor had chased away plenty of demons in their time together. But this one was different.

"Not till I talk to him," Kate said.

Hadley looked at her long and hard, then reached over and gave her a hug.

Kate glanced across the living room at *Foggy Night*. When Belinda fell, she had broken the frame and torn the canvas. There was a long vertical tear, straight through the ghostly lighthouse that James Suydam had so poetically painted. One of the Ocean House staff had delivered it here last night, after the rehearsal dinner's awful end.

"I want to take the painting upstairs," Kate said. "I'll wrap it up so Maeve can take it to the conservator."

"I'm glad you're going to keep it," Hadley said. "And I hope Conor is there so you can talk this out."

"So do I," Kate said. She hoped she would find him there. It was an unbreakable habit—to love him so much and be excited about seeing him. This time it was tempered by a million other feelings. She wanted to yell at him, make him tell her what went on between him and Belinda. She felt humiliated by last night's scene, but that was nothing compared to feeling betrayed by Conor.

She stood to go, lifted the painting as carefully as she could to avoid damaging it further. Hadley followed her to the door, and Kate saw her pick up her key card from the table in the foyer.

"Where are you going?" Kate asked.

"Up to the Tower Suite, with you," Hadley said.

"You don't have to," Kate said.

"Yes, I do. I'm sticking with you," Hadley said.

Kate didn't feel like arguing. They walked to the beautiful old elevator and pushed the button for the fourth floor. The door slid open, and they headed to the Tower Suite. Now Kate's heart was really racing. Conor had to be there, waiting for her. She imagined facing him, him assuring her that Belinda had been lying. Both of them wishing they could go back twenty-four hours, go back to the way they'd been before last night.

She unlocked the door, stepped into the foyer, and called his name. She listened for his footsteps upstairs on the suite's main floor, for him running down to hug her.

But nothing. It was silent. Conor wasn't there.

She tried to hide how upset she felt from Hadley, but that was impossible. She walked into the bedroom, the blue accents bringing the sky and ocean inside. Housekeeping had made the bed, straightened up the room so well it looked as if she and Conor had never even stayed there at all.

The closet loomed straight ahead. Her palms felt sweaty; she put the painting on the bed. Then she went to the closet. She stood in front of the closed door for several long seconds. She knew her wedding gown was inside, hanging in its garment bag. She thought of how much she loved the dress, how exquisite the fabric and details.

She took a deep breath, pulled the closet door open, and looked inside.

It was gone. There was no sign of the garment bag, of the dress, of anything to remind her of the fact that she was supposed to get married today. Until she got upstairs and saw her veil, cut into a million tiny pieces. She gasped and ran to it, trying to gather all the shreds, as if she could put them back together.

She heard a knock on the suite's door.

"I'll get it," Hadley said.

Kate didn't know who it could be, and she was too stunned by Conor's absence, the empty closet, and the destroyed veil to really care. Then, through the fog in her mind, she heard Maeve's voice. It was high and wild, and the words Maeve cried rang in Kate's ears.

"They took Conor to the police station," Maeve was saying, as Kate walked into the foyer.

"What are you talking about?" Kate asked.

"She was wearing your dress, Kate! He slit her throat, and it turned red with her blood, the darkest red I've ever seen," Maeve said, the words spilling out. "She's dead!"

"Maeve, who's dead? Who was wearing my dress?"

"Belinda," Maeve said. "She was murdered, and they're saying Conor did it."

8

Saturday, July 3; 12:00 p.m.

Sam was used to seeing Kate in total control. Even when times were tough—after Sam's mother had died—Kate had tempered grief with strength, helping Sam make sense of it all. Now, Sam wished she could be that steady person for Kate, but that didn't seem possible. Sam was keeping a secret from her.

Word about Belinda's murder spread fast, but the beach was the last place to receive the news. It was as if the sun and salt air, the cheerful blue umbrellas and yellow chaise longues, formed an invisible shield, protecting the peace and sanctuary of the sand for the beachgoers.

Sam knew the whole story, though. Hadley had told her and asked her to keep CeCe busy, to keep her from hearing anything about it, so she had taken her down to the beach. CeCe ran ahead to the damp sand at the water's edge, and Sam got her started building a sandcastle.

Sam drizzled wet sand to make turrets, trying to settle her mind. It was that old question: If you know something that will hurt another person, do you tell them? Or do you hold it inside and let them go on not knowing, blissfully ignorant? Which is kinder, more loving?

Not that Kate was in any way blissful at this moment, but this would make it much worse. Sam was lost in dark thoughts when she heard her name. Anne waved from one of the white-curtained cabanas at the top of the beach.

"Mike just called," Anne said, holding her cell phone. "He told me what happened. That woman from last night was murdered? Her throat was cut, how gruesome!"

Sam nodded.

"And Conor's a suspect?"

"Well, they're questioning him," Sam said.

"That is insane," Anne said. "Mike will straighten it out."

Sam didn't reply. She knew that as a judge, Mike was probably used to throwing his weight around, but she couldn't see how he could straighten out a murder. And Conor either did or didn't kill Belinda. Sam wanted to believe he didn't, but the thoughts tormenting her made her wonder.

Anne talked on and on about how much she and Mike loved Conor, how he could never have done what he was suspected of, how ridiculous it was to even entertain the idea. Then she skipped to talking about the wedding being postponed.

"Good lord," Anne said. "Last night with that woman was a shock, but Conor will be cleared. It's early in the day—the wedding can go on." She paused, looked sideways at Sam. "What *did* happen last night? We all saw the ruckus, but what caused it?"

"I don't know," Sam said, even though she did. She had been there when Kate had told Hadley about the baby picture, heard how Belinda had said the child was Conor's.

CeCe came running up, and Sam was relieved for the distraction. Anne and Mike were members of the private club within the Ocean House, and they were able to use the cabana. It had a plate of fresh fruit and a small refrigerator full of water and juices. Sam made CeCe drink a glass of water and eat some grapes so she wouldn't get dehydrated; CeCe immediately ran back to her sandcastle. Sam felt as if she was on autopilot, just going through the motions.

A friend of Anne's walked up to the cabana, and Anne introduced her as Nola Aldrich. Sam heard them talking about the murder, how terrible it was, such a shock, who could have done it, there was no way it had been Conor. Nola was saying something about the psychology of a murderer who would slash the victim's throat, how it could be sexual in nature, how it exhibited passion. Sam briefly wondered if Nola was a psychologist or in law enforcement.

But then she blocked out their voices, and she spun back in time.

It was the night of the summer solstice—June 21—less than three weeks before the wedding. Sam was on the terrace outside the library at home at Cloudlands, stretched out on a wicker sofa. There had been a blazing sunset, but the vivid reds and purples had faded into peaceful darkness. The French doors into the library were open to the warm breeze. All the lights were off in the book-lined room, and she was half asleep, exhausted from work.

She heard someone in the library, but they didn't turn on any lights. Sam craned her neck to look over the back of the sofa and saw that it was Conor. She was about to say hi, but he was bent over the desk with such purpose, she held back. Then he walked back to the door from the hallway and looked both ways—as if checking to make sure Kate wasn't coming—so Sam stayed silent.

Conor stood by the desk. He turned on the green glass-shaded desk lamp—curved to keep most of the room in darkness—and focused it on an envelope he held in his hands. She saw him stare at his phone until it buzzed. He answered instantly. Sam had the feeling he'd been waiting for the call.

"Why did you send this to me?" he asked, his voice strained, without any greeting.

The person on the other end of the line must have had a lot to say, because he stood there in silence, listening for a long time.

"I want no part of it," Conor said after a while. "Don't contact me again." He hung up without another word. Sam hunched down in the sofa; now she really didn't want him to see her. She heard a desk drawer open, then close. He turned off the light and left the room.

Sam had the feeling she had just witnessed something no one in the house was meant to see or hear. She stayed very still, her heart pounding. She had grown up in a house of secrets, and she knew they were the reason her family had shattered. Lying on the sofa, she debated with herself what to do next, but she knew she had to look. She walked over to the desk and opened each of the drawers.

The envelope was in the bottom one. Sam pulled it out and saw that it was addressed to Conor. It had been slit open. Sam hesitated, then looked inside. She stared for a few long seconds. It was dark in the room, but she could see well enough. Her mouth went dry; she couldn't even swallow.

She couldn't stand holding that envelope. She quickly shoved it back into the drawer and closed it.

She wished she could have pushed her thoughts into a drawer too. For all those days between then and the wedding date, she had kept the secret. She considered asking Conor about what she had seen or blurting it out to Kate.

But she didn't. She didn't want to meddle; she shouldn't have been snooping. It was a bad habit she'd picked up as a child, looking through her parents' drawers, trying to find answers to her family's unhappiness.

So, she kept burying her fears. She had to believe that there was some crazy explanation. In fact, she was pretty sure she had overreacted. Conor deserved his privacy. She was sure that he had either already told Kate, or he would. Either way, it was none of her business. She kept kicking herself for prying, and she hadn't let herself make sense of what she had seen until the rehearsal dinner last night.

Now it made all the sense in the world—and it should have right away, that night of the solstice, in the library at Cloudlands. She had just refused to acknowledge the obvious. It was all perfectly clear.

Sam wished she hadn't opened that drawer.

9

Saturday, July 3; 3:00 p.m.

Conor was on the wrong side of the interrogation table at the Wickford Barracks of the Rhode Island State Police, in North Kingstown. It was ironic, because during the Maddie Morrison case, he and Joe had sat across this exact table from their suspects.

But today, Garrett Milne had ordered Trooper George Bouchard to drive him here. George had seemed embarrassed and apologetic. At first he said he was sorry but just following orders, yet he was quiet on the drive.

Even though Conor knew him from the earlier investigation, he realized that George was most likely wary—suspicious of Conor for how he had behaved that morning. George had led him into the room, asked if he wanted coffee. Conor had said no. He asked about Kate, and George said he hadn't heard anything. Conor felt like climbing the walls. Anything could be happening to her and he was trapped here.

Garrett kept him waiting. At first Conor was kept busy giving forensic samples. As a police officer, most were already on file in Connecticut, but Rhode Island had its own procedures. He was fingerprinted; he agreed to let them swab him for DNA and to take hair samples. He had been photographed at the scene, but now a different photographer took more detailed pictures before they let him wash off the blood.

Conor would have done the same in most cases—let the suspect sit alone till he was sweating, overthinking what he was going to say to get himself out of there. Two hours went by. Garrett kept passing the door, shooting Conor sharp looks but not saying anything. At one point, Garrett opened his mouth as if to speak, then just stood there, glaring. Conor felt his face turning red.

He knew he had to stop letting Garrett get to him. He had plenty of time to think, and he couldn't help feeling as if he was being set up. He thought of how he had received the "help her" text, how he had been lured to the murder scene. Maeve had made the call to the police, and the officers were already there. Conor's reaction—throwing himself on Belinda's body—made him look guilty.

What part was Garrett playing? His tough act was over the top. Was it simply jealousy over Belinda's apparent feelings for Conor and her story about the baby? Or was it something deeper? How long had he and Belinda been together? Did he see Belinda's outburst last night as a betrayal of what he thought they had? Could he have been angry enough to have killed her?

He wondered where Joe was. He hadn't seen him since they had returned to the hotel after searching for Kate. He wanted to get out of here, but he also wanted Joe to observe Garrett in action, confronting Conor. Conor was tempted to walk out—he hadn't been arrested, he had the right to leave—but he thought that if he stayed, Garrett might reveal something that would help Conor understand what was really going on and how it might relate to Belinda.

Eventually, Garrett walked in, holding a folder. He opened it and stared at the contents without saying a word or making eye contact with Conor. Conor refused to react, but he recognized Interrogation 101. Staring at a sheaf of papers, Garrett was trying to make him think the evidence was stacking up.

"Sorry to keep you waiting so long," Garrett said eventually. He took a seat across the table. "But we've been busy."

"I can imagine," Conor said. "You're investigating a murder."

"The interesting thing," Garrett said, "is that all the evidence leads straight to you."

"Okay," Conor said.

"And we have a lot of it."

Conor waited.

"Your footprints in the blood," Garrett said. "Your prints on the victim."

"Well, you know I was there," Conor said.

"Yeah. George and Miles said you and your brother came running down the street when you saw their car. And our witness said you tore up the stairs, ran straight into the room—as if you already knew what you would find. And as if you wanted her—and the arriving officers—to see you."

Her. Conor realized the witness had to be Maeve. George had told him and Tom about how the 911 caller had said she saw blood seeping under the bedroom door. And Maeve had been waiting to be interviewed when Conor ran past her, up the stairs.

"We have Belinda's cell phone," Garrett said. "And we'll get a warrant to examine it. To check the records. Will we find calls from you? Or from her to you?"

Conor felt like explaining things to Garrett, telling him his suspicions about the anonymous texts, but he held back. He thought of investigations when subjects had deleted calls, thinking that by doing so they could erase the evidence. He knew that forensic specialists could examine phone data and uncover the missing calls. Conor had had cases like that, and it was much worse than if the person had just let the call stand; deletion indicated consciousness of guilt.

"We're going to get your phone too," Garrett said.

Conor stayed silent. He knew that if he was honest and put it out there—if he explained that he had deleted the calls and texts not to hide them from Kate or the police but just because he wanted to distance himself from the craziness, the stalking. He didn't want the reminder on his phone. But he knew that saying too much at this stage of the investigation was a mistake. Even with a genuine desire to be helpful, a person could say more than they should, sometimes contradicting themselves. Their desire to "set the record straight" wound up being a gift to the prosecutor to use against them in court.

"So why don't you just give your phone to me?" Garrett asked. "You know we're going to get it anyway. If you're innocent, you have nothing to hide, right?"

"I don't have it."

"Convenient," Garrett said. "Where is it?"

Conor didn't reply.

"I have to ask myself, what would be your motive, killing her? I assume it has something to do with that shit show last night," Garrett said.

Conor thought of the look on Kate's face, of the way she had run away from him after their rehearsal dinner. He couldn't help letting out a long exhalation.

"You're at the center of a whole lot of trouble," Garrett said. "Everything's falling apart for you, isn't it?"

Conor didn't say a word.

"Even aside from the murder. Your wedding. Your fiancée finding out about your relationship with Belinda."

"There was no relationship," Conor said.

"You're saying you didn't have one?" Garrett asked, glossing over the question. "Belinda told me all about it once we got back to the room. She showed me the baby photo. Suzanne was there too. She knew all about it."

"Suzanne?" Conor asked. He tried to place the name, but he felt outraged that Belinda had been lying about him, and his head was spinning.

He knew the worst thing he could do was to let Garrett see his emotions. He took a deep breath, steadied himself. He had to keep his focus, concentrate on staying calm. He began to wish Uncle Mike's friend Leo Kennedy would hurry up and get there.

"Belinda ruined everything, didn't she?" Garrett asked. "Spoiling your rehearsal dinner? Springing the news on Kate?"

"Springing it on you too," Conor said. "She was your date."

The left corner of Garrett's mouth twitched. He kept his hands flat on the table but flexed them twice, as if he wanted to make fists. Conor felt anger pouring off Garrett, and he knew he had struck a nerve.

"That's what this is about, right?" Conor asked. "You're blaming me for that, for whatever you think went on between me and your girlfriend. So you want to hold me here, treat me like a suspect? Go for it, Garrett."

Conor stood up. He kept close watch on Garrett's reaction. At first, Garrett looked shocked, then dismayed—like a kid who'd been beaten on the playground.

"You can't leave," Garrett said.

"I've been courteous to you and let you play this game with me. But you know how it works. Arrest me, or I'm walking out."

Garrett tapped the folder on the table. An expression of smugness crossed his face. "Go ahead and leave. But the statements from guests at the dinner last night, and witnesses of you running into the house this morning, make you a person of interest. Witness reports and photographs of you covered with Belinda's blood make you a suspect. And once we get a statement from Suzanne, we'll have all we need."

Conor waited to hear Garrett read him his Miranda rights, but the words didn't come, and Conor held himself back from asking why Suzanne's statement was so important—she was just the calligrapher, helping Maeve with some wedding details. Garrett was doing an intense job of staring him down and barely even noticed when the door opened.

Conor hoped it was the lawyer Mike had called, but instead Joe stepped into the interrogation room.

"What's going on?" Joe asked.

"I'm about to place Conor under arrest," Garrett said.

"Let's hold off on that," Joe said. The senior detective had a way of speaking that left no doubt, without raising his voice, that it was more an order than a suggestion.

Garrett held his dagger gaze on Conor for a few more seconds, then tapped his folder and left the room without another word.

"Thanks for coming," Conor said to Joe.

"You're welcome," Joe said. "And you'll thank me more once we get to the car and you find out what I was doing. Come on."

10

Saturday, July 3; 5:00 p.m.

It was 5:00 p.m., the hour that Kate and Conor should have been married, and Kate still hadn't been able to speak to Conor. She thought of the lovely Watch Hill Chapel just across the street from the Ocean House and the wedding tent. She and Conor had loved it the minute they had walked inside last August. Cozy yet airy, over a century and a half old, with warm natural wood walls and a tall ceiling with beams that curved like the ribs of a ship.

The curtain behind the altar was deep blue, and so were the organ panels with chapel mottos done in gold lettering. Kate was particularly moved by one: *"In Essentials, Unity: In Non-Essentials, Liberty: In All Things, Charity."* She felt that nothing between her and Conor was more essential than unity.

The chapel was seasonal; Kate and Conor had thought of all the summer weddings that had been held there, all the couples who had said their vows and walked out the door, believing they were united forever.

"We'll be just like them," Conor had said, holding her hand.

"Together forever," Kate had said.

"Well, we already are," Conor said. "We don't need vows or a paper to prove it."

"No, but is it okay that I want all that? That I want it to be official?"

Conor lifted her left hand to his lips and kissed it. "I wouldn't have asked you to marry me if I didn't want it too."

After visiting the chapel, they had crossed Bluff Avenue and returned to the Ocean House. They remembered the night they had gotten engaged: Christmas Eve, when the railings and columns were wrapped in evergreen laurels and twinkling white lights. The blizzard had passed, and the sky was so clear it had seemed as if every star was close enough to touch.

Kate remembered that August day last year, how they had sat at a table on the verandah, talking about how wonderful their wedding would be. They had gazed across the street at the chapel and at the wide lawn where the tent for their reception would be, and they talked about who they would invite, all the people they loved most. And they confirmed the date with the Ocean House: July 3. Someone else's misfortune was their good luck: A couple had reserved that date over two years earlier, but they broke up, and that first Saturday in July had suddenly become available.

Now July 3 was here—the date Kate and Conor had come to consider the luckiest in the calendar—and Kate felt the luck and happiness draining away. She still loved Conor—that could never end. The hour of her wedding had passed; her hurt and confusion had cut her to shreds, just like her veil.

She had informed Frances, the wonderful director of events who had helped her every step of the way, that the wedding was off. She didn't give a reason, but she didn't have to. Everyone on the property had heard about the rehearsal dinner disaster, and details about the murder were spreading fast. Kate was touched by the staff's kindness. It bolstered her and made her feel cared for.

Right now, Conor should be standing at the altar, waiting for her. Sam had asked if she could give her away, and Kate had said yes. Kate would be walking down the aisle toward Conor. She would see the look on his face and know he was feeling what she was too. Nothing but the love they had both yearned for their whole lives and found in each other.

She would be wearing the dress she had adored from the moment she saw it—a simple white column, no lace, no embroidery—just a crystal neckline that glinted like the snow and stars the winter night of their engagement.

But now—nothing. It had all been a dream. Her hopes, the words she and Conor had spoken, were dissolving. They were receding like the tide, nothing more than spindrift being blown off the wave tops, disappearing into the salt air.

When the time on her iPhone clicked to 5:01 p.m., she felt a stab of grief—followed by relief.

At least the wait was over—she didn't have to dread the hour anymore. The time had passed, and she had somehow survived. Most of their guests had rooms reserved until Monday. Kate and Conor had planned a three-day weekend celebration, starting with the rehearsal dinner, then the wedding and reception, and, on the third night—the Fourth of July—fireworks and the annual Ocean House Independence Day Beach Ball.

The whole weekend was Kate and Conor's treat. Kate had been the sole heir of her grandmother, Mathilda Harkness. Mathilda had been her role model in most things. She had served as a WASP in World War II and had taught Kate to fly a plane, run an art gallery, and wait until she found the right person to love. She had helped Kate find the bravery in herself. And she had left Kate a fortune—a true fortune, going back generations.

So treating their guests to a wedding weekend at the Ocean House, the most romantic place in New England and beyond, had filled Kate with joy. Mathilda had not found Ruth, her true love, until later in life, but once she had, that was it. She would approve of Kate and Conor throwing the best party possible to celebrate what they had.

Her grandmother had been tough, generous, and romantic. She had lived long enough to meet Conor but not know that he had proposed.

Kate had been sad about that, but now she was glad Mathilda wasn't here to see what had happened.

The guests felt so bad for her and didn't know what to say. She didn't know what to say to them either. She just let them enjoy the beautiful day and evening at the Ocean House; she had something less pleasant to do.

Conor was the detective, but Kate had a mystery she needed to solve on her own. Belinda had swept into her life last night, Maleficent spoiling the celebration, turning it into a dark fairy tale. She had stolen Kate's wedding gown and been brutally murdered while wearing it.

Kate steeled herself to walk through the lobby; she felt as if everyone knew her connection to the crime and was staring at her. The front desk staff smiled when they saw her, as warm and friendly as ever, and without any hint that they knew what had happened. She appreciated that.

But then Christina, one of the managers, leaned forward, holding out an envelope.

"Miss Woodward, this was left for you," she said.

"Thank you," Kate said. She opened it right away.

> I need to talk to you, I know all about Conor's daughter. Come to the house across the street, I'll be waiting.
> Suzanne

Kate stared at the signature. Suzanne was the young calligrapher Maeve had hired at the last minute. She and Kate had barely had the chance to speak, and now she was saying she knew all about Conor's daughter? Kate felt as if she'd been punched in the gut.

"Do you know when the note was left?" Kate asked.

"It must have been very early this morning," Christina said. "I came in at seven, and it was already here."

Kate stared out the open door, at the house where Belinda had been murdered. The house across the street. Suzanne had wanted Kate to meet her there and had left the note before seven—when Belinda's body had been found. Had Suzanne been setting a trap? If Kate had gone, would she have been the victim instead of Belinda?

Kate pulled out her phone and called Maeve's mobile. Maeve had the list of all the room numbers—she was efficient that way, wanting to make sure that all the cards and welcome gifts Kate had prepared for her guests were delivered to the right place. Kate was anxious to get together with her and ask how she knew Suzanne, how she had come to hire her. But mostly, she needed Belinda's room number.

The phone rang, and Maeve didn't answer. The call went straight to voicemail, as if the phone was turned off. She went back to the front desk, asking to be put through to Maeve's room. Lincoln answered.

"Hey, Kate, are you okay?" he asked.

"I'm fine, thanks, Lincoln," she said. "Is Maeve there?"

"She's gone out," he said. "And I'm about to meet her."

"She's not answering her phone. Is she all right?"

"Not really," Lincoln said.

Kate was so fond of Maeve; her sensitivity made her ideal as an assistant—she was a careful art historian and interpreter of artists' work. Kate couldn't bear the idea of her faced with a blood-soaked murder scene.

"I want to talk to her," Kate said. "To see how she's doing."

"Thanks, Kate. Right now, I think she just needs the beach—we're going to Napatree, walk the whole way to the point."

Kate pictured the tremendous beauty of that long spit of sand. The soft dunes of Napatree Point stretched along the Atlantic on one side, then curved into Little Narragansett Bay and Watch Hill Harbor on the other. She could imagine it soothing Maeve.

"Lincoln, I need some information. Do you know if the calligrapher she hired—Suzanne—was staying here at the hotel?" Kate asked.

"No, I'm pretty sure she went home last night."

"Okay," Kate said. "Another question. Maeve kept a list of where each of the guests is staying in the hotel. Do you see it anywhere?"

"Yeah, it's on the desk."

"Good," she said. "Can you please take a look, tell me the room number for Garrett Milne and Belinda Tyler?"

"I don't even have to look," Lincoln said. "Their room is right next door to ours. Belinda accidentally walked into our room last night, through the adjoining door. Families book these when they don't want the kids out of sight." He paused. "Maeve wasn't happy to see her, after what she did at the rehearsal dinner. That was terrible. And now, knowing what happened to her, it's freaking Maeve out."

"I can imagine," Kate said.

"I'd better go—I don't want to keep her waiting," Lincoln said.

"Of course," Kate said, her thoughts racing. "Could I ask you a favor? Could you leave your room unlocked or give me the key? Maeve has all the paperwork for the weekend, and I need to check on some things."

"Sure," Lincoln said. His voice dropped down. "I'm really sorry about the wedding, Kate. It sucks."

"It does," Kate said.

Lincoln came down to the lobby and gave her the key. He was tall and had to bend over to give her a big hug, and she was relieved he didn't say anything more about the wedding.

She let herself into the room he shared with Maeve. It was as tidy as Kate would expect from her fastidious assistant. She saw a pile of papers on the desk, including the list of guests. Her heart was pounding as she walked to the adjoining door and turned the knob. She knew the next part would depend on whether Garrett and Belinda had locked the room from their side.

They hadn't.

She was in.

The bed was unmade, covers pulled back. The room smelled of whatever perfume Belinda had been wearing last night, when she'd stood close enough to Kate to shove her phone into her face. Kate didn't know what she was looking for, so she scanned every corner of the room. She stepped into the walk-in closet. Two terrycloth robes hung on posh satin hangers. The velvety-soft Ocean House slippers remained unworn, in their wrappers. There was a set of drawers, and she opened each one to find it empty.

The marble bathroom was next. Wet towels had been left on the floor and draped over the side of the deep-soaking tub. An empty packet of scented bath crystals lay on the teak tray. The wooden body brush was on the white tile floor. Bottles of Molton Brown shampoo and conditioner stood beside the faucets, and their scent was fresh and blocked out Belinda's perfume in the other room.

Kate returned to the bedroom and glanced around. There were no apparent clues—what had she even hoped to find? She knew, deep down, she was looking for anything that would tell her about Belinda's supposed connection to Conor. She walked to the desk. There was a green leather blotter on the surface. A pad of Ocean House notepaper, with a whimsical drawing by Ludwig Bemelmans, sat in a small leather tray.

Inside the tray was a crow quill pen—with the smallest nib possible, perfect for calligraphy. Beside it was a bottle of India ink. Kate knew it well; it was the brand of ink she had bought for Maeve to provide to the calligrapher. It came from England and was of the highest quality, the smoothest consistency. The inkwell itself was distinctive: clear glass in an octagonal shape. The price sticker from Giddings, the London art supply store she had ordered it from, was affixed to the side.

Kate turned back to the desk drawer and saw a box of blank place cards. She used the tip of the crow quill pen to lift the cards, and buried beneath were receipts from Giddings, showing that the pen and ink had been charged to Kate's account. Kate's heart rate shot up. What were these things doing in Belinda's room?

Her gaze fell upon the wastebasket beside the desk.

Crumpled paper had been tossed in. She tilted the basket with her foot, and everything spilled out. There were several folded cards that had been calligraphed with the names of her wedding guests. She noticed that each one had a blot of ink or a misspelling and had obviously been discarded.

Kate had ordered the cards herself from Smythson, her favorite stationery store: white tented place cards, bordered in Nile blue. She and Maeve had admired them when they had arrived at the gallery. Maeve had told her she would hire the best calligrapher in the area and that they would be finished long before the wedding so Kate could approve them.

But Kate had been busy with the gallery, and planning the wedding and honeymoon, and she had left the approvals to Maeve. Maeve had found Suzanne to help with the lettering. And here were calligraphed place cards thrown into the wastebasket of the room where Belinda had been staying with Garrett.

Suzanne must have sat right here, showing Belinda the place cards.

Among the discarded cards, Kate spotted a crumpled-up paper. She pulled it out and saw that it was a marina receipt. It was a yellow paper, like a duplicate, with faded writing, as if the person hadn't pushed down quite hard enough with the pen. It was undated. The business name was printed on top: East Cove Marina. And the scrawl said *Dockage fee, Suzanne McKinney.*

Kate wanted to show it to Conor. Maybe the receipt was a lead, or maybe not, but Kate felt that the connection between Belinda and her wedding calligrapher had to mean something. It felt strange, to be excited about an investigation with Conor, when her heart was so broken. It was habit to want him and rely on him and be unable to wait to tell him everything. But she felt blocked—as if she were walled off—like the character in that Poe story, "The Cask of Amontillado." She felt as if she couldn't get to Conor—she could barely get to herself.

The marina was a start. No one was more familiar with the boatyards of southeastern New England than Tom, so she took out her phone to call him. It was a step toward Conor, calling his brother, asking him to go with her to check it out and find out what it meant to Belinda and Suzanne.

She used her iPhone to photograph the receipt and place cards. And then she dialed Tom's number.

11

When Conor walked out of the state police barracks, he breathed in fresh air and felt the relief of freedom. He had never been detained by law enforcement before, had always been able to enter and leave police stations and jails at will. This had shown him a different reality, one he hoped never to experience again. He and Joe walked into the parking lot, and he saw his brother leaning on Joe's black Crown Vic Police Interceptor. Tom came toward him, looked him straight in the eye, and clapped him on the shoulder—the Reid brothers' version of a hug.

"Let's get you out of here," Tom said, opening the front passenger seat door and standing aside to let Conor in.

"Thanks," Conor said.

"You okay?" Tom asked.

"I'm fine," Conor said. That was Irish Catholic code for the exact opposite—*I'm not fine, I feel like shit.* "What about Kate? Have you seen her?"

"She stayed with Hadley and CeCe last night. Call her," Tom said, handing Conor his phone.

He dialed her number, but it went straight to voicemail. He stepped away from the truck to leave her a message. "Kate, I love you. It's all going to be okay, I promise. I just need to talk to you, and we'll be fine." When he disconnected, he wondered why he had said "fine"—considering it was Irish for *anything but.*

"You might be wondering why I brought your brother along," Joe said, pulling out of the parking lot.

"I wasn't wondering that," Conor said. "Just glad that you did. But since you mention it . . ."

"A few things have come up. Tom can help with one in particular," Joe said.

"You did say I'd thank you when you told me what you've been doing," Conor said.

"The house and Belinda's connection to it," Joe said.

"Okay," Conor said.

"The caretaker came by. He knows the cops, and one of them called him, told him to get over there. He said there's a succession of young women who stay there. Like college-aged."

"A party house?" Conor asked.

"Not at all. No noise complaints, no one trashing the property. The opposite, in fact."

"In what way?"

"He said it's like a nunnery. Everyone is very quiet. Polite." He paused. "One of the girls was Suzanne McKinney."

"Wait, Garrett mentioned a Suzanne . . ." Conor said. "Who is she?"

"She was around last night," Tom said. "Working at the dinner, and Maeve said she'd hired her to do the place cards."

"Okay," Conor said, picturing her. He wondered about the house, about Suzanne, and what Belinda's connection to them had been.

"The caretaker does the garden as well as the house. He said hardly anyone seems to go to the beach or walk down the hill to Bay Street—they don't socialize. But every so often he sees a Mercedes pull into the drive. An older woman gets out, enters the house through the back door. He has the feeling she didn't want him to see her face. She stays for a while, then leaves with one or more of the girls."

"Maybe she owns the house," Conor said.

"Turns out the owner of record is a business—Leprince de Beaumont Associates, LLC."

Conor knew that it was not uncommon for homeowners, especially wealthy ones, to put their houses under the names of their trusts, corporations, or limited liability companies. These were time-honored ways to protect the owner's privacy and provide tax advantages. It was hard to crack the shield and learn the identities, but there were ways around it.

"What's Leprince de Beaumont Associates, LLC?" Conor asked.

"No clue. I checked out the secretary of state's website and found the listing. There's a registered agent but no actual owner listed. I left a message with the agent's service, and I'm waiting for a callback," Joe said.

"What about that truck that was parked outside? Can you trace it?" Conor asked.

"That's registered to a different corporation—1740 LLC."

"That number was stenciled on the truck's door," Conor said, picturing it. "Are there any other leads?"

"A few," Joe said. "Starting with Maeve Longacre. She's our 911 caller—she saw the blood."

"Why was she at that house?" Conor asked.

"She said she'd gone out for an early walk," Joe said. "She heard screams and ran to look through the open door."

"Who did she think it was?" Conor asked.

"Kate," Joe said. "See, Maeve had gone to check on her, and when she found the Tower Suite empty, she saw the cut-up veil and realized that the dress was missing. She was on high alert for Kate."

"Kate had no connection with that house," Conor said, doubting that scenario. "Why would Maeve have assumed it was her?"

"She didn't know," Joe said. "Her nerves were raw after the scene last night. She was worried about Kate."

"And instead she came upon Belinda dead. Wearing Kate's dress," Tom said.

Conor nodded. "You said a few leads. What else?"

"Suzanne McKinney," Joe said. "She apparently had an agenda."

"What about her? How did Maeve come to hire her?"

"It's the other way around," Joe said. "Suzanne found Maeve."

"How?" Conor asked.

"Maeve's boyfriend is a musician—"

"Lincoln Adams," Conor said. "His father buys paintings from Kate's gallery."

"Okay," Joe said. "I'll have to talk to him. Because Lincoln played at a wedding in Jamestown, and Suzanne approached him—told him that she'd heard about a big wedding at the Ocean House—yours—and that she wished she could get hired to do assistant-type stuff and the calligraphy."

"So Lincoln put her in touch with Maeve?" Conor asked.

"Yes. Suzanne made it seem she had no idea who was getting married. But that doesn't ring true, considering other developments—we'll fill you in, but it seems Suzanne had a connection to Belinda. Could Lincoln have lied to Maeve, told Suzanne from the start?"

"I don't know him that well," Conor said. "But Kate does—through his father, then through Maeve. Sometimes she has music at gallery openings, and he's played a few times. She said he seems like a good guy. But wait—what connection to Belinda?"

"She might be living on a boat," Tom said. "There was a marina receipt made out in her name. The bizarre thing is, it was found in Belinda's room."

"So they knew each other?" Conor asked.

"Seems so," Joe said. "We'll ask Suzanne when we find her, hopefully soon."

"Where is she?"

"According to the receipt, she's off-grid, at one of the dumpiest marinas in Rhode Island. We're going to check it out now," Tom said.

Joe pulled into the parking lot at Westerly State Airport. This was where Kate kept her plane. The knowledge made Conor's heart tighten.

"Where are we going?" Conor asked.

"The marina's on Bellevigne Island. It has a grass strip, and flying is the fastest way to get there," Tom said.

Joe drove straight toward the tarmac, where private planes were parked. Conor spotted Kate's Cessna. Joe pulled into a space and turned off the engine. Then Conor saw the pilot standing by the cockpit door, arms folded, hair tossed by the summer breeze. It was the most beautiful sight he'd ever seen.

"Here's our ride," Joe said dryly.

"Kate," Conor said, getting out of the car.

Kate took a step toward him, then stopped. Her eyes were full of emotions, too fleeting for Conor to translate. All he cared about was seeing love in her eyes—he thought he saw it, along with sorrow, hurt, confusion—so he moved closer to her. He wanted to put his arms around her. He hesitated, and then he did. Tom and Joe were standing right there, but he felt as if he was alone with Kate.

She leaned her head against his chest. "Oh, Conor," she said.

"Kate, I am sorry . . ."

"Don't say that right now," she said. "I want to hear everything, I want us to talk, but not here."

"I know, Kate. I have a lot to tell you. I can't work, do anything right now, until I can explain what happened. It's so important. And I'm so fucking sorry—about our wedding. I swear, if I hadn't been in police custody, I would have been right there with you. We would have done it, Kate. We would have gotten married, no matter what."

She didn't reply to that. She leaned back, stepped out of his embrace. Her eyes filled with tears, and Conor's heart fell. Was she saying she wouldn't have married him? Was the damage between them too great for her to go on with him?

"We would have, right?" he asked.

She nodded, but no words came out.

"Please say it," he said.

This time she looked down at her feet, as if she wasn't sure—or worse—as if she had decided she couldn't. He knew she was thinking of Belinda, the silver ring, the baby picture. He could feel all her doubts and suspicions pouring off her.

"Let me tell you the whole thing," Conor said, feeling desperate. If only he could explain, put the truth in perspective, he would have her trust again. He would tell her the whole story about what had happened; he would come clean about it all.

"Not right now. Tom told me you're still under suspicion. I'll fly you to the island so you can go to that marina, get Suzanne to put it all together. You have to get out from under this. People think you killed Belinda."

"Do you think that?" Conor asked.

"No. I know you didn't," Kate said. "But you need to prove it to everyone else."

Conor nodded and felt a flood of relief. At least Kate believed him. He heard Tom clear his throat, and he knew that he and Joe were getting impatient to take off and start the investigation on Bellevigne Island.

"It's time," Kate said, nodding her head toward the others.

Their fingertips touched. It wasn't another hug, but it was something.

Conor watched her pull herself together and get into pilot mode.

"Our flight will be smooth on the way over," she said to the group, "but there's weather coming. There are a few storms tracking north of us. They won't impact us directly, but they could cause turbulence on the way back. We have about two and a half hours until dark, and we should plan to be on our way back again."

Kate and the three men climbed into the plane. Joe and Tom took the back seats, leaving Conor to sit up front, next to Kate. He glanced over at her. She was always cool and focused when flying. The only sign that she was still feeling emotional was the flush spreading upward from her neck to her cheeks. She ran through her preflight checklist and started the engine.

The propeller began to turn. The airport was small and didn't have a tower, so she tuned the radio to 122.8, the frequency monitored by pilots.

"Westerly traffic, this is Cessna 2122 Quebec departing runway 5, northeast bound. Crossing midfield," she said into the mike, stating her intention.

Then she taxied, and they took off.

Conor had taken off from this airport with her a hundred times. She flew with grace and confidence. Her eyes never stopped scanning the horizon and the airspace around them. He felt proud to have Tom and Joe in the plane, to see her as a pilot. The plane gained altitude, flying over the marshes and salt ponds, banking over the long barrier island, heading out over Block Island Sound.

They quickly climbed to three thousand feet, and he saw ferries and pleasure boats down below on the glass-smooth water. The sky was still bright blue, but the sun was moving west, just enough to touch the ocean's surface with gold. Gazing down, Conor thought of the people on all those boats, of how they had chosen the perfect weekend for their cruises.

And it hit him hard, to think that it was also a perfect evening for a wedding. Of how wonderful it would have been, there under the white tent, holding Kate close and dancing her around the floor.

He wanted to look over at her again, but he couldn't. Instead, he turned his head to the window and stared out to sea, beyond Block Island, past the windmills, out toward the banks where the ocean was too deep for any light to pierce.

12

Saturday, July 3; 6:00 p.m.

Sam sat at a table on the Ocean House verandah, drinking lemonade and listening to distant thunder. The sky that had been blazingly blue all day began to darken until it was the color of a ripe plum. The bright-blue sea had turned a shade of deep gray green, and white caps began to kick up.

Kate had told her that she had found a receipt in Belinda's room. Written in Suzanne's distinctive handwriting, it listed the address of a marina on a small island. Kate was flying out there with Conor, Tom, and Joe. Sam had no idea what they hoped to find. She could imagine the tension in the plane, given the fact that two of the occupants had just canceled their wedding, but she was guardedly glad to think of Kate with Conor for any reason. She just hoped that he had told her about the envelope he had stuffed into the desk at home.

Sam gazed across the croquet lawn, past the tent and bowers of hydrangeas, at Bluff Avenue. Two police cars and a forensics van were still parked there. Crime scene personnel had been in the house for hours. They had searched the yard and the street in both directions. It looked as if they were wrapping up—loading up the van, closing the door to the house.

She watched them impound a vehicle parked in the driveway—a navy-blue Ford F-150 pickup truck with an insignia stenciled on the driver's-side door. The number 1740 was printed in white, set inside an oval that looked like a vine of thorns. She had seen Suzanne driving it yesterday morning. Now she saw it being taken away on a flatbed.

Sam knew her trucks. Kate had inherited an estate from her grandmother Mathilda. Cloudlands, the stone mansion at the top of Sachem Hill, overlooked a hundred acres of fields, a pine and cedar forest, and tidal wetlands. Kate kept a pickup truck there so they could care for the property and drive the dirt roads into the less accessible regions. Kate's truck happened to be a Ford F-150, and it made sense to Sam that she would need it at Cloudlands.

But what would Suzanne, a calligrapher, be needing with a pickup? In the short time Sam had observed her, Suzanne had seemed prissy. Sam pegged her as a girl who'd wear makeup to an 8:00 a.m. class, lived in ALICE + OLIVIA, and wore Celine sunglasses even after the sun went down. Sam had noticed the red soles on Suzanne's sandals. Because a girl in her dorm had worn them, she knew they were Louboutin. Thousand-dollar sandals.

And, considering all that, what was Suzanne doing with a Ford truck?

Sam spotted Maeve and Lincoln approaching the shingled house where Belinda's body had been found. They spoke to one of the last police officers on the scene, and Maeve seemed upset. At first Sam assumed it was because of finding the body, but then Maeve raised her voice and began gesturing, pointing at the front door. Lincoln put his arm around her shoulders, as if trying to calm her down. The police officer shook his head vehemently, and Maeve and Lincoln walked away.

They came into the hotel's circular drive and up the wide, curving stairs. Sam caught Maeve's eye and waved. Maeve waved back, and then she and Lincoln joined her at the table.

"What's going on?" Sam asked.

"I can't believe this," Maeve said.

"Maeve left her purse in the house this morning," Lincoln said. "And she needs to get it back."

"It has everything in it," Maeve said. "My wallet, credit cards, the notebook I use for the gallery, even my passport."

"The house is a crime scene," Sam said, thinking that should be obvious, considering the yellow tape around the perimeter. "They're not going to let anyone in."

"It's not in the house anymore. The cops took it for evidence," Lincoln said.

"It's crazy," Maeve said. "I had nothing to do with the murder. My address book is in there! All my family's numbers!"

"Don't you have them in your phone?" Sam asked. *What person our age has an address book?*

"Some are," Maeve said. "But it's a special book that means a lot to me. It was my mother's. It reminds me of her."

At that, Sam nodded solemnly. It sounded as if Maeve's mother was dead, and if there was one thing Sam considered sacred, it was a dead mother and the feeling of missing her.

"I hope you get it back soon," she said.

"She will," Lincoln said, taking Maeve's hand.

Sam liked his attitude, the way he was being so supportive. Miranda, Bernard's girlfriend, waved and started toward them.

"I wish I'd never met Suzanne," Maeve said, staring at the house, oblivious to Miranda. That must have given her the vibe that she'd be intruding, because she turned and walked away.

"How *did* you meet Suzanne?" Sam asked.

"Through me, playing at weddings," Lincoln said. "It's a small world of Rhode Island wedding vendors, and we share contacts."

"So you told Suzanne that Maeve needed a calligrapher?" Sam asked.

"It's much weirder than that," Maeve said.

"Actually," Lincoln said, "she completely tricked me. She'd heard about a big Ocean House wedding, and she asked if my band was playing it."

"And he said no, but he's dating the bride's assistant," Maeve said. "And she jumped on that. I swear she knew all along. She got to me through Lincoln."

"And to Kate through you," Sam said.

"Yes, and I feel horrible for hiring her."

"Where is she from?" Sam asked.

"Not sure," Maeve said. "Do you know, Lincoln?"

Lincoln paused for a few beats. He blinked fast and looked down.

That one motion triggered something in Sam.

After her mother was killed, Sam had developed a strange fascination. You'd think that the daughter of a homicide victim would do anything to avoid watching shows about violent crime, but she had gotten obsessed with profiling and behavior analysis. She had read a ton of books and watched YouTube videos of experts breaking down the behavior of criminals. She thought that if she had known such things, she would have been able to recognize her mother's killer in time to warn her.

Lincoln's blink rate was through the roof, and the left side of his mouth was twitching up a storm. Something was clearly bothering him, and Sam had the feeling he was carefully constructing his answer, weighing whether to lie or not.

"Yeah, I do," he said. "She mentioned it one time . . . I'm trying to remember."

Sam stared at him and thought he *did* remember but just didn't want to say. Is that why he was being furtive? Maybe he'd known Suzanne all along. But then he sighed and put up his hands.

"I've got to tell you something," he said. He paused, looked toward the ocean, at a sailboat heeled over in a still breeze. "Suzanne didn't just want to work a big wedding—she specifically wanted to be at Kate and Conor's wedding, and it had to do with Belinda."

"How do you know that?" Maeve asked, sounding shocked.

"Yesterday I saw her going into Belinda's room, before the rehearsal dinner. They hugged, and they were laughing and talking," Lincoln said.

"Why didn't you tell me?" Maeve asked.

"Because I'm the one who introduced Suzanne! You would never have hired her if I hadn't. It's my fault," Lincoln said.

"How could you have known she had other motives?" Sam asked.

"I don't *know* it. But looking back to when she first asked me, it was as if she was leading me. She could have easily found out that my dad is tight with Kate's gallery and that I'm dating Kate's assistant. It was as if she already knew the wedding details and needed to find a way in."

"Why?" Sam asked.

"I don't know. But, looking back, she was so secretive," Lincoln said. "The fact she knew Belinda and kept it hidden is dark."

"Very," Maeve said. She closed her eyes, as if trying to summon a memory. "When I went looking for Kate last night and found her veil sliced to pieces, I was really scared. It was so creepy, it made me think that someone had hurt Kate."

"You didn't think Kate might have cut it up herself?" Lincoln asked.

"Of course not!" Maeve said.

"She's right," Sam said. "You don't know Kate at all if you'd think that was possible. Someone else did it."

"I want to talk to Suzanne," Maeve said. "Where is she now?"

"I don't keep track of her, Maeve," Lincoln said sharply. "We're not close friends or anything."

"Maybe she's still here," Sam said. "She definitely didn't leave in her truck, because I saw the police take it away."

"They must suspect her of something," he said.

"What does 1740 mean?" Sam asked, picturing the number painted on the side of the blue pickup.

"No idea," Lincoln said.

"If it's true that Suzanne knew Belinda," Sam said to Lincoln, "and if she really did angle to get the job, maybe ruining the wedding was her goal all along."

"Like they were in it together?" Maeve asked. "Belinda and Suzanne?"

"Could be," Sam said. "Destroying the veil was vicious. Symbolic. I keep thinking this could be a fairy tale. Belinda showing up the night before the wedding with tales of a secret baby. Then someone—Suzanne—slashing the veil."

"Cursing the wedding," Maeve said.

"You left out the part about murder," Lincoln said. "How someone murdered Belinda."

The ultimate curse of all, Sam thought.

13

Saturday, July 3; 6:30 p.m.

The plane hit turbulence as they approached the island. Kate had checked radar just before taking off, and it looked as if the closest storm cell was trending northwest, so she wasn't too worried. But that was certainly a sharp downdraft, and she heard Joe quietly swear in the back seat. She came in straight, the wheels touched the grass strip, and she taxied to a stop.

"Sorry, that was a bumpy landing," she said.

"It was expert, as usual," Conor said.

He always praised her flying. She felt his gaze and turned to meet his eyes. She had always loved how startlingly blue they were, but just then, they reminded her of the baby picture Belinda had shown her, and she nearly flinched. Everyone climbed out of the plane, and Conor stood waiting for her. Tom and Joe walked ahead.

"I'm just so glad we're together right now," he said. "It's been terrible without you."

"For me too," Kate said. She was overwhelmed with questions that she was afraid to hear the answers to. She was almost glad that they weren't alone; it would give her more time to be ready for the conversation.

She had flown over this island but had never landed here before. She looked around and saw a red barn—the hangar, she assumed. There were a few white houses a short distance away, and she could see the curve of East Cove and a few masts.

"Is that the marina?" she asked, pointing.

"Yes," Tom said.

"We don't man this island," Joe said. "So no State Police vehicles for me to commandeer. We're going to have to walk it."

"Is there a harbormaster?" Conor asked.

"There's barely a harbor," Tom said. "You'll see."

The four of them set off along a dirt road toward the water. It was just two weeks past the longest day of the year, and they had over an hour until sunset. Flying at night wouldn't be a problem, but getting around on the island might be. Fields were scored by stone walls, overgrown with vines and brambles. Barberry, bittersweet, and poison ivy were everywhere.

So far, they hadn't seen a vehicle, but when they reached the town, Kate noticed cars parked in the driveways of two of the houses. One single street ran along the waterfront, with alleys sloping down to the docks. Many of the houses looked run down. She wondered if they were even occupied.

There was a building that was half general store, half post office with a single gas pump out front. The doors were locked, shades drawn. What had Suzanne been doing here, Kate wondered. It felt like a ghost town.

"The town that time forgot," she said.

"If time ever knew it," Tom said.

"I didn't realize there were any islands in this part of the world that hadn't been built up," Conor said. "Where are the tourists?"

"The island is privately owned," Tom said. "Two families who could never decide what they want to do with it—they've been feuding over it for years. One family wants to preserve everything the way it is now, the other wants to sell out to developers."

"They'd make a fortune," Joe said.

"If it's private property," Kate said, "are we allowed to be here?"

"I'm a detective with the Rhode Island State Police, and Tom is a Coast Guard commander, and this is an official investigation," Joe said. "So, yes. We are."

Kate scanned the docks. There were three, jutting out into the cove. Two needed repair and were unusable—their pilings were tilting, from lack of maintenance and the continual battering of the sea. The third one had two boats tied to either side: two fishing boats that looked to be in decent shape, a Boston Whaler, and a classic sailboat.

Joe took out the receipt made out to Suzanne that Kate had found in the wastebasket and scanned it.

"All it says is 'dockage fee.' Nothing more specific, so it's anyone's guess which boat she was paying for," he said.

"I'm betting against the fishing boats," Tom said. "They belong to a couple of guys with recreational lobster licenses. It's got to be the sailboat."

"Pretty," Kate said. "My grandmother and Ruth used to charter Hinckleys up in Maine every summer. Beautiful designs."

"Your grandmother had good taste," Tom said. "This one's a Hinckley Pilot—I've seen her around Fishers Island, Watch Hill, Stonington."

They stood beside the Hinckley. She had a gleaming black hull with highly varnished brightwork—someone took very good care of her. The companionway door, leading down a steep, brightly varnished ladder to the boat's interior, was half open. Kate could see that the wood frame was splintered, and the hinges had been jimmied. There were some rusty-looking drops on the deck.

"Is that blood?" Kate asked.

"Could be, and looks like we have a break-in," Joe said. "I'm going to call for the police boat."

"I'm going to board her," Tom said.

"I thought you needed a warrant," Kate said.

"The police do," Tom said. "The Coast Guard doesn't."

Tom announced himself loudly, but there was no response from inside. Kate, Conor, and Joe watched him step over the lifelines onto the deck, move quickly to the companionway, and peer inside. A moment later, he disappeared down below. Kate knew it had to be dark there; she saw the beam of his flashlight moving behind the windows. A moment later, she heard him exclaim. He poked his head up.

"You are going to need that police boat," he said. "And I'll get my team out here too."

"What is it?" Conor asked. Kate watched him and Joe step aboard and follow Tom down below. Kate climbed onto the deck. She leaned over to look through the doorway. She saw the two Reid brothers and Joe Harrigan standing in the main salon, staring at something. She went down the ladder; it took a moment for her eyes to get used to the dark.

Kate had done a lot of sailing, been on many boats, including the Hinckley Bermuda 40 her grandmother and Ruth used to charter. At first glance, this interior looked like others she had seen before. She saw hunter-green settees on either side, a folded-up dining table in the center, a small galley to the left of the companion ladder. Nestled into the corner was a small tile fireplace—a rarity on boats.

The beam of Tom's flashlight was directed at one of the settees—padded benches along the bulkhead. He shined the light upward, and she saw chains bolted into the wood. Her gaze followed them down, where handcuffs attached to chains lay on either side of the mattress.

"What is this?" Kate asked, hardly able to speak.

"Someone was held prisoner here," Conor said.

Kate watched as the flashlight beam moved in on the galvanized metal clasps. They were streaked with something dark, and she saw that there were maroon spots on the settee fabric.

"Blood," Conor said. "Whoever was restrained here struggled to get free."

"The handcuffs chafed her wrist," Kate said. She used the pronoun *her* with no doubt that a woman had been held here. Her eyes met Conor's, and he nodded.

Tom put on gloves and tapped the bulkhead. A corner of the wood was loose, and he pulled it free to look behind. "There's foam insulation in there. This boat has been soundproofed," he said.

"So no one could hear her scream," Kate said.

The four of them climbed back onto the dock. The sun was starting to set. Butterscotch rays spilled through thunderheads, over the waves, and through the town. Kate felt sick. Tom stood beside the boat, noting the registration number. Kate walked to the stern to look at the name. In the declining light, the letters looked ephemeral, as if they'd been scrawled by a spirit, and she could barely make them out: *Psyche*.

Tom tried to make a call, but it wouldn't go through.

"No reception," he said. "Big surprise. I need to call this in. Joe, you, too, right?"

"We need a crime scene van," Joe said. "But there's no ferry service, so how am I going to get it out here?"

"You're right, there's no scheduled ferry," Tom said. "But there's a boat ramp. It's how they get supplies delivered." He walked over to the cracked asphalt sloping down into the cove and gave it a skeptical once-over. "The ramp's not in great shape, but it's workable. You can get whatever you need onto the island."

Joe looked toward the white houses along the main street. "You think anyone has a landline?" he asked.

"We can use my radio," Kate said. "But since it's getting so late, maybe you should just come with me, head back here tomorrow."

"Someone has to stay and preserve the crime scene," Conor said. He scanned the village. "This place seems deserted, but you know if anyone's home, they're watching us right now. We don't want anyone tampering with evidence. And we should start questioning them."

"Why didn't anyone say anything?" Kate said, gazing back at *Psyche*. "Someone was tortured on that boat. The people in those houses or the ones who own the fishing boats . . . Even if they didn't hear screams, they must have noticed something."

"Well, we're here now, and no one is getting on or off the island without our seeing," Joe said. "And you can be sure we'll question everyone."

"Where are you going to sleep?" Kate asked, gazing at Conor.

"Who's going to sleep?" Joe asked.

They returned to Kate's plane, and Tom and Joe took turns using the radio to call their headquarters and request assistance. Conor and Kate stood a few yards back. She felt him staring at her. Her heart was beating hard. There was so much they needed to say to each other, but she had no idea where to start. He stepped forward, touched her arm.

"Kate," he said.

She shook her head.

"We should be . . ."

"Married by now," she said in a low voice. Their wedding should have happened over two hours ago. They should be having dinner under that magical white tent. The band should be starting to play, and any minute now they would have started dancing.

"I know," he said. "Kate, I want to fix this."

"Fix it how?"

"Tell me. I'll do anything."

Her thoughts were scrambled, and she tried to put them into words. "I wish you had told me everything from the beginning."

He nodded, as if agreeing with her.

"I felt so blindsided. I didn't know what to think when she showed me that picture—I still don't. We've always said we could tell each other anything, that we wouldn't keep secrets," she said.

"Kate, I wasn't keeping a secret. Belinda came out of nowhere with those lies. There was nothing to tell you—I haven't thought of her in years," he said.

"You didn't seem honest yesterday," Kate said. "Starting when I saw you with her in town. I felt like you wanted to hide something."

"I was just shocked to see her," Conor said.

Kate tilted her head. Even now, her antennae were up. He wasn't telling her the full truth.

"Really?" she asked. "That's all?"

"Kate," he said, trying to hold her hand. She backed away, and she gave him a look that told him to stop.

"The reason I'm here," she said, "is that I searched Belinda's hotel room, looking for something, anything, to explain what's going on. Belinda and Suzanne were very much connected. You were questioned by the police today, Conor. You might have been arrested if Joe and Tom hadn't gotten you out of there."

"I didn't belong there," he said. "That was spite on Garrett's part. Because Belinda was his girlfriend, and she obviously had an ulterior motive in getting him to bring her to our wedding as his date."

"Belinda told me she had your child," Kate said slowly. "And Suzanne spent time in her room. She left her pen and ink and cards right there, in the desk."

"Well, maybe they knew each other," Conor said.

Kate barely heard him. She was focused on his face, that handsome Irish face that she loved so much. There was a faint rust-colored streak on his left cheekbone.

"You have blood on your cheek," she said.

"I thought I washed it all off," he said, his hand straying to the side of his face.

"From when you touched Belinda's body," Kate said.

"Because I thought it was you," he said, his voice tight. "She was wearing your dress."

"Conor," Kate said, looking down and imagining what that must have been like for him.

At the same time, a realization had been building inside her. It had started last night, when Belinda had shown her the photo. Thoughts and impressions had filled her mind, when she was both sleeping and awake, but until now she had been able to push them away. She wished she could keep them from adding up into a whole that she would give anything not to see. She pictured Suzanne last night and remembered how she had noted that the indigo flowers printed on her maxi dress matched her eyes.

"The ages are right," Kate said.

"Whose ages?"

"Belinda's and Suzanne's. Yours and Suzanne's. About twenty years apart."

Conor's expression darkened. Was it because he was catching up with her logic, figuring it out? Or was he upset that Kate was working out the puzzle pieces?

"The eye color is right too," she said.

"What are you talking about?"

"Suzanne's your daughter," Kate said.

"God, Kate—no!" Conor said.

"Your eyes," Kate said. "The same blue as the baby in the photo, the same blue as Suzanne's." She paused, composing herself. "Had you ever met Suzanne before? Did you hold her when she was a baby?"

"This is crazy," Conor said. "Kate, I didn't have a child with Belinda."

His voice broke, and it sent shocks through her whole body, cracking her bones as if they were ice. She wanted to reach for him, to steady herself and to hold him. He sounded so upset, and she had to believe he was telling the truth—at least as far as he knew it. What if Belinda had had his baby and just never told him about it?

"She said you call her 'Belle,'" Kate said.

"What?" he asked.

"*Beauty and the Beast*," Kate said. "You're the Beast, and she's Belle. The great love story, your own private fairy tale."

"I have no idea what that means," Conor said. "I've never called her anything but Belinda."

"That's not what she said."

"She lied about everything," Conor said. "Tell me you believe me."

Kate gazed at him, wanting to say yes, but feeling churned up and unsure in a way she never would have thought she could feel about Conor.

"Kate, thanks for letting us use the radio," Tom said, interrupting them. "We've got the police and Coast Guard on their way out here. You might as well head back to Westerly."

Conor moved toward Kate, as if he was going to get into the plane with her, but she stopped him. "You're staying here with them, aren't you?" she asked quietly, so Tom and Joe couldn't hear.

"I want to be with you," he said.

"I don't know what's happening out here," Kate said. "But someone was held prisoner on that boat, and Suzanne plays some part in it. The dockage receipt is in her name. We've gotten pulled into a nightmare, and we need to get out of it."

"You want me to stay out here and work the case with them?" he asked.

Kate wasn't sure what was right—all she knew was that she wanted to get back on even ground with Conor, and that couldn't happen with the mysteries of Belinda and Suzanne and murder and lies swirling around them.

"Yes," she said. "I want that."

Conor nodded, then turned to Joe and Tom.

"I'm staying," he said.

"It's my crime scene," Joe said. "This is Rhode Island, remember. And you're not off the hook."

"Then let's solve the case and get me off the hook," Conor said.

Kate saw Tom smile. He knew that once Conor made up his mind to do something, there was no talking him out of it.

And so did Kate.

Tom and Joe looked at her, waiting for her to get into the plane and take off, but she didn't move. Her eyes were locked on Conor's. She had always been able to read him, since the beginning. She could sense his mood, read his thoughts—as he could read hers. Sometimes it seemed they shared a heart, the way their emotions synced.

Tom and Joe began walking back toward the dock, leaving Kate and Conor alone.

"Maybe I won't go either," Kate said. "I can stay and help however I can."

"Before you decide what to do," Conor said, "I need to hear you say something."

"What?"

"That you believe me. That you know I never had a child with Belinda."

Kate stared at him. Her heart was racing because she knew they were at a crossroads and that everything that would happen in the future would begin right here.

"She was obviously troubled, messed up," Conor continued. "She wasn't living in reality. She had some kind of fantasy that began when we lived next door to each other. For the longest time, I had no idea how seriously she took it. It was never real." He moved so close to Kate, she could feel warmth pouring off him. "Please, Kate. Believe me—I am telling you the truth."

"And you won't lie to me, ever?" she asked.

"I promise," he said.

"Then tell me this," she said, her heart beating so fast she was almost breathless.

"Anything," he said.

"Did you ever sleep with her?" she asked.

He looked straight at her, but then he bowed his head, and he didn't say anything for almost a minute. She knew then. His silence was enough of an answer for her, but then he said the words out loud:

"Yes," he said. "I did."

Kate stood very still. She gazed at those eyes she had fallen in love with, that smile she had memorized, the arms that had held her. He was

Conor, he was the same man. But just then she felt so numb inside, she might as well be standing beside a stranger.

"It was before," he said. "Before you and I were really together."

She nodded.

"Say something, Kate. Please."

"*Really* together?" she asked, hearing him qualify it. "Like when we were only a little bit?"

"No, Kate. It's not like that."

Kate waited for him to continue and tell her what it *was* like, but he was silent. She had thought about staying on the island until the backup police and Coast Guard arrived, but now she turned away and climbed into her plane.

She went through the motions as she did her preflight check and started the engine. She told herself she couldn't afford to be numb; she needed all her senses to fly. On the other hand, numbness was probably safer than the alternative—giving in to a broken heart. Without looking back at Conor, Kate taxied down the grass strip and took off into the wind.

It wasn't until she did a wide, banking turn that she looked down at the island, at Conor. He was standing right where she had left him, at the edge of the runway, looking up at her plane as it flew away.

14

GIRL #3

Mid-May; two months earlier

It was as if he magically knew when she was getting ready to drift into another realm, into death, that he came to the boat to rescue her. He told her he had learned his lesson, by what had happened to the girls before her. He would never let her die on the boat. He told her the woman had gotten very angry with him. She had taught the girl every-thing she knew, it had taken a lot of effort and training at the Finishing School, and the girl was valuable to them.

So he would unlatch the companionway door, enter the cabin, kneel by the mattress, speak to her in a low, soothing voice. He would remove the restraints and gently wash her places where the metal cuffs had chafed her skin. He always brought fresh water and an antiseptic that stung. He would fill the cup and tip it against her lips. He would bring a dark-green thermos and feed her consommé with a silver spoon, and she would sip hungrily, as if she were a wounded bird being fed with a dropper.

The woman had trained her, but she hadn't said anything about handcuffs or being fed with a dropper. She had left those parts out. The training had only been about parties and gowns and makeup and conversation and promises of trips to the island and to Europe and sailing on yachts and how the men loved it when you acted shy.

Sometimes this man spoke to her in French, using a phrase here and there. He told her that he would take her to France—to Alsace or the Loire Valley—places where the story began, where châteaus—real castles—were located. She had studied French in school—she had read novels in French such as *L'Étranger* by Albert Camus and *Bonjour Tristesse* by Françoise Sagan; poems by François Villon and Arthur Rimbaud. His accent was terrible, and she had to pretend to take him seriously.

Then, when she was strong enough, he would blindfold her again. He would tape her mouth shut. He would lead her into the fresh air, across the dock's rough boards, across the grass, and up the hill. They would enter the house. She had never seen the house from the outside, but she sensed it was grand. When they reached her bedroom, and he untied the blindfold and ripped the tape off her mouth, she could see, feel, and smell all the beautiful things.

He reminded her the walls were made of stone and the locked door lined with lead, and that even if she screamed, no one would hear her.

Although there was no real light in the boat, here in the mansion, in her special bedroom, there was plenty. A chandelier with crystal prisms sent rainbows dancing all around the room. Gilded lamps stood on ornate white tables on either side of the big bed. The walnut headboard was carved with flowers and angels, antiqued with gold. The mattress was thick and so comfortable, covered with crisp white sheets and a featherlight white down comforter.

The floors were polished wood, covered with plush blue-and-white Aubusson rugs that he told her were very old. He had bought them at auction, just for her. Or for the girl before her, she was never really sure. There was a marble fireplace with brass andirons shaped like monsters, and when the fire was lit, their eyes glowed orange and flames shot from their mouths. Above the mantel hung a black-and-white photo—a still from the film they always watched. They read the books, too, and sometimes the imagery seemed so different, it was hard to believe it was the same story.

She felt nervous, waiting for the party to begin.

One wall had bookshelves from the floor to ceiling, and they were filled with hundreds of books. Novels, volumes of poetry, atlases, books about history, nature, dreams, psychology, travel, and more. She read all the time, sometimes a book every day. Mostly, the books were about them—about him. Well, not him by name—but his inspiration for all of this, for the gifts he gave her.

He gave her a diamond ring, to wear on her left hand. It was too big, so they made it fit by wrapping a piece of adhesive tape around the band. The stone was enormous, shaped like a pear. But she wondered if he had once given the ring to a girl who was bigger than she was, who the ring would fit better. Had that been the girl who had died on the boat? The girl who had scratched marks into the glass of the porthole?

Her reading pleased him. In the days before the party, he would visit her in the evening. He brought her dinner, served on a tray with gold-rimmed porcelain plates and sterling silver forks embossed with a coat of arms—he never gave her knives. If dinner was meat, he would cut it up for her himself. Then he would sit in the silk-covered armchair by the fire and watch her eat. After dinner, they had tea from a blue-and-white teapot, and he asked her to tell him about what she had been reading.

Especially what he called the legacy books: the various editions of "La Belle et la Bête." He loved when she read in French; he kept interrupting her to make sure she knew that he was her special one, that other men might attend the party, but she had to know that she was his. Of course he didn't know that all the men wanted that, and the woman had trained her to make them believe that each was the most important.

There were several editions of "La Belle et la Bête," each one an antique volume with pages as fragile as butterfly wings. She liked the oldest version, printed forty-nine years before the French Revolution. So did he. Occasionally they watched the film—the original, an old black-and-white print, in French. He told her that ordinary girls—the other girls who came to the party—liked the animated version, but that she was not an ordinary girl.

There were tall windows with long pale-blue velvet draperies tied back with gold cords. But the window glass was wavy, the kind that gave privacy, that allowed light to enter the room but did not allow her to see anything outside. The only thing she was sure of was that a tall tree grew close to the house, and sometimes she saw the branches moving in the wind, and the light would cast shadows of the leaves on the blue-and-white carpet.

She imagined breaking the window glass and jumping on the branch closest to the wall, shinnying down and escaping.

The woman had instructed her about many things. There weren't many rules in her bedroom, but there was one that had to be obeyed without fail: She had to close the curtains at night—or anytime she turned the lamps on. If she did not obey, if she forgot, she would be taken to the boat and left there until she was too weak to lift her water glass.

So she never forgot and always obeyed.

He told her he would love her until one of them died. That the rule about the curtains was to protect her—to protect him too. To make sure they could stay together. Because if light escaped the room, and someone saw the windows illuminated, they would be torn apart forever. He said that the last girl who had stayed here—not the party visitors, but one like her, who had been his special girl—had disobeyed and opened the curtains after dark. He said that after she did that, she had gone away.

Gone where? she asked.

It doesn't matter, he said. *The point is, we couldn't be together after that. I don't want that to happen to us.*

She acted as if it would be the worst thing in the world, to be sent away from him. But she didn't feel that way at all. Sometimes, when she lay awake in the warm bed, she felt as if she might explode with anxiety and rage. She would think of things he had told her: that tragedies sometimes happened on the boat. That she should be glad it was dark in there, so she couldn't see dark swipes on the walls, where the woman had tried to clean up the blood. And that tree outside the window would beckon.

He had said there were layers of disobeying, that not closing the curtains was just the first layer. He said that she wouldn't want to find out what the deeper layers were, as Girl #2 had found out before her.

Did Girl #2 drown? she asked.

No, she died in a different way.

What about Girl #1? she asked.

She is fine, he said, *she is just fine.* But in the way he blinked hard and looked away, she didn't believe him.

He would always assure her that she was his favorite by far, the most beautiful of all the girls who had come before her. He would tell her that her beauty was intoxicating, more powerful than the richest wine. His words slipped and slid; he couldn't keep track of his lies. He told her whatever he thought she wanted to hear—if only he knew how pathetic she considered him, that she never believed one word he said.

She would think of the boat, and the restraints, and how she knew the girl before her had died there. And those thoughts led to this plush bedroom—all the luxuries, even the marble bathroom and the lavender-scented bath oil, and the thick white towels—and she felt as if this bedroom was even worse than the dank, cold, smelly place with its rust-red streaks and grimy windows.

He told her that this bedroom was her castle—their castle—but she knew that wasn't true. It was her prison, her tomb. He said they would be together until one of them died, and deep down, she knew that she would die in here or in the place, just like Girl #2. Even if she tried to jump to the tree branch, it was a long way down to the ground; she could fall and die.

But she could try.

And then he told her how she could be set free. He told her she only had to do one thing.

It was time for her to graduate. She would no longer be a pupil; she would be a teacher.

She pretended to go along with him, because maybe "graduation" would take her to a different place, somewhere she could escape from. And she would take him down—for herself, and for all the women.

15

Sunday, July 4; 8:00 a.m.

Instead of staying with Hadley and CeCe again, Kate had slept in the Tower Suite on what should have been her wedding night. She woke up, reached across the bed to touch Conor, and remembered. Her heart fell, and she lay there staring at his pillow for a long time. She heard his voice answering her question last night. Yes. He had slept with Belinda. She turned over and tried to go back to sleep.

But of course, she couldn't. She wanted to face him again and hear the whole story as soon as possible, and at the same time, she never wanted to hear another word out of his mouth. She hated the way she was feeling: distrustful of the love of her life, jealous of a poor, murdered crazy woman. She got out of bed and caught a glimpse of herself in the mirror. She looked nuts.

She had once had a therapist who advised her to practice self-acceptance, to gaze into her own eyes and say *Hello, I love you, Kate.*

That wasn't happening this morning.

Get over it, idiot, she said instead. But that didn't feel right either.

When she eventually went down to the lobby, she saw that the thunderstorms had cleared out the heavy air, and it was another sparkling blue-sky summer day. She stepped outside, onto the verandah. It was the Fourth of July, and a row of American flags attached to the hotel's south-facing side fluttered in the sea breeze. The ocean was calm, with gentle waves tumbling onto the beach, advancing up to the tide line.

A crew of workmen was efficiently disassembling her wedding tent. She leaned against one of the staid white columns, watching them lower the wooden poles, fold the enormous white sailcloth canopy. It disappeared before her eyes into the back of a truck. When the truck drove away, she returned to the lobby and walked to the sleek Italian coffee machine.

"Well, there you are," Anne said, hurrying across the lobby before she could get herself a cappuccino. "Where's Conor?"

"He's with Tom and Joe. They're working on a lead."

"Mike is anxious to talk to him," Anne said. "And his calls go straight to voicemail."

"Why is Mike anxious?" Kate asked.

"You know him. He can't relax until he knows everyone is all right. He was worried about Garrett bringing Conor into the station for questioning."

"From what I hear, it went well," Kate said.

Conor's uncle Mike walked over with a tall, strong-looking man appearing to be in his early fifties.

"Kate, this is Leo Kennedy, the lawyer I told Conor about," Mike said.

"Hello, Leo," Kate said.

"Nice to meet you, Kate," Leo said. "I'm sorry I couldn't get back in time to go with Conor to the police barracks—I'm on vacation, and I was out fishing on my boat." He swiveled his head, and Kate noticed that he had the same Irish American sunburned skin as the Reids, along with curly brown hair and eyes the color of Galway Bay.

"Sorry you're interrupting your vacation," Kate said. "He's with his brother and a friend, working on the case."

"That concerns me, Kate," Mike said. "Joe is a Rhode Island detective. He might be Conor's friend, but this is an active investigation. Garrett Milne very much considers Conor a suspect, whether Joe does or not. I want to catch Conor before he says anything he shouldn't to Joe."

Good luck with that, Kate thought. "Conor has never turned away from a homicide investigation in his life," she said. "Don't expect him to start now. Especially with this one."

"He won't be able to investigate anything if he winds up in custody," Leo said.

"Mike," Kate said. "Given what happened at our dinner, Garrett has it in for Conor. He heard his girlfriend say that she and Conor have a child. I think he's acting out of jealousy. It's no basis for him to suspect Conor of anything."

She was shaking as she spoke. She thought of how she had linked Belinda and Suzanne through the place cards and quill pen, and in spite of Conor's denial, she couldn't get the idea of Suzanne, with her blue eyes, out of her mind.

She had also started to wonder whether Garrett, who had been staying in the same room as Belinda, knew some of these things too. And whether he was ignoring—burying—them to make Conor his scapegoat.

"I'll have my investigator look into Garrett," Mike said. "And whyever he might be going after Conor."

"You have an investigator?" Kate asked.

"Yes. Anne," he said and chuckled. "Well, and the rest of our crew. Now that I'm retired, I've been branching out. We're kind of like private detectives, sometimes working parallel to the police, other times in a completely different direction."

"In this case, looking into Garrett Milne, it's most certainly in a different direction," Leo said. "The police will want no part of going after him."

"A lot of jurisdictions take care of their own," Mike said. "Cops don't investigate cops. Mainly, I'd like to hear everything possible about his girlfriend. Belinda is the murder victim—she's the key to everything."

"She lived next door to Conor in New London when they were kids," Kate said. "And then she seemed to fall off the face of the earth. Just disappeared, when she was very young."

"Maybe she went away to school," Anne said.

"I didn't get that feeling," Kate said. "Another thing—she was married once, and her husband died."

An older couple approached, and the man raised his hand in greeting. Then he and the woman hugged Anne and Mike, and Mike introduced them.

"Kate, I'd like you to meet two of Anne's and my dearest friends," Mike said. "Edward and Nola Aldrich."

"Lovely to meet you," Nola said, and Kate shook hands with her and Edward.

"Listen, Kate," Mike said. "We are here to help Conor. You can count on all of us—we'll put our heads together."

"Leo doesn't talk about his cases, but most of them wind up in the news," Nola said. "So we do a lot of hypotheticals. Of course, the media is full of plenty of unsolved crimes, so mostly we just talk about them. I teach a course in criminal behavior at Brown, and some of my students are very good at profiling. Honestly, I learn a lot from them."

"We weigh in on message boards, and we've done quite well on our cases," Edward said.

"Some friends play bridge, we solve murders," Mike said. "Or try to."

"We're lucky because Edward has all kinds of databases, connections with the right people," Anne said.

"Databases?" Kate asked.

"Like Mike, I retired a few years back. I owned a private security firm," Edward said. "And I keep up the subscriptions."

"We'll do our best," Nola said. "One hundred percent for Conor's defense."

"Only if he needs a defense," Anne said with strong emotion in her voice. "There is no way that Conor hurt that woman. Belinda. I don't even want to say this . . ." She paused, then took a step closer to Kate.

"What?" Kate asked. "Tell me."

Anne took Kate's hand and looked into her eyes.

"I think the murder was a case of mistaken identity. Belinda was never the intended victim," Anne said.

"Then who was?" Kate asked.

"The killer saw Belinda wearing your wedding dress and thought he was killing you," Anne said.

"Conor thought it was me, when he found the body," Kate said quietly. She felt a cold chill run down her spine. In spite of how she felt about Belinda, her heart seized to think of her so violently killed—even worse if it had been a mistake.

"What do we know about the actual murder?" Nola asked, pulling a notebook from her purse.

"From what Conor told me," Mike said, "Belinda was attacked from behind. The killer reached around to cut her throat."

Nola listened, taking notes.

"Exactly," Anne said. "So the killer wouldn't have seen Belinda's face. And it was early morning."

"The sun was just coming up," Kate said slowly. "There would have been shadows in the room. The light would have been dim."

"There are a few obvious issues," Edward said. "What is Belinda's height in relation to Kate's? Kate, you're what—five six?"

"About," Kate said.

"So the murderer had to be at least that tall, probably taller—to reach around and make his cut," Nola said.

"I'll get the medical examiner's report from one of my contacts on the state police," Edward said. "That will tell us a lot. And I'll get him to pull Belinda's driver's license. It will have her height. Does anyone have a photo of her?"

Kate scrolled through her phone, found a couple of shots she had taken the night before, with Belinda in the background. Edward gave her his number, and Kate texted them to him.

"Thank you," she said, looking around the group. "For helping with this."

"Of course," Mike said. He put his arm around Kate's shoulders. "We're family, Kate. And our friends are very good at what they do. We'll figure this out."

Kate nodded, and then she left the five old crime-solvers to keep working on Conor's case. She had to walk away from them before she cried.

16

Sunday, July 4; 11:00 a.m.

Sam and Hadley took CeCe to the Ocean House pool. It was located a level below the lobby, with a wall of glass that opened onto a terrace lined with hydrangeas, with a view of the sea. The pool was long and serene, with turquoise water sparkling in light slanting in from outside. A semicircle of shallow water, with a gentle fountain glittering in the sun, curved onto the wide terrace, reaching toward the ocean. Hadley played in the pool with CeCe while Sam sat on a lounge chair, staring intently at her laptop. She googled Belinda Tyler. Many websites advertised all the information anyone would want about any Belinda Tyler in the United States, including current and past addresses, family members, and background reports. Most of them required payment. But there were much simpler and obvious ways, where she could actually see pictures and, sometimes, snippets of real life. She could go to any of the major social media sites—Facebook, Instagram, and X—and type in the name. Sometimes she would get a hit. Even though she didn't consider "Belinda" a common name, quite a few Belinda Tylers were coming up.

One bit of data might help her narrow things down: the fact that Belinda had grown up on the same street in New London as Conor and Tom Reid. Their families had been neighbors. Sam knew from experience that available online information could go back many years, even decades. There could be multiple addresses. She didn't know the name of the street, so she typed Conor and Tom's parents' names into the search bar.

She found the address for John and Mary Reid:

613 Montauk Avenue

New London, CT 06320

That made it easy. She had no idea of Belinda's parents' first names, but she remembered Conor mentioning her maiden name and typed:

Quinn

Montauk Avenue

New London, CT 06320

And then she hit the jackpot. Google gave her names and an address that she thought had to be Belinda's parents—Clement and Rosalie Quinn, 611 Montauk Avenue, New London, CT 06320. The search also brought up a full page of mentions and articles about the family from *The Day*—the local newspaper.

Clement Quinn had been named Citizen of the Year in 1978. He had owned a printing company and was honored for all the work he did at discount prices for nonprofit organizations and young business owners. There was a photo of Clement—it was blurry, but Sam could see that he was wearing a blazer and tie and had a wide smile, a seventies mustache, and sideburns. The article mentioned his family: wife, Rosalie; three-year-old son, Clark; and infant daughter, Belinda.

Sam scrolled through the hits and found a less honorable mention. Ten years later, in 1988, Clement appeared in the *Day* police blotter for risk of injury to a minor, second-degree unlawful restraint, second-degree threatening, third-degree assault, and disorderly conduct. The article did not name the victim.

One year after that, in June 1989, there was an article about Whaling City Community College having paid the Quinn Company two thousand dollars for printing costs. They didn't receive the materials, and when the registrar contacted Clement Quinn for a refund, she discovered that the company had gone out of business and left no forwarding phone number or address.

A follow-up article stated that the Quinns had withdrawn Clark and Belinda from school, left their house having defaulted on their mortgage, as well as an unpaid lease on their Cadillac. The car had been parked on Bank Street, behind the printing company, with the keys in the ignition.

Sam found no articles after that one. She searched all the names, not limiting the geographic area, but there was nothing until a July 2010 wedding announcement in the *Providence Journal*:

Belinda Quinn weds Dr. J.W. Tyler III

Belinda Quinn and Jonathan Whitman Tyler III were married yesterday at their home in Narragansett, R.I., by the Rev. David M. Dorset, a Congregational minister.

The bride is the daughter of the late Mr. and Mrs. Clement P. Quinn of New London, Conn. Her husband is the son of Dr. and Mrs. Jonathan W. Tyler Jr. of Providence, R.I.

The bride is an artist. The groom is the medical director of the Maynard-King Center in Narragansett, Rhode Island. The bride's daughter was flower girl.

Sam focused on that phrase: the bride's daughter. Could the flower girl have been Conor's daughter? Kate and Conor were the best couple she knew. They were her family, and they gave her hope that life was good, that people were who they seemed to be. She had grown up with a painful legacy: a family broken by violence and cheating.

Kate and Conor had done so much to make up for all that.

But if Conor had really had this secret life, that meant he had tricked Kate. And fooled Sam too—just like her father. In the back of her mind was that call that Conor had taken in June, when he had been so secretive. She felt scared to find out what Conor had been up to, but no matter what, she wanted to know the truth—and that meant learning whatever she could about Belinda.

The wedding announcement said that Belinda's husband was director of the Maynard-King Center. Sam googled the Center, and its website came up. The home page showed a bright picture of a stately white clapboard building in a parklike setting. The type said: It takes bravery to get better. Better from what? she wondered.

Above the photo of the bucolic scene, there was a row of headings with clickable links to explore elements of the site.

What We Do * Who We Help * What We Treat * Why Maynard-King * About Us

She clicked on What We Treat and read the list:

- Co-Occurring Disorders
- Anxiety Disorders
- Mood Disorders
- PTSD Caused by Domestic Violence
- Psychological Trauma
- Borderline Personality Disorder
- Dissociative Disorders
- Psychotic Illnesses

Obviously, Maynard-King was a psychiatric hospital. She ignored the list of mental health conditions and clicked on the About Us tab, expecting to find Dr. Jonathan Tyler listed as medical director, but he wasn't. There was no Dr. Tyler mentioned at all.

She closed the hospital website and typed *Dr. Jonathan W. Tyler III* into the search bar. Her search yielded many links to newspapers and television stations, all with similar headlines, and her blood begins to thump through her veins.

Police Identify Victim in Halloween Hospital Homicide

Doctor Is Victim of Halloween Murder

Prominent Psychiatrist Murdered

All Hallows Homicide at Exclusive Mental Health Center

"It's a Very Sad Day"—Details in "Princess" Killing Emerge in Death of Dr. Jonathan Tyler III

Sam clicked on the first article and read it:

> Rhode Island State Police have identified the victim in a homicide investigation at the Maynard-King Center as Dr. Jonathan W. Tyler III. At midnight on Tuesday, October 31, officers were called for reports of screams coming from within an office in the Norton Two Unit. They discovered a male suffering from stab wounds to his neck. Lifesaving measures were unsuccessful, and Dr. Tyler was pronounced dead at the scene.
>
> Dr. Tyler was the medical director of the Center, specializing in the treatment of trauma patients. He was one of the nation's foremost authorities in treating dissociative disorder.
>
> One witness reported seeing a "masked princess in a silver gown running from the scene." Another described her as a "faceless witch in a flowing white dress." An iridescent face mask was found on the property. Authorities have declined to say whether they believe it was worn by anyone connected to the crime,

but one witness reported that it was covered with blood spatter.

Earlier in the evening, a Halloween party had been held for the patients. "Dressing in costumes was allowed as long as masks were not worn," said one staff member who declined to be identified. She continued, "Facial coverings can trigger trauma patients and bring on feelings of anxiety, terror, claustrophobia, and entrapment, and induce a 'fight-or-flight' reaction. No masks were allowed or discovered during room checks, so we are confident that both the holographic face mask and the perpetrator came from outside the hospital."

The case remains under investigation. Police are requesting anyone with information to contact Detective Martin Matthews of the Rhode Island State Police.

Next, Sam skipped down to "It's a Very Sad Day"—Details in "Princess" Killing Emerge in Death of Dr. Jonathan Tyler III

After a prominent psychiatrist was murdered in his office at the exclusive Maynard-King Center on Halloween night, police spokesperson Armand Braga stated that there are no suspects, and the investigation continues.

A nurse at the center greeted a reporter in the lobby. "It's a very sad day," she said. "Dr. Tyler was loved by patients and staff alike. Our hearts go out to his wife and stepdaughter." The tearful nurse declined to give her name.

Fear reigns throughout the twenty-five-acre hospital campus. Witnesses report seeing someone dressed as a masked phantom leaving the Norton Two Unit shortly after the 911 call reporting screams was made.

"The screams were chilling," one witness reported.

"Bloodcurdling," said another, who added, "Shrieking, pure terror. Poor Dr. Tyler. He only wanted to help people."

"Can you imagine how terrified he must have been, being stabbed to death by a princess? A wicked princess?" one distraught patient asked.

Norton Two is a locked unit serving patients suffering from a variety of trauma-induced illnesses. Most of the physicians at Maynard-King kept offices in a different building, but several staff members said that Dr. Tyler preferred to be with his patients.

"None of the Norton Two residents are suspects at this time," spokesperson Braga stated.

The medical examiner's report reveals that Dr. Tyler died of exsanguination. "A long and deep, oblique incision was found on the front of the neck. There were no defense or hesitation injuries. Death was caused by a homicidal cut by a right-handed person standing behind the victim, using a bladed weapon such as a knife or a razor."

The weapon has not been found. However, a mask that is believed to be the murderer's was found near the cemetery on hospital grounds.

"No one could survive an attack like that," a witness said. "Everyone here is freaked out. If it could happen to Dr. Tyler, it could happen to anyone. They say the killer isn't a patient, but who else could it be? It happened on a locked ward. There's no getting in or out of there. Except staff. Scary to think the killer princess could be someone who works here."

"Why was she wearing a white dress?" asked a staff psychiatrist who requested anonymity. "The answer to that question is excruciatingly obvious. The killer wanted to wear his blood. A throat slashing would cause propulsive arterial spray. Blood would have covered the killer, turned a white dress scarlet. This is a very violent individual. Was Jonathan targeted, or was this a thrill kill? We don't know. I have encountered individuals to whom killing is the entire point. Murder from which pleasure is derived. But I doubt that in this case. I would say that passion played a role, passion directed very specifically at Jonathan."

Dr. Tyler's widow, Belinda Quinn Tyler, had no comment. Police reports indicate that at the time of her husband's killing, she was in Black Hall, Connecticut, over an hour away from Narragansett. She was with her brother, Clark Quinn, and an unnamed childhood friend. Law enforcement sources state that Mrs. Tyler and Mr. Quinn are not suspects in Dr. Tyler's murder.

The investigation continues, and anyone with information is asked to contact Detective Martin Matthews of
the Rhode Island State Police.

The last article Sam read was Jonathan Tyler's obituary. It listed his accomplishments and awards, said that he left his wife, Belinda, and a stepdaughter—again, the child's name was not mentioned—and that he was buried in the Maynard-King cemetery.

That struck Sam as odd—a cemetery with the same name as the hospital? Was it the spot where the holographic mask was found that Halloween night? The article stated that many of the dead buried there had been patients or staff. It also said that the cemetery was the only part of the hospital property that was open to the public.

Sam closed her laptop again. Did the police investigating Belinda's murder know that her husband had died because someone had slashed his throat—the same method that had killed her? Did Kate and Conor know?

It couldn't be a coincidence. Sam stood up from the lounge chair by the lovely pool, waved to Hadley and CeCe, and hurried to find Kate, to give this evidence to Conor. When she got to the top of the stairs, she saw Lincoln talking to Bernard's girlfriend, Miranda. They seemed deep in conversation, but when Lincoln saw Sam watching them, they stepped apart, as if they didn't want to be seen together.

"Hey, Sam," he said as Miranda hurried away.

"Are you leaving?" she asked, gesturing at the overnight bag slung over his shoulder.

"Yeah, I'm checking out," he said.

"Did the police give Maeve back her stuff?" she asked.

"Most of it," he said.

"Mainly, she wanted her address book," Sam said. "Did she get it?"

Lincoln seemed not to hear the question. "She's staying in case Kate needs her," he said. "How about you?"

"Me?" Sam asked.

"Yeah," he said. "How long are you staying?"

"Our reservations are until tomorrow. We were supposed to have the big fireworks tonight."

"They'll still go on, right?" Lincoln said.

"Yes," Sam said. "You and Maeve have your room for another night too. Don't you want to stay?"

"You want me to?" he asked, grinning.

It felt weirdly as if he was flirting with her, but he seemed to realize that he'd made her uncomfortable and backed off. "I really have to get home," he said. "Too much stuff to do." He paused, then added, "Work. I have a lot of work piling up."

"Playing music?" she asked.

"Yes. Well, writing it," he said. "I have a side job composing strange little jingles for this guy who will never tell me what they're for."

"That sounds . . . interesting," Sam said.

"It's bizarre, but it pays the bills," he said, taking a step closer to her. "You should come to my studio sometime. I'll play for you. You won't believe this stuff he wants me to write."

"Thanks," she said. "I'll keep it in mind."

He gave her a hug that lasted a few seconds too long and walked away. She watched him go. Maybe it was an innocent enough invitation, to hear him play the strange music he'd been commissioned to write, but there'd been a tone to his voice that made Sam wonder.

Lincoln was Maeve's boyfriend. He had introduced Suzanne to Maeve, brought her into their lives. Sam wondered what he and Miranda been talking about so intently. Sam had the idea that they had known each other before this time in Watch Hill.

She decided that her next search would be for Lincoln Adams. But first she had to tell Kate and Conor about Belinda's murdered husband.

17

Sunday, July 4; 1:00 p.m.

Conor and Joe had spent the morning interviewing the residents of Bellevigne Island while Tom investigated the boats and dock buildings along the waterfront. Their efforts centered around East Cove Marina—the marina itself and the small village that surrounded the harbor. Conor tried to focus on learning whatever he could about the receipt in Suzanne's name—and now, how it connected to those handcuffs they had seen on *Psyche*.

But concentration was almost impossible. He hadn't slept last night. He kept seeing the look in Kate's eyes when he'd answered her question about Belinda. Standing beside her plane, he had watched her nearly melt onto the tarmac. Or maybe that was him—he couldn't stand seeing her so hurt and knowing that he was the cause.

He forced himself to get his head in the game. Joe had taken photos at the rehearsal dinner. He had gotten a good shot of Belinda with Garrett, sitting together and smiling at the camera. He had also, inadvertently, captured Suzanne, when she was standing beside Kate at the Harbour Room door. The Ocean House concierge had printed out copies of the photos, and Joe showed them around now.

Crime scene investigators from the Rhode Island State Police had arrived by helicopter. They were processing *Psyche*—taking photos, fingerprinting surfaces, collecting DNA from the mattress and bulkheads.

Conor knew that they would drive or tow the boat back to the mainland, but it was protocol to secure basic evidence before the move.

Some of Tom's crew had come out from Station Point Judith in a CG45—a forty-five-foot response boat—to meet him at East Cove Marina. Conor could see his brother down by the dock, talking to crew members.

The fact that it was the Fourth of July meant that many of the islanders had the long weekend off; some had headed off island for various mainland celebrations. Conor and Joe found several residents at home and showed them the photos of Belinda and Suzanne. No one said they recognized them. Everyone was curious about what the police and Coast Guard were doing there. One woman said she had been walking her dog late one foggy night last week and had heard an engine. As the sound grew louder, she saw *Psyche* motoring alongside the dock. She hadn't noticed who was at the wheel, and she hadn't seen anyone boarding the boat or leaving it since.

Conor and Joe approached the last house on the street. Like several others, it looked run down. The yard held blue plastic fish barrels and a stack of barnacle-encrusted lobster pots.

But Conor noticed that it also had a tidy herb garden and a bed full of colorful cosmos and zinnias—some of the same flowers Kate grew at Cloudlands. A rustic arbor in the side yard was covered with grapevines; a woman wearing a black dress sat beneath it in the shade. She had been needlepointing, but at the sight of Conor and Joe, she lowered the canvas and stared at them intently.

"Hello," Joe said, showing her his badge and ID.

"Rhode Island State Police," she said, examining his ID.

"Yes, I'm Detective Joseph Harrigan."

"Who are you?" she asked Conor.

"Conor Reid," he said. "I'm a detective from Connecticut."

"A Nutmegger," she said, using a nickname for Connecticut people.

"Yes," Conor said.

"What brings you here?" she asked, directing the question to Joe. "Someone on the island in trouble?"

"Not necessarily," Joe said. "Were you thinking of someone in particular?"

"There's a bunch of idiots out here," she said. "They have no respect. I've called in complaints before. They know it's me who reported them, and they throw bottles in my yard, shout names at me on my walks to the water. But it's okay. I've lived here my whole life. I'll outlast them."

"Good for you. That's a strong attitude," Joe said. "What are the complaints about?"

"Bad things," she said.

"Like what?" Conor asked.

She glared at him and didn't answer at first. Then, "I forget."

Conor gazed at her face. She had sun lines across her forehead and around her mouth, but her eyes were bright. She looked to be in her late forties, not much older than he was, so he didn't think her confusion was due to age.

"Yes," Joe said.

"What is your name?" Conor asked.

"Grace Matos," she said.

"Well, Grace," Joe said. "I'd like to ask you some questions. Is that okay with you?"

She nodded. "Go ahead."

"Do you know anyone named Suzanne McKinney?" Joe asked. "Who might keep a boat at East Cove Marina?"

Joe showed her the pictures of Suzanne and Belinda, and Conor saw her lips tighten.

"You recognize them, don't you?" Conor said.

"I'm not sure," she said.

"You mentioned that you walk down to the water," Conor said.

"Every day," she said.

"When you take your walks," Conor said. "Have you ever noticed a sailboat tied to the dock?"

"Sailboat," she said, shaking her head. "That's for leisure, for rich people. We're working people here. No one here has sailboats." She paused. "Except the people who have money. You know, like the rich one who has the parties. Him and that woman."

The tone in her voice when she said *woman* caught Conor's attention. It was a combination of anger and derision. "Do you sometimes see the woman on the sailboat?" he asked.

"A few times."

"What do you know about the boat?" Joe asked.

"I was hoping you would ask about that," she said. "I have been hoping for a long time. When the police come to see about the bad things . . . I always hope they'll go to the boat. But they never do. That's because they're paid off. Money can buy anything. It can buy your way out of trouble."

"Why do you want the police to go to the boat?" Conor asked.

She blinked hard and looked away, as if deciding how much to say.

"Do you know who owns it?" Conor asked.

"No," she said, shaking her head. Then, "Maybe."

Conor watched her face. She seemed to be wrestling with something she wanted to say but felt she shouldn't.

"How long has the boat been here?" Joe asked.

"It just got here," she said. "This time."

"You mean it comes and goes?" Joe asked.

"Yes," she said.

"You mentioned seeing the woman on it," Joe said. "Do you know who she is?"

Grace shrugged.

Conor's mind was racing with a line of questions, but he held back from asking them—he wasn't officially here, and he was trying to stay on his side of the line. He exchanged a glance with Joe, and Joe ran with it.

"Are there other people with her?" Joe asked.

"A man. Well, sometimes more than one. And the girls. They come for the parties."

"Tell me about the parties," Joe said.

"They're up there," she said, gesturing up the hill. "They're the real reason I call the police."

"Because they're loud? Disturbing your peace?" Joe asked.

"No, they're quiet. The whole point is for no one to know they're celebrating. They all arrive in boats—in yachts. Or sometimes in a plane. But you can never hear music. Silent parties. Silent nights."

"Okay," Joe said. "Who are they?"

"The girls are like me," she said, gazing into the distance. "Except they're not like me. They're Ghost Girls."

"Ghost girls?" Conor asked. She didn't reply. She gazed into the distance, as if seeing specters of the girls who had visited the island.

"It's a riddle," she said. "I don't mean they're like me now. They're like the way I was. We're ghosts of how we used to be."

Conor and Joe waited for her to go on.

"I was one of the first." She paused, and her chin began to wobble. "Poor things, they've been sick too. Like me. They've been in treatment. They are frail. They're not ready for parties, or for seeing those people."

"What kind of treatment?" Joe asked.

"Maybe they just don't want anyone to see them at night," she said, ignoring his question.

"At night?" Conor asked.

"That's when they get here," she said. "Just after dark, and they stay until midnight. They wear white dresses and float up the hill like spirits. Ghost Girls can go anywhere and be almost invisible. Like me." She frowned. "Do you think they are real?"

Conor watched her clasp and unclasp her hands. She was drifting in and out of reality; he sensed that the treatment she'd spoken of referred to some sort of mental health intervention.

"Maybe they're dead. Maybe the girls really *are* ghosts. They leave no footprints. Why is it that I survived when some of them don't? I get a bad feeling from them. Some of the dead are good, and some are not," she said.

"Which ones aren't good?" Joe asked.

She frowned and looked away.

"Do you ever hear any sounds coming from the boat?" Joe asked. "Voices?"

She nodded. "Just like the wind," she said.

"The sound of the wind comes from the boat?" Conor asked.

"Oh yes," she said. "A terrible wailing, you know, the way the wind sounds when we're having a real nor'easter, or even a hurricane before the eye passes over, when the barometer falls. Just that ungodly shriek. Makes you think your house is going to come apart. But oh, that wind on the boat. It's the same thing. Howling."

Conor felt the hair on the back of his neck stand up. He couldn't hold back. "Could it have been a person instead?" he asked. "Screaming, maybe?"

"I don't like to think about it," she said. "It makes me upset."

"Does that sound come from the house too, Grace?" Conor asked. "The wailing?"

"No!" she said, shaking her head hard, as if trying to dislodge memories or sounds. "I told you, the house is silent."

"Tell me another thing," Joe said. "You mentioned that the girls from the sailboat are like you but not like you. They're like you because they were once sick, and in treatment, but how are they different?"

"Because I'm here," she said. "I have my life. They didn't take it."

Conor had the feeling she meant it very literally: that she was alive while other women were dead. While some of what she said seemed to come from delusion, he felt that she was absolutely solid in saying that she had her life. He saw her take a quick glance toward the dead end of her road. A chain was stretched between two wooden posts: Beyond the chain, a gravel road meandered through a field, up a rock-strewn slope, and into a grove of trees.

"What's up there, Grace?" Conor asked.

"That's where they have the parties, in a big mansion. The Finishing School. You can't see it from here. It's on the hilltop, behind the trees."

"Finishing school?" Joe asked.

"*One* of the finishing schools," Grace said.

"You said the parties last until midnight," Conor said.

"The clock strikes twelve," she said.

"What happens then? Where do the people go?"

"Back on the boats," she said. "And away. They leave the island."

"On *Psyche* . . ." Conor began, but she put her hands over her ears.

"I don't like to talk about it. You have to go now."

"Okay," Conor said. "We will." Then, leaning closer, he looked at the canvas she was needlepointing. "That looks pretty."

"Thank you," she said.

Conor could see that she had been stitching a tableau of a big stone building surrounded by trees, in the middle of a vast green lawn. At first the canvas seemed to depict a painterly bucolic scene, but then he saw that the tree branches were bones, the stones in the yard were human skulls.

"What is that place?" Conor asked, pointing to her canvas.

"The mansion." She pointed at the hill and looked worried.

Conor took the pictures of Belinda and Suzanne from Joe's hand and showed them to her again. "You've seen them, haven't you, Grace? These two women."

"The young one," Grace said, pointing at the photo of Suzanne. "Yes, I've seen her. She was here last fall."

"But not the other one?"

"Maybe," Grace said, lips tight. "But not here, and it was a long time ago."

"Where?" Conor asked.

"Somewhere else."

"Where?"

"The place they get the girls," she said, swallowing back tears. The words thudded as Conor thought of the restraints he had seen on the boat.

"What about the man?" Conor asked. "Do you know his name?"

"I made a mistake," she said, avoiding the question. "I didn't mean to, but when I was sick at MK, I told the woman about the mansion on the hill. And she came to see, and she brought one of the men. And it was perfect for what they needed, so they come back again and again, with the girls. Girls are being taken, and it's my fault."

"Grace, what do you mean, 'taken'?" Conor asked. "Kidnapped?"

"Are they there now?" Joe asked. "In the mansion?"

"What is MK?" Conor asked.

Without replying, Grace stood up and gathered up her needlework. Conor watched her start walking toward her house. Then she stopped and turned around. "Don't tell the man or the woman how you know about MK. Don't say it was me who told. Do you promise?"

She didn't wait for an answer, as she had stopped believing that promises could ever be kept. She turned her back on Conor and Joe, then stepped through her door and closed it behind her.

"She's obviously confused," Joe said. "Ghost girls? Can we trust anything she said?"

Conor knew that not all of Grace's words had made sense, but her emotions were genuine. He felt the guilt pouring off her when she'd said it was her fault that the man and woman brought girls to the island.

"I think we have to," Conor said. "What else do we have to go on?"

Joe nodded. "Okay," he said.

Then the two detectives walked to the dead end beyond Grace's cottage, stepped over the chain, and followed the gravel road toward the mansion on the hill.

18

Sunday, July 4; 2:00 p.m.

In preparation for the Ocean House Independence Day Beach Ball, the wide and beautiful strand directly in front of the hotel had been set with round tables and chairs for six hundred people. Vases of blue and white hydrangeas adorned the center of each table, and long, white tablecloths were secured with discreet clips, to keep them from blowing off the tables in the sea wind. The seating area was flanked by raw bars, barbecue grills, enormous pots full of steamed lobsters, and stations of salads and local delicacies. Garlands of twinkling lights crisscrossed overhead.

A band had set up beside the beach restaurant—Théa at Dune Cottage—and the deck was ready to transform into a dance floor. Fireworks would commence after dark. Some of Kate and Conor's guests had planned to stay for the festivities; given the fact that the wedding had been canceled, many had decided to skip the beach party.

Kate found a corner table on the Club Room terrace to sit and think. Brian kept her glass of sparkling water full. She had seen Mike and his fellow crime-solvers sitting in the Bistro's bar, huddled over a table with pens and pads of paper. She kept her eye on the door. She hoped that when Conor came back from Bellevigne Island, he would look for her here.

Her phone buzzed, and she stared at the screen. It wasn't Conor; it was her niece.

I'm in the car out front with Maeve. We have an idea. Can you come with us? Sam texted.

Where are you going? Kate asked.

But she received no response, so she headed through the lobby, down the stairs into the circular drive. Maeve was at the wheel of her navy-blue BMW. Sam was in the passenger seat, but when she saw Kate, she got out to let her sit in front.

"No, you stay there," Kate said.

When she climbed into the back seat, she saw the painting propped up beside her—*Foggy Night*, with a corner of its broken gold frame poking out of the brown wrapping paper. Kate felt a pang and touched it, tore a little of the paper away so she could see the canvas.

Maeve looked in the rearview mirror, saw Kate gazing at it.

"I'll take the painting to the conservator, Kate," Maeve said. "As soon as he opens after the holiday."

"Thanks, Maeve," Kate said. She didn't ask which conservator. She had two that she favored, but right now, she barely cared.

They started to drive away from the hotel, but Dermot the valet waved for them to stop.

"Miss Woodward," he said, jogging over to the car. "Miss Forrest gave me this gift a few minutes ago and asked me to see you got it."

"'Forrest'?" Kate asked.

"Miranda Forrest," Sam said. "You know, Bernard's girlfriend."

Kate took the box from Dermot and thanked him. It was about four inches square, wrapped in pale-yellow paper and tied with a turquoise bow. An envelope was tucked under the ribbon. Kate opened it and read the note inside:

> Kate, I don't even really know you, but I can only imag-
> ine how you're feeling . . . My heart hurts for you. There's
> something I'd like to tell you, if you have time to talk before
> we check out. In the meantime, this memento is for you.
>
> All my best, Miranda

Kate stared at the note. She knew that Miranda must have meant well. But getting a sympathy note from a near stranger made everything feel even more raw.

"What is it?" Sam asked.

"I'll open it later," Kate said. She set it on the seat beside her, wondering whether it had initially been intended as a wedding gift. "Where are we going?"

"A place called Maynard-King," Sam said.

"What's that?" Kate asked.

"A psychiatric hospital in Narragansett," Sam said.

"It's a very private place," Maeve said. "I'm pretty sure they pay a publicist to keep anything about them out of the media. But, you know, stories leak . . . and if you're a pop culture junkie, it's kind of common knowledge that celebrities get treated there." She named a few—an actor, a famous athlete, the wife of a politician.

"What does it have to do with us?" Kate asked.

"How much do you know about Belinda's first marriage?" Sam asked.

"Nothing, except that her husband died," Kate said.

"He didn't just die," Sam said. "He was murdered."

Kate didn't think she could feel any more shock after the last few days, but she did. She heard herself asking, "When? How?"

Sam explained as they drove north on Route 1. Kate listened to how Sam had researched Belinda online, learned that in 2010 she had married Dr. Jonathan Tyler—a psychiatrist who was the medical director of Maynard-King—and that he had been murdered in 2014.

"The killer slit his throat," Sam said.

"Same as what was done to Belinda," Maeve said.

Kate took that in. "What does that mean? It can't be a coincidence."

"I agree," Sam said.

"But what's the point of going to the hospital right now?" Kate asked.

"Just to see it, maybe ask questions," Sam said. "That's where her husband was killed."

"If it's a psychiatric hospital," Kate said, "we won't be able to get onto the grounds."

"There's a way," Sam said.

"It's the Fourth of July, Sam," Kate said. "People are on vacation, no one will be there to answer any questions."

"Just wait and see, okay?" Sam asked.

"Okay," Kate said.

They headed east. Traffic was heavy, with people on their way to the beaches and the Block Island Ferry. There was a slowdown approaching Point Judith, but soon they were driving through town with Narragansett Bay sparkling blue in front of them.

GPS had sent them up Boston Neck Road, then a right onto Lovecraft Lane. They stopped at a gated drive. Kate looked at the closed wrought iron gate and the stone pillars for any sign that they were at the entrance to Maynard-King, but the property was completely unmarked. The bay was visible through the trees. Sun glittered on the surface. A small stone building stood inside the fence. Kate saw a camera pointed at them, mounted on a pole. A uniformed guard came out and stared at the car.

"May I help you?" the guard asked.

"We're here to visit the cemetery," Sam said.

"This is a private facility," he said.

"I thought the cemetery was open to the public," Sam said.

There was a long pause. "Pull in and wait. Someone will be down shortly to take you there."

Maeve drove in as the gate slid open, then immediately closed behind them. They parked as directed. From here, there was no sign of the hospital building itself. To the right, a paved road lined with beech trees curved up a hill. To the left, a dirt path led behind what looked like a maintenance shed.

A few minutes later, an ATV came speeding down the hill. The driver was a young woman with brown hair flowing out from under her helmet. She wore a khaki uniform with an insignia and name tag, and she gestured for them to follow her. She drove fast, leading them the way she had come, up the gentle hill.

The road curved up through the beechwood forest. Dappled light penetrated the leaves and branches. Kate noticed a small gazebo set in a sunny glade. Two people walked along a path, watching them as they passed by. A little farther, there was another clearing with a tennis court, and, across the drive, a large swimming pool. At the top of the hill was a large white building, with Ionic columns at the front door. Large stone planters overflowed with white geraniums.

The ATV turned onto a narrow lane that passed some smaller buildings and stopped at the entrance to the cemetery. From here, Kate looked over the gravestones and across an expansive lawn, sloping to the edge of Narragansett Bay. A long dock, with two powerboats tied alongside, stretched into the bay. Twenty yards off the end of the dock, a sleek sailboat sat on a mooring. Two kids were fishing in a rowboat; it bounced in the wakes of larger boats passing by.

Kate, Sam, and Maeve climbed out of the car. The ATV driver pulled a clipboard from a storage box on the vehicle and walked toward them.

"Thanks for getting us here," Sam said to the woman.

"You have to sign in," the escort said, handing Sam the clipboard. Kate read her name tag and saw that her name was Jennifer. The insignia looked like a monogram, the letters MK entwined together—Maynard-King.

"No problem," Sam said, signing her name.

"I need all three of you to sign," Jennifer said. "And I need your drivers' licenses. Plus, put down your car's make, model, and license number."

"Wow, you have a lot of security," Sam said. Kate pulled out her license and watched Jennifer take a photo of it, as well as Sam's and Maeve's.

"Here are the rules," Jennifer said. "Other than the cemetery, the grounds are completely closed to visitors. You can be right here, but that's it. I will stay until you're ready to leave."

"Okay," Sam said. "Thank you."

Jennifer nodded.

"Just out of curiosity," Kate said. "Why is the cemetery open to the public, since the hospital is so private?"

"Well, because people want to pay respects and visit their loved ones who have passed," Jennifer said, gesturing at the graves. "No one's going to stand in the way of that. Maynard-King is a place of compassion, above all else."

"That's kind of you," Kate said, thinking that Jennifer's words sounded very formal, as if memorized from a pamphlet.

"How do we find someone's grave?" Sam asked.

"You don't know where it is?" Jennifer asked with a frown of suspicion. "You've never been here before?"

"No," Sam said. "This is our first time."

"I have a map," Jennifer said, removing a laminated card from a compartment in her dashboard. "What is your loved one's name?"

"Dr. Jonathan Tyler III," Sam said, and Kate watched for Jennifer's reaction. Her expression was impassive. Jennifer stared at all three of them and took a long time to answer.

"He's D3. Last row on the right. He has a large headstone—you can't miss it," Jennifer said.

"Thank you," Sam said.

Jennifer nodded. She stowed the clipboard. She looked at her phone and half turned away, a signal that she was dismissing them. Kate, Sam, and Maeve walked through an opening in a low stone wall, toward the graves. When Kate turned to look over her shoulder, she saw Jennifer watching them intently.

Even before they reached Dr. Tyler's gravestone—enormous, topped with an angel—they could see that someone had left a bouquet of white roses there. The roses were tied together with a trailing vine. Kate spotted a small white envelope tucked into the flowers, camouflaged by the white petals. She knelt, reached in to remove it, and pricked her finger on a tangle of thorns. A dot of blood dripped onto the envelope. Her finger hurt, and she brought it to her lips.

She read the message on a card inside:

1740

With love

Always

She felt a chill run through her whole body. It was one of her wedding place cards. The words were calligraphed, the ink was that signature glossy blue black she had ordered from London, and the style of penmanship was precisely what she had seen on the discarded cards in Belinda's room at the Ocean House.

Sam reached down, took the card from Kate's hand, and read it.

"1740," Sam said, looking at Kate.

Maeve stared at the card but didn't say anything.

Kate nodded, examining the handwriting. Her scratched finger had left a bright-red print on the side. "I think Suzanne wrote this," she said.

"She did," Maeve said, sounding bitter. "Definitely. That's her writing."

"Why would she leave a note like this on Belinda's husband's grave?"

Kate held the card, her thoughts racing, an answer coming into focus.

"Belinda and Jonathan's wedding announcement said the flower girl was Belinda's daughter, obviously from a previous relationship," Sam said.

"Suzanne," Kate said.

"Maybe," Sam said, her eyes meeting Kate's.

"And the 'previous relationship'?" Maeve asked.

No one answered, and Kate was glad. She didn't want to hear anyone say "Conor."

They heard the squawk of Jennifer's radio, and all three turned in unison to look at her. Without them noticing, she had climbed off her ATV and had moved closer to them. Kate wondered if she had heard what they'd been saying.

She caught sight of Jennifer texting, but Jennifer saw her watching and quickly put her iPhone in her pocket.

"Are you finished here?" Jennifer asked.

"Yes, we are," Sam said.

"Okay, I'll lead you back to the gate," Jennifer said.

"I have a question," Kate said, gesturing at the grave. "Do you know who left these white roses?"

Jennifer shrugged. "No idea. People bring flowers all the time."

"Specifically for this grave?"

"Dr. Tyler was very important here," Jennifer said. "He was beloved. Patients and staff pay their respects to him often."

Kate noticed Jennifer gazing at her, Sam, and Maeve, the gaze lingering on the two younger women.

"I guess he meant a lot to you too?" Jennifer asked. The question was open ended, as if she was hoping for an answer or explanation.

"Very much so," Sam said. Kate caught the lie—but it wasn't really. He meant a lot to them in terms of solving Belinda's murder and the mystery of Suzanne.

"You're one of us?" Jennifer asked.

"'Us'?" Sam asked.

Jennifer reddened and looked away.

"What do you mean by 'one of us'?" Kate asked.

"Nothing," Jennifer said. Then hurriedly, as if regretting her question and covering her mistake, "Just that people admire what he did here. He cared so much for his patients."

"You were a patient?" Sam asked.

"If you're ready to go, I'll take you to the gate," Jennifer said brusquely.

"Jennifer," Kate said. "Did you know Dr. Tyler personally?"

But Jennifer just revved the engine and gestured for them to drive ahead. Kate, Sam, and Maeve climbed into their car and headed down the hill. This time, instead of leading them, Jennifer brought up the rear.

When Sam reached the main road, she waved at the guard. He acknowledged her with a nod, and the gate slid open. Kate glanced out the rear window. She saw Jennifer staring after them. Then she began typing on her phone screen.

Kate wondered who she was reporting to.

19

Sunday, July 4; 4:00 p.m.

Conor and Joe climbed up the hill, toward the highest point on Bellevigne Island. In the far distance, Conor saw Watch Hill shimmering across the water, almost like a mirage, a place he had merely imagined. He felt haunted by love, as if what he and Kate had had moved into another realm, like Grace's Ghost Girls.

Kate had done the math and said that given their ages, Suzanne could be his daughter. But when Conor remembered details from the biggest mistake of his life, he knew that there was no way. Even so, the truth was bad enough—he had been involved with Belinda long after they'd been next-door neighbors, and he hadn't told Kate. And now, he was out here with Joe, looking for leads in Belinda's murder.

Grace was right: There was a mansion on the hill's crest. Built of gray fieldstone, it had a portico with tall columns that were covered with vines. Two of the front windows were broken, repaired with squares of plywood. The steps were overgrown. Birds had built nests in the eaves. The mortar holding stones in place was cracked. A storm had sent a branch from a tall tree crashing onto the slate roof, sending slate tiles cascading to the ground next to the chimney. The house looked as if it hadn't been occupied for years.

"Is this the right place?" Joe asked doubtfully. Conor didn't answer.

The two detectives walked around the perimeter. Untrimmed hedges grew close to the foundation. Curtains were drawn across most of the windows, but it was possible to look through the French doors, into what appeared to be a living room. The furniture was covered in white sheets, and so were paintings on the walls—a practice of summer house owners, to protect upholstery and art from being damaged by sunlight and dust.

Conor and Joe continued their circuit, looking for a way in. After seeing the scene on the boat and having Grace direct them to this mansion, after speaking about girls being "taken," the detectives realized that timing could be critical. Conor pictured those blood-smeared handcuffs on the boat and knew that someone could be held prisoner inside. They rounded the house and came upon stone stairs leading down to a basement door. Conor tried the knob. It turned, and they were inside.

Daylight slanted in through dirty windows. The cellar was damp and musty, and the air glittered with dust motes. Steep, rough wooden stairs led to the main floor; Conor followed Joe up them and stepped out into a corridor.

"What's that smell?" Joe asked.

Conor noticed it too. It was sweet, like flowers, but more concentrated, almost oppressive.

"Perfume?" Conor asked.

"Yeah," Joe said. "Or candles?"

They moved quickly through the first floor, clearing each room before entering the next. Kitchen, dining room, living room, library, bathroom. So far, they had observed nothing suspicious, but the sweet smell grew stronger.

A wide staircase in the center hall swept up to the second floor. Conor and Joe split up, checking rooms on each side of the upstairs hallway. And this was another world. It didn't seem to belong to the same house. Everything was pristine; it felt exclusive. Conor felt as if he had walked into a private club. It couldn't be more different from the dilapidated exterior and the shabby downstairs.

This reminded Conor of other aristocratic homes he'd been in. Connecticut, where he was a detective, was full of them. Sordid crimes didn't care about class. The furniture was solid, antique, with a burnished glow. An office had a carved wooden desk, red leather armchairs, and green-shaded library lamps. There was a Windsor chair with the Yale University "Lux et Veritas" gold insignia on the back. Bookcases were full of rows of matching red leather-bound books—they appeared to be more for show, he thought, than for reading.

The carved keyhole desk held a brass tray full of coins, pens, a tarnished silver money clip, a few loose keys—things that looked as if they'd come out of someone's pocket. He glanced at the desktop but kept moving down the hall.

There were four bedrooms, each with queen-size beds covered with white comforters. The last door on the hallway was locked. Not only that, but the door appeared to be reinforced with steel. He bent down, to see if there was a space under the door, but there was none: The reinforcement material extended all the way down to the gleaming parquet floor. He pounded hard on the door. The sound of his hand banging on steel was barely a dull thud.

"Soundproofing," Conor said. "Like on the boat. Someone's in there."

"Could be," Joe said.

"Let's get her out."

They tried ramming the door, kicking it, putting their shoulders into it, but it didn't budge.

"This is no good," Joe said. "We'll get the team up here."

Conor stared at the door. Extra security plates had been installed around the door latch, so trying to jimmy the lock would be useless. Everything Conor had seen in the rooms, and the hardware on the other doors, appeared to be old bronze, from another era. But the Schlage lock was new and looked to be made of stainless steel or zinc. He pictured the pile of metal things in that tray in the office.

"Got gloves?" he asked Joe. He usually had some in his jacket pocket, but he hadn't thought he would need tactical gloves on his wedding weekend. Joe handed him a pair, and he snapped them on.

Conor moved quickly down the hall to the desk in the library. With a gloved finger, he rummaged through the loose change. There were several keys in the tray, but only one Schlage. Conor took it to the locked room, inserted it into the knob, and turned. He heard the tumblers click, and he pushed the door open.

Conor and Joe stepped inside.

The room felt royal, as if it belonged in a castle. And it felt lived in: Air was circulating, not stale and musty like downstairs. There were no windows open. The fresh air came from vents in the ceiling. They saw the source of the sweet smell they had noticed downstairs: a cut glass diffuser with rods sticking up, spreading the scent of some essential oils through the room. It gave him a headache.

Crystal prisms dangled from a chandelier hanging over the large, canopied bed. The walnut headboard was ornately carved with flowers and angels. The white muslin canopy stirred very slightly in the moving air. A white linen coverlet, embroidered with gold threads, had been pulled back, and the sheets were rumpled.

Conor touched the mattress to feel if it was warm. It wasn't, but it appeared that someone had lain here recently.

The polished wood floors were covered with blue-and-white Oriental rugs. Conor noticed that they were threadbare in places—they looked very old and valuable, probably made of silk like ones he had seen in Newport with Kate. A pair of pale-blue silk-covered armchairs flanked the marble fireplace.

A large black-and-white photograph over the bed showed a lion lunging over the bed of a young girl. It was shocking and violent, a disturbing tableau. It had a sepia tinge, indicating age. There was a feeling of motion, of stop-action, as if it was a still photo from a black-and-white film.

Conor took a photo on his iPhone. He noticed he had two bars of cell service—being high on the hill gave him some reception—so he texted the picture to Kate. It was habit, when he came upon artwork in an investigation, to ask her about it. He stared at the screen, wondering if the picture would go through and if there would be a reply. He couldn't stop thinking of how she had looked at him after his confession about Belinda.

He looked at the image above the bed and realized it wasn't a photo of an actual lion, but of a man wearing an animal disguise. The man loomed over the sleeping girl, her blanket made of white fur. The gauzy white canopy curtains softened the scene, illuminated by a candelabra. The room in which he stood was identical to the room in the photograph, as if a designer had come to the mansion and re-created the old photograph.

But how old was the photo? Maybe it had just been colored to make it look vintage.

"I've got to say, maybe that shit is staged, but it looks like a sex crime," Joe said, standing beside Conor to stare at the photo.

"You think the picture inspires him?" Conor asked and pointed at the unmade bed. "Someone was just here."

"You think he brought her in on the boat, like Grace said?" Joe asked.

"Maybe," Conor said.

They were standing by the bed and turned their attention from the photograph to the sheets. Conor saw traces of blood at the foot of the mattress and roughly halfway down. It could have come from wounds on someone's ankles and wrists. He thought of the handcuffs on the boat. Had the blood on them come from a current victim or one of the other women Grace had seen arriving on other nights?

Joe had grabbed a Bendix mobile when his team had arrived, and he used it now to call Danica Bouchard, the senior crime scene tech, and tell her to come up to the house as soon as she finished with the boat. Conor's phone buzzed with a text. It was from Kate. The sight of her name jolted his heart.

The message was straightforward.

The photo is a still from a film by Jean Cocteau.

Conor took the hit. True, she hadn't ignored him, but considering what she had just typed, her brevity spoke volumes. Conor replied:

Cocteau! Wow, Kate!

Conor had taken her to the south of France for her birthday, wanting to make a long-standing dream of hers come true. They had landed in Nice, rented a car, and driven to Villefranche-sur-Mer, a port town on the Mediterranean, where Cocteau had lived. Conor had made a reservation at the waterfront Welcome Hotel, where Jean Cocteau lived in 1924. Conor had loved surprising her by arranging for them to stay in his exact room.

Conor stared at his iPhone screen, wanting Kate to reply. When she didn't, he wrote:

What film is it from?

A long wait before her reply, then:

La Belle et la Bête. A fantasy inspired by the fairy tale Beauty and the Beast. Sound familiar?

Unfortunately, it did. Belinda's bullshit about their supposed nicknames.

She made that up, Conor wrote.

He wanted not to be texting Kate about this. He had to hear her voice, so he called her number. She didn't answer. It was a gut punch, being accused for something so crazy. Time was spinning, and he needed to hold her. He needed her to listen to him, let him explain the truth. He tried her again, and still no answer.

"Kate can identify the picture," he said to Joe after he hung up. "It's from a French film based on *Beauty and the Beast*."

"Interesting, because check this out," Joe said, standing by a tall bookcase.

"What have you got?"

"Someone's got a fixation going," Joe said, gesturing at the top shelves. They were full of various editions of *Beauty and the Beast*. Some looked very old, with cracked leather spines and flaking gilt titles. Several were foreign, and he recognized *La Belle et la Bête* from the French phrase Kate had just used.

"Maybe the fixation continues," Conor said, pointing at the black-and-white photograph above the bed.

"Strange," Joe said. "My daughter liked the Disney movie, she watched it constantly, along with a bunch of others, but I always got them mixed up—*Little Mermaid*, Esméralda, they all blended together. Except *Beauty and the Beast*. That one always bothered me."

"Why?" Conor asked.

"Basically, the story is about how someone puts a spell on a prince and turns him into a beast, and this old guy picks a rose outside the Beast's castle, and the Beast flips out and tells him that he's got to trade his daughter for his freedom. I mean, what the hell! And Belle—his daughter—gets sucked into wanting to save her father, then feeling sorry for the Beast. What a shit father, incidentally."

"Yeah, I'd say so," Conor said.

"Of course, Belle falls in love with the Beast, because even though he's ugly as shit, she tells herself he's so kind to her. Right, he's given her this choice—stay with him, or her father dies? Typical domestic violence scenario, power and control."

"Dark," Conor said.

"Hell yeah, it is," Joe said. "And that's just the Disney version. Not the French one Kate mentioned. Wait, tell me it's not all artistic and black and white, like that photo?" He pointed at the picture above the bed.

"It is. It's black and white."

"So that's probably even nastier. Edgy, right? It reminds me of every domestic I've ever been called to."

"Except this one is in a castle," Conor said.

"Like in Newport," Joe said.

Conor nodded. Newport, Rhode Island, the Gilded Age summer playground of robber barons and their modern-day counterparts. Lots of castles on Bellevue Avenue and throughout the Ocean Avenue environs.

Conor glanced at the table beside the bed and noticed that it had a lower shelf. On it was a small crystal decanter. There was an inch of amber-colored liquid inside. A white muslin towel was crumpled beside it, stained the same brownish color.

Something had spilled on the table, thickened into a dark, sticky mess, like coagulated blood. In the center of the spill was the image of a rose. It jolted Conor—he had seen it before. At first he thought it was a drawing, scrawled into the fluid, but then he realized it was an imprint, like a seal left in melted wax by a stamp.

Conor took a photo with his iPhone, so he could enlarge and see it more clearly. He moved closer and crouched down to examine the towel, about to tell Joe about the imprint, but the smell brought on a blast of dizziness so strong, he thought he was going to fall over.

"Whoa," Joe said, catching his arm.

Conor stumbled into the hallway, leaned against the doorjamb. He struggled to keep himself from passing out.

"Take it easy," Joe said. "Sit down." Conor stood where he was, still holding on to the wall.

"He's drugging his victims," Conor said, shaking his head to get rid of the fog. "Are you okay?"

"Yeah, I'm fine," Joe said. "I didn't have my nose in the bottle like you did. What's that substance?"

"Some kind of sedative," Conor said, feeling sick and still reeling. "Let's get out of here."

They went downstairs and left the house, walking into the fresh air. Conor leaned over, hands on his knees. He breathed in and out, steadying himself until he could stand upright again. They stood looking at the house for a while.

"Do you think our guy is reenacting the story?" Conor asked.

"Story?"

"*Beauty and the Beast.* The photo, the books."

"Who knows? Maybe," Joe said. "In the Disney movie, the Beast will stay a monster forever unless someone can love his sorry-ass self. So of course it turns out to be Belle, and once she comes through, he goes back to being a prince. It's so fucked up."

"Transformation," Conor said. "Maybe that's what this is all about."

"This?"

"The boat, the room. Maybe he thinks that if the girl—one of the girls—loves him, she'll restore him to someone he used to be."

"He'll turn back into a fucking prince?" Joe asked.

"Maybe. In his mind, anyway," Conor said.

"What's in it for her?" Joe asked.

"She gets to have her throat slit," Conor said.

His phone was burning in his hand, with Kate's text saying Belinda had said that she was Belle and he was the Beast. He knew he needed to get back to Watch Hill as soon as possible, to return to the house where Belinda had been murdered. Because even through the drug's haze, he remembered where he had seen the imprint beneath the bottle before, where he had seen a rose stamped in blood.

And he knew that figuring that out was his way back to Kate.

20

Sunday, July 4; 5:00 p.m.

After that visit to the Maynard-King cemetery, Kate felt incredibly relieved to return to the Ocean House, her sanctuary. She went up to the Tower Suite and took a long, hot shower. She put on the white robe and walked upstairs from the bedroom into the living room, and she sat on one of the window seats looking south, out toward the lighthouse. Her finger hurt from where she had pricked it on the rose at Jonathan Tyler's grave. Her heart hurt from where it had been broken by Conor.

She looked at her phone, at the photo he had sent her just a short while ago. He had seemed not to realize how upset she would be by the *Beauty and the Beast* reference. Had he truly not heard what Belinda had said, there in the Harbour Room?

Why would she believe Belinda instead of Conor? But images kept flashing through her mind: Conor and Belinda huddled together on that bench by the harbor, the picture of the blue-eyed baby on Belinda's phone, the silver ring, her words about him calling her Belle. Him saying he had slept with her.

Slept with her.

It was undeniable that the dark fairy tale somehow played a role in the mess they had found themselves in. It kept popping up—Belinda's words, the Cocteau film still—so it had to be significant. Kate thought of the various interpretations. She knew the Disney version because when Sam was a little girl and came to spend the weekend with her, or when Kate had gone to her sister's house to babysit, they had snuggled together on the sofa and watched the animated movie—the tale of Belle and the Beast.

The Cocteau film was avant-garde and certainly a different art form—even, almost, a different story. Shot in black and white, it was unbearably romantic. It was dangerous and erotic. Kate found it to be an emotional, most unlikely, love story. Outwardly, the Beast was frightening, but at heart, he was gentle. Belle was a delicate beauty, with a caring spirit that led her to see beyond his physical ugliness and fall in love with him. And save him.

Kate had seen the movie many times. She spoke fluent French—studying French and German had been a requirement for her master's degree in art history—and she found that the French language added to the film's romance and mystery. Cocteau was a surrealist, and to view his work was to enter a fantasy.

Kate had felt that—and she knew Conor had too—when they had stayed in Cocteau's room at the Welcome Hotel on the quai in Villefranche-sur-Mer—a pink hotel by the azure Mediterranean. Conor had planned it, just for her. That first day, they barely got out of bed. They didn't want to let go of each other. The scent of jasmine and bougainvillea was hypnotic, and they fell in and out of sleep until almost midnight when they woke to the glow of moonlight on the harbor.

Then they got up, went out to look for a late supper at one of the cafés on the Quai Courbet. They stopped in front of the Chapelle Saint-Pierre. The Romanesque chapel belonged to the Fishermen's Guild, and in the fifties, Cocteau transformed the walls. The exterior was wild with color, frescoes, and two unblinking eyes on the top story. The door was ajar.

"Can we go in?" Kate asked Conor.

"Well, the door is open, so . . ." he said, putting his arm around her waist as they walked inside.

It seemed like a magical invitation, that they could enter so late at night. Kate had known, in an abstract way—from her studies—what the interior would hold, but seeing it illuminated at midnight left her breathless.

Cocteau had filled the walls with images, connecting spirituality and art, paintings of angels and archangels and soldiers and ladders to heaven, all dedicated to Saint Julian, the patron saint of fishermen. The altar was painted in shades of rose; the rear of the chapel shimmered blue and silver, like the moonlight on the water that had wakened them. It all felt eternal, like a dream. It felt sacred.

"I wish," Kate whispered.

"What do you wish?" Conor asked, holding her.

"That we could live here, in Villefranche-sur-Mer," she said. "And come here every day."

"You'd open a branch of the Woodward-Lathrop gallery right on the harbor. And I'd be a cop. Guess I'd have to learn French, though."

"I'd teach you," she said.

They stayed for a few more minutes, then walked outside into the night air. One café was still open, so they sat at a table by the water. The half-moon was still up, tracing a silver web on the harbor. Kate remembered that night now, how she and Conor had held hands and shared a dream. They had gone back to their room and stayed awake until dawn. The moon had followed them into sleep. She was sure that one of the reasons they both loved *Foggy Night* by James Suydam was because it reminded them of the chapel and their moonlit stay at the Welcome.

Thinking about it, with the way they were now, was excruciating. Kate needed something to do, to get her mind off him. She thought about how the number 1740 kept coming up, starting with the decal on Suzanne's truck. She grabbed her laptop from the low table in front of the fireplace and googled *1740*.

First, a page of real estate sites appeared, with properties that had "1740" as their house number:

1740 Pearl Street

1740 Fifth Avenue

1740 Broadway

And so many more. Next, she found a list of world events that had taken place in the year 1740:

The War of the Austrian Succession begins.

Frederick II becomes king in Prussia.

The University of Pennsylvania is founded.

Anna Strong, one of the only female members of the Culper Spy Ring in the American Revolution, is born.

George Frideric Handel composes *L'Allegro, il Penseroso ed il Moderato*, based on two poems by John Milton.

Johann Sebastian Bach begins to lose his sight.

Kate's mind kept going back to the chapel, how it had felt as if Jean Cocteau and his paintings had blessed her and Conor. And he was connecting them now, but through that disturbing image from his film. Kate thought of all the elements from this case swirling together—Belle, the Beast, the film, and the number 1740.

That made her put two things together, and this time she googled *1740, Beauty and the Beast*.

She felt a jolt when she saw what came up. The original fairy tale had been written in 1740 by the French novelist Gabrielle-Suzanne Barbot de Villeneuve. The name "Suzanne" jumped out at her. She read about how Villeneuve's work had inspired many versions. Eventually the tale became the story that modern readers were most familiar with, adapted by French author Jeanne-Marie Leprince de Beaumont.

Villeneuve's work had its own origins. It had been inspired by ancient Greek stories, including "Cupid and Psyche." In school, Kate had read that powerful myth about overcoming obstacles to love. Back then, she had never realized that it was connected to *Beauty and the Beast*, but now she saw it.

Psyche was the name of the boat Conor was investigating on the island.

And Suzanne was the name of the girl so closely connected to Belinda. Was her name coincidence, or had it been chosen very consciously, an homage to the author of the fairy tale and a connection to 1740?

Kate looked at her phone, wondering when Conor would get back to Watch Hill, knowing he needed to hear all this. And knowing that she needed to sit down with him and hear the whole story of what had happened with Belinda. She was tired of being stuck with Belinda's words in her head, with the baby photo emblazoned in her mind.

She heard a knock on the door. Her immediate thought was that Conor had forgotten his key, and she ran downstairs to let him in. Instead of Conor, she saw Miranda Forrest standing there in the hallway.

"Hello, Kate," Miranda said. "I don't want to intrude, but I was hoping to have that chat with you."

"This isn't a good time," Kate said.

"Please," Miranda said. "It's important."

Kate hesitated, wanting to get back to reading about 1740. But she stood aside, letting Miranda enter. She led her through the foyer and upstairs, past the small gallery of vintage *New Yorker* covers done by Garrett Price, an artist who had painted with the nearby Mystic Art Association. They were cheerful depictions of summer and sailing scenes. She and Conor had found them charming, perfect for the Tower Suite, but now her mind was on darker art, and she barely noticed them.

"What an amazing view," Miranda said when they reached the living room. She walked from window to window, surveying the vista of three states. Then she looked up at the tall spiral staircase leading another full story up to the Crow's Nest.

"Bernard and I were wondering what it was like up here," Miranda said. "It must be the most romantic spot in the hotel . . ." Then as if she realized how that must affect Kate, she touched Kate's arm. "I'm sorry for saying that. I don't want to bring up something hurtful."

"That's okay," Kate said. She wanted to rush Miranda through whatever she wanted to say and be alone again, to get back to her reading—and waiting for Conor. But Miranda just stood there, saying nothing.

"Thanks for having me here this weekend," Miranda said. "I've always wanted to see what the Ocean House was like inside—especially up here in the tower."

"Well, you're Bernard's date," Kate said.

"Yes," Miranda said. "It wasn't easy, engineering that."

Kate tilted her head at the odd statement. "But you're his girlfriend," she said.

Miranda paused. "That's a recent development."

"Okay," Kate said, waiting for her to say more.

"Did you open my gift?" Miranda asked.

"No," Kate said. She had forgotten about it until that minute. She glanced at the dining table, where the box sat unopened.

"Could you do that now?" Miranda asked with an anxious edge to her voice.

Kate figured she might as well open it, to send Miranda on her way. The two of them sat at the table. A door opened to a terrace overlooking the beach. Kate didn't want to look down there, to see the Independence Day Beach Ball being set up. She and Conor had been looking forward to it—it was going to be the last chance to gather with their wedding guests.

She picked up the small square box, untied the blue ribbon, and ripped the yellow wrapping paper. When she lifted the lid, she saw a thin, tiny silver ring on a bed of white cotton.

"What's this?" Kate asked.

"Don't you recognize it?" Miranda asked.

Kate stared at the object and realized it was a piece of wire, twisted at the ends to make a ring. She knew exactly where she had seen it before.

"A child's wedding ring," Miranda said. "Something a little boy might have made for a little girl."

"Belinda's," Kate said, raising her eyes to look at Miranda. "The one Conor gave her."

Miranda nodded.

"How did you get it?"

"I took it off her finger while she was sleeping," Miranda said.

Kate's mind was spinning. "But why? How did you get close enough to her to do that?"

"She's my cousin, Kate. She's the whole reason I found a way to meet Bernard. Just like she found a way to meet Garrett. She and I both really needed to come to your wedding." She paused. "For different reasons."

"Why?" Kate asked, shocked.

"Belinda, because she's obsessed with Conor. Me, because I was afraid of what she would do," Miranda said. "I wanted to stop her."

"From telling me about her and Conor?" Kate asked.

"No, Kate," Miranda said. "From killing you."

21

Sunday, July 4; 6:00 p.m.

The Ocean House Independence Day Beach Ball was a dream event, the quintessence of a New England summer. At six o'clock, the sun was making its way west, behind the hotel and chapel and houses on the bluff, and the sky was turning deep blue. Emerald-green waves rolled in, translucent as they broke, then exploded into frothy white spindrift. The air was warm, with an early-evening breeze blowing off the water; Sam wore a white cashmere sweater that had been her mother's. She loved it because it reminded her of her mom; it still smelled faintly of the Diptyque perfume she used to wear. It had pockets to hold her phone and room key card.

Chefs were busy at their stations, the dance floor was set up for later, and servers came around with bottles of wine.

Sam, Hadley, and CeCe sat at one of the tables closest to the water. Their tablemates were Mike and Anne Reid and their friends—the Old Detectives, as Sam had started thinking of them: Nola and Edward Aldrich, and Leo Kennedy. CeCe seemed restless, so Hadley took her down to the water's edge. Sam was saving seats for Maeve and Lincoln; he had changed his mind about leaving. Maeve had said that they would meet her here, but they hadn't shown up yet. There was a sense of festivity all around, but Sam felt desolation. This was supposed to be the last party of the wedding weekend.

"What's with the long face?" Uncle Mike asked, giving Sam a wry smile.

"Isn't it obvious why?" Sam asked.

"Of course," Mike said. "It's been a hell of a time. And Conor and Kate should be sitting here with us. But we have to keep our spirits up, in order to be useful."

"'Useful'?" Sam asked.

"To help Conor and Kate," Anne said. "To solve this."

"Conor could still be arrested. Garrett Milne is awfully gung ho, and he seems to have a personal problem with him," Mike said.

"Even without an arrest," Leo Kennedy said, "Conor's reputation could be damaged. Rumors and innuendo can hang over a person's head forever. That would be the kiss of death if he wants to advance in his career."

"So that's where we come in," Nola said. "Being useful."

"I'm in too," Sam said. She paused, thinking of the trip she, Kate, and Maeve had taken to Maynard-King earlier. She thought about all they had seen at Dr. Jonathan Tyler's grave, especially the handwritten card. "I think Suzanne is the key. Plus the number 1740."

Mike frowned. "That was the number on the blue truck. I saw it at the murder scene. What does it mean?"

"Not sure," Sam said. "But it seems to be recurring." She told them about the grave and the note. She wrote it out on a napkin and passed it around, and she watched each of them examine it.

1740

With love

Always

"There it is again," Mike said. "And you know, it's reminding me of something. A murder case, about ten years ago. A woman was about to go on trial for killing a man she claimed had kidnapped her. There were allegations of sexual abuse and that he had held her for an extended time. The state offered her a plea deal, but she swore she hadn't done it—that there had been another kidnapper, a woman, and that the woman had been the one who killed him. She was out on bond, and just before trial began, she disappeared. She had left a diary, and I think it mentioned that number." He glanced around the table. "Does this ring a bell with anyone?"

"Yes," Leo said. "Her name was Lilian Jones. I remember thinking I could have done well for her if she had hired me, but she went with a different firm. Nola? You were my investigator. We were intrigued by the case, weren't we?"

"Yes, we were," Nola said. "I was hoping to meet her in the prison, but she made bail before I had the chance. I read the arrest report, and she seemed so vulnerable. The details of what she said she went through convinced me that she was innocent. But, Mike, I don't remember anything about a diary. Or the number 1740."

"I wonder what happened to her," Mike said.

"The police were never able to verify her claim of being kidnapped and held, but from everything I read, I believed her," Nola said.

"Abuse, trafficking, exploitation," Mike said, shaking his head. "Cases like hers get to us. They are so hard to let go."

"That's you all the way, darling," Anne said to Mike. "You care about the people who wind up in your courtroom, even after the final judgment. And even ones who never actually make it to trial."

"We all have cases that affect us," Leo said. "Mike's not alone in that."

"Maybe it's why we've all wound up in this field," Nola said. "Criminal law."

"You're a lawyer?" Sam asked.

"No," she said. "My research is in criminal behavior and victimology."

"Victimology?" Sam asked.

"Yes," Nola said. "Studying the victim of a homicide can often give us clues about her killer. What drew him to her? What habits of hers could have put her at risk? Where did her attacker first encounter her—were they neighbors? Coworkers? Did she always go to a particular grocery store? Gas station? Victimology can help answer the where and why of murder."

"Isn't it blaming the victim?" Sam asked. "To ask where she grocery shopped or got gas? As if by going to those places she brought it on?"

"Not at all, Sam," Nola said. "She was just living her life. Going about her day. Monsters can find their victims anywhere. In many ways, it's like a shark attack. If the person entered the water a minute earlier or later, the shark might have swum by. Sometimes timing and location are just very bad luck." Nola paused and gave Sam a sad smile. "It's never the victim's fault, Sam. No one asks to be attacked."

"Have you ever studied actual killers?" Sam asked, thinking of the person who had murdered her mother. She had never stopped wondering what the driving force had been.

"Many times," Nola said. "I often go to the ACI—the Adult Correctional Institute—here in Rhode Island to interview inmates, trying to understand their motivations. That's where I would have met Lilian. Most often, I've spoken to survivors. Victims of assault or attempted murder, who lived through it. I really believe that Lilian was a victim, and she needed an advocate. I wish I could have been that for her." She paused. "I always try to talk to family members who can tell me about the one they lost."

Sam nodded. She wished that she had had someone like Nola to talk to after her mother had died. Kate had done her best. She had always been there for Sam and had sent her to therapy. But losing a parent to murder wasn't like losing her to illness or an accident, so talking to someone who didn't understand crime, who really just thought Sam needed to "process her grief," hadn't been that helpful.

"There's always a victim . . . and we all care," Mike said. "We want to solve the crime. Now we have a great clue about this one—1740."

Then a chime rang, signifying it was time for dinner, and a parade of servers came around carrying trays heaped with bright-red lobsters. Sam's spirits lifted a little not because of the food but because it helped to know there was a team on Conor's side. It felt as if something was happening, as if, to use Mike's word, they were being useful.

Melted butter was poured into individual bowls, wines were served, and music played. Sam tried to eat, but she had zero appetite. She looked across the festive tables, toward Dune Cottage, and saw Lincoln standing there, beckoning her. She excused herself and walked over.

"Where's Maeve?" she asked. "You're going to miss dinner."

"I don't know where she is," he said. "After I decided to stay, we planned to meet in the lobby, but she's not there. I thought she might have come down already. You haven't seen her?"

"No," Sam said. "Is she all right?"

"Not really. She's incredibly shaken up."

"I can only imagine," Sam said.

"Look," Lincoln said, sounding nervous. "Will you come with me to look for her? She's been acting strange. I'm getting worried."

"Strange how?"

"Super distracted. She keeps stepping away to make calls."

"It's probably about Kate," Sam said. "Touching base with the conservator, to fix the painting."

"Maybe," Lincoln said. "But it feels like something else—as if she doesn't want me to hear what she's saying. Never mind, I'll go look for her by myself."

"Of course I'll go with you," Sam said. "We have to find her, make sure she's okay. Let me just let everyone know what I'm doing."

"Thanks, Sam," he said, giving her a quick hug as she hurried over to the table to excuse herself and say she'd be back after she found Maeve.

22

Sunday, July 4; 8:30 p.m.

Conor didn't return from the island until just before dark. They had crossed Block Island Sound in one of Tom's Coast Guard RIBs, speeding over the mirror-calm surface. The Ocean House loomed in the distance, the sunset light striking the yellow tower. He stared up at it, wondering if Kate was there waiting for him. He had to make things right—even though he knew it would hurt her to hear the truth.

They slowed to navigate the rocks and currents of Watch Hill Reef. Tom had told Conor that there had once been a Coast Guard station located just north of the lighthouse on Watch Hill Point. Many lifesaving missions had originated there, but it had been decommissioned in 1947. They came around Napatree Point and into the harbor, and the helmsman dropped Conor, Tom, and Joe off at the dock where the Fire District rescue boats were stationed.

The three men walked up Plimpton Road. House lights were coming on, and the Ocean House glowed from within. The murder house was twenty yards ahead, and Conor knew he had to get inside. He had the boat and mansion fresh in his mind, and he had to compare what he had seen there with the murder scene. He knew equally well that because Garrett's suspicion had made him a suspect, he would be prohibited from entering. Aside from protocol, he knew that it could be perceived that he was trying to remove, alter, or destroy evidence.

"That's odd," Joe said as they got closer.

"What?" Tom asked.

Joe gestured toward the murder house. "The crime scene tape's been taken down, and I don't see a patrol car."

Depending on the police force, a crime scene could be blocked off and guarded for several days. In this case, although the tape had been removed, Conor saw a notice attached to the front door, and he knew its basic message would be "off limits." He felt torn, because he wanted to see Kate right away, but this felt urgent.

"Joe, I want to see the room again. Can we go in there right now?"

"No, you're not going in," Joe said. "You know that. I mean, how many more rules do you want me to break today?" He stopped and looked at Conor. "Why do you want to?"

"To compare what we found on the boat and in the mansion with what was left behind in that room."

"A lot of blood," Joe said. "That's what was in that room."

"With your footprints in it," Tom said. "You've got to stay out of there, Conor. You could get hit with a tampering charge."

Conor stared his brother hard in the eyes. "You could go in," he said. "With Joe."

"What's my reason? How would I have jurisdiction?" Tom asked.

"The marina connection," Conor said. "The dockage receipt with Suzanne's name on it. A Coast Guard investigator would want to chase that down, wouldn't he? *Psyche* is a crime scene too."

"He's right," Joe said.

"Okay, say I go in with Joe," Tom said. "What would I be looking for?"

"An imprint in the blood," Conor said. He pulled out his phone and showed his brother the photo he had taken in the bedroom at the mansion, of the indentation left in the sticky substance beneath the bottle.

"What is it?" Tom asked, taking Conor's phone and looking at the screen.

"A rose," Conor said. "I took this at the mansion on Bellevigne Island. I saw the same mark in the blood here."

"The murderer took the time to draw a flower?" Tom asked, looking skeptical.

"At first, I thought it looked drawn, but now I think it was made by a stamp or a seal—you know, like a notary embosser. Some kind of tool."

Tom had been down at *Psyche* while Joe and Conor had gone through the mansion, so Conor let him scroll through the rest of the shots he had taken of the bedroom, including the one of the large black-and-white still from the Cocteau film. Then Tom went back to the photo of the mark left under the bottle containing the drug.

"I think it's an impression left by a signet ring," Tom said. "A rose insignia, maybe."

"Like a family crest?" Joe asked.

"I think it's connected to the fairy tale," Conor said. "And I think the killer used it to sign his kill." *Or kills, plural,* he thought, picturing the blood on the handcuffs, on the sheets.

"The crime scene techs will have clear photos," Joe said.

"I want to see the real thing," Conor said.

Joe stared at him. "I told you, you can't go in. I'll get the key, and I'll call Tom when I have it. I'll go too."

Conor was all for that. Dermot greeted them at the turnaround, and the three of them hurried up the wide stairs. Tom and Joe went into the lobby. Conor stood on the verandah and stared down at the beach where the Fourth of July festivities were underway. He thought of the wedding weekend schedule—how the whole party was supposed to be down at the Beach Ball for fireworks.

Something told him that Kate would be feeling about as in the mood for fireworks as he was, so he went into the lobby and took the elevator up to the Tower Suite. He knocked first, then used his key.

She met him at the door, as if she had been waiting all day. Her dark brown hair was uncombed and fell across her green eyes. Conor stepped forward to hug her, but he stopped himself. They weren't that way anymore. She didn't belong in his arms.

Except she did. She was the one to step toward him. She leaned into his body. His heart pounded. Everything felt right, the way it always had. They held each other. Her head was against his chest. He felt her kiss his shoulder. Then she tilted her head back. She looked into his eyes.

"You were waiting for me?" he asked.

"Yeah," she said.

His heart was racing. Would she ever wait for him again after what he had to tell her? He was about to ask her to sit down on the sofa with him, but she spoke first.

"I have stuff to tell you," she said.

"How did you know when I'd be here?" he asked.

"I was standing on the widow's walk," she said. "Above the tower. I saw the Coast Guard boat come in, and I knew you were aboard."

"How did you know that?" he asked. "It could have been a patrol boat. It could have been anything. How did you know?"

"I just knew," she said. "I was watching for you."

She reached up to hold him.

"Kate, wait," he said.

But she shook her head, and then she kissed him. It was the kind of kiss that changed both everything and nothing. He felt it in his skin. Kate was his life, the way his bones and blood were his life. This kiss brought him back to the beginning yet told him that nothing was the same. They'd never be the way they were. He wanted to take her to bed. He wanted to pick her up and carry her over the threshold, the way he should have after their wedding.

The wedding that never happened.

He couldn't do that to her, but he couldn't help himself from wanting to walk her into the bedroom. He stopped himself and took a deep breath.

"You said you have stuff to tell me," Conor said. "But I have to go first."

"I'm not sure I'm ready for it," she said.

"Please, Kate. It's eating me up," he said.

She gazed at him for a long time, and then she nodded. "I get that," she said. "It's the same for me."

He took her hand and led her to the sofa in front of the fireplace. He sat down, about an arm's length away from her. He didn't want to be too close—he needed a little distance because he wanted to look right into her eyes, see her reaction.

"You kissed me just now," he said. "I wasn't sure you'd want to, after what I told you on the island."

"I would block it out if I could," she said. "I keep telling myself it doesn't matter, whatever you did before you met me. But then I find myself wondering when it happened . . . you sleeping with Belinda . . . was it after you and I?"

"Kate, you and I weren't together yet," he said. "Not really."

"But sort of?" she asked.

"Well, you and I had met, but we hadn't started seeing each other," he said. "It was between the two cases." He meant the cases where he had helped solve Kate's mother's murder, and, later, her sister's.

"You were dating Belinda then?" Kate asked.

"No, not at all. You know we knew each other when we were kids, when she lived next door. But I had forgotten all about her." He gathered his thoughts, trying to remember the sequence. "I began getting calls from an unknown number. I'd answer, hear someone breathing, and then they'd hang up. There were emails from an unfamiliar address, sent to my work email. They were unsigned. At first, they contained what I thought were poems—at least, that's how they sounded. It turned out that they were lines from a book. Can you guess which one?"

He watched Kate; after a moment, he saw the sharp look in her eyes.

"*Beauty and the Beast*?" she asked.

"Yes. Throughout this whole time, I had no idea who was sending the messages. I wrote back and asked who it was. That's actually against the advice of our cyber investigators. The instruction is to delete and not reply. But I was so curious."

"And she answered?"

"No. Instead, the calls and emails stopped. But a few weeks later, I got a call at my office from Belinda. Totally out of the blue. She said that she had read about me in the paper—ironically, in an article about how I'd worked on your mother's case. She said that she'd moved away and had come back to the area, and would I like to meet for lunch."

"So you did."

"Yes," he said. "And at first, it was good to see her. We had a lot to talk about—old times in New London. She remembered things I had totally forgotten, like how our first-grade teacher said that we were the two best readers in the class. Like when I fell out of a tree and broke my arm, and she signed my cast. She made the *B* in Belinda into a heart."

Kate didn't say anything.

"I gave her that stupid wire ring right after that," Conor said.

Conor noticed Kate glancing over toward the dining table. He wondered what she was looking at, but she didn't say anything.

"Anyway, after that lunch, we went on a few dates. I liked her—she was funny and smart, and she told me all about this interesting life she was leading—studying historic houses, traveling around New England to document them." Conor stopped. "I don't like telling you this," he said.

"I want you to. I need to know."

"We began as friends, but it turned into something else. Or it started to. One weekend, she asked me to go with her to Salem, Massachusetts, to visit a Colonial house connected to the witch trials. So we went. We stayed in a bed-and-breakfast. And that's when we slept together. It was the only time."

"Really?"

"Yes. And we never went out again after that weekend."

"Why? What happened?"

Conor exhaled hard. "She had brought that little ring with her," he said. "She put it on, in the middle of the night, and she was wearing it when we woke up. She told me that she had worn it ever since I'd given it to her. That she had taken the ring as a promise that we would always be together—that we would get married when we grew up."

Kate's eyes widened. "Wow," she said.

"She said she was sure that I felt the same way," Conor said. "And that it was such a gift that we were finally together again, that now we could start planning."

"Planning what?"

"Yeah. I asked her that too. She said that it was destiny, that we were meant to be a couple. She told me that she had been sending me emails for months—she was the anonymous emailer—and that the quotes were from *Beauty and the Beast*. She said that she was Belle, and I was the Beast."

"Just like she said to me," Kate said.

"Yes," Conor said. "She asked where we would live. Basically, she wanted to know if it should be her place or mine. I was so shocked, I hardly knew what to say. I didn't want to hurt her, but I also didn't want to lead her on. And even more—I felt that she was crazy. Deluded doesn't cover it. She was truly out of touch with reality."

"Sounds it," Kate said.

"I kept my voice very steady and told her that we were just getting to know each other again, that it wasn't possible to plan a future when we hadn't seen each other since childhood. It felt bizarre to even have to say that—it was so obvious. The look in her eyes changed in that second—from dreamy to furious. She accused me of using her, basically just taking her away for the weekend when all I wanted was sex, how I was a user, a bad guy, and how she was going to tell everyone in my department what a shit I was. She was going to spread the word."

"Did she?" Kate asked.

"No," Conor said. "But she wrote to me. She mailed the letter and emailed a copy. It was pages long—just spewing vitriol, how I'd thrown the best thing in my life away, how I thought I was so special, too good for everyone. What a phony I am, what a liar, what a player. She said I needed therapy to address how toxic I am. How I would never have love in my life because I was incapable of feeling or giving it. She told me that she had lots of men after her—guys smarter, better looking, and richer than me. She said she could marry a doctor tomorrow if she wanted and that I didn't know what I was missing."

"A doctor," Kate said. "That's interesting. Did she keep contacting you?"

"Not at first," he said, wondering why she had homed in on the doctor part of Belinda's rant. "She disappeared. At first, I was sure she'd be back—I kept waiting for her to show up. Or for the calls and emails to start up again. And they did—always anonymously. At one point, I received an envelope with a baby tooth and a lock of hair in it."

"It was from her," Kate said.

"I assume so," Conor said. "There was a note inside, but it wasn't signed. I never saw or heard from her again until Friday—until she came here with Garrett."

"When I saw you at the seawall?" Kate asked.

"Yes," Conor said. "That's when she showed me the ring and also the baby picture. She told me it was my daughter—from that one night."

Kate was silent for a moment, staring across the room. "Could that be true?"

"No," Conor said. "I hate getting specific about that night, Kate. But I have to, because I want you to know. I used protection. I brought it with me."

Kate nodded. Conor knew he'd said enough, and when she looked at him, he could see a certain resolution in her eyes. "I believe you," she said.

She slid closer to him and put her head on his shoulder. They sat there for a long time. The sun had completely gone down, and the living room was dark. Through the door that opened to the terrace, they could hear music and voices drifting up from the beach.

"Hear that?" she asked after a few minutes.

And he did—the first explosion, the start of the fireworks.

"They're for us," she said. "They mark the end of our wedding weekend."

"The end of us?" he asked.

"No," she said, smiling. "We're still us."

He held her tighter.

"Should we go watch the fireworks?" she asked.

"Down on the beach?" he asked.

She shook her head and took his hand. There was a terrace off the dining area, facing northeast across the beach toward Weekapaug and Block Island. But instead of stepping outside, she took him up the circular staircase to the Crow's Nest—the small and cozy nook with the daybed. From there, she started climbing straight up a ladder to the roof, and he followed her.

To the widow's walk, at the very top of the Ocean House.

Conor followed Kate through the hatch onto the tower. They stood in a tight square surrounded by an ornate wrought iron fence. They looked around in four directions and saw Rhode Island, Connecticut, and New York, salt water everywhere.

They saw the Atlantic Ocean, lighthouses on the horizon, too numerous to count. The Block Island windmills blinked red. Watch Hill Harbor was filled with boats, masthead lights twinkling, red-and-green running lights casting reflections in the water. They saw East Beach curving below them, a crescent embracing the ocean, the same view as the one in the painting Kate had given him.

When they looked straight down, they saw all the tables and all the celebrants at the Ocean House Independence Day Beach Ball. And when they looked up, they saw the fireworks. They saw canopies of white stars, waterfalls of red fire, treetops of green and yellow, exploding orchids, trailing vines and roses.

Conor was gazing at Kate instead of the sky. She must have felt it, because she reached up and touched his cheek. She left her hand there for a few seconds, and then he pulled her close. He felt her heart beating against his chest. He held her so tight, and she whispered something. He couldn't hear the words over the sound of the fireworks, but he was pretty sure he knew what they were.

23

Monday, July 5; 8:00 a.m.

Kate and Conor had stayed up for hours, sitting on the widow's walk until the fireworks were over, until the revelers had left the beach, and the staff had stowed the chairs and tables. They sat quietly, feeling the stillness. The only sounds were the tumbling waves and the bell buoy marking Watch Hill Passage.

She didn't want to leave the tower. Being up here felt enchanted, in the same way as when they'd stayed in the Welcome Hotel. They sat side by side, holding hands. She barely noticed the time passing, but then the dark sky began to turn gray, and the first pink line of dawn appeared on the eastern horizon. Conor put his arm around her, and she leaned her head on his shoulder until the sun had risen and turned the ocean pure gold.

After sunrise, they climbed down the ladder, into the suite, and Conor made coffee in the kitchen—the way he always did at home. She sat at the table by the door to the terrace and watched him, feeling something new. They had been together for years, they had been engaged since two winters ago, but after last night, she felt that they had started over in some mysterious way.

"Good morning," he said, handing her a cup of black coffee.

"Thank you," she said.

"Are you tired?" he asked. "After staying up all night?"

She shook her head. "No, are you?"

"Not at all."

They drank their coffee for a while. She didn't want to talk or break the spell; she didn't want to return to reality. She wanted the magic of the tower, of last night, to stay with them and keep them safe. But eventually she sighed.

"I want to show you something," she said. The box that Miranda had given her was across the table, and she opened it and handed Conor the little wire ring. She watched his face, for his reaction.

"Belinda's?" he asked, turning it over in his palm. "How did you get it? She gave it to you?"

"No, Miranda gave it to me," she said.

"Bernard's girlfriend?" Conor asked.

"It seems they're not really together, though I'm not sure he knows that."

"Then why is she here?"

"Because Belinda was her cousin."

Conor looked up. "Okay . . ." he said.

"They both wangled invitations to our wedding," Kate said. "Belinda got close to Garrett, and Miranda began seeing Bernard."

"But why?" Conor asked.

Kate took a deep breath. "Miranda said Belinda wanted to kill me, and she wanted to stop her."

Conor stared at Kate, seeming stunned. He reached for her hand.

"There's another element," Kate said. "It's insane, literally. Sam and Maeve found out that Belinda had been married before, and her husband was murdered in the exact same way as she was. His throat was slashed. Belinda was right when she told you she could marry a doctor—she did. He was a psychiatrist at a hospital . . ."

"Where?" Conor asked.

"Maynard-King," Kate said. "It's a psychiatric hospital in Narragansett, not far from here."

"There's a woman out on the island," Conor said. "Her name is Grace. She said she had been in treatment, like other girls—'Ghost Girls,' she called them. She talked about girls going to 'MK.'"

"MK—Maynard-King," Kate said.

Conor nodded. "That must be the same place. She said that she survived, but some of the other girls didn't."

"Survived what?" Kate asked.

"I don't know," Conor said. "But women are being taken, held captive, and murdered."

"How do you know?"

"You saw *Psyche*," Conor said. "The restraints on the bulkhead. He—whoever he is—uses the sailboat to bring them to the island, and then he locks them in a room. The *Beauty and the Beast* room."

"Where the photo is?" Kate asked, thinking of the text he had sent her, with the image from the Jean Cocteau film.

"Yes," Conor said. "He has some sort of obsession with the fairy tale."

"But who is he?" Kate asked. "If there's a connection to Maynard-King, could it be another doctor there?"

"Possibly," Conor said. "He has a whole bookcase full of different editions, including translations. Some are vintage, probably valuable, which—along with the boat and mansion itself—makes me think he has money."

"Who owns the house?" Kate asked.

"Joe is on that," Conor said. "Another thing—the way the number 1740 runs all through this."

Kate nodded, excited. "The year Gabrielle-Suzanne Barbot de Villeneuve wrote and published *La Belle et la Bête*. It's the oldest known version of the story . . . *Beauty and the Beast*," she said.

"The date was stenciled onto the door of Suzanne's truck," Conor said.

"It was at the grave too," Kate said. "Someone left a note by Jonathan Tyler's headstone, along with a bouquet of white roses."

"Roses?" Conor asked sharply.

"Yes, roses are an important part of the story. They are the reason Beauty became the Beast's prisoner."

"In what way?" Conor asked.

"Beauty's father stole roses from the Beast's castle, and the forfeit he had to pay was his daughter. He gave his daughter to the Beast," Kate said. "So it makes it even stranger that Belinda calls you both by those names. Because if you're the Beast, it means you somehow imprisoned her."

"But I didn't," Conor said.

Kate touched his hand. "I know," she said. "Of course you didn't. But someone did, and obviously she would have suffered trauma."

Conor was quiet for a minute. He walked over to a window and stared out across the ocean, toward the island. When he turned back to Kate, he shook his head.

"I think it's the other way around," he said. "Talking to Grace, I have the feeling that the girls became more traumatized *after* they went to Maynard-King. Maybe the doctor was reenacting the fairy tale—or someone was. And whatever happened there took away their hopes of getting well. Or got them killed."

"How do you and I figure in?" Kate said. "She started calling you Beast on that weekend in Salem . . . but what about me?"

"She hated you because I love you," Conor said.

"She did everything she could to ruin our wedding . . ."

"And she got killed instead."

"By someone who thought she was me."

Conor was silent for another minute. "Or maybe he didn't think she was you. What if he meant for Belinda to die? What if she was the intended victim? The killer is someone passionate about *Beauty and the Beast*. I keep thinking of *Psyche* and of that house on the island—there are so many references to his obsession. And when he killed Belinda, he left a rose imprint in her blood."

"Or she," Kate said. "It could have been a woman."

"Possible," Conor said. "What if it was Suzanne who did it?"

Kate considered that. "Her name tracks—it's an homage to the author, to Gabrielle-Suzanne Barbot de Villeneuve. She might well have left a rose—in Belinda's blood, but also at the hospital grave site."

"Could they really have been mother and daughter?" Conor asked.

"I don't know," Kate said. "Maybe you should get the tooth and hair DNA tested."

"I'm already on that. It was weird and disturbing to get them, but they weren't associated with a crime, so I just stuck them in a drawer. I'll get them to our lab."

"Is there any way Suzanne would have intentionally murdered her own mother?" Kate asked.

Conor didn't answer. He didn't have to. Kate knew that over the years he had worked on the worst, most unbelievable murder cases. So often the killer was someone who had once loved—or should have loved—the victim.

"I want to get a copy of that note we found on Tyler's grave," Kate said. "I should have made one myself, but I left it to Maeve. Maybe something in it—the 1740 reference—will make more sense considering what you found on the island."

Kate texted Maeve:

Hi, I'm with Conor and want to show him that note. Can you send me a photo?

They drank another cup of coffee while waiting for her to respond. It took so long, Kate wondered if Maeve was sleeping late. The sun was fully up, and people were starting to stroll down to the beach. Kate checked her watch. It was almost nine, and Maeve was an early riser. Maybe she was all packed up, checking out of the hotel, possibly even on her way home. She could be taking the slashed Suydam painting to the conservator.

"She's not answering?" Conor asked.

"No, and I'm surprised. She's always got her phone with her."

"Give her another minute," Conor said.

"Maybe she's already checked out," Kate said. She met Conor's eyes. The whole wedding party was supposed to check out today. "I guess we should too." She stood up.

Conor didn't answer. She wondered if he felt the way she did. They had spent the whole wedding weekend apart. This was the first time she'd started feeling as if they could be together again. She didn't want to leave. She wanted to stay with him, right here in the Tower Suite.

"What are you thinking?" he asked, pushing his chair back and standing up.

"That Maeve might be on her way home," Kate said. "Or maybe she's already taking the painting to the conservator, to have it repaired."

"I don't mean about Maeve," Conor said, taking a step closer to her. "Or the painting. I mean what are you thinking about us."

"Don't you already know?" she asked. She felt energy pouring off him, electricity that rocked her.

She took his hand and led him down the stairs, past the joyful Garrett Price *New Yorker* covers, into the master bedroom. When she had packed for her wedding last week, anticipating the most important day of her life, she had folded each item perfectly, with great care. Yesterday, anticipating leaving the Ocean House, she had pulled out her suitcase and tossed everything into it. She hadn't been at all careful; she had packed her clothes the way she felt—as if nothing mattered anymore.

But that was yesterday, she thought. Now everything mattered again: How quickly things could change. The bedroom, like the rest of the Tower Suite, had windows facing the ocean, all the way out to Watch Hill Point, and Montauk beyond, across Block Island Sound. She stared down at the waves, as if they were telling her the most wonderful story, and then she turned to Conor.

"Don't you already know?" she asked again.

"About us?" he asked. "Yes, I do."

"And I'm sorry that I forgot who we were for a while. Did you too?"

Conor reached for her hand. They stood there, looking out the window at the summer morning, at the blue-green Atlantic Ocean. They didn't move. They hardly breathed.

"Never," Conor said. "I never forgot, not even for a minute."

And he kissed her, and Kate knew that they were staying. They weren't going anywhere.

24

Conor and Kate walked through the lobby, and he spotted Sam and Lincoln standing in front of the model of *Aphrodite*. Sam ran over when she saw them.

"Maeve's missing," Sam said.

"That's a little dramatic, putting it that way," Lincoln said, hurrying to catch her. Conor noticed the cool, almost annoyed, tone in his voice.

"We haven't seen her since yesterday," Sam said. "She was supposed to meet us on the beach, for the ball last night. We saved a seat for her, and she never showed up."

"I haven't heard from her since we got back from the cemetery," Kate said, sounding alarmed. "I've been texting her, but no answer. She wasn't with you, Lincoln?"

"No, she wasn't," he said.

"You haven't seen her all night?" Conor asked him. "Is it normal for her to stay away without letting you know where she is?"

"We don't answer to each other," Lincoln said. "We do our own things and get together when we want to."

"I thought you lived together," Sam said, turning toward him.

"Did you have a fight?" Kate asked.

"Look, I admit I'm getting a little concerned," Lincoln said, and Conor noticed he didn't answer the question. "But I can understand why she might have needed to go off alone and center herself. She's not over the shock."

Conor saw Kate's troubled expression. Ever since last night, when he'd told her everything and they'd shut the world out of the Tower Suite, they had stopped worrying, stopped thinking about anything but each other. But now he could see worry building in her eyes. "This isn't like her," Kate said. "I wanted to show Conor that note we found, and I texted her about it. She still hasn't answered me."

"The one we found at the grave?" Sam asked. "I know where it is—in her car. I saw her put it in the center console as we were leaving the cemetery."

Kate hurried toward the valet stand in the foyer, and Conor followed her. Dermot had just come through the door after bringing a guest's vehicle around.

"Hello, Ms. Woodward," Dermot said to Kate. "Need your car?"

"Not yet, Dermot," she said. "I'm checking on my assistant, Maeve. Can you tell me if she picked up hers yet?"

Dermot didn't even have to look at the master list. He shook his head, then paused as if remembering something. "No, I'm sure she didn't."

"Why are you so sure?" Conor asked.

"Well, she came out yesterday and gave me the ticket. I went to get her car, and when I drove it up, she was gone. I parked it in the upper lot, kept it close for her, thinking she would come back for it any minute, but it was still there when I left for the day. And it was right where I parked it when I got here this morning."

"Where is it now?" Conor asked.

Dermot pointed at the lot across Bluff Avenue, and Conor walked straight over. Maeve's dark-blue BMW was backed into a space, ready to go. Conor peered into the driver's window, then walked slowly around the car.

He noticed that the painting Kate had bought for him was resting upright and leaning against the back seat. The cracked frame and torn canvas were clearly visible. Conor knew that meant that at one point, Maeve had been planning to go to the conservator. Had something interrupted her?

Kate crouched by the left front tire, reached into the wheel well, and came out with a magnetic metal box—the kind Conor knew some people used to hide a spare key. Kate started to use it to unlock the driver's-side door. But the door was already unlocked. She leaned inside and opened the center console.

"The 1740 note's gone," Kate said, turning to Conor.

"Did you say 1740?" Dermot asked.

"Why do you ask?" Conor asked.

"I saw that number, drawn on a truck," Dermot said, gesturing across the street. "For a while it was parked over at the house where the woman was murdered. It belongs to Suzanne."

"Do you know her?" Kate asked.

"Not really. She told me she was working with your assistant, for the wedding," he said, and looked apologetic, as if he didn't want to cause pain.

"It's okay, Dermot," Kate said.

He nodded and gave her a smile. "Anyway, I asked her about the 1740 on the door—because the lettering was beautiful. Lots of cars have stenciling on them, but that was different. I thought I might get some on mine."

"What did she say?" Conor asked.

"She said she'd done it herself. That her specialty was calligraphy, so why not put it on her truck? But then she said something I didn't quite get. She said the number was sacred. It was a symbol that protected her and gave her life."

"She said 'gave her life'?" Conor asked.

"Yes," Dermot said.

Conor took it in, the extreme phrase that Suzanne had used. He felt charged, the way he did when puzzle pieces began to fit together. The idea a number could give Suzanne life went along with the idea of obsession that he'd been forming about the case. Symbols—the number, the rose, the recurring theme of *Beauty and the Beast*, even Suzanne's name—perhaps inspired by that of the original author, were obsessions that ran all through the case.

"When's the last time you saw Suzanne?" Conor asked.

Dermot thought for a few seconds. "Early this morning," he said. "I'm not sure of the time. She hasn't valeted a car with us, but she's always walking around. It's been so busy."

"Of course," Kate said. "It's Fourth of July weekend."

Not to mention all the guests for a big wedding that never happened, Conor thought. "Can you tell me who unlocked Maeve's car?" he asked.

"We always keep guests' vehicles locked," Dermot said. "We hold the keys in a safe place."

"Then it was Maeve herself or someone who knew where she hid the extra key," Kate said. "Used it to open the door, then put it back in the box in the wheel well."

"They'll be on camera," Dermot said.

"Thanks, that's helpful to know," Conor said. Then he texted Joe and said to meet in the lobby right away.

Conor went to the front desk and asked to see the person in charge of security, and Joe arrived at the same time Augustus Lande called them into his office. Joe showed his badge and explained what they needed. Kate had narrowed the window of time down to when she, Maeve, and Sam had returned from Maynard-King.

"You can start in the upper parking lot around 3:30 p.m. yesterday," Conor said. Against the wall were several monitors. Augustus cued up yesterday's parking lot footage and fast-forwarded it through yesterday afternoon, until Conor saw movement near Maeve's BMW.

"Stop there," Conor said. The exact time was 6:13 p.m.

They watched the screen. Maeve approached the driver's side of the vehicle with someone wearing a ball cap and a windbreaker, shoulders hunched. Maeve crouched by the front tire, removed the hidden key, and clicked the remote so that the car lights blinked and the side door mirrors flared out, indicating that the door had just been unlocked.

"Can you tell who that is with her?" Joe asked, leaning forward.

Conor stared at the screen. The hoodie was bulky, the face obscured. Head held low, the ball cap hid the eyes and most of the face as if Maeve's companion was aware there were cameras. Even his height was hard to assess, because of his bent-over posture. Conor had the impression he was quite a bit taller than Maeve but trying to hide that fact.

Kate leaned forward to get a better look.

They watched Maeve lean into the front seat of the BMW and emerge holding what looked like a small white card or piece of paper.

"The note from Tyler's grave?" Conor asked, looking at Kate.

"It could be," she said.

The man had his back to the camera; looking down the street, he made a quick gesture, and a black Range Rover drove alongside the BMW. The front passenger door swung open.

"Can you zoom in on the windshield?" Joe asked. "Get a look at the driver?"

Augustus did his best, but it was impossible to see the person's face. Because the Range Rover was broadside to the camera, the license plate was unreadable.

"Maybe our lab guys can enhance the image," Joe said.

"Wait—did you see that?" Kate asked.

"What?" Conor asked.

But Kate just stared intently as the video kept playing.

They watched as the man shoved Maeve, trying to force her into the front seat. The motion was so rough, Kate gasped. Maeve resisted, trying to squirm away. He pushed her harder, and she tumbled into the front seat. They watched as the man slammed the door behind her. Kate was gripping Conor's hand as they watched the person climb into the back seat behind Maeve and the Range Rover speed away and out of sight.

"What did you see?" Conor asked.

"He hurt her," Kate said, her voice shaking. "And just before he pushed her, she looked straight at the camera and said something. She was trying to send a message. A word—did you see?"

"Can you rewind?" Conor asked Augustus.

Augustus clicked the keyboard and slowed down the video playback to half speed, until Kate said stop. Conor saw what Kate had meant about Maeve staring at the camera, mouthing a word just before she was forced into the vehicle.

But Maeve also made a subtle action, easy to miss. She held her right arm tight against her body, as if to make sure the man didn't see. Conor saw something glitter as she let it slide through her fingers onto the road.

He hurried out of Augustus's office—onto the hotel verandah, down the curving steps, and a few yards along the short path between perfectly manicured hedges, onto Bluff Avenue. He stopped in front of the stone wall that bordered the upper parking lot. And he saw what he had missed before.

Kate and Joe were right behind him, and Kate bent down to look at the object. She didn't touch it; through her own experience, and from being around Conor, she knew it might be evidence. Cars drove past—sightseers visiting Watch Hill, people circling around in search of a parking spot so they could go to the beach.

"It's Maeve's," Kate said, gazing at the fine gold chain that Maeve had surreptitiously let fall onto the road. Conor saw it lying on the tar: a long, glinting S-shaped necklace, almost invisible in the shade of the wall. "She always wore it—she would never have dropped it on purpose unless it had a meaning. She wanted us to know . . ."

"Know what?" Joe asked.

"That she's been taken," Conor said.

"Like the others," Joe said.

"What was the word she mouthed to the camera?" Conor asked.

"'Help,'" Kate said. "I think she was saying 'help.'"

25

Monday, July 5; 1:00 p.m.

Kate watched Garrett cross Bluff Avenue and approach Joe. He had just returned from the State Police barracks, and she overheard him tell Joe that he had gotten his text about the video of Maeve and had stopped in the security office to review the footage.

Conor took Kate's hand and began to step away, to give the Rhode Island detectives privacy. She noticed that Sam and Lincoln were standing on the hotel verandah, so she and Conor started toward them, but Garrett called out.

"Conor," he said.

"Yeah?"

"You're cleared."

Conor turned to face him, showing no emotion, as if he'd known all along that he would be cleared. But Kate saw his shoulders relax, and she knew what a relief it was to hear it—it was a relief for her too.

"You understand why we had to look at you, right?" Garrett asked.

"You did what you had to do," Conor said.

"Look, you were soaked in her blood. Your fingerprints and footprints were all over. I couldn't just automatically rule you out."

"What cleared me?" Conor asked.

"I talked to Tom and other witnesses," Garrett said. "Your alibi holds up. Plus, the medical examiner's report just came in. Joe, did you get it? I emailed it to you."

"Haven't had the chance to check email," Joe said.

"What did the ME find?" Conor asked.

"Homicidal cut-throat," Garrett said. "Right to left—left-handed aggressor."

Conor nodded, and Kate saw him relax even more.

"The killer was behind Belinda," Garrett said. "The cut began just under the right ear, two quick hesitation marks. Then deeper, extending across the entire neck. It slanted down somewhat in the center, then moved upward to the other ear. The weapon slashed the carotid arteries, accounting for the arterial spray . . ."

"So I'm cleared because I'm right-handed?" Conor said.

"Yes, along with your alibi," Garrett said. "Plus, we found the murder weapon."

"What is it?" Conor asked.

"An Opinel. Curved blade."

"That's an odd choice," Conor said.

"Why?" Kate asked.

"An Opinel is a French knife, relatively uncommon in the United States," Conor said. Then, to Garrett: "Where did you find it?"

"A guy was on the dinghy dock yesterday, about to get into his Zodiac and head out to his boat. He looked down—must have been low tide—and saw the knife in the shallow water. He scooped it up, and he was planning to keep it, till he heard about the murder. He gave it to a Westerly cop."

"It's not necessarily the murder weapon," Conor said. "It could be anyone's knife, right?"

"No," Garrett said. "It's our knife. There were strands of white silk from the wedding gown caught in the hinge, several hairs that match Belinda's length and color. Obviously, the lab will test for DNA."

"Prints?" Conor asked.

"It was in salt water for a while," Garrett said. "So we'll see. Maybe we can narrow down to where it was purchased. It's not a common knife, at least not in the States."

"So I really am off your list?" Conor asked.

"Yeah," Garrett said. "You never should have been on it in the first place. Just . . . I got caught up in something."

"Belinda?" Conor asked.

"She intended to get to you, Kate," Garrett said. "She obviously had it in for you. I had no idea until I saw what she did at the rehearsal dinner. By the time I got to the ER, she was already done with me. The only reason I was her date was because I could get her here, into the Ocean House for your wedding weekend."

"And Miranda did the same with Bernard?" Kate asked.

"Apparently," Garrett said. "Belinda and Miranda were very close. She told me they were like sisters. I wonder if they really *were* sisters."

"Belinda had one brother, no sisters, when I knew them as kids," Conor asked.

"They're cousins," Kate said. "Miranda told me."

"Yeah," Conor said. "She had cousins who spent summers in Groton Long Point. The girl was our age."

"Maybe," Garrett said.

"I remember that the cousins' father—Belinda's uncle—was an actor," Conor said. "They lived in New York, and he was well known for doing Shakespeare. The family came out to Groton Long Point nearly every July so he could perform at the National Playwrights Conference, at the O'Neill."

"He could have named his daughter after Miranda in *The Tempest*," Kate said. "If she grew up in the theater world, that's how she could have met Bernard. It would make sense that their paths crossed."

"Or she targeted him," Conor said.

"Miranda came to talk to me, to give me this," Kate said, digging into her pocket and pulling out the wire ring to show Garrett. "She took it off Belinda's finger while she was sleeping."

Conor leaned closer to examine it.

"This isn't the same one," he said. "I didn't realize that before, when you showed me upstairs. I had wondered how it could still fit her—a ring she wore in first grade—but this isn't the one. I used soldering wire from my dad's workbench. It was much thicker than this. I should have noticed first thing."

"So she made it just to wear here, to your wedding," Garrett said to Conor. "To get a reaction from you."

"And from Kate," Conor said.

"I wonder what happened to the original ring," Kate said.

"I'd say we could ask Miranda about it," Garrett said, "but she's on her way back to LA. I just got word that Bernard's jet took off from Groton–New London Airport an hour ago."

"I doubt Miranda went with him," Kate said, thinking of how she had confessed to tricking Bernard, just as Belinda had manipulated Garrett. With Miranda's mission accomplished, there was no reason for her to continue the charade.

"I thought everyone was supposed to stick around, not leave till the investigation was over," Conor said.

"That's right," Garrett said. "But Bernard chartered a private jet. He drove to Groton–New London Airport, got on board, and as they were taxiing, he texted me he has a big scene tomorrow and will be back on the weekend."

"No way he's planning to come back," Joe said.

"He is French," Garrett said. "He could easily have an Opinel, and since he's flying private, he'd have no problem getting it on his jet and bringing it here. But what would his motive have been? Belinda had never met him before Friday, at the rehearsal dinner."

"Do we know that for sure?" Conor asked. "Belinda was Miranda's cousin. Bernard could have met her anytime."

"I know this is all very important," Kate said. "But what about Maeve?"

She pointed at the gold chain, still on the ground in the shadow of the wall. Joe had left it there until it could be photographed, collected as evidence.

Everyone but Conor looked down at the necklace. Kate saw his eyes narrow as something up on the hotel verandah caught his attention. Lincoln and Sam were still standing there. Sam had her back to the road and was looking toward the ocean. Lincoln stared, intent on what the police detectives and Kate were doing.

"They're worried about Maeve," Kate said. "That's why Lincoln is so interested in what's going on here."

"Yes, of course," Conor said, smiling at her. He gave Lincoln and Sam one last glance, then turned to watch Joe put on gloves and crouch down to pick up the fine gold chain.

But Kate knew Conor, and she knew there was more to what he had observed in Lincoln than he was saying.

26

Conor was so happy that things with Kate were getting back to a good place again, he wanted to forget everything else and just be with her. But details in the two cases—Belinda's murder and Maeve's abduction—were swirling around, and he was following the leads. The rose imprinted in Belinda's blood and the note taken from Maeve's car indicated that the crimes were connected to 1740. And that meant that they were linked to each other, as well as to the handcuffs on *Psyche* and the mansion on Bellevigne Island.

He had sent Dave Liggett, a Connecticut State Trooper who reported to him, to Cloudlands. He told Dave to look in the top drawer of the library desk, to retrieve the envelope that held the hair and baby tooth, and take it to the crime lab for analysis. Conor had extended his and Kate's stay at the Ocean House. Not only did they need time together, but they also both wanted to be near the center of the investigations. He walked through the lobby and found Tom in the Bistro, sitting at one of the tables by the fireplace and typing on his laptop.

"Hey," Conor said, taking a seat across from his brother. "What are you doing?"

"Hey," Tom said, looking up. "Making notes about the case. Laying out a chronology and documenting what we found on *Psyche*. Anything new here?"

"Maeve is missing," Conor said.

"Kate's gallery assistant? She found Belinda's body?"

"Yes," Conor said.

"Did they hold her for questioning?"

"They're questioning everyone. She was first on the murder scene, and she hired Suzanne to do the calligraphy. Big connections there. So, yes, Joe spent time talking to her. But she's not a suspect."

"That you know of," Tom said. "It's possible Joe and Garrett are keeping that confidential, even from you."

"Certainly possible," Conor said. "But I seem to be back in Garrett's good graces."

"That's good to hear. When did Maeve go missing?" Tom asked.

"Yesterday. 6:13 p.m."

"That's specific. Where did you get that?"

"We checked the security footage and saw the time stamp." Conor told Tom what had been on the video and the conclusions they had made based on Maeve dropping her necklace and the fact that the note was missing.

"So, someone doesn't want you to find the note," Tom said. "Fingerprints, DNA, handwriting? And the fact it was found at that psychiatric hospital. Doesn't a place like Maynard-King treat the human psyche? Did someone there name the boat?"

"Maybe," Conor said. "But there's also the myth of Cupid and Psyche. Kate says that ties in with *Beauty and the Beast*. This guy is obsessed with it."

"The boat is the key. The handcuffs and all that blood," Tom said. He handed Conor the paperwork he had gotten from the marina owner, stating that Suzanne had paid for dockage throughout the summer, until late September.

"Why would she pay for it? The boat owner would," Conor said.

"Maybe she was the owner," Tom said.

"That doesn't make sense—it was obviously used as a place to hold women before the guy took them to the mansion," Conor said, remembering Grace's disjointed story about the boat transporting girls from the mainland.

"Suzanne was involved somehow," Tom said. "The dock records prove it. Come on, we'll find out who owns *Psyche*."

The Reid brothers walked down the hill, into town. Conor knew that Tom's office at his main post in New London was more equipped to research maritime matters, but the USCG maintained a space next to the harbor, on Bay Street—tucked between a clothing boutique and an antique store—that held a secure computer system.

Several years ago, Tom and Conor had uncovered an art-smuggling operation centered in southeastern New England. It had started with one painting stolen from Kate's gallery and had escalated into a major investigation of art theft and how it was a cover for larger crimes.

Tom had requested that command restore an outpost of the decommissioned USCG Lifesaving Station to active but secret use, and they had acquiesced. Watch Hill was a prime location to monitor northbound-ship traffic through three critical bodies of water: Long Island Sound, Block Island Sound, and the Atlantic Ocean.

Tom punched a code into the keypad beside the door, then leaned close to a small lens so an eyeball scanner could verify his identity. He and Conor were buzzed inside. The officer in charge greeted them, and they walked to a desk at the far end of the long room. The space had once been an antiquarian bookshop that specialized in volumes of local history; several remained on shelves that lined a windowless wall.

Conor pulled up a chair beside the desk. Tom had his laptop, but he set it aside and logged in to a desktop computer. Conor knew that his brother could access databases connected to many aspects of inshore, nearshore, and offshore marine interests. This office computer would have a higher level of security and access than Tom's personal one.

"Wouldn't it be easier to just ask the harbormaster who owns the boat? Or wasn't there a registration on board?" Conor asked.

"The harbormaster runs a pretty loose show out there, and from what I could see, there was no paperwork on the boat. The state police will do a thorough search—I didn't want to be in their way—but I suspect the boat is documented."

"What are you talking about?" Conor asked, watching Tom type parameters into the computer.

"There are two ways to register a boat. One is with the state where the boat owner lives and where it will be docked. The other is to document it with the federal government—that means me."

"You?"

"The Coast Guard," Tom said. "Documentation, as opposed to standard registration, makes it easier to travel to foreign waters. It helps with clearing customs, and it gives the owner US protections."

"International travel," Conor said, jumping on that. "You think Suzanne—or whoever—plans to sail *Psyche* abroad? Like Europe?"

"It's one possibility, but we don't know yet," Tom said. "You see it with yachts that race outside the States—ones who do the Bermuda Race, St. Maarten Heineken Regatta, St Barths Bucket, Antigua Race Week, things like that . . . Canada, the Caribbean—the destination doesn't have to be Europe."

"So *Psyche* is a racing yacht?" Conor asked.

"No. The fireplace and some of the other modifications add weight that wouldn't work for racing," Tom said.

"Like the restraints," Conor said in a flat tone.

"Definitely. But she's a Hinckley and obviously has a pedigree. She could be making international trips for other reasons." Tom paused, squinting at the monitor. "Yep—here she is. *Psyche* is documented."

"Does it show the owner?" Conor asked.

Tom nodded, pointing at the screen. "Leprince de Beaumont Associates."

"Holy shit," Conor said.

"What?" Tom asked, looking at him.

"Same as the house," Conor said. "Joe was supposed to check with the registered agent to get through the corporate firewall—to try to track down the principal of the LLC." He was already calling Joe when Tom stopped him.

"Hold on," Tom said. "There's an address."

Conor leaned over and read *Leprince de Beaumont Associates, 13 Lovecraft Lane, Narragansett, RI 02906.* It gave a phone number with a Rhode Island area code. Tom searched the address online, and Conor punched the number into his cell phone and put the call on speaker. They got the information at the same time.

Conor was reading it on Tom's screen when his call was answered.

"Maynard-King Hospital," the operator said, and Conor could hardly believe it. His pulse sped up.

"I'm trying to reach Leprince de Beaumont Associates," Conor said.

"You need the business department," she said.

"The business department?" Conor asked.

"Yes," she said. "LP de BA—Leprince de Beaumont Associates—is the corporation that owns the hospital."

"Is their office there in the hospital?" Conor asked.

"Not in the hospital, but on the grounds," she said. "They have their own building. Let me put you through to them."

"Thanks," Conor said. The line rang, and he got voicemail.

"You have reached the office of Darla Vandeveer. I am not available right now, but please leave your name and number, and I will return your call as soon as possible."

Conor hung up without leaving a message.

"No one's there," he said. "But I have a name—Darla Vandeveer." He immediately called Joe. There was no answer, so he texted him the information.

Tom was staring at the Maynard-King website. The home page contained a short, unsigned message saying that MK was a safe place for all people, a sanctuary full of compassion and the desire and experience in promoting healing.

Conor watched his brother click on the What We Treat tab. It listed the many services the hospital offered, the conditions its physicians treated. Conor read over his brother's shoulder as Tom opened each link on the list. When he got to Psychological Trauma, they saw that the page was blank except for some hyperlinked letters: VIS.

"What's 'VIS'?" Tom asked.

"I don't know. Let's see," Conor said.

Tom clicked on the link.

The new screen contained a photo of women with blurred-out faces, standing in a circle and holding hands. Conor read the page:

Victims of Involuntary Servitude

According to the United Nations, human trafficking affects every country around the globe. While you may think it can't happen in your city or town, it can, and it does. Victims of sex trafficking—most of them women, many of them minors—are being held captive in some of the loveliest, "safest" neighborhoods in America.

We at Maynard-King offer trauma-informed care for victims of trafficking. We understand the effects of trauma on the mind and body. We know that survivors have been torn away from their families and held against their will, often restrained.

In some cases, they are forced to work with no pay. Some are required to perform sex acts with a promise of freedom after they comply with their captors' demands. The sad truth is that many are never released; they may disappear, never to see their families again.

Even for those who do regain their freedom, life can be its own prison. Cruel treatment at the hands of some of their captors takes a psychological toll that may be difficult—even impossible—to recover from. Self-hatred is a persistent emotion, accompanied by feelings of worthlessness. Victims often blame themselves for what they have been through. They may turn to addiction or other self-destructive behaviors. Nightmares and night terrors are common.

An inability to form healthy and satisfying relationships is but one effect of being held in involuntary servitude, but it is perhaps the most tragic.

Maynard-King is a safe space to receive care. Survivors can connect with each other, heal by discussing shared experiences, all in the safe embrace of our compassionate community. Self-hatred will melt away, replaced by self-respect. You will learn lessons that will serve you well. When you complete the initial treatment recommended by your doctor, you will be ready for the finishing school of life.

We prepare you for life.

We care.

We will love you until you can love yourself.

You are not alone.

"Okay," Tom said. "So now we know that *Psyche* is used for trafficking humans."

"The handcuffs, yeah," Conor said. He reread the last paragraph. Something was pricking at his memory, but he couldn't bring it to the surface.

Tom had been saying that documented vessels often made international trips, and Conor knew that the common perception was that women were trafficked into the United States, across borders from other countries. But the fact was, much trafficking was local—sometimes across state lines, but often victims were transported within a much smaller distance.

"Yeah. Can it be a coincidence, that what we've been thinking happened on *Psyche* is what they treat here?" Tom asked.

"The company that owns the hospital also owns the boat and also owns the house where Belinda was killed," Conor said. "Leprince de Beaumont Associates."

"And what? They traffic women, then treat them at the hospital?"

"Or they 'treat' trafficked women at the hospital," Conor said. "Then traffic them again—on the boat and the island. They know the victims have already been broken down—that makes it easy for them. They harvest them—women at their most vulnerable." He felt rage even saying it.

Tom nodded. Joe was busy getting warrants. Conor knew that would take time, especially when he told Joe what they had just discovered. He watched his brother scroll through the website, looking at the photos of the Maynard-King hospital grounds, ending on the contact page with a map of the property.

"It's waterfront," Tom said. "Directly on Narragansett Bay." He typed the location into a website that had nautical charts and found the one that corresponded to the Maynard-King location. It showed water depths, reefs and other dangers, aids to navigation, and the shoreline. He zoomed in to the hospital property and pointed. "They have a dock."

"That makes transporting victims easier," Conor said. "And it makes our investigation easier too."

"Yeah," Tom said, nodding. "Coast Guard business. You said you have a name? A contact at Leprince?"

"Yes. But let's not call her. Face-to-face would be better. Do you feel like a road trip?" Conor asked.

Tom didn't even have to answer. They were walking outside toward Tom's truck when Kate caught up to them.

"Where are you going?" she asked.

"The place where you found the note," Conor said. "Maynard-King."

"Do you know how to get there?" Kate asked.

"We'll use GPS."

"You don't have to," she said. "I can show you."

Conor held her gaze for a few seconds, saw her start to smile. "It's always good to have a guide," he said.

"Then let's go," she said, and they continued on to Tom's truck. Conor checked to see if Joe had texted back, but he hadn't. They all climbed into the truck and headed out of Watch Hill, driving east toward Narragansett.

27

Monday, July 5; 4:30 p.m.

Kate directed Tom to Lovecraft Lane and the wrought iron gate that marked the entrance to Maynard-King Hospital. Tom flashed his CGIS badge—and the same guard that had been there the day before leaned down to examine it.

"What can I do for you?" the guard asked.

"We're here to speak to Darla Vandeveer," Tom said.

"You have Coast Guard business with Ms. Vandeveer?" he asked, sounding skeptical.

"I'll discuss that with her," Tom said.

The sentry glowered at him but stepped into the stone guardhouse to call. He returned a moment later. "She's not in her office right now."

"That's okay," Tom said. "Let us in anyway."

"No way is that happening. I don't see what right you think you have to just come in here without permission from Ms. Vandeveer. I mean, what does the Coast Guard Investigative Service have to do with the hospital?"

"It's more about the waterfront," Tom said. "Narragansett Bay is my jurisdiction, and you have a dock. So let us in, and we'll be out of here soon."

Conor stared at the guard, knowing that he had no idea Tom was the sector commander, doing the enforcement division's dirty work only because the case meant something personal to him.

"Whatever," the guard said. "But like I said, she's not in her office."

"That's fine," Tom said. "I want to go down and look at the dock. Can you tell me anything about boats that tie up there regularly?"

"No, sir," the guard said.

"Well, I'll take a look myself," Tom said.

The gate rattled open, and they drove in. Conor had explained how they had connected Leprince de Beaumont Associates with Maynard-King. Kate didn't know where Darla Vandeveer's office was located, but she had an idea of who would.

"The dock is that way," she said, pointing east. "I saw it from the top of the hill when we went to Jonathan Tyler's grave. Let me out here, though."

"Why?" Conor asked.

"I want to walk up to the cemetery," she said. "We can text each other and meet up after you check out the dock."

"Kate, stay with us," Conor said. "This place is in the center of it all."

"I'll be fine," Kate said, giving him a reassuring smile as she got out of the truck. He was being protective and didn't look happy, but he didn't try to stop her.

She watched the Reid brothers drive away, toward the dock. Then she turned in the other direction and walked up the rise toward the graveyard. As soon as she entered the beech grove, she heard the rumble of an ATV. The young woman she remembered from last time drove out from behind the shed and stopped in front of Kate.

"Hi," Kate said.

"Hi," Jennifer said. "Where are your friends? The other two you came with before."

"My niece is back in Watch Hill," Kate said. "Our friend Maeve . . . well, that's a mystery." She thought she saw a look of recognition in

Jennifer's eyes, at the mention of Maeve's name. "We don't know where she is. She's missing."

"That's horrible," Jennifer said. "You must be so worried."

"Very," Kate said. "We think she was taken."

Jennifer seemed to take that in. Then she asked, "Like, kidnapped?"

"Possibly," Kate said.

Another long pause before Jennifer spoke again. "Who would do that?"

"We're trying to figure that out," Kate said.

"I hope it's not true, that she was kidnapped," Jennifer said. "I hope she just went away on her own. She'll come back. Right? Don't you think? It's too awful to imagine her being taken."

Kate noticed an anxious tone in Jennifer's voice. Her words weren't casual—they seemed very urgent, and Kate wondered if Jennifer had heard about Maeve—or perhaps other women—going missing before.

"I want to visit Dr. Tyler's grave again," Kate said. "Would that be okay?"

"Yeah," Jennifer said. "Hop on, and I'll give you a ride."

Kate climbed onto the seat behind Jennifer and was struck by the fact that she seemed more friendly than last time. The ride was quick but very bumpy, and Kate was glad when they got to the cemetery. They parked at the entrance and walked through the headstones toward D3.

"How did you wind up working here?" Kate asked.

"Uh, just, I needed a job, and they needed someone on the grounds crew."

"It seems as if you're mostly stationed here, at the cemetery."

"I am, someone has to keep it up. Keep everything trimmed and neat."

"I'm sure the families appreciate it," Kate said.

"I hope so," Jennifer said.

Kate knew the way to Jonathan's grave from last time. She could see the large stone angel as they walked toward it. Her heart sped up the closer they got. She wondered whether there would be another note.

But when they stopped in front of Jonathan Tyler's grave, she could see that the ground was bare. No note, no white roses.

"Do you want to be alone for a minute?" Jennifer asked. "I guess he must be really important to you, to visit twice in such a short time."

"I don't need to be alone," Kate said. "I never knew him."

Jennifer looked surprised. "Then . . . why are you here?"

"Because of who he was married to," Kate said.

"Belle?" Jennifer asked. "You know *Belle*?"

The shortened name sent prickles down Kate's back. "I knew her as 'Belinda,'" Kate said. "That was her name."

"We called her Belle here," Jennifer said.

"She came here?" Kate asked. She took note of Jennifer's use of the past tense.

Jennifer nodded. "She sure did," she said. She turned away and took a few steps toward the gravestone.

"When was the last time?" Kate asked. But Jennifer had crouched down and was pulling out some weeds that had sprouted around the stone. There was a distant drone of a powerboat speeding up the bay. Kate glanced down the hill. She could see Tom's truck parked by a boathouse. He and Conor were standing on the dock, beside one of the boats tied alongside.

"How well did you know 'Belle'?" Kate asked.

"We all knew her," Jennifer said, still tending to the weeds. "You might say she was Maynard-King royalty. The lady of the house."

"Why?"

"She was married to Dr. Tyler."

"Why does that make her royalty?"

"He was everything to us," Jennifer said, finally turning around. Her face was red, and she had what Kate took to be fear in her eyes.

"Last time I was here, you asked my niece if she was 'one of us.' Was Belinda—Belle—one of you? Was she a patient here?" Kate asked, and Jennifer's eyes narrowed.

"We're not allowed to say who was and who wasn't a patient here," Jennifer said. "Everyone who comes here is promised privacy, and we keep that promise."

"Fair enough," Kate said.

"I'm glad you understand."

Kate wanted to get around Jennifer's devotion to patient confidentiality. She decided to confront her. She knew that Belinda's name had not been released to the media yet. It was being held back pending notification of next of kin.

"You spoke of Belinda in the past tense. Why is that?" Kate asked.

"Because she hasn't been here in a while," Jennifer said.

"Is that the real reason?" Kate asked.

"What else would it be?" Jennifer shrugged and looked down at the ground.

"Did you hear what happened to her?" Kate asked. "She was Dr. Tyler's widow. And now she's gone."

Jennifer nodded. She raised her head, her eyes glittering with tears. "We all know. They told us she was murdered. I can't believe it. She was so special, so good to me and all of the girls."

"All of the girls?" Kate asked. "What girls?"

"Just . . . never mind. You knew Belle?"

"I did. And I know Suzanne." Kate stared at Jennifer, wondering how she would react to her next statement. "I feel so bad for her daughter."

"Oh my god. Losing a mother, especially Belle. No one could love a daughter more . . ."

"Were Belinda and Suzanne close?" Kate asked, her heart pounding. Jennifer was so close to saying that Belinda was Suzanne's mother.

Jennifer seemed to freeze.

"Suzanne did the calligraphy for my wedding—she is very talented," Kate said, changing course. "I have the feeling she calligraphed that beautiful note we found at the grave, the last time we were here."

"She did. You shouldn't have taken it," Jennifer said. "It was for Dr. Tyler."

"He was her stepfather," Kate said.

"I didn't say that!" Jennifer said.

"But if Belinda were her mother, then it stands to reason that Dr. Tyler must have been her stepfather. We found the wedding announcement, and it said that Belinda's daughter was their flower girl. She would have been Suzanne's age."

"I've got to get back to work," Jennifer said.

"You don't want to talk about Suzanne?"

"Not really."

"You know, I had the feeling you recognized Maeve's name when I said it before. When I said she's missing," Kate said.

"No, I didn't," Jennifer said.

"I wasn't sure whether it was her name you recognized or whether you've heard about other girls and women going missing—being taken."

A flash of alarm crossed Jennifer's eyes.

"Why would I know anything about that? It sounds terrible," she said.

"Is that who you meant by 'all the girls'?" Kate asked. "The ones who've been taken?"

"You'd better go now," Jennifer said.

"Can I ask one more thing? You mentioned that Dr. Tyler was loved and that people miss him. I saw white roses on the grave last time. And Suzanne's note. Do a lot of people leave things there?"

"Yes, many gifts," she said. She seemed to relax slightly, because the question had nothing to do with Belinda or family connections.

"Like what?"

"Well, roses always. They were his favorite flower. But other things. Mementos, little trinkets. We leave things that mean something to us, that we know would have touched his heart. See, he taught about self-less love. If you loved, truly loved someone, you would give them whatever is most important to you."

Chills ran down Kate's spine as Jennifer opened a compartment in her ATV. Kate watched her remove a small pale-cream satin jewelry pouch. She held it out to Kate, and Kate leaned forward to see what was inside.

There were dry rosebuds. There were fragments of blue robins' eggs. Pieces of sea glass. Moonstones and wishing stones. A pile of cards, stationery, folded yellow legal paper. And many single earrings.

"What are all of those?" Kate asked.

"Treasures. Gifts and notes left on the grave. I usually let them stay there for a week or so, then gather them up to make room for more."

"What about those earrings?" Kate said. "Mismatched?"

"Not really. People visit and decide to leave an earring."

"Why would they do that?"

"An offering," Jennifer said. "A sign of love and respect."

"Are those real jewels in those earrings? That one looks like it's set with sapphires and diamonds," Kate said.

"Probably," Jennifer said.

"Is that one a real pearl?" Kate asked, pointing at a single-stud earring.

"Looks it," Jennifer said. "But just because they're jewels doesn't make them more precious than the rosebuds. Gifts are all about the intention."

"Another reason for you to remove them from the grave is that someone might come along and steal them—especially the diamond and pearl ones."

"No one would do that." Jennifer laughed. "You really don't know how much everyone loves him. To you, these are just objects. To the people who leave them, they are signs of love, a way of giving back. Diamond love."

"What is 'diamond love'?" Kate asked.

"Look, I have to work now. Sorry about your wedding being canceled," Jennifer said curtly, as if aware she had said too much.

"How do you know about that?" Kate asked.

Jennifer reddened, as if realizing she'd slipped up.

"Anyway, I'm going back to the maintenance shed. Do you want a ride?" Jennifer asked.

"No, thanks," Kate said. "I'm meeting someone down at the dock. But first—where is Darla Vandeveer's office?"

"It's between the main building and the gazebo," Jennifer said. "It's a little white house, and there's a stone statue in front of it."

Kate thought it unusual that the business office would be in a house. "Does she actually live there?" she asked.

"Not Darla, it's not her style. It hasn't been used as that kind of house in years. It's just for offices." Jennifer started the ATV and put it into gear.

Kate stared at her. There was something furtive, almost feral about Jennifer. She was a keeper of secrets. How had she first come to Maynard-King? Was she one of the trafficked girls?

"Jennifer!" Kate called over the sound of the engine. "What's 1740?"

Jennifer stepped on the brake and turned toward Kate.

"1740 is everything," Jennifer said. She gave Kate a radiant smile, then drove away.

28

Monday, July 5; 5:00 p.m.

Conor had watched Kate coming down the hill from the hospital cemetery toward the Maynard-King dock. She was almost running; she seemed excited, as if she couldn't wait to tell him some news.

She did have things to tell Conor and Tom, and it was a lot. Jennifer, the groundskeeper, had confirmed that Suzanne had left the note on Dr. Tyler's grave. She had let it slip that Suzanne was Belinda's daughter and then tried to take it back. And she had said "1740 is everything" when Kate had asked her about the date's meaning.

"It's all interesting," Tom said when Kate had finished reporting on everything she had seen and heard at Tyler's grave. "We have suspicions about this place, and now about this young woman—Jennifer—but what does it add up to?"

"Jennifer knew about Maeve—I'm sure of it," Kate said. "And she knew our wedding was canceled."

"But that doesn't prove anything definitive," Tom said.

"She knew about Suzanne. And she was secrctive about it."

"Another piece of the puzzle," Conor said.

"We have plenty of pieces," Tom said. "Now we need the whole picture on the front of the puzzle box."

"She admitted that Suzanne did the calligraphy on the note. And she calls Belinda 'Belle' and says she came here. I felt . . ." Conor watched Kate pause and gather her thoughts. "I felt as if Jennifer has been through it—whatever is going on here. The other day, she asked if Sam was 'one of us,' 'all the girls.'"

"She takes care of the cemetery?" Conor asked.

"Yes. I have the feeling she was a patient—and either she doesn't want to leave, or they won't let her." Conor felt Kate's gaze on him. "She keeps a case full of notes and jewelry that people leave on Tyler's grave. Really expensive things. She mentioned 'diamond love' and giving back—I guess because he took such good care of them when they were here."

"Sounds as if she really opened up to you," Conor said.

"She started to, then she shut down. Do you think the gifts are from the girls, the ones who were aboard *Psyche*?" Kate asked.

"Why would anyone subjected to that kind of treatment on *Psyche* want to give gifts to the person who did it?" Tom asked.

"We don't know that Tyler did anything," Conor said. "The hospital seems like ground zero, but we don't have the evidence to prove he was involved, whether hands on or even in the background. Since the crimes are still occurring, someone else is calling the shots."

"That's all true, but I think your question is really good, Tom," Kate said. "Victims would give gifts to a captor because they have been conditioned to love him. You saw the website: 'We'll love you till you can love yourself.'"

Conor gazed at her, knowing that her wisdom on the subject came from something she had experienced when she was only sixteen.

"Can't Joe get a warrant for the hospital?" Kate asked.

"Not yet," Conor said. "There's not probable cause. We have a lot of threads, but that's all. We'll see what Joe gets back from the crime lab, as far as evidence from *Psyche* and the house on the island, and that might help for a warrant for those places. We still don't have enough for Maynard-King."

"Have we defined the crime?" Tom asked.

"Take your pick," Conor said. "Murder, trafficking, kidnapping, unlawful confinement, sexual assault, torture."

"But who is doing this?" Kate asked. "Say the girls are taken from here, from Maynard-King, who plans where they will go, what they will do? Who gives those orders? There has to be one person in charge."

"We'll talk with Darla Vandeveer," Tom said. "If she's in charge of the corporation, she'll have paperwork on the boat, house, and hospital. That will be a good start."

Conor nodded his head. They stood on the dock, looking at the boats tied beside it. Were these vessels involved with 1740? One was a vintage eighteen-foot varnished wood Chris-Craft, the other was a million-dollar Hinckley Picnic Boat 37, a beauty with a wide deck and comfortable cabin.

The Chris-Craft didn't have a name; the Hinckley's was *Zémire*. Tom had checked the whaler's Rhode Island registration and the Hinckley's documentation. No surprise, *Zémire* was owned by Leprince de Beaumont Associates. The Chris-Craft's ownership was more straightforward—its owner was Darla Vandeveer. Because it was a small, open runabout, with no cabin, there wasn't much to hide.

"Are there handcuffs in *Zémire* too?" Kate asked, standing beside the larger boat, trying to peer through the windows. One was slid open a crack, but the curtains were closed. "Anyone in there?" she called.

"We can't just board her," Tom said.

"Why not? You boarded *Psyche*," Kate said.

"That was different. The door had been forced open, and there were blood spots on the deck," Conor said. "Exigent circumstances. We don't know anything about this boat."

"Conor, *Zémire et Azor* is an opera based on *Beauty and the Beast*," Kate said. "The boat names are connected. What if they have someone on board here? What if it's Maeve?"

Tom tapped Kate's arm and beckoned her away from *Zémire*. Conor followed, knowing Tom wanted to move away from that open window, in case anyone was inside and was listening.

"It's possible, Kate, but we don't have any real reason to think so," Tom said.

"With *Psyche* out of commission, they need a new boat, right?" Kate asked.

"They probably do, if we're right about the vessels being used in a trafficking operation," Conor said. "And I'm going to tell Joe about it, and he'll have the whole Maynard-King property searched. And he'll question the directors and medical staff."

Kate kept staring at the Hinckley, as if her gaze could solve the mystery, protect anyone who might be on board.

"I'm going to assign a team to watch this dock," Tom said. "And we'll tell Joe everything we've learned today and see where he wants to go."

"What about talking to Darla?" Kate asked. "Jennifer told me where her office is."

"Let's go," Conor said.

They left the dock and drove through the sprawling and manicured grounds of Maynard-King. Conor noticed the gardens, the graceful trees, the large white building with columns on either side of the door, flowers blooming in planters beside the steps, a wide porch. It seemed peaceful, a sanctuary. But through years of police work, he knew that secrets hid everywhere, and sometimes the most apparently beautiful people and places were not what they seemed.

They parked outside a small white house that looked as if it belonged in a neighborhood, not on the grounds of a psychiatric hospital. Considering that it was just past five p.m., he wasn't sure the office would be open, but he knocked on the door, and it was answered by a young woman looking very businesslike in slim black pants and a jacket.

"May I help you?" she asked with a wide smile.

"We'd like to see Darla Vandeveer," Conor said.

"Do you have an appointment?"

"No. I called earlier, and I'm just following up."

"You're the one who left the message?" she asked.

"Yes," Conor said.

She smiled. "I got it. I'm Gabrielle, Darla's assistant, so I check her voicemail and relay it to her. She's not here."

"When will she be here?" Conor asked. "It's very important that I speak with her."

"Can I ask what this is about?" she asked.

"I have some questions about the 1740 property owned in trust by Leprince de Beaumont Associates. LP de BA," he said, watching for Gabrielle's reaction. He saw a small furrow crease her brow when she heard him mention the trust's name. "The operator told me Darla would be the best person to talk to."

"The hospital operator?" she asked. "Hmm. I'll have to speak to her. She's new."

"Why, she's not supposed to put calls through?"

"We're just careful with information," Gabrielle said. Her smile had gone briefly away but came back strong. "It's very sensitive, dealing with institute matters. I'm sure you can understand that. We're a psychiatric facility, and privacy is a main concern."

"Of course," Conor said. He thought her smile was due to training, not a friendly feeling. There was something pacifying, manipulative about it, a bit like a magic trick to distract her visitors from their quest. "You have my number. Please ask her to call me when she can."

Monday, July 5; 6:00 p.m.

Sam sat on the Club Room terrace, listening to the waves and feeling anxiety build in her chest. The table had been reserved by Anne and Mike for dinner, but neither they nor the rest of their party had arrived yet. Sam and Leo Kennedy were the first to be seated.

Brian came over to take drink orders. Leo asked for a Glenlivet on the rocks, and Sam said she'd stick with water. Her stomach was flipping. It felt incredibly weird to be sitting in this beautiful place while

Maeve was missing. She could be anywhere, something terrible could be happening to her. She looked at Leo.

"Edward and Nola are your investigators, right?" she asked.

"They have their own work, but yes—sometimes."

"What kind of things do they investigate?" she asked.

"Matters concerning my cases. My clients. In a criminal case, for example, they will investigate witnesses or other potential suspects. Sometimes after a deposition, when the witness has given answers under oath, Edward and Nola will investigate to see how truthful, or untruthful, the testimony actually was. They trace family connections, property ownership, financial irregularities. And Nola has a specialty in profiling and criminal psychology."

Sam nodded, remembering the work Nola talked about when she went to the prison. "Do they ever look for missing persons?" she asked.

"They don't do that sort of work for me," Leo said. "Why do you ask, Sam?"

"Haven't you heard about Maeve?" Sam asked.

"Yes, of course," Leo said. "Forgive me—I didn't realize you were referring to her. You haven't heard from her?"

"No."

"Are you close?"

"Well, not really," Sam said. "But we know each other. She works for Kate. She and Kate adore each other—Maeve is almost like another niece. They work with each other every day."

"Might Maeve have gone off on her own?" Leo asked. "Maybe she feels upset about the wedding being called off—especially if she really cares about Kate. Not only that, but she was also the first to find the murder victim. It makes sense that she would have to get away."

Sam ran that through her mind and shook her head.

"I can see the wheels turning," Leo said. "Do you want to tell me what you're thinking?"

"Just that . . . I don't think she left on her own," Sam said.

"That's troubling," Leo said. "Have you talked to Conor and Joe about it? Let the police in on the situation?"

"Yes," Sam said. "They're investigating. I think it's all connected. Kate and Conor do too."

"What's connected?"

Sam found herself wanting to tell him all of it. "Belinda's murder and Maeve being taken."

"Taken?" Leo asked.

"Yes," Sam said. "It all goes together, Leo. It's crazy, but it all has to do with the number 1740. That was stenciled on the door of Suzanne's truck, and it links up to this doctor—Jonathan Tyler, a psychiatrist at a hospital in Narragansett—who was murdered in the exact same way as Belinda. Maeve, Kate, and I went to the hospital where he worked . . . and we found a note . . . and it's gone, along with Maeve. I think it's the reason she . . ."

She was interrupted by Brian dropping off their drinks just as Mike, Anne, and the Aldriches approached the table.

"You can't stop there," Leo said to Sam. "Keep going."

"What have we missed?" Anne asked.

"The most extraordinary story," Leo said. "Connections we never dreamed of. Edward and Nola—Sam asked if we do work to find missing persons, referring to Maeve. I said no, but I am rethinking it. The elements are completely in your wheelhouse."

"I couldn't agree more," Mike said, slapping the table. "I have been thinking the same thing. The police are on it, focused on the murder. But this is all of a piece. And '1740' is the thread we need to follow."

"Sam, can you tell us more?" Nola asked.

"Yes, start at the very beginning, even if you think we already know it," Edward said.

"Sure," Sam said. She watched Nola pull a notebook from a canvas bag. As Sam began to talk, Nola began to write. Sam kept her voice low, so people at nearby tables couldn't listen. That might not have been necessary. The older people leaned in close, to hear what Sam had to say, and she felt a wave of comfort wash over her—a feeling of hope.

29

Shortly before sunrise, the Coast Guard had towed *Psyche* to New London, where Tom's investigative unit was stationed. Tom and Conor were waiting at the dock. Last night's moon was setting in the west, and Tom watched the sloop glide through the dawn mist. She looked ethereal, a moonlit ghost. Many times, Tom had investigated boating incidents where fatalities had occurred. It could be anything from someone slipping on a wet deck and going overboard to an accidental crack on the head from a wildly swinging boom. Whenever he encountered a vessel where death had occurred, he saw it differently. It was as if not only the human aboard had died—he felt as if life had gone out of the vessel as well.

The Reid brothers boarded *Psyche*. She had initially been processed at her berth on the island—finger and palm prints lifted, blood samples from the handcuffs and the bulkheads swabbed.

Tom knew that the boat had been gone over by the forensics team from the Rhode Island State Police. The Coast Guard investigated crimes such as human and drug smuggling in the maritime realm. Given suspicions that *Psyche* had been used to imprison women, Tom had an interest in the case. Right now, he and Conor would be searching for anything related to 1740 or Maynard-King.

Tom knew that the Hinckley Pilot's length was thirty-five feet overall, but that was on deck—bow to stern. At the waterline, the sailboat's length was twenty-five feet, with plenty of overhang fore and aft, making *Psyche* a sleek-looking beauty. Tom and Conor climbed down the companion ladder into the cabin. The beam—the width of the boat—was nine feet, making the salon quite narrow.

The sloop had once been elegant, outfitted for style and comfort. But the bulkheads and the door to the forward cabin had been soundproofed with layers of foam, and chains had been bolted into the sole—the floor of the boat. There were bookcases and storage lockers behind the insulation. The team had pulled down sections of foam in order to look inside the lockers, and lumps of it were scattered around.

"Do you really think Suzanne lived aboard?" Conor asked.

"She had the dockage receipt."

"But living in a torture chamber?"

"Let's figure that out," Tom said.

"Do you think she—or anyone—really used that?" Conor asked, pointing toward the small mosaic-tile fireplace—more like a woodstove—tucked into the corner. "Or is it just for show?"

"People do use them," Tom said.

"The Coast Guard must love that," Conor said. "An open flame on a sailboat out at sea."

"Yeah," Tom said. "One of our favorite calls—a drunk captain who forgot to close the stove door before turning in, a spark lighting the boat on fire."

"Must be hard for you to get fireboats to the scene out at sea in time," Conor said.

"Yep," Tom said, glancing at his brother. "Making small talk? You must be nervous."

"Why would I be nervous?"

"I can think of a few reasons."

"Look," Conor said. "The way I see it is that Joe Harrigan is in charge. Officially I have no say. But you're a Fed, and you've got jurisdiction on this boat and any other boat, and I'm helping you. Right?"

"You're a shadow investigator," Tom said.

"Whatever you want to call me," Conor said. "Can we get going here?"

"Sure," Tom said. He noticed that Conor's frown had deepened. He knew his brother better than anyone. And he knew that to Conor, solving the case would get him back on track to the altar. The devastation of the last few days had made their wedding seem cursed. Conor and Kate needed each other.

The two brothers split up in the small space. Tom watched Conor head into the forward cabin. Tom stayed in the main salon. He looked in all the open lockers. They were empty, and he was sure that the police had collected their contents for evidence. Law enforcement agencies didn't always work well together, but Tom had a good relationship with Joe, and he was confident they would share information. He had to peel back insulation that was covering the bookcases, and he found an interesting array of volumes.

There were folders of nautical charts, books about marine science, field guides to birds and marine mammals, books about stars and the night sky, books of poems, a few thrillers and romance novels, *Moby-Dick*, *The Perfect Storm*, and some blank journals. He half expected to find at least one edition of *Beauty and the Beast*, but there were none.

"Hey!" Conor called from the forward cabin. "They missed something."

Tom went to meet him. The cabin was shaped like a triangle, the apex being the bow of the boat. There was a V-shaped platform covered with cushions cut to measure. It formed a double bed. Conor had pulled the cushions off. At first, the platform beneath them appeared to be solid. But Conor used a pocketknife to pry up the center section, revealing a shallow compartment containing a stash of photographs.

Each six-by-four photo showed a young woman wearing an old-fashioned white gown. Each woman's face was hidden by a black mask. They wore jewelry—earrings, necklaces, bracelets, and rings. Two of the photos had been taken right here, with the subject lying on the V-berth. No restraints or wounds were visible. Three shots were unmistakably of the bedroom in the stone mansion on Bellevigne Island. The rest of the photos appeared to have been taken elsewhere—a location Tom had not seen before.

"I can't tell," Conor said, leafing through the photos, "if they are alive or dead."

"I was thinking that too," Tom said. "We can't see their eyes behind the masks. Is it the same mask, by the way? And are these different women, or are there multiple photos of the same one?"

"Judging by hair color, some are different," Conor said. "Unless he made them wear wigs."

"Wigs?" Tom asked.

"He dresses them up," Conor said. "The gowns look Victorian—as if they belong in a museum. And he wants them to look like princesses. Ruffles and lace, prim and proper. Even the jewelry." He pointed at one photo. "Three strands of pearls here . . ." He flipped to another shot, another girl. "And here."

"What's that?" Tom asked, pointing at a shiny object on a bureau in the background. "Is that a crown?"

"Looks like a tiara," Conor said.

"Same thing," Tom said.

"He likes shiny things," Conor said. "Look at the hands. Each woman is wearing a diamond ring."

"As if they're engaged. Does he kidnap women who are about to be married?"

"I think he fantasizes that the women belong to him—possession, a promise to love him," Conor said. "Each one is engaged to him, and no one else can have her. But maybe you're right. Maybe destroying other people's love is what he wants."

Tom figured that was projection. He stared at his brother, knowing that he had just experienced someone trying to destroy the love between him and Kate: Belinda.

Conor continued searching the cabin. Tom left him there and went out into the galley to seal the photos in an evidence bag. Once that was done, he began searching through cupboards, the ice chest, and the oven. Nothing stood out. The sun had risen over the dockside buildings, throwing shards of light onto the harbor. He glanced out a porthole on the starboard side, but his attention was drawn to the glass itself. It sparkled, and there appeared to be a flaw. He put his face very near the surface to examine it.

Marine glass was thicker than regular window glass, tempered to withstand the impact of rough weather and collision as well as extreme temperature variations. These side ports were fixed and did not open. When he looked at the porthole straight on, he saw nothing but a view of the harbor. But when he tilted his head and looked at it askance, he saw tracing—lines as fine as spiderwebs.

"Hey, Conor," he called.

"What?" Conor asked, coming out of the forward cabin.

"See this?" Tom asked.

Conor leaned close to look. "It's there, and then it's not," he said.

"Right," Tom said. "It's very faint. Focusing depends on how the light hits it. But what does it look like to you?"

"Not sure," Conor said. "Someone drew on the glass?"

"Or wrote on it. Are those words?" Tom asked. "Or numbers?"

The brothers stared at the shimmering, disappearing traces. Tom snapped a photo with his iPhone. Conor moved along the bulkhead to look at the other portholes—two on each side.

"There's some here too," Conor said, pointing at one on the port side.

Tom examined the faint tracing. He moved his head close to the glass and, without touching the surface, tried to look at the marks sideways, to see if there was any sign that they had been drawn or scratched on the inside of the glass. He went up on deck, walking from one side of the cabin to the other, and looked at the portholes from those perspectives. Nothing was visible, but he took more photos and returned to the cabin.

"Who drew these things?" Tom asked. "And with what?"

"I don't think they're drawn," Conor said. "Those marks are etched right into the glass itself."

"You can't scratch this stuff," Tom said. "It's hard as a rock. Marine glass is sand-casted—heated and cooled and reheated. Tempered glass."

"I've seen marks like this before," Conor said. "I was working a murder at a girl's boarding school—an old-money place, one of the First Ladies went there—and some of the windows had initials and dates scratched in."

"With what, glass cutters?" Tom asked.

"Diamond rings," Conor said.

"Seriously?"

"Yes," Conor said. "The girls used diamond rings to leave their marks—so they would be remembered. It was the kind of school where generations from the same family attended, and daughters would find their mothers' or grandmothers' old rooms by looking for their names in the windowpanes."

"That's another world," Tom said.

"Diamonds are harder than tempered glass," Conor said.

"Apparently," Tom said.

Tom and Conor stared at the delicate, glittering lines in the glass, and they knew that someone had wanted to be remembered.

Or to be found.

30

Tuesday, July 6; 8:00 a.m.

Sam walked out of the water after a morning swim. She stood on the wet sand, squeezing salt water out of her long hair, and feeling charged up. The ocean had been flat calm for days, but waves were building offshore, and she felt the energy. She glanced up at the cabanas and saw four of the Old Detectives huddled over a low table. Although she couldn't hear what they were saying, Anne, Mike, Nola, and Edward were talking animatedly. Sam knew they had taken the wedding mysteries to heart and were doing their best to solve them, to help get Kate and Conor back together.

Sam saw Miranda and Leo walking along the tide line from the point. She felt surprised to see them together. Miranda was dressed in yoga clothes; while Sam was still swimming, she had noticed the beach yoga class offered by the hotel. She had also seen Leo jog past, along the hard sand.

"I thought you left," Sam said to Miranda.

"I decided not to," Miranda said. "Bernard and I are over. Besides, there's so much going on, and I feel I need to be here."

"I don't get many chances to run on the beach," Leo said. "Must be kismet—it was nice to bump into Miranda. We hadn't met before."

Miranda ignored that. "Sam, is there any news about Maeve?"

"No," Sam said. "I checked with Kate first thing this morning, and she hadn't heard anything."

"This is just incredible," Miranda said. "I don't know Maeve well at all, I just met her, but I hate to think of something happening to her. She seemed so sweet."

"And she seemed devoted to Kate," Leo said.

Sam felt jarred by the fact that they had both used the past tense. "Don't say 'seemed,'" she said. "She's coming back."

"Oh, I didn't mean it that way," Miranda said, grabbing Sam's wrist. "I just meant at the time I first met her—three days ago, at the rehearsal dinner."

"Same here," Leo said. "I'm sure she's *still* devoted to Kate. Ongoing, Sam. I guarantee you she's okay."

Sam's head was spinning. She wanted to ask Leo how he knew that. She knew she was being extra sensitive, that one terrible thing after another was taking a toll. "Sorry," she said. "I just wish I knew what happened to her."

"I feel as if I brought bad luck," Miranda said.

"Hmm, isn't that a little dramatic?" Leo asked.

"No," Miranda said. "I helped Belinda get this whole thing started."

"On purpose?" Sam asked. "You knew she was going to confront Kate with that ring and baby picture?"

"Sam, I didn't know what she was going to do," Miranda said. "She was my closest cousin when we were kids. She's gone through a lot, and I was just so glad when she called me, told me she had this amazing plan."

"What plan?" Sam asked.

"Crashing the wedding of the boy next door. I knew she used to have a crush on him. She made it sound so lighthearted and fun—like going back in time, being girls again. She was a widow, I'm divorced. Life gets to be so serious—mortgages, health stuff, getting older."

Sam couldn't believe what she was hearing. This person actually thought it was fun to have destroyed Kate and Conor's wedding? Miranda must have read her expression.

"Honestly, it was a stupid prank. She told me she thought Conor would get a kick out of it. It wasn't until we'd set the whole thing in motion—you know, getting ourselves invited along with Garrett and Bernard—that she told me about Conor being the baby's father."

"What did she say?" Sam asked.

"That she had had a child with Conor. And that he never took responsibility for it."

"That's disgusting," Sam said. "That is not who he is. If she did have his child, he would have stepped up. But she was lying."

"I'm figuring that out," Miranda said.

"If you were such close cousins, why did she wait until this summer to tell you that she had had a baby?" Sam asked.

"I knew that part," Miranda said. "Of course I knew she had a daughter—I just didn't know who the father was. She never talked about him. And she didn't tell me that Conor was the father until just before the rehearsal dinner. Once she told me, things fell into place—her real reason for wanting to crash his wedding."

"To destroy his life?" Sam asked.

"More like to destroy Kate's. I tried to stop her, but by that time, we were with Bernard and Garrett, and I told myself she wouldn't do anything crazy in front of everyone," Miranda said.

"She must have been a very sick person," Leo said.

Miranda nodded. "She was. She had very bad depression and anxiety, and she wound up in a hospital when she was very young. She was there for over a year. I always thought that was where she got pregnant."

"Maynard-King?" Sam asked.

"You know about that?" Miranda asked, sounding surprised.

"Yes. And she married the head of the hospital. Dr. Tyler."

"Yes," Miranda said. "Jonathan was her doctor when she was a patient there. But they didn't get married until several years later. After she'd gotten well—or at least gotten better—and had a daughter with another man."

"Conor," Leo said.

"Not Conor," Sam said sternly.

"Like I said, she never told me," Miranda said. "It was always a big mystery. I actually figured that Jonathan was the father, and they had to keep it secret because it would have been a scandal . . . for the head of MK to get a patient pregnant. The board would have fired him immediately."

"They certainly would have," Leo said. "I can promise you that."

"How do you know?" Sam asked. "Are you connected to the hospital? Are you their lawyer or on their board?"

"No," Leo said after a few seconds. "But Rhode Island is a small state, and I've known members of their board. Besides, it's universal truth that fooling around is one thing. Getting caught is another. Especially for a man in authority."

That put Sam's back up. Was Leo saying that it was okay for a doctor to sexually abuse a patient as long as he kept it secret?

"Anyway, Sam," Miranda said. "I feel terrible about what Belinda did. I think she really lost her mind when she found out Conor was getting married. She was obsessed with him."

"That seems obvious," Sam said. "You know, Miranda . . . considering that Belinda was your cousin, you don't seem all that sad about her death."

"I'm sad," Miranda said sharply. "You don't know how I feel. But I'm also angry at her, the way she tried to use her daughter to manipulate Conor and drive Kate away."

"Who is the child?" Sam asked. "What's her name?"

Miranda didn't answer that question. "Could I be in trouble? For being involved with getting Belinda here? Could I be a suspect?"

"Miranda, I'm a lawyer," Leo said. "If you want me to advise you, we can step away, and you can tell me whatever you know about Belinda, her daughter, and anything else. That way it will be just between us."

Miranda seemed to consider his offer, but she didn't reply.

Leo gestured toward the cabana, where the Reids and Aldriches were sitting together. "Let's go up there," he said. "I want to take some notes. Even if I don't represent you, we're working together to get some answers. It can only help."

Miranda shook her head hard. "No, thanks," she said, starting toward the hotel. "Sam, I will see you later."

"That is strange," Leo said, watching Miranda go. "She seemed to want to talk, but she shut down when you asked her Belinda's daughter's name. What's she afraid of?" He gestured for Sam to follow him up the sand to the cabana, and they walked there together.

Sam looked down at the table where the four of them sat. There were index cards and what looked like an old-fashioned phone book. From the cover, she could tell that it was South County's telephone directory.

"Not everyone researches on the internet," Mike said. "We've been tracking down 1740 ever since we heard about it."

"We had an old phone book in the cottage," Anne said, flipping through the book, pointing at a particular page. "Look what we found."

Sam took the empty chair beside her and saw several advertisements. Each one was set within borders, in its own square. There were different sizes, fonts, and images. Anne tapped her finger on a listing positioned in the upper right corner:

1740 Events

Fantasies our specialty

Let us make your fairy tale come true

Discretion guaranteed.

There were a phone number and line drawing of a beautiful woman and a monster—they looked to Sam like *Beauty and the Beast*.

"Wow!" Sam said. "That's it!"

"This ad is too old for it to matter," Leo said. "It's out of date. Let's move on."

"I agree with Leo," Nola said. "Just from my own experience, dealing with violent offenders, especially in sex crimes, they are not going to advertise. They operate in secret. This ad was for something else—they're party planners."

"But it says 'fairy tale,'" Sam said. "And look at the drawing—it's *Beauty and the Beast*. Have you tried the number?"

"Of course," Nola said. "As soon as we saw the ad. The person who answered had no clue about the company or anything to do with 1740. He said he has had the number for fifteen years."

"See? It's out of date," Leo said. "Maybe this particular operation went out of business back then, and the number was reassigned."

"Well, people have been known to lie," Mike said.

"We are better off focusing on present day," Leo said. Sam stared at him, wondering why he seemed so opposed to looking into what seemed to her to be a good lead.

"I'm sure that's what Conor, Tom, and Joe are doing," Mike said. "And Kate too. Sam, didn't you and Kate go to Maynard-King and find some sort of note mentioning the infamous 1740?"

"Yes," Sam said.

"So let's run this down," Mike said. "Go in a different direction."

"Backward," Leo said.

"Come on, now," Nola said. "Don't be negative."

"I don't get any of this," Anne said. "Especially the part about Maynard-King. It's always been such a respected place for people to go when they have breakdowns or addictions. Mike and I have gone to fundraisers for the hospital, and we know people who have gone there, who've been helped. I just can't imagine it being a center for what's been going on."

"But it is," Sam said. "We're positive about that. Belinda was married to Dr. Tyler, and she was murdered the same way he was. And that 1740 note someone left there, on his grave . . . that note is missing now, along with Maeve."

"Dr. Jonathan Tyler," Leo said. "He was a visionary. He did groundbreaking research in the trauma field. His death was such a tragedy."

"You knew him?" Anne asked.

Leo didn't answer for a few seconds. "I can't really go into it. Even though he's dead, there's an attorney-client issue," he said.

"He was your client?" Mike asked.

"I didn't say that," Leo said sharply. "There's just . . . an issue. Let's leave it there, Mike."

Sam was slightly shocked, the way he spoke to Mike. His words were clipped, and his tone was almost rude. She could tell that Mike noticed it, too, the way his eyes widened, then looked away. He seemed both surprised and annoyed.

Leo's phone buzzed. He excused himself and stepped out of the cabana to take the call. Sam watched him walk down to the tide line for privacy as he talked on the phone. The others began discussing dinner plans, whether to eat at Dune Cottage or walk down the hill to the Olympia Tea Room, and wondering if they could get a reservation last minute.

The phone book was still open on the table. Sam pulled out her iPhone and snapped a picture of the ad. She glanced down at the water and saw that Leo was still on his call, talking animatedly. She hadn't acknowledged this to herself till now, but she had the feeling that Leo and Miranda meeting on the beach hadn't been an accident. Something told her they had known each other before.

By itself, that wouldn't be all that strange. But if they had known each other before, why would they keep that a secret? Maybe it was the fact that Miranda was Belinda's cousin, too close for comfort to the murder. And why was Leo so negative about investigating the ad in the Yellow

Pages? To Sam, it proved that 1740 had been in existence for at least twenty-five years, the age of the phone book—a very valuable lead.

She said goodbye, and she headed up toward the hotel. Even though they had called the phone number in the listing, Sam was going to call it herself and see what she could learn. She would do it from her car—it had been a few days since they had checked the house and picked up mail. Steve, their postman at the small South Lyme Post Office, always held it for them when they were away for a while. It was only forty-five minutes away, and she would be glad for the break.

Tuesday, July 6; 9:00 a.m.

Kate sat at the suite's dining table, working on her laptop. A weather front hung just offshore, dispatching high clouds through the blue sky, kicking up waves, and sending a strong breeze through the open door. Conor had gotten up early, gone to meet Tom and continue investigating the boats—*Psyche* and *Zémire*.

On Kate's screen was the photo that Conor had sent from the house on Bellevigne Island. It showed the image above the bed. Last night, she had rewatched Jean Cocteau's 1946 black-and-white film—the one from which the enlarged photo had been taken. The film was a magical, romantic, and frightening fantasy, full of Freudian imagery. In the movie, Belle loved her father and would do anything to save him—even leave her home and family to live in the Beast's castle.

Kate had made notes while watching Cocteau's eerie and extravagant film, and she consulted them now as she stared at the photo Conor had texted.

She had written down a line in French, the Beast telling Belle that she was in no danger. Had Belle believed that?

And she had noted what a lonely creature he had been.

She thought of how the entrance to the Beast's castle was filled with statues that were alive, that spied on the Beast and Belle.

Voyeurism? she had written. Was that part of the current scenario? If girls were being taken, trapped aboard *Psyche* or elsewhere, was there just one perpetrator, or were there others who watched? Or participated?

The Beast had prepared clothes for Belle, and when he carried her into her chamber, the white nightgown was waiting for her. He called her his queen.

Kate thought of the opulent room Conor had described. She could imagine royal garments chosen for whomever was brought there. It seemed that the man who took the women idealized them—or at least wanted to present them with a type of luxury—at some point during their captivity.

Did he start out intending no harm, and did his plans change along the way, when his instincts took over? Because instead of the love the Beast felt for Belle, the perpetrator felt some sort of deep-down hatred that manifested in violence—irons and chains. She remembered her impressions of *Psyche's* cabin; in her brief moments on board the boat, she had sensed that any woman being held there would feel unimaginable fear.

Beast's intention was to make Belle his bride. Kate thought of Belinda Tyler. She didn't believe the nickname was a coincidence—Belle. And if her daughter was indeed Suzanne, that was the same as the author's middle name. Belinda had been dressed as a bride—in Kate's dress. Someone had murdered a bride—the "Beauty" of the story.

Kate's mind was spinning with too much fantasy and allegory, so she turned to her email and began to read. Most of them concerned gallery business. Her regular framer wanted to know whether she preferred a gold frame with a medieval and elaborate gothic pattern or a simpler design. This was a common question. Did an ornate frame give the painting the respect it deserved, or did it steal attention from the painting?

She read some inquiries from collectors regarding works on the website or ones they had seen on visits to the gallery. Then she opened one from Fernando Harris, her main conservator. The time stamp was eight a.m.—just an hour earlier—and the message heading was FOGGY NIGHT.

Hello Kate,

Maeve just dropped off *Foggy Night*. What an extraordinary painting. It might just be the best James Suydam work that I have ever seen, and I include the ones shown at that National Academy Exhibition.

The damage is not as extensive as it appears at first. It is a clean tear. I will rejoin the fibers and back and reinforce the canvas. Once I finish that, I will turn to the paint itself. Even though it will take some time, I will put this project ahead of everything else on my worktable. Maeve told me a little bit about the incident—I can't believe someone tried to destroy this masterpiece. It is horrific to me that this person stopped your marriage. But rest assured, *Foggy Night* will be ready to give to your husband in time for your rescheduled nuptials.

All the best,

Fernando

Kate felt shocked. She had Fernando's number stored in her phone and dialed it as she ran out of the suite. Instead of waiting for the elevator, she ran down the stairs. She got Fernando's voicemail and left him a message to call her back as soon as possible. The hotel drive was full of cars, with valets loading cargo areas with the luggage of departing guests. Kate hurried across Bluff Avenue, into the upper parking lot.

Maeve's BMW was nowhere in sight.

She called Conor, and he answered right away. She told him about the email and how Fernando said that Maeve had delivered the painting an hour ago.

"Her car is gone," Kate said. "How is it possible?"

"Could we have misinterpreted what we saw on the video? Could she had driven off on her own?"

"No," Kate said. "We saw her saying 'help,' and she purposely dropped her necklace. She was in trouble, sending a message."

"Yet somehow she delivered the painting to Fernando," Conor said. "So that means she wasn't taken—she must not have been. She returned to the Ocean House this morning, got into her car, and took it to him. Is he sure it was her?"

"He said so," Kate said.

"Does he know her by sight?"

Kate thought about it. She had had several assistants over the years. Damaged paintings were not common, but when she had one, she sent it to one of two conservators. Of the two, Fernando Harris was her most gifted and reliable, the one she used most often. She knew that Maeve had personally delivered more than one work to be repaired, but had it been to Fernando or to Kate's other conservator? She couldn't remember offhand.

"I think he does," Kate said. Just as she said that, she spotted Dermot and asked him if he had seen Maeve that morning.

"No, Ms. Woodward," he said. "Her car was gone before I arrived."

"Thanks, Dermot," she said.

"I heard," Conor said, from the other end of the line.

"This is so bizarre," Kate said. "Why hasn't she called me? Fernando hasn't called back either. I have to double-check." She looked at her phone again—nothing. "I can't wait to hear from them—I'll go see him now."

"Let's double-check together," Conor said. "I'll go with you."

Kate hesitated. "I thought you were busy with *Psyche*."

"Joe and his team are on the boat now," Conor said. "But Tom and I have photos of those tracings on the porthole, and we're trying to decipher them. I'd be happy to take a break and go with you. Where is Fernando located?"

"Mystic. I've already left him a message," Kate said. "He always has music on when he works, and he might not have heard the phone. I'll head over now. It's not far. You keep going on the tracings."

Conor was silent. Kate felt her heart beating hard. She knew he might be taking this as a rejection. She didn't mean it that way, but she was upset about Maeve and wanted to get to the bottom of what she was doing.

"Are you sure?" he asked.

"Positive," Kate said. "Everything's okay. I'll call you as soon as I talk to him. I'm sure he's in his studio, oblivious to all this. I know there's an explanation about Maeve."

"The way things are going, I wonder," Conor said. "And even if there is one, will it make any sense?"

Her phone beeped, indicating another call.

"Maybe this is Maeve or Fernando," she said. She hung up quickly and answered, but not in time. She glanced at her phone screen to see who had called. She didn't recognize the number. She tried dialing it back, but the call went straight to voicemail with the default standard greeting.

Glancing around, she saw Dermot and asked him to get her Volvo. She texted Conor back to let him know that she missed the call and told him she'd be back by lunchtime. She thanked Dermot for her car and the bottle of water he handed her, and she drove west, toward Mystic, Connecticut, on her way to find Maeve.

Tuesday, July 6; 9:15 a.m.

Conor watched his brother at the computer terminal in the USCG Bay Street office. Tom had transmitted the photos of the window writing to

Joe and Garrett, and now he downloaded them from his iPhone onto his work computer. Using an advanced enhancement program, he was able to clarify the tracings.

"Tell me about the diamond rings," Tom said.

"Some of the girls at Langtry Academy had them."

"High school girls? Isn't that a little young to be engaged?" Tom asked. "Who gives a girl that age a diamond?"

"They were mostly heirlooms, passed down through their families."

"And the girls used them to write on the glass?"

"Some did," Conor said. "Mostly they scratched their initials, and some dates—going back into the 1800s. The school was founded in 1843."

"And you were solving an almost two-hundred-year-old murder?"

"No," Conor said. "It was five years ago. There were two roommates, and one killed the other in their senior year. They had been best friends even before boarding school and had roomed together for two of the four years."

"What happened?" Tom asked.

"No one had any idea. They had seemed close, with no problems that anyone at the school could see. We interviewed students, faculty, and family members. Every person we spoke to was shocked. I went back to their room a week after the murder, and it was just like on the boat. The light was different. I glanced at one of the windows and saw something traced in the glass—the letters 'NW.'"

"Northwest?" Tom asked.

"We didn't know at first. I didn't know if it had any bearing on the case, and I had no idea who had written it and how they'd done it. I assumed a glass cutter. But the writing could have been done anytime during the last two centuries, so even though it piqued my interest, I didn't really think of it as evidence. At first."

"But it was?"

"Yes," Conor said. "Abby Jenkins—the victim—was wearing a diamond ring when she died. It was the middle finger of her right hand, so apparently not an engagement ring. I asked her parents where she had gotten it, and they didn't know—they had never seen it before. It didn't come from the family. Helen Wagner, the roommate . . ."

"And suspect?" Tom asked.

Conor nodded. "She wasn't talking to us. Her father was a lawyer in Hartford, and he'd immediately gotten her a top defense attorney. The murder was so brutal, the prosecutor had requested no bail. I was in court the day of her bail hearing, and I noticed a clear hostility between Helen and her father. Helen practically spit at him when he leaned toward the defense table to talk to her."

"So that caught your attention," Tom said.

"Yes. It was extreme. It was more than 'if looks could kill.' Another thing—her mother was there but not sitting with her father. I checked, and they were not divorced, but they had recently separated. Like a week before. And Helen wanted her mother—that was obvious. She was crying, reaching out her arms toward her as the marshals led her out of the courtroom."

"Did you talk to the mother?" Tom asked.

"Tried to, but she wouldn't see me at first. A few weeks went by. I had gone back to the girls' dorm room and seen the scratched glass. I'd reexamined everything we'd collected from the room, including schoolbooks, papers, letters, clothes, everything. Abby had a book of poems by Pablo Neruda—it was called *Love Poems*. Inside the front flap was an inscription: *For you, always. Nicholas.*"

"N from NW on the window?" Tom asked.

"Yeah. It took me a while to put it together. I kept thinking about that family dynamic in the courtroom, the way Helen had been toward her parents. And I'd found out about a big fight they had all had a few weeks earlier—very loud and public, at parents' weekend. Helen's mother had started screaming at Abby."

"What did Abby do?"

"It was more like, what did Helen's father do? His name was Nicholas Wagner, and he had been having a sexual relationship with

Abby for over a year. He gave her a diamond ring that had belonged to his grandmother, and she'd worn it all that time. It had been in a safe-deposit box, and Helen had never seen it, but when his wife went to parents' weekend, she spotted Abby wearing it."

"And she flipped out."

"Yep. It was a bad scene. After the parents left, Helen confronted Abby in their room, and Abby admitted it. Helen saw her family breaking apart, blamed Abby for it, and she killed her. Hit her over and over with a crystal paperweight," Conor said, remembering the trail of blood from where Abby had tried to crawl away.

"Abby was just a kid, though," Tom said. "It wasn't her fault. That 'relationship' was sexual assault."

"Yes, it was. And we charged Nicholas with it. Meanwhile, Abby had thought it was love. He had convinced her it was. Now Abby is dead, and Helen is serving a sentence for first-degree manslaughter," Conor said. "I don't know if I'd have solved it if Abby hadn't used the ring to scratch his initials in the window glass. NW."

"Wow," Tom said. "So she was in love, but she wound up leaving a clue that revealed who her killer was."

"Unwittingly, yes," Conor said.

Tom leaned closer to the computer screen. "Do you think we have something similar here? A victim writing something that might identify her killer?"

"That's a possibility," Conor said.

"And what, he gave her a diamond ring before chaining her up?"

"It tracks with the part of him that wants to treat her like a queen."

"I'm starting to see double," Tom said, rubbing his eyes and pushing his desk chair back. "You take a look."

Conor was glad to, anything to take his mind off Kate heading to Mystic without him. They were independent, they had always done their own things. As much as they loved being together, they each had work and separate interests. Kate knew that he was investigating the violence on *Psyche*, and it made sense for him to stick with it and for her to go there alone.

He was thinking of Kate, but as he stared at the window markings, he suddenly saw clearly, and letters came into focus.

"Hey," he said, pointing.

"What?" Tom asked.

"There's a word," he said. "Or at least some letters." Some of them had been written backward, but the closest Conor could get was SFALON.

He typed it into the search engine, but nothing came up.

"What does it sound like to you?" Tom asked.

"S. Falon? Could that be a name?" Conor kept staring. "Or is that 5? 5FALON. A license plate number?"

"Or a letter-number combination," Tom said. "To a mailbox? Or a keyless lock?"

Conor texted Joe:

Can you check RI DMV for this registration? SFALON or 5FALON.

Will do. What's up?

Conor didn't reply right away. He was already accessing the Connecticut Department of Motor Vehicles, noting the fact that there was no such registration number in his state.

Nothing, Joe texted back at the same time Conor was coming up empty on the CT DMV site. Why you ask?

Written on the boat glass. Can you see it?

Negative.

Look again—SFALON.

And now that Conor had told Joe what to look for, the scrawl was legible, and Joe shot back:

Got it. But still no plate coming up. Must be something else. Where are you now?

Tom's office, Bay Street.

Conor waited for a reply, but before he received one, he heard Tom answer a call on his desk phone.

"Where?" Tom asked. "Do you have an ID?"

Conor froze at the sharpness in Tom's voice and the look in his eyes when he disconnected the call.

"What is it?" Conor asked.

"A fisherman just found a woman's body," Tom said. "My crew got the call."

"Who is it?" Conor asked, thinking immediately of Maeve.

"They haven't identified her yet," Tom said. "They're transporting her body to our dock in Galilee. Come on, let's go."

31

Tuesday, July 6; 10:00 a.m.

Kate drove into Mystic, Connecticut, just thirty minutes away from the Ocean House. There had been a traffic jam on Route 1, with cars stopped dead until the accident was cleared. When she got close to the center of town, the bascule bridge had swung open for boats that couldn't clear it.

So she waited in more traffic, watching the classic steamboat *Sabino* chug upriver toward Mystic Seaport, and she felt anxiety building. Fernando Harris still hadn't returned her call, and in spite of what she had told Conor about him listening to music while he worked, she expected that he would have checked his messages.

When the bridge lowered and the road was open again, she inched through the town crowded with tourists, past shops and restaurants, until she could take a right onto Gravel Street. With the Mystic River on one side, and elegant nineteenth-century houses on the other, Kate could well understand why Fernando lived and had his studio here.

She pulled into a driveway behind a stately white Federal-style house with black shutters and a columned porch. Pots of white geraniums flanked the front door. Fernando's van, with his logo on the side, and a dark-gray Range Rover were parked in back. She occasionally encountered collectors and curators, waiting for Fernando to work his magic on their damaged artworks. Some of them had bought paintings from her gallery, and she usually enjoyed hearing about their collections. But she wasn't in the mood for that today.

The house's main entrance was in front, facing the river, but the back door led into Fernando's studio. The bell chimed when she stepped inside—it was programmed to announce arrivals.

She walked into the room where he did his framing. Classical music played through speakers in the ceiling. There were numerous frame samples stuck by Velcro to fabric-covered walls. A wide, square worktable filled the room's center. Did the fact that the music was on mean that Fernando would be back soon?

After a few moments, she cut behind the framing table and walked down a short hallway. She stopped in front of the heavy door to what he always referred to as his inner sanctum. She knew that the door was made of steel; it was alarmed and triple locked because of the valuable works in his studio. There was an intercom off to the side; she pressed the buzzer and waited.

It took so long, she was beginning to think that in spite of his van being in the driveway, he wasn't there. She thought about Maeve, and panic filled her chest—she needed answers. She was about to leave, when the heavy door finally opened.

"Kate," Fernando said. "Didn't you get my email? I haven't started working on the painting yet. But come in." He stood aside to let her pass.

"That's not why I'm here," she said. "I called and texted you—"

"Sorry, I've been in a meeting and had my phone off. What's up?"

"You said that Maeve dropped off the painting," she said.

"Yes," he said. "I have it in back."

"Are you sure it was Maeve?"

He looked confused. "Of course. Who else would it be?"

"Fernando—have you met her before?"

"No," he said. "This was the first time. I knew that other assistant of yours, a couple years back. I forget her name . . ."

"What did the woman who dropped it off today look like?" Kate asked.

"Dark-blond hair, blue eyes. Blue—kind of turquoise—nail polish," he said.

"Suzanne," Kate said, feeling a chill ripple across her skin. "That was Suzanne. It wasn't Maeve."

"Who is Suzanne?" Fernando asked.

Kate was shaking. "I need to see the painting."

Fernando nodded. He gestured for her to follow him through a library with shelves overflowing with art books, into the intimate chamber where he did his restoration work. He took very few clients, so the space was small. It was filled with the tools and paints he needed to do his meticulous repairs. He stored finished work in archival boxes, but the ones yet to be restored were upright in racks in a large walk-in closet.

There were no windows, which kept the overall light dim, to not damage fragile works on paper, using only a spotlight to focus on torn or stained canvases. Kate's eyes took a moment to adjust to the dark, and she felt startled to see a man standing in the shadows. When he stepped forward, she saw who it was—Crispin Adams, her friend and one of her biggest collectors.

"Good to see you, Kate," he said.

"Crispin, hello," she said.

"I'm here to drop a painting with our esteemed friend," Crispin said, smiling toward Fernando. "I have an Allen Butler Talcott landscape—a beauty of a crescent moon setting over the Connecticut River—that was apparently stored in a barn. The canvas is mildewed."

"The damage isn't too terrible," Fernando began.

"But I couldn't help hearing you asking about Maeve," Crispin said, talking over Fernando. "I know that Lincoln is very concerned about her. Any word?"

"No, not at all. I was hoping she was the one to deliver *Foggy Night* to Fernando, but it was someone else."

"How odd," Crispin said.

"Fernando, you were going to show me the painting," Kate said.

Fernando went into the storage closet and came back with the James Suydam oil. He laid *Foggy Night* carefully on the oak table in the room's center. Kate looked at the heartbreakingly broken gilt frame, the ragged tear in the canvas.

At first glance, the painting looked as it had right after the incident at the rehearsal dinner. But when she leaned closer, she saw that someone had scratched a crude circle into the paint, ringing the moon just above the lighthouse.

"That wasn't there," she said, pointing at the circle.

"Maybe there's something in the instructions," Fernando said.

"What instructions?"

"She left an envelope—said there was a letter from you inside—but I haven't had the chance to read it yet," Fernando said.

He went to a mahogany desk, lifted the envelope from the green Florentine leather blotter, and handed it to Kate. Kate noticed the return address engraved on the back—Maynard-King on Lovecraft Lane in Narragansett. She slit it open and pulled out the stationery inside.

The note had been calligraphed with black ink in ornate script.

A ring for a ring.

Miranda stole my mother's promise ring from Conor to give to you.

I am returning the favor, a ring around the moon, a circle in the sky.

Don't look up at the sky, Kate. Just turn around.

Kate's heart began to skitter in her chest. She hesitated, but then she swiveled her head. Fernando's head was bowed.

"I'm sorry, Kate," he said, not meeting her eyes. "They made me mention Maeve in the email. They would have destroyed me."

Crispin stood there, smiling at Kate. The room was so dark, at first she didn't see the third person stepping forward, holding out a hand as if to take Kate's.

"Kate," came the familiar voice. "We knew that email would call you here. We knew you would come."

32

Conor stood with his brother on the dock in Galilee, waiting for the Coast Guard vessel carrying the woman's body. The Block Island ferry steamed away with a loud blast of its horn, and trawlers returned to port, seagulls wheeling and screeching over their white wakes in hopes of fish scraps.

Meeting death as a detective had trained him to remain detached, to not get emotionally involved. But training was just that: behaviors to be studied, lessons to be learned. Deeper down, Conor never failed to be affected: Someone with hopes and dreams and family and secrets had died. Someone who had yearned for love and happiness.

As soon as the Coast Guard boat docked, Conor and Tom climbed aboard. They went belowdecks, to where the body had been placed. Conor approached, afraid not so much of what, but of whom he would see.

The woman wasn't Maeve. Her face was unfamiliar to Conor, and he let out a long exhalation. Relief, he supposed, that Kate would be saved from heartbreak. He quickly put emotion aside and clicked into detachment.

From appearances, the woman hadn't been in the water long. Her face was bluish white, and there were strands of eelgrass tangled in her long brown hair. She wore a high-collared, long-sleeved cream-colored lace garment that could have been a dress or a nightgown. Bits of seaweed clung to the fabric.

Conor watched Tom pull on black nitrile gloves. This wasn't Conor's crime scene, so he kept his hands in his pockets to avoid any temptation to touch the body. And he was tempted, because he saw three things that needed closer examination: a deep ear-to-ear gash just beneath the lace collar, an indentation on the swollen fourth finger of her left hand, and a single pearl earring on her right ear.

"Sir, Rhode Island State Police are arriving," someone called down from the deck, and Conor went to greet Joe. Joe had obviously gotten his message, and he and Garrett arrived in their black Dodge Durango Slicktop, with a crime scene van directly behind them.

"You got them here fast," Conor said, gesturing at the crime techs.

"Perfect timing," Joe said. "We were just finishing up with *Psyche*. Who's the victim?"

"Don't know yet," Conor said.

"Not accidental drowning, I'm guessing? Since they called us?" Joe asked.

"Correct, it's not accidental," Conor said.

Conor led him and Garrett down below and pointed at the cut where the woman's throat had been slit.

"That's familiar," Joe said.

"Yeah," Conor said, picturing Belinda.

The body was positioned so that both arms were straight at her sides. Her skin was wrinkled and discolored from being in the ocean. The left hand rested palm down, her broken or dislocated ring finger jutting out at an unnatural angle. She wore pink nail polish, but her fingernails were dirty, and one had been torn off.

"She fought back," Garrett said.

"I think she was wearing a ring, and someone pulled it off," Conor said.

"Why?" Joe asked.

"Conor has a theory about how rings connect with these cases," Tom said.

"Tell me," Joe said.

"Whoever was imprisoned on *Psyche* wore a diamond ring," Conor said.

"Are you kidding me?" Joe asked. "How do you come up with that?"

"Because 'SFALON' was scratched into the window glass. I think she left a message before he killed her."

"What makes you think a diamond made the scratches?" Garrett asked.

"Because I've seen it before. Diamonds are hard enough to cut glass. Even tempered glass," Conor said.

"Okay," Joe said. "Say you're right. How does that connect with this victim?"

"She could be the woman kept prisoner there," Conor said. "The white dress goes along with what Grace described. Her finger could have been broken by the killer, when he removed the ring."

"While she was alive? Or postmortem?" Joe asked.

"Since her fingernail is broken, I'd say he did it before he killed her," Conor said. "Like Garrett said, she fought back."

Joe slipped on his gloves. He crouched down and carefully rolled up the long sleeves on her arms. Both wrists were rubbed raw, scored with abrasions.

"These wounds could have been made by handcuffs," Joe said.

"On *Psyche* or in that bedroom," Conor said.

"Yes. We need an ID on her right away," Joe said. He stood up and turned to face Conor. "Tell me what you're thinking about the ring. Say that you're right, and she was wearing one. What's the significance?"

"I think the killer gave it to her," Conor said.

"Like an engagement ring?" Garrett asked.

"In his mind, maybe," Conor said. "But not really. It's part of his *Beauty and the Beast* fantasy. He's a romantic."

"A romantic psycho," Joe asked.

"Something like that," Conor said.

"Is it one man, or are there more?" Garrett asked.

"Grace said there were men, plural. She also mentioned a woman, who seemed to be part of the same group," Conor said.

"It seems likely that whoever killed Belinda killed this woman too. The wound looks identical," Joe said. "A right-to-left cut. A left-handed killer. But there are no hesitation marks this time. He's getting more confident."

"This kill took place after Belinda?" Garrett said.

"We'll need an autopsy for that," Joe said. "So, what do we think happened here? He decided to kill her, then took the ring off her finger?"

"Maybe," Conor said.

"Because he didn't mind throwing her overboard but didn't want to lose the diamond?"

"It could be more symbolic than that," Conor said.

"By taking the ring, he was breaking up with her?" Tom asked.

Conor nodded, picturing the romantic stage set created in the mansion. "Maybe she let him down, disappointed him, didn't return his 'love'? Stopped participating in whatever fantasy he has going on?"

"Or maybe he's just a psycho who likes to torture women," Joe said.

"I think we all know that part's true," Conor said. "But there's more. He's prettied it up, at least in his mind."

"Psycho on *Psyche*," Garrett said. "So he took back the ring but left a valuable pearl earring—if it's real?"

"It's real," Conor said. "Our killer likes luxury. He'd want only the best for his victim."

"Why only one earring?" Garrett asked.

"The other could have come off in a struggle or slipped away in the ocean," Joe said.

"We should go talk to Jennifer, the young groundskeeper at Maynard-King. Kate said she keeps a collection of single earrings in a compartment of her ATV. I thought at the time that they could be trophies," Conor said. "And maybe the other pearl earring is too."

"A young woman keeping trophies?" Joe said. "That seems unusual. You think Jennifer is the killer? It would be very rare."

"Unlikely, but she could be involved," Conor said.

Conor's phone buzzed. An unfamiliar number came up, and he stepped away to answer the call.

"Reid," he said.

"Conor?" a very faint woman's voice asked.

"Yes," he said. "Who's this?"

"It's Miranda," she whispered. "Kate's going to be next."

"What do you mean—next?" Conor asked, his heart crashing.

"You have to keep her safe, or she'll be taken just like the rest. I can't talk more. He'll hear me."

"Who's 'he'? Where are you?" Conor asked.

But the connection was broken, and Miranda wasn't on the line anymore.

33

Girl #3

Tuesday, July 6; 10:30 a.m.

It was her turn to teach.

She had been well trained by the woman, and now she was expected to pass her knowledge along to the next girl and the one after that. She was shaking, to know what they had done to the one before her. That girl was gone; her blood had flowed from where they had cut her throat, and her life had drained into the ocean.

This setting was unfamiliar and brand new. Girl #3 had become used to the boat and the mansion on the island. But after they killed Belinda three days ago, and the new girl yesterday, it was too dangerous for the group to stay in those places.

They told her the police would tear *Psyche* apart, and they would search the mansion for any clues that would lead them to the woman and the men. The girl felt a combination of panic and hope when she thought of the message the other girl had left on *Psyche*'s window. The woman and men hadn't noticed it, or she wouldn't be here now.

She hoped the police saw it and that it would lead them to saving her.

The new location was just as opulent, filled with—as the woman said proudly—"understated luxury." The girl knew that the "understated luxury" had nothing to do with her, it was all for the men. It was a fairy tale just for them.

When she asked about Belinda, they had at first told her only that she had died, just died. As if a woman Belinda's age had just dropped dead from natural causes. But the girl hadn't believed that. She had known there was more to it.

She had felt the handcuffs on her own wrists and ankles, had been dressed in a flowing white gown and taken to the parties. Now that the last girl was dead, they gave her the diamond ring. They warned her forgetting any of the lessons would call forth the knife. The woman had traced the blade across her throat—not enough to draw blood, but enough to make every muscle in her body tighten in fear.

That's when the woman told her that Belinda had been murdered. The other girl too.

"She did not work out," the woman said. "And it's your fault."

"Why, what did I do?"

"You taught her to be afraid, not to please. Fear has its place, but it never left her—she couldn't break through it. She wore it in her eyes, all the time. She would never fit in. She would never be able to fulfill our clients' dreams, make their fantasies come true."

"Where is she now?"

"In the ocean, darling."

"The knife?" the girl asked, her knees turning to jelly.

"Yes," the woman said. "She earned the blade. Just make sure you don't. There will be new students, and you will train them, just as I taught you. Remember—they need to feel loved and happy. I don't want to see dread in their eyes every time I look at them. That poisons them. They need to save their fear and their fight for the right moment. When the men require it. For the handcuffs and the ring. Do you understand?"

"Yes."

"They need to be Beauty when they meet the Beast. As you did, so brilliantly," the woman said, leaning close to stroke her hair. "That's why I've chosen you to follow in my footsteps. Because you've accepted the mission. And you'll be rewarded as long as you remember your lessons."

The girl nodded, keeping terror out of her eyes. *In the ocean, in the ocean.* They had murdered again, and she could be next. The warning was there—if she remembered her lessons.

How could she ever forget them?

Tuesday, July 6; 10:45 a.m.

Conor's calls to Kate went unanswered. They went straight to voicemail, and he knew that her phone was turned off. She had told him that she had gone to Fernando Harris's studio and that it was in Mystic, but Conor didn't have the address. After Miranda's call, Conor was out of his mind needing to find Kate. Even without an exact location, Tom was already driving them toward Mystic when Conor texted Sam:

Sam—what is Fernando Harris's address?

He stared at his phone, but she didn't reply.

Conor and Tom didn't talk. Conor kept checking his phone, and finally Sam called.

"Sorry," she said. "I went to the house first, and then the post office. Guess I got sidetracked talking to Steve. I don't have Fernando's address. Why do you need it?"

"I'm looking for Kate. She was heading to his studio. He emailed her and mentioned Maeve. He said Maeve had just dropped off *Foggy Night* today, and obviously that got her attention."

"I know how I can get it," Sam said. "Let me text Lincoln real fast. He's been to Fernando's with Maeve, and he'll have the address."

Conor waited, and then Sam came back on the line. She gave him an address on Gravel Street in Mystic.

"Lincoln is really freaked out about Maeve, and so am I," Sam said. "And now about Kate too. Conor, it has to do with 1740. I have an idea, and I just asked Lincoln if he wants to research it with me."

"You're right about the connection," Conor said. "What are you researching?"

"Uncle Mike and the others found an ad in the Yellow Pages from twenty-five years ago," Sam said. "It said '1740 Events—Fantasies our specialty,' and it gave a phone number."

Sam was on speaker, and both Conor and Tom could hear everything.

"Did they try the number?" Conor asked.

"Yes, and so did I," Sam said. "No answer—I just got voicemail. It's a florist."

"I'm glad no one answered," Conor said. "Don't get too involved. Young women are the targets—you're right in that age group."

"I know," Sam said, and she paused for a moment before continuing. "Conor, there's something else. It's about Leo Kennedy."

"What is it?" Conor asked, bracing himself as Tom swerved to avoid some orange cones marking the spot of a recent accident. Route 1 from Westerly into southeastern Connecticut was full of typically heavy summer traffic.

"He and Miranda were walking down the beach earlier," Sam said. "They acted as if they were separate and just ran into each other, but I had the feeling it was the opposite—they had just pulled apart when they got close to me."

"You saw Miranda?" Conor asked, thinking of the call he had just received. "When?"

"Around eight," Sam said.

Conor thought about what Miranda had said, how she couldn't talk because "he" might hear her. Had she been referring to Leo?

"Do you know where she is now?" Conor asked.

"No, last I saw her was on the beach."

"I need to talk to her," Conor said. "She warned me that Kate will be next."

"'Next'?" Sam asked.

"Taken," Conor said.

"Kate is too smart and careful to get taken."

"You be smart and careful too, okay?" Conor asked, thinking of how many intelligent, cautious women had been tricked into letting down their guard. No one ever expects the worst to happen.

"I will," Sam said, and hung up.

"You think Sam has a point about Leo Kennedy?" Tom asked.

"I don't know," Conor said. "But if she's right about him hiding a connection with Miranda, it would at least be strange."

"Call him," Tom said. "See what he says."

Conor had Leo's number saved in his contacts. He stared at it for a minute. He wanted any information he could get, that might help Kate. He had tried calling Miranda back at the number on his screen, but she hadn't answered. Was she in danger, and did Leo have anything to do with it? He hesitated, then rang Leo's number on speaker.

"Detective Reid!" Leo said, answering immediately. He spoke loudly, over the sound of an engine in the background. "What's up? Don't tell me they have you in custody again."

"No," Conor said. "They don't."

"Then to what do I owe the pleasure of this call?"

Conor hesitated. He decided to show his cards and approach Leo head on. "I want to ask you about Miranda Forrest," he said.

A long pause. "Funny, I just saw her on the beach," Leo said.

"Do you know where she is now?" Conor asked.

"No, why would I?" Leo asked.

Conor's senses pricked up at the defensive response. It reminded him of interrogations, of the tone people took when protesting their innocence.

"Well, you said you saw her on the beach," Conor said. "Do you know where she went after that? I really need to know. This has to do with Kate."

"I have no idea where she went—it's not like she would tell me. I just met her. What's going on, Conor? Is Kate okay?"

Conor took a breath. He didn't want to out Miranda, in case Leo was the person she was afraid might hear her. "She's fine, I'm sure. I'm just being extra careful and need to speak with Miranda about something."

"Look, Conor," Leo said. "You've been through hell this weekend. If it makes you feel better, I've checked with Criminal Division, and they don't have any charges brewing against you. You're in the clear."

"Good to know."

"I've got to go now," Leo said. "I'm on my Hatteras, about to go fishing. I'd invite you to come along, but clearly you have more important things to do. Call if I can help. I hope you find Kate."

"Hey, Leo," Tom said. "It's Conor's brother, Tom. What's running, what are you going out after?"

Conor shot his brother a look across the front seat.

"Tuna," Leo said. "Are you a fisherman?"

"Sure am. Tuna, nice. Are you heading out to the canyons?" Tom asked, and Conor knew he was referring to the deep water on the far side of Montauk.

"No, that's too ambitious," Leo said. "Just the Gully, out past Block Island. I want to come home tonight. The canyons are too far."

"Good luck," Conor said.

"You too," Leo said and disconnected.

Conor looked at Tom. "Did you catch that?" he asked.

"Yeah," Tom said. "You didn't mention anything about needing to find Kate."

He knew he didn't have to ask Tom why he had inquired about Leo's fishing destination. Leo had just risen to the top of his 1740 list, and both Conor and Tom wanted to know where he could find him.

Tom dialed a member of his team, and Conor heard him instructing him to look for a Hatteras sportfishing boat, focusing the search in—but not limited to—the waters around Block Island. He said to check registrations and identifications and stay alert for—but don't detain—a boat owner named Leo Kennedy.

"Leo might have just told us Block Island and be going somewhere else entirely," Conor said.

"That's why I said don't limit the search," Tom said. "We don't know if Leo has anything to do with it. But the thing is, if we are right about there being a trafficking enterprise, and he's involved, a large Hatteras would be perfect transport. It's spacious, fast, and long range."

"He knew I was looking for Kate without my telling him. That's enough for me. We should find out if his boat has been seen at either the Maynard-King or Bellevigne Island docks," Conor said.

Traffic was moving slowly into downtown Mystic as they inched toward the big flagpole in Mystic. The bascule bridge was closed, and cars were barely creeping across. But then a loud alarm sounded, and Conor swore. He knew that once the bridge swung open for boats to pass through, they'd be stuck in that line of tourist traffic for at least another twenty minutes.

"You got the Gravel Street address, right?" he asked, quickly turning to look across the front seat at Tom.

"Yeah, but . . ."

"I'm not going to wait. Meet me there," Conor said. He jumped out of the truck and started to run.

The alarm was still going off when Conor sprinted toward the bridge. It had not started to open yet, and he ran across it. If he were on duty and saw someone else doing that, he would have arrested them. He was in Connecticut now, his jurisdiction. His badge was in his pocket, and he would have flashed it in a second if someone stopped him, but no one did. He had to get to Kate.

34

Tuesday, July 6; 11:00 a.m.

Sam figured the Tower Suite was the best place to work on her 1740 research. Kate had moved in for the duration, and Sam was staying in the adjoining room on the lower floor. She climbed up to the main level and saw Kate's laptop on the table by the terrace door, so she and Lincoln set up their workstation there too. The suite was quiet and inspiring, with light streaming through the round windows in the mansard roof.

Everything about the last few days—the rehearsal dinner drama, the wedding cancelation and her aunt's unhappiness, the tension she felt coming from Conor, and most shockingly, the murder—made Sam feel wildly off balance.

Sam's mother had been murdered when Sam was sixteen. Every year that passed meant another 365 days since Sam had last hugged her. Her parents had been going through an ugly divorce at the time of her mother's death, and Sam had been acting out, angry, not speaking to either of them.

Those facts were always with her; they were part of who she was. Not only did she love and miss her mother, but she also had to live with the fact that she had been furious at her mother when she died. Worst of all, she hadn't been there. Maybe she could have stopped her mother from being strangled by someone she had trusted, even loved.

Had that been the case with Belinda? Had someone she'd known well, cared about—someone she'd thought loved her—walked up behind her and slit her throat?

The wedding dress must have played a role; it was bizarre that Belinda had stolen it from right here in the Tower Suite, put it on, and had been wearing it when she was murdered. Sam pictured the white fabric soaked with blood. Had the killer been repulsed by that sight, or had it fed a sick fantasy? It all seemed beyond the realm of reality, and Sam wondered if either or both victim and killer were insane. It seemed to her that they had to be.

She remembered that she had gone a little mad after her mother's murder. There was no possible way to exist in normal life, among regular people, while her entire mind was swimming with images of the lace imprints left in her mother's neck from where the elastic of her underpants had dug in, of her mother dying, watching the person strangling her, feeling her heart break as the life drained out of her. Had that happened with Belinda? Had she looked into the eyes of her killer, had it been someone she loved?

Sam knew that having crazy thoughts and dreams as the daughter of the victim was one thing: But what about a killer? And what about a victim who dropped into a pool of blood wearing someone else's wedding dress? She thought of delusions, paranoia, dissociation, the inability to stop reliving a terrible moment.

And she thought of that envelope she had seen Conor take from that drawer in the library desk at home, when he thought he was alone. Seeing what it contained—a tiny tooth and a lock of hair—had activated a ton of suspicion in Sam. But that had passed—when she was home, just an hour ago, she had checked the drawer and found it empty. On top of the desk was a receipt and a note from Trooper Dave Liggett saying he had taken the envelope to the crime lab.

Sam figured the envelope had come from Belinda, and that brought her back to 1740.

"Maynard-King is the center of it all," she said out loud. "It has to be."

"Why do you say that?" Lincoln asked, not looking up from what he was doing.

"I think some of them were in the hospital for treatment, and they met each other there," she said.

"We can put it on the list of things to check out," he said. "But what makes you think it?"

"Because I know what it's like to lose touch with reality."

"Sorry," Lincoln said. "That must have been awful. When?"

"After my mother died."

"So why do you think Maynard-King is the center of this?"

Sam didn't answer right away. She thought of how she had spiraled after her mother's death. Every night for months she had dreamed her mother was alive. They were wonderful dreams, full of love and comfort. She could hear her mother's voice, feel her arms around her.

But after a while, her dreams changed. She began having nightmares about her mother's last day on earth. She had visions of her mother in their garden, tending the roses and hydrangeas. Her mother had been pregnant, and Sam remembered how they would talk about what the baby's name would be. But the killer would be waiting there, hiding in the garden, waiting for Sam's mother to go inside the house. And then her mother would be murdered, and Sam would never see her again.

Those nightmares, and the grief Sam felt, had made her want to die herself. Kate saw Sam falling apart and arranged for her to be admitted to McLean, outside Boston. It was one of the best psychiatric hospitals in the world.

The reason Sam felt so strongly that Maynard-King was key was that she related to sad, lost girls, and she knew how easy it was to fall off the edge of life. It would be even easier if there was someone evil standing there, giving them a push. But she didn't say all that to Lincoln.

"That note at Dr. Tyler's grave," she said, because she knew it was a more acceptable response that wouldn't require her getting too personal. "'1740, With Love, Always'"

"We don't have the note, do we?" he asked. "Maeve grabbed it just before she got into that Range Rover."

"But I saw it," Sam said. "So I know what it said." She paused. "Lincoln, the way you say Maeve 'got into that Range Rover' makes it sound as if you think she did it of her own free will—instead of being forced in."

Now he looked up from his keyboard, reached up with one hand to push his long hair out of his eyes. "Sometimes I do think that."

"Then why hasn't she called you? Or Kate?"

"She was freaked out by seeing all that blood run down the stairs from Belinda's body," he said. "Wouldn't you be?"

Sam nodded. She knew she would. Add that to the list of ways to lose your mind.

"And it messed her up, knowing that Belinda was killed wearing Kate's wedding dress. She was obviously obsessed with Conor. Even though she was a widow and had a kid, I guess she never got over her fantasy of getting married to the boy next door."

Fantasy, Sam thought. Just like in the old Yellow Pages ad.

1740 Events: Fantasies our specialty.

She looked at the photo she had taken of the ad. Even though Sam had called the number earlier, she wanted to try again. Maybe someone would answer this time. She dialed it on her phone.

"Who are you calling?" Lincoln asked. Sam put a finger to her lips because she had just reached voicemail again, and she wanted to listen more carefully. When it finished, she hung up and turned to Lincoln.

"It's a florist," she said.

"Well, I guess we can cross that off the list, then," Lincoln said. "A florist is pretty far from an event company."

"I don't know," Sam said.

"What's bothering you?"

"The message said, 'Make someone's dreams come true.' Dreams aren't that different from fantasies," Sam said.

"What's the name of the place?" Lincoln asked.

"Enchanted Petals," she said.

"I know where that is," he said after a moment. "It's in Narragansett, and it's not just a florist shop—it's a nursery. They have greenhouses, big fields full of flowers. I've seen them—there's a hiking trail along the edge of the property."

Sam replayed the message in her mind. Dreams, enchanted petals. A shiver ran down her spine. She thought of that ad, placed in the Yellow Pages so long ago, and she suddenly had a growing feeling that 1740 was somehow alive and well at the garden center.

"I want to go there," Sam said to Lincoln.

Tuesday, July 6; 11:00 a.m.

Conor found Fernando Harris's house and thought it looked more like an 1800s sea captain's home than a framing and art restoration studio. It blended in with all the other historic houses on Gravel Street, along the Mystic River. There wasn't a sign out front; the neighborhood was residential, not commercial, and for a moment he wondered if he had the right place.

Cars were parked on one side of the waterfront street. He didn't see Kate's, so he walked down the driveway that ran alongside the house. Part of the backyard had been paved to create a parking area for a few cars. Conor saw a van with Fernando Harris's logo on the side; behind it, just out of immediate view, was Kate's car. He let out a big sigh of relief and began to walk toward the house.

There was a back entrance, so Conor headed up the stairs and knocked before he saw the small sign:

BY APPOINTMENT ONLY, UNLESS IT'S YOUR LUCKY DAY AND I HAPPEN TO BE HERE.

Conor pushed the door open. He walked through a room lined with samples of picture frames, with a massive work surface in the center, and a small oak table and two armchairs off to the side. There were a few art magazines and exhibition catalogs stacked on the table.

He had clocked a security camera above the outside door, and there were two more set in upper corners of this room. At the far end was a narrow hallway that led to a white steel security door. To the right of the door was an intercom panel. Conor pressed the button. He listened for a faint buzz on the other side of the door but didn't hear one. His phone was in his pocket; he took it out and checked to see if he had heard back from Kate.

He texted her: I am at Fernando's now—I see your car, where are you? Nothing.

He stepped back from the door, in case she was inside and hadn't had time to respond yet, but he felt his blood pressure rise as he waited. He stood by the table and fanned out the top three catalogs. The top one was from the Woodward-Lathrop gallery, displaying the shadow boxes of gallery artist Claire Beaudry Chase. The second was a brochure from the Mystic Museum of Art's exhibition a few years earlier, "Magic Hour: Art between Waking and Dreams." The third was from Botanicum/Animalium, a gallery Conor had never heard of. The title of the show was "Judge not, Lest ye be Judged."

Odd title for an art show, he thought. He stared at the brochure's cover and was sure he had seen the painting depicted there—a still life of a bowl of peaches, four perfect and one rotten, brown and dotted with blow fly larvae, brown juice spilling out of the bowl and staining the white tablecloth on which it sat. He couldn't remember who had painted it or where he had seen it before, but he recalled being repulsed by the decaying fruit and the way the juice reminded him of fluids leaking from a corpse.

He used the side of his fist to bang on the white steel door. It had been realistically painted to look like a cross-and-bible Colonial-era door but was in fact a bank-grade vault door, like ones Conor had seen in panic rooms—and like the one to the bedroom in the Bellevigne Island mansion.

"Kate!" he called. "Fernando, open the door!"

Conor knew that Fernando stored valuable paintings and other artworks here, and that definitely explained the extra security measures. Kate had recently upgraded the system at the gallery, adding alarms to every window—including the small sidelights, too narrow for any would-be thief to slip through, high-definition cameras that recorded continuously instead of just being motion activated, and extra-sensitive glass-break detectors. If Fernando had those in place here, wouldn't Conor's entry have tripped some of them and caused Fernando to come out?

He heard a door open, and when he turned around, Tom was entering from the parking area.

"Her car's here," Tom said.

"Yeah, and I rang the bell," Conor said, gesturing at the steel door, "but Fernando's not answering."

"Just walk in," Tom said, heading toward the door, then stopping in his tracks. "Where's the doorknob?"

"There isn't one. It's a safe room."

"In a framing gallery?" Tom asked.

Conor didn't answer, just concentrated on the door.

"How does he open the door?" Tom asked, running a hand around the perimeter of the doorframe.

"He probably has remote access, uses a key fob or a program on his phone," Conor said. He pointed at a small matte triangle, flush with the steel. "I think that's the access site."

"Okay," Tom said. "But with high tech, there always has to be a fallback. You know, in case the grid is attacked, or the Wi-Fi goes out, and your electronics stop working. Isn't there a standard lock? You could get in that way."

Conor felt frustration rising. He walked outside and around the house to the front sidewalk. Looking up at the house, he noticed that all the first-floor curtains were drawn. He walked up onto the wide front porch and rang the doorbell. He could hear the tone through the door, unlike the reinforced one in the studio.

From this perspective, the house looked completely normal—regular doors and windows, nothing to suggest that inside it was a fortress. He didn't see any special reinforcement, which led him to believe that only the back section, where Fernando worked on paintings, was fortified. He rang the bell, then banged hard on the front door.

"Connecticut State Police," he called. "Open the door."

Tom pushed through the boxwood hedge that ran along the front of the house, getting close enough to peer through the closed curtains of the first-floor windows.

Conor pulled out his phone and called his office at the Connecticut State Police Western District Major Crime Squad. He gave his location to the dispatcher and asked her to send a unit. He stood back, surveying the house again. His heart was racing.

"Does Harris have a family?" Tom asked. "Wife, kids?"

"No idea," Conor said. Again, he pounded on the door rapidly, with the side of his fist. "Police! Fernando Harris, open the door!"

"We both know Kate could be in there," Tom said. "You need a warrant, but exigent . . ."

"Fuck it," Conor said, interrupting him. "I'm not waiting."

He eyed the lock on the front door. It looked standard, and from the outside, he couldn't see if there was a dead bolt. He took a big step back, raised his right foot, smashed it into the wood just beside the doorknob. The wood cracked loudly, and the next kick sent the splintered door flying open.

The forward momentum sent Conor stumbling into Fernando Harris's foyer, with Tom right behind him. Everything looked in order, with the kind of decor Conor was used to seeing in houses of well-off people, especially those who lived in this maritime part of the world: antique mahogany furniture, Oriental rugs, paintings of sailing ships in gilded frames, brass candlesticks on the mantel, birch logs tidily held in a polished copper bin. There was an air of genteel unflappability, as if this was the kind of home where nothing bad ever happened.

The Reid brothers split up. Conor took the first floor while Tom went up the stairs. Conor made his way through each room, including closets, looking for Kate. She wasn't there, and neither was Fernando. Tom came downstairs and shook his head.

The door to the studio, in the back of the house, was located off a hallway lined with bookcases. Conor examined the door and saw that it was fortified just like the one at the rear entrance. It had a lock on it. It made sense to Conor that Fernando might hide a key somewhere close by, so he began removing books and looking behind and under them. Each section was about three feet wide and seven feet tall, and each held ten shelves, spaced in ways to hold books of varying heights.

He worked his way down the row until he came to a spot where the bookcases were uneven. One section tilted slightly out from the next, leaving an inch gap between them. He pulled on it and realized that that section was a door.

"Tom," he said, and his brother walked over, and they opened the door.

It led into a space that was completely dark. It was obviously an interior room and had no windows. A chill ran through Conor, Kate's name racing through his mind. He fumbled his hand along the walls on both sides of the door, feeling for a light switch. He found one about shoulder level on the left side, and he switched it on.

"Holy shit," Tom said.

The walls were covered with silk and there was a pale-blue rug on the floor. A black-and-white photo—the same still from Cocteau's *Beauty and the Beast*—hung above the bed. There were old editions of the book, and there was a crystal decanter that held the same sickly sweet liquid that had nearly knocked Conor out on the island.

"How many of these rooms are there? The island, here . . . where else?" Conor asked.

The bedroom was an exact replica of the bedroom in the mansion on Bellevigne Island.

The bed was made, but the covers were mussed up, as if someone had lain on top of them and failed to straighten them out. Conor touched the indentation to see if it was still warm. It was not. But he could hardly breathe when he pulled back the sheet and saw reddish-brown streaks of blood.

"Conor, that's not Kate's blood," Tom said, reading his mind. "It can't be—it's dry. This stain has been there awhile."

"You're right," Conor said, incredibly relieved but still shaken. "It's old, it's not Kate's."

Conor walked around the perimeter of the bedroom until he came to the closet. When he opened the door, lamplight from the bedroom streamed inside. It was a cedar closet; bolted into the wood were hand-cuffs, just like the ones they'd seen on *Psyche*. There was dried blood on the metal and on the floor.

"So Fernando's part of it. And he lured Kate here." Conor stared at the irons, then back at the bed. He wanted to explode, to tear Fernando apart.

There was a commotion coming from the front of the house, and Conor knew that the team from his police barracks had arrived. He and Tom stood and went to meet them. Conor thought of how, once again, he had stepped into a crime scene, but he would do anything to find Kate, so he didn't care.

"Where's Kate now?" Conor said to Tom. He was trying to hold himself together, his mouth so dry he could barely speak.

"Let's go find her," Tom said.

And Conor didn't even answer. He didn't have to.

35

Tuesday, July 6; 1:00 p.m.

"Enchanted Petals," Sam said, sitting beside Lincoln in the front seat of his Mercedes SUV.

"Strange name, right?" he asked, giving her an amused sideways glance. "Like, flower petals have magical powers?"

"You know how to get there?" Sam asked.

"Like I told you, I've seen it. There's an awesome trail that runs basically from Point Judith all the way up Narragansett Bay to Providence. I did it with my dad once, and I've walked parts of it other times. It goes right past the garden center."

"How far is it?" Sam asked.

"I don't know—twenty-five minutes? Why, what's the rush? Why do you feel it's so important to go there?" Lincoln asked.

Sam couldn't explain that. They had driven from Watch Hill along Route 1, through South Kingstown, toward Narragansett. She knew they were heading in the direction of Maynard-King, but then Lincoln turned slightly inland from the shore and drove roughly parallel to Narragansett Bay. They passed fields crisscrossed with old stone walls, a chicken farm, a small village with shops and a gas station. They hit a traffic signal next to a funeral home, and Lincoln stopped at the red light.

"You're close to Kate, aren't you?" Lincoln asked, surprising Sam with his out-of-the-blue question.

"Very," she said. "She's never tried to be my mother—she knows that I only had one of those—but she has always been there for me. And she doesn't have kids of her own, so I know I'm like a daughter to her." Sam paused. "I'm not the only one she loves, though. She'd fight for a few of us. Conor, of course. Hadley and CeCe. And Maeve."

"That makes two of us," Lincoln said. "I'd do anything for Maeve. But Conor . . ."

"What about him?"

"Why would Kate fight for him, after what he did to her?"

"Did to her?"

"With Belinda. That whole thing had to devastate Kate. Whatever parts of it are true, whether Belinda had his kid or not, or whether they just hooked up—man, that would be hard to live with. Being cheated on, lied to."

Sam blinked hard and looked out the window again. They had left the small town and were back in a rural section. They passed a one-story motel with an attached restaurant and a half-empty parking lot, then a lake surrounded by pine trees.

"I don't know if any of that Belinda stuff is true," Sam said. "And neither does Kate. She loves Conor. They're going to get back to how they were."

"I wouldn't," Lincoln said, still speeding, taking his eyes off the road to momentarily look over at her. "Guys sometimes lie, Sam. They might act one way, but they're hiding their true selves. They hurt the women they're with and supposedly love."

Sam snapped her head to look at him. "Are you talking about yourself?" she asked. "And Maeve?"

"I would never do that to Maeve," he said in a low voice.

They came to a stop sign, and Lincoln took a right. Now they were on a straight road, and they were silent. After a few minutes,

Sam caught a glimpse of the water in the distance. She knew they were heading east, toward Narragansett Bay.

"This looks familiar," Sam said. "I've been here before, with Kate and Maeve. We went to Maynard-King—is it near here?"

He glanced over and smiled at her. "Yes," he said. "You have a good sense of direction."

"I thought we were going to Enchanted Petals."

"We are—the nursery property abuts the hospital's."

"Really?" she asked.

"Yes," he said. "The land used to be owned by the same family."

"Whose family?" she asked.

"Mine," he said.

36

GIRL #3

Tuesday, July 6; 2:00 p.m.

They kept calling her *Three*, as in Girl #3, to remind her that she was just a number, expendable, without any identity. But she had a name. Sometimes she thought they wanted her to forget her name was Caroline. It was weird, because in a way she wanted to forget—she didn't want these things to be happening to Caroline, to the girl she had been. But she knew she had to hang on to everything she knew about herself. That's how she would beat them.

Girl #3—Caroline—wore a tiara. She also wore the diamond ring. The woman did her hair so the tiara would stay put when she moved. They wanted her to believe that if she did what they wanted, all the jewelry would be hers one day.

She didn't care one bit about any of that. When William, her true love, had proposed to her, he had told her he wanted her to pick out the ring—he hadn't wanted to get her something she didn't like. She had kissed him and said she didn't need one. He said he wanted to give her something, though. It didn't have to be a diamond, but he wanted it to be something that would last their whole lives.

A desk, she had said. Maybe a desk?

They had shopped for one. They had had so much fun going to antique stores, tag sales, and the big flea market in Norwich, but he had died before it could be delivered. William was such a fine sailor. He had been captain of the sailing team at the United States Coast Guard Academy, and he had been asked to crew on *Alastair*, a maxi boat in the Newport to Bermuda Race.

Caroline didn't know that much about sailing. She had met William in New London, where she had attended Connecticut College.

She had majored in art history and minored in psychology and loved how they both told stories. In her art history classes, she would sit in the dark in the auditorium, gazing at paintings up on the screen, hearing her professors point out details that unlocked the world of the artwork. Psychology did that too—unlocked the mysteries and secrets of people's lives.

It would be understandable to imagine she had met William at a college event, because Connecticut College was right across the street from the United States Coast Guard Academy, where he had attended. But that's not how it happened. They had met at a bar on Bank Street.

She had known instantly from his haircut that he was a Coast Guard cadet. He had looked at her and smiled.

She had said, "Hi, Coastie."

He had said, "How can you tell?"

"Hmm," she said.

"Okay," he said, smiling.

"It's obvious," she said.

"Why?" he asked.

"Things," she said. He was so handsome, and she loved his eyes, and everything in her body swirled into a tornado.

"I don't know what you mean."

"I just . . ." she began.

"The way I look," he said.

She said, "Not the haircut."

"No, then what?"

"Your eyes," she said.

She had gazed strong and hard into his eyes and knew that they had already spent a lot of time staring at the sea. Then she lowered her head and tried to think of how she could tell. When she looked up at him, she saw beautiful sage-green eyes that had gazed at the horizon but that were at that moment focused only on her.

"Because you want to save people who are lost at sea," she said.

"Well, I am in the Coast Guard," he said, and they both grinned.

Oh, and the time that had followed. They met each other's families. After graduation, she got a job as an archivist at a museum. He shipped out, and it had been nearly unbearable for both of them. Somehow, they had survived his first deployment, gone crazy in love over his home-coming, and he had proposed. He had loved the fact that she wanted a desk instead of a ring.

After searching for a while, they had finally found the right one at an antique shop in Black Hall. It was a tiger maple roll top with three drawers. She couldn't wait until they could find a house together.

But that would never happen.

That year, he was chosen out of many sailors to crew aboard a yacht competing in the Bermuda Race.

"I don't want to do the race," he told her.

"Why?" she asked.

"Not sure," he said. "I just have a feeling."

She had gazed at him, into his eyes. She had never heard him say anything like that. William wasn't superstitious; he didn't have premonitions.

"There must be a reason," she said.

He nodded. "There is. The boat owner seems very interested in you. He keeps asking about you."

"That's bizarre—I have no idea who he is," she said. "What does he ask about?"

William seemed to think about it. "It started when I told him I'd asked a girl to marry me, and he wanted to know all about you. The strange thing is, I have the feeling he already knew the things I was telling him. That you attended Conn College, studied art history, worked in a museum."

"How would he know that?" she asked.

"No idea," he said.

"What does he do?" she asked.

"Basically, he's rich. He likes toys—his yacht, his cars, his Rolex, his art collection."

"How did he find you?" Caroline asked. "To ask you to be part of the race crew?"

"He follows everything about sailing, and he knew I was captain of the team. We'd met a few times, when he came to watch the races. He went to Yale, and he used to compete against the Academy back in his day."

"Maybe he's just an old romantic," she said. "And he's happy that you're in love. You are, aren't you?"

"Yeah, I am," he said.

"So go do the race and win it for me."

"I can do that," he said. He kissed her, and the whole world fell away, and it was just Caroline and William, and she forgot all about the creepy boat owner.

The entire fleet of the Bermuda Race blasted off from Newport, and they had fair winds the whole way down. They were leading in their class, and William P. Mayhew died of a head injury. No one saw it happen, but they had hit a storm ten miles north of St. David's Lighthouse in Bermuda. William was found unresponsive on deck, and the crew assumed he'd been struck on the head by the boom. The boat owner was the one who called Caroline to tell her the news.

He had told her that he would help her through it. He knew how much William had loved her, and considering that her true love had died on his boat, it was the least he could do. He asked if she needed anything. She said no.

Six months after William's death, the owner sent Caroline an invitation to a memorial that he was holding for William on board the yacht where he had died. All the guys who had sailed with William on that race would be there. They wanted to honor their crewmate, and they planned to unveil a plaque dedicated to him.

Caroline didn't respond.

Her grief over losing William was so great, she stopped being able to get up in the morning. Sunlight scalded her eyes, and she couldn't bear the blue sky because it was so beautiful, and William would never see it again. She couldn't eat. She didn't want to live. The boat owner insisted she get the best care possible, and he arranged for her to be admitted into Maynard-King. It was such an expensive, private psychiatric hospital, and Caroline said she couldn't afford it, but the owner said she shouldn't worry. Out of respect and love for William, he would cover the cost.

And from there, Caroline became Girl #3. Now, when she looked at the jewelry, the diamond the woman made her wear, she thought of William, and of the desk, and of how they hadn't needed anything shiny or fancy or expensive to cement their love.

She would go along with the people of 1740. She knew how to fake a smile—not just with her mouth, but with her eyes.

That was called a Duchenne smile. She had learned about it in college, in one of her art history classes, where they had studied portraits for clues to the subjects' psychology. The professor had told them to look for signs of happiness or grief, tension or anger. He had told them how to examine the faces in the paintings, to pay attention to their smiles. A Duchenne smile was genuine, full of true happiness, and it showed throughout the entire face, especially in the eyes. It had to show in the eyes. It was very hard to fake.

Sometimes she thought that William's death hadn't been an accident. *William died because of the boat owner,* she thought. *Because he wanted me to become Girl #3, he had to get rid of William.*

She would go along with them for now, wearing the ugly diamond, pretending to be who they wanted her to be.

But she would make them pay.

37

Tuesday, July 6; 3:00 p.m.

When Sam and Lincoln arrived at Enchanted Petals, there was a sign on the gate saying **CLOSED TODAY**. It seemed strange to Sam that a garden center would be closed on a July day. Possibly even stranger was what Lincoln said to Sam when he apologized for it.

"I feel shitty, lying to you," he said. "I know this place very well. I just felt really weird because of the whole 1740 fantasy place Yellow Pages ad—I don't want you to think it's connected at all. I have no idea how my relatives wound up with their phone number."

"Relatives?" she asked.

"Yeah," he said. "Like I said, our family owns the property."

He got out of the car and opened the gate. Sam watched him, feeling odd about the coincidence. They drove into the driveway, through a meadow, up to a white Victorian house with ornate gingerbread trim. The side door bore the sign *Enchanted Petals*—Sam could see that it was the flower shop. Behind the house were a red barn, the greenhouse, and vast flower beds.

"Where's the trail?" Sam asked. "That you told me you hiked on?"

"It's on that rise," he said, pointing to a hill at the edge of a pine forest beyond the barn.

"But you didn't have to actually hike it, to know that this place was here," Sam said. "I mean, you made it sound as if you spotted it from far away and made a haphazard discovery. That's different from saying you're related to the owners."

"I know," he said. "I'm really sorry for leaving that part out."

"Why did you, then?" Sam asked.

Lincoln exhaled. "Honestly, when you called the number and told me it rang at Enchanted Petals, I was blown away," he said. "Part of me wanted to talk you out of coming, because I feel so embarrassed—confused, actually—about my family winding up with that 1740 fantasies phone number. But I'm glad we came, so you can see how innocent this place is. It's really beautiful—do you want a tour?"

"Sure," she said, hiding how rattled she still felt.

"Let's start inside," he said. "There's an amazing library of nature books, especially about horticulture. My dad owned property in Grasse, France, where they grow flowers to make perfume. He'd like to do that here, but the growing season is different. Rhode Island is colder than Provence."

Sam thought about Crispin Adams, how she knew him only as a collector who bought paintings from Kate's gallery.

"Guess your dad has a lot of interests," Sam said. "Art, flowers, perfume . . ."

"They intersect, if you think about it. My dad likes beauty," Lincoln said.

He turned the front doorknob, but it was locked, so he walked a few steps and tried the shop door without success.

"Usually someone's here, even when the shop is closed. I don't know what's going on. Let me make a call, I'll get us in," he said.

"It doesn't matter," Sam said. "Let's just look at the grounds." Her instincts told her that she'd been right to want to check this place out—that it still had a connection to 1740—but she didn't like the fact that Lincoln had lied about his family owning it.

Lincoln ignored what she said and dialed a number on his phone.

Sam walked away from him, toward a walled rose garden. She heard him making a call, asking someone why the garden center was closed, then asking if there was a hidden key. He must not have gotten the answer he wanted because she heard him swear and then make another call.

The lawn was manicured, the hedges were trimmed, and the rose garden was well tended. The roses were in full bloom, some shades of pink and red, but mostly white and pale-cream flowers—like the ones that had been left on Dr. Tyler's grave.

"Well, that's embarrassing," Lincoln said, walking over to her.

"What?"

"I kept the big secret, that I'm related to the owners, and then I tell you all about it, and I couldn't even get us into the building," he said.

"That's really okay," she said, feeling nervous about being there at all.

"But good news—my dad is bringing us the key," he said.

"Your *dad*?" Sam asked.

"Yes," Lincoln said. "Let's go for a walk. I'll show you the green-houses and the hiking trail while we wait."

Sam hesitated. She loved nature and hiked whenever she had the opportunity, but just then she felt uneasy. Lincoln seemed too relaxed, considering Maeve was missing and the weird surprise that his family was connected to this property. Sam didn't want to go wandering off with him; in fact, she realized that she didn't even want to be there at all.

"Let's go back to the Ocean House," Sam said. "Call your dad back and save him a trip."

"He's already on the way," Lincoln said.

They walked into the greenhouse, hot and humid from sunlight pouring through the glass and moisture from the sprinklers. Long rows of benches were covered with pots of geraniums and petunias. Baskets hung overhead, artfully planted with summer flowers. A large adjacent annual garden was enclosed with a wire fence. Sam could see cosmos, zinnias, dahlias, and other bright flowers. Several plants appeared to have been gnawed down almost to the ground. Lincoln walked over to examine them.

"Damn squirrels," he said. "Wait here."

Sam watched him run into the barn. A few minutes later, he came back with a large black plastic box. He stepped over the wire enclosure and began looking for a place to put it.

"What is that?" Sam asked.

"Pest control. Rodenticide."

"No," she said. "Don't put it there. Animals eat the poison, and it causes internal bleeding, they bleed to death. It's horrible—they suffer."

"And they stop eating our flowers."

"Do you realize that if you poison the squirrels, it will also poison anything that eats them? Cats, owls, hawks?" Sam asked.

"People should keep their cats inside," Lincoln said sharply. "Outdoor cats don't stand a chance in the country—too many predators. You can't worry about everything, Sam."

Yes, you can, Sam thought. "Lincoln, please don't do it."

He completely ignored her and began walking along the rows of plants, looking for a place to hide the black plastic box. She wanted to yank it out of his hands, but he gave her a strange smile that sent prickles down the back of her neck, and she froze.

"Fine," he said. "I won't poison the rodents."

"Let's go back to the Ocean House," she said again.

"What's the difference, there or here? We're still going to be waiting."

"I want to see Kate."

"She hasn't even been answering your calls," Lincoln said.

His mood had changed dramatically since speaking to his father. She felt as if something was about to happen, and it scared her. She wasn't sure she felt it directly from Lincoln or from the garden property, but she knew she wanted to get away from there.

Just then, she heard tires on gravel. The driveway wasn't visible from here, over by the barn. Lincoln looked surprised. He walked halfway to the lodge, leaned to see around the building, and saw the car that was approaching. Then he hurried back to Sam.

"Come on, let's hide," he said.

"Who is it?" she asked.

"My dad and someone I don't want to see," Lincoln said. He reached for Sam's hand and tugged her toward the barn. "Don't let them see you."

"Why, what's wrong?" Sam asked.

"Tell you later," he said. "Just hide, Sam." He pushed her into the barn, threw the poison box into a corner, and slid the door closed behind him.

With the door closed, the barn was dark, but slivers of light came through cracks in the boards. Sam's thoughts were racing. Why was Lincoln so insistent that she hide? Was he embarrassed to be with her? Maybe he was afraid that his father would wonder why he was with her instead of Maeve. Sam felt foolish and annoyed, hiding in a barn, so she decided to just walk out into the sunshine and say hello.

But she heard the barn door creak as it was opened, her gut told her to do the opposite. She made herself very small and hid behind the firewood rack.

"I told you, Dad—no one's here," Lincoln said.

"Then whose purse is in your front seat?" Crispin Adams asked.

"A friend's. She forgot it when I dropped her off earlier," Lincoln said.

"What friend?"

"You don't know her, Dad," Lincoln said.

"How old is she?" his father asked.

There was a long silence when Lincoln didn't answer. Sam's heart was pounding. What a strange question—what would his father care about Lincoln's friend's age?

"How old is this friend?" his father pressed. "Is she a possibility?"

"Forget it, Dad," Lincoln said. "Let's get out of the barn, okay? It's damp, and it smells like mold."

"I'd like to know what you were doing in here," his father said. "You seemed very secretive when I saw you closing the door behind you."

"No," he said. "I was just looking for some rat poison. Some animal has practically decimated the annuals. I was going to put traps in the greenhouse and garden."

"Little fuckers," his father said.

"Yeah, the dahlias are basically gone."

"I'm glad you called. I need your help, and this can't wait, Lincoln," his father said. "The police are getting close. We have to move the party, got it?"

"Got it," Lincoln mumbled, dropping his voice.

"Don't sound so sullen. You're my son, and this is your inheritance. Be proud."

"Thanks, Dad," Lincoln said.

Sam stayed where she was until their voices faded and she heard the rasp of the barn door being pushed shut. She poked her head up, saw that the door was still cracked open a few inches, and crept forward. She glanced outside and didn't see anyone, so she squeezed through the door's narrow opening. She walked softly to the edge of the barn and peered around the corner to see the driveway.

Parked right behind Lincoln's Mercedes was a black Range Rover just like the one Sam had seen on the video, stopping on Bluff Avenue to pick up Maeve and her captor. Lincoln was standing there with his father and a woman with her back turned. She heard someone calling loudly from inside the Range Rover and practically jumped. Was that Kate's voice?

"This is beyond the pale. Can you shut her up?" Crispin Adams asked.

"Of course, Crispin," the woman said.

When she turned to Lincoln, Sam saw her face and gasped.

"Maybe your father believed you about no one being in the barn, but I don't," Maeve said. "I recognize that purse in your car. It belongs to Sam Lathrop. Were you really so stupid as to bring her here?"

"Maeve . . ." Lincoln began.

"You idiot. Now Sam is part of it. Go get her, and we'll bring her with us, along with her aunt."

Sam held her hand to her mouth. *That* is *Kate in the car,* she thought.

"No way," Lincoln said. "Leave Sam alone."

"You're an idiot. I'll get her myself," Maeve said, sounding furious.

They have Kate, they have Kate, and Maeve's part of it, Sam thought, shaking with panic. She pulled back, hiding around the corner, just as Maeve started toward the barn.

Sam stayed out of sight until Maeve entered the open door, and then she began to run.

She had no idea where to go, but she knew she had to get out of there. Her eyes stung with tears and fury at Maeve's betrayal as she dashed for the woods, needing to lose herself in the trees so they couldn't see her. She made sure to avoid the trail Lincoln had pointed out—they would look there for her. As soon as she was a relatively safe distance away, hidden in the forest, she stopped to call Conor for help.

That's when she realized that her phone was in her bag, the one Maeve had seen in the front seat of Lincoln's car. She couldn't go back for it; her only chance was to start running again, to keep going as fast and as far away as she could.

Tuesday, July 6; 3:30 p.m.

"We've got to locate Miranda," Conor said, focused on finding Kate. "And given the connection Sam noticed between her and Leo, we should find him too."

"Could Miranda be on the boat with him? Did you hear an engine in the background when she called?" Tom asked.

"There was background noise, but I'm not sure what it was. She talked in a low voice—someone was there, and she didn't want them to hear what she was saying about Kate."

"About Kate being next," Tom said.

"Kate's already been taken," Conor said, berserk over that fact.

"You don't know that."

"You saw that room in Fernando's house. Her car's there, and she's not. They've got her somewhere. I should have gone with her."

"Let's focus on what we know," Tom said.

Conor had called Uncle Mike to ask if he knew the name of Leo's boat or where he docked it. Mike didn't know the boat's name, but he remembered that Leo had mentioned that he kept it at Breakwater Marina in South Kingston. Tom said he knew the manager there, so he made the call. Both calls steps in finding Kate, but time was ticking by. Conor knew that anything could be happening to her, and every minute that passed meant that she was farther away from him, in greater danger.

He waited impatiently while his brother spoke with Henry, the boatyard manager. It was a short conversation—summer days at any New England marina meant busy times and long hours for yard managers. Clearly Tom and Henry had known each other for years, so Tom used sailor shorthand to get the information he needed.

"What did he say?" Conor asked.

"First, Leo told Henry the same thing he told us—that he's heading to Block Island. He said that Leo sometimes takes women out on the boat, rarely the same one twice, and he doesn't remember anyone named Miranda. He saw Leo when he was getting ready to leave today, and he had a friend with him. A judge from Providence."

"A judge? Did he give you a name?" Conor asked.

"Yes," Tom said. "Randall Flook. Do you know him?"

"No, I don't know many Rhode Island judges. We can ask Uncle Mike about him. What else did he say?" Conor asked.

"He told me the name of Leo's boat," Tom said. "You're not going to believe this."

"What?" Conor asked.

"*Rosebud*," Tom said. "Like in *Citizen Kane*—it's the last word spoken in the movie, the main character's obsession—he says it on his deathbed. Guess Leo's a film buff."

"That's not it," Conor said, his heart smashing in his chest. "An obsession, yes, but of a different kind. *Beauty and the Beast*."

"How does that work?"

"Belle asks her father to bring her back a rose from his business trip. He picks one, but it's from the Beast's garden, and the Beast says he has to trade his daughter if he wants to stay alive. The father hands Belle over to him . . . she becomes the Beast's prisoner."

"Like the women on *Psyche*," Tom said.

"And maybe on *Rosebud*," Conor said, feeling sick. "This can't be a coincidence—it's all too close. Leo is in on this, Tom. He's part of the whole thing."

38

Tuesday, July 6; 3:45 p.m.

Kate sat in the back seat of Crispin's Range Rover as they drove away from Enchanted Petals, feeling as if she was living in a nightmare tableau staged by a surrealist. Jean Cocteau couldn't have done it better. She was sitting between Suzanne and a girl she had never met before. Crispin sat in the front passenger seat.

To cap the grotesque dream quality of her day, the young woman Kate had loved like another niece was driving.

Maeve was with 1740.

Kate's heart had been pounding with shock and heartbreak ever since Maeve had stepped out of the shadows in Fernando Harris's studio. They hadn't been alone, so Kate had so far been unable to look her straight in the eye. But she couldn't hold the word, the question inside any longer, and she asked Maeve: "Why?"

She felt weak, as if the fight had taken everything out of her, and she wondered if she had actually said the word out loud. But she must have, because everyone in the car—except Maeve, at the wheel—turned their heads to look at her: Crispin, Suzanne on her right, and the girl she had never met before on her left.

"Why?" she asked again.

"Is that a rhetorical question, Kate?" Crispin asked. "Because I have an answer, but you wouldn't understand it."

"I'm not asking you, Crispin. I'm asking Maeve."

Maeve didn't reply. Kate could see that she was gripping the steering wheel tightly. Her eyes flicked to the rearview mirror, but as soon as they met Kate's, they quickly looked back at the road.

"You can't even look at me," Kate said.

"Shhh," Suzanne said, patting Kate's knee, making Kate flinch. "Don't make it worse."

Kate wasn't sure how it could be worse—except if they had gotten Sam too. But why had they taken Kate? Suzanne, Maeve, and the girl whose name Kate did not know were young—in their early twenties. Kate was twenty years older, certainly not the age that Crispin and the others seemed to target. And that question, like the word *why*, spilled from Kate's lips without her planning it.

"If Maeve won't answer me, why don't you tell me, Crispin?" she asked.

"It's a club," Suzanne said. "You wouldn't understand."

"That seems to be the party line," Kate said, looking at her. "First Crispin, now you. What wouldn't I understand?"

The girl on her left leaned close. "Don't challenge them, just go along with it for now," she whispered.

"What did you say, Caroline?" Maeve asked sharply.

"Caroline, you're not permitted to speak to our guest," Crispin said. "She's not part of us. She's not one of you."

"What am I not part of?" Kate asked, focusing on Caroline's words *for now*. Had she meant that she knew they would get through this, to some sort of other side?

"The club," Suzanne said.

"1740?" Kate asked.

"You know about that?" Suzanne asked.

"It's hard not to. The number was on your truck, on the note you wrote and left on Jonathan Tyler's grave. You gave yourself away."

"It's important to me," Suzanne said.

"Was it important to your mother too?" Kate asked.

"My mother?" Suzanne asked.

"Belinda," Kate said.

Suzanne tried to hide a smile but didn't reply.

"1740 has to do with Dr. Tyler, doesn't it? Your mother's dead husband. Something that started with girls when they were patients at Maynard-King."

"You don't know anything," Suzanne said.

Kate let that go. "Whenever it started, it's centered around *Beauty and the Beast. La Belle et la Bête.*"

"You know the French," Suzanne said, almost admiringly.

"Did Belinda name you 'Suzanne' after the author?" Kate asked. "Gabrielle-Suzanne Barbot de Villeneuve?"

"Maybe I chose the name myself," Suzanne said. "We come into the world with the names our parents gave us. But when we learn from the right teacher, we become someone brand new."

"The right teacher?" Kate asked.

"How do you know so much about *Beauty and the Beast?*" Suzanne asked, sounding genuinely curious. Kate looked at her, realized how young she really was. How young and brainwashed. Was the club really a cult?

"Cocteau," Kate said. "One of my favorite artists. The photograph is a still from his film. You know, the one with the Beast looming over the sleeping woman. The black-and-white photo above the bed in the mansion on the island."

"Kindly shut up, Kate," Crispin said.

Kate was squeezed so tightly between Suzanne and Caroline, she felt Caroline trembling at the mention of the Beast and the bed. Or was that Kate herself, shaking to think of what these young women had gone through?

"You need to be trained," Suzanne said. "We have to introduce you to our lady."

"That sounds religious," Kate said.

"It's spiritual," Suzanne said. "It transforms us. She teaches us the correct behavior and how to please."

"To please men who use you?" Kate asked.

"You don't know anything yet," Suzanne said.

"Where are we going?" Kate asked. "Where are you taking us, Maeve?"

"To the Finishing School," Maeve said. "The secret garden, where the roses grow."

And where, if you pick one, there is a forfeit to be paid, Kate thought.

Tuesday, July 6; 4:00 p.m.

Sam stumbled through the woods. Her mind was on fire, thinking of Kate. The sound of her aunt yelling from the back of that car filled Sam with the worst helplessness she had ever felt. She reeled with the shock of realizing that Maeve—and Lincoln—had fooled everyone. They were all in on it, Crispin and Suzanne too. And they had Kate.

She crashed through thick brush, snagged by briars that tore at her clothes and scratched her legs. Eventually she stumbled upon a very narrow trail that made the going easier. She hoped that it wasn't the same one that Lincoln had talked about—she didn't think it was, because he had pointed up toward a hill, and this ground was flat.

Besides, the trail seemed too haphazard to have been cleared by humans; she thought perhaps it was a track used by deer or other wildlife. She hadn't seen any houses, so she assumed that she was still on Lincoln's family's property.

Why had he even brought her to Enchanted Petals? Now that she knew how involved he and Crispin were with 1740, she wondered if Lincoln had been setting her up. Had he planned to do something to Sam, then changed his mind when they were in the barn and his father showed up?

Sam was furious at herself for leaving her phone in the car. She wanted to call Conor that minute and tell him to hurry, find Kate, save her *now*. Her only hope was the fact that Miranda had warned him that Kate was about to be taken. Conor had snapped into action. *I'll help him*, Sam thought. *We're going to save Kate.*

That became her mantra, and she timed the words with the rhythm of her steps as she lengthened her stride and ran faster: *We're going to save Kate.* Knowing that she had a mission made her feel brave, made her think about Kate instead of being scared for herself. Kate had been her champion, her cheerleader, not just her aunt, but a friend and, at times, a stand-in for her mother.

Every so often, she caught a glimpse through foliage of blue water off to her right. Was that a lake, or could it be Narragansett Bay? If it were the bay, and she kept it to her right, it meant she was traveling north. At some point, the trail had to intersect with a road. She would come upon a house, a neighborhood. But deep down, she remembered what Lincoln had said: that the Enchanted Petals property abutted the Maynard-King grounds.

And Sam admitted to herself that that was where she was heading. This evil had originated at Maynard-King, with Dr. Jonathan Tyler. His grave was where she, Kate, and Maeve had found the note in Suzanne's handwriting. Maeve's act had been so convincing. Neither Sam nor Kate had had any idea that they were being played. But Sam knew that now, and that knowledge was her power.

The woods began to thin out, and up ahead she spotted an expanse of green grass. It was a clear line of demarcation between forest and lawn; she suspected it might be the spot where the Enchanted Petals property met that of Maynard-King.

A white rail fence ran the length of what appeared to be a well-tended lawn. She stood still and stared at the top rail. If the fence were electrified, there would be electrodes and wires running between the posts. There were none. She figured that the hospital had a sophisticated security operation, so she scanned the area for cameras. She couldn't see any place where they would be mounted, but then she heard a faint beep.

She knew immediately what it was. Both Cloudlands and Kate's gallery had advanced alarm systems that relied on cellular connections to transmit data to the monitoring company. When the satellites passed over or the cell tower misfired, the systems lost signal, and the console began to emit an intermittent beep.

The sound seemed to be coming from one of the fence posts. She walked closer and saw the camera—the rim of the lens was white and camouflaged the camera by blending it into the white fence. She saw a red light, indicating that the camera was offline, so she jumped the fence and ran fast across the lawn until she reached a copse of birch trees.

The grounds of Maynard-King began to look familiar. She skirted the lawn until she came to the boxwood hedge that marked the back edge of the cemetery. The late-afternoon sun struck the granite head-stones with golden light. Up ahead was the angel that marked the grave of Dr. Jonathan Tyler.

It should have been a demon, not an angel, Sam thought. She looked around. Unsurprisingly, she seemed to be the only person here. It was early July, and people should be doing summer things, not visiting the dead. She wasn't exactly sure what she was hoping to accomplish here, but it seemed like a good place to start—seeing if there were any more messages at Dr. Tyler's grave while she contemplated how to find a phone and call Conor.

She ducked between headstones and arrived at Dr. Tyler's memorial. There were notes stuck into the angel's wings. Earrings and bracelets and seashells and a bird's nest were piled on the ground. Sam was tempted to read the notes; maybe there was one from Suzanne or Maeve or any of the other sad, sick girls offering up their lives to the dream—whatever it was—of the murdered doctor. Or to the memory of his wife, Belinda. Sam knew that there could be clues in their writings.

She sat on the grass, catching her breath after her long run. She was about to reach for one of the folded pieces of paper when she heard the whine of an engine behind her. Sam turned and saw Jennifer hopping off her ATV, running over to stand above her.

"You shouldn't be here," Jennifer said.

"I know," Sam said, staring at the walkie-talkie in the holster on Jennifer's belt. "Please don't call anyone. I'm leaving now."

"They're looking for you," Jennifer said. "We've all been told to report if we see you."

"Please," Sam said. "Let me leave, I won't bother anyone . . . I just want to cut through the grounds, okay?"

"Come with me," Jennifer said. "I don't want them to find you. And hurry, they're checking everywhere. They'll be down here soon."

Jennifer climbed onto the ATV and gestured that Sam should get on behind her. Sam hesitated, scared and confused. After what had just happened with Lincoln and Maeve, she didn't trust anyone.

"No," she said. "I'll be fine on my own."

"You won't," Jennifer said. "You don't know them. Get on! We don't have time . . ."

Sam stood frozen, pressure building inside her chest. She thought of the way Maeve had come charging toward the barn, where Sam had been hiding. The look in her eyes was wild, almost mad, and Sam had known that Maeve meant her harm.

"Are you coming?" Jennifer asked.

Sam held her breath, trying to decide. But did she really have any choice? Not knowing if she was making the biggest mistake of her life, Sam climbed onto the ATV behind Jennifer.

"Hold on," Jennifer said. "It'll be a bumpy ride."

Sam reached her arms around Jennifer's waist. They set off so fast, Sam nearly fell off. Jennifer sped them down the hill, through a grove of pines, and onto a dirt access road. Sam heard gravel under the tires. Dirt flew up into her mouth and eyes. She blinked hard to clear her vision, but her eyes stung and she couldn't see, so she just closed them and felt the ATV hit rut after rut and hoped that Jennifer wasn't delivering her straight to 1740.

Tuesday, July 6; 4:00 p.m.

"Okay, what's all this about?" Mike asked when Conor and Tom found him on the Ocean House verandah, having an iced tea.

"Who is Judge Flook?" Conor asked.

"Randall Flook?" Mike asked, resting his book on the table in front of him. "He's a Superior Court judge. A good friend of mine. Why?"

"He's also a friend of Leo's?" Conor asked.

"Yes, we play golf together, often in the same foursome. Sometimes they go fishing," Mike said.

"That's what they're doing right now," Conor said. "Or at least that's what Leo says."

"What are you getting at, Conor?" Mike asked. His expression was perplexed, bordering on angry. "Ever since you called me, I've been wondering. You think Leo's lying?"

"He is," Conor said. "He's part of it, Uncle Mike. He's in 1740, and I have to find him and get him to tell me what he knows so I can find Kate."

"You're not making any sense," Mike said. "Sit down and explain what you're talking about."

Conor let out a huge sigh of frustration, put his hands on his head, and paced in a circle. Conor *knew* he wasn't making sense, and he was glad when Tom took over.

"Uncle Mike," Tom said. "The bottom line is that Kate has been taken. Her last known location is a crime scene, and there is evidence that it was used by 1740."

"Explain more," Mike said, sitting up straighter. "Where is this crime scene?"

"Fernando Harris's studio in Mystic, Connecticut," Tom said.

"Kate was there? You're sure? When?"

"This morning," Conor said, jumping in. "She was going to see her art conservator. When we got there, her car was in the driveway, but she was gone. We went through the house, and there's a bedroom just like the one we found on the island—it's tricked out for someone's fantasies, and it has restraints for holding women."

"God," Mike said in such a deep voice it sounded like a prayer. "Holding women? You're sure?"

"Yes," Conor said. "There's blood on the handcuffs and on the bedsheets." He felt sick, thinking of what could be happening with Kate.

"Early today," Tom said, "a young woman was found murdered, dropped into the ocean, with wounds on her wrists consistent with having been restrained."

"Sexual assault?" Mike asked.

"We won't know until the autopsy," Conor said. He stepped closer, then sat down next to their uncle. "Right now, I just need to find Kate."

"Of course. But what does any of this have to do with Leo and Randall?" Mike asked.

"I don't know about Randall, but things are adding up about Leo. They are on Leo's boat now."

"You think they've got Kate on board?" Mike asked, sounding shocked.

"They could," Conor said. "It's one possibility."

Mike was silent for a long moment, obviously pondering something. Conor had the idea he was weighing whether to tell them what he was thinking. Finally, he did.

"The rooms," he said. "With the restraints. It sounds to me as if women are being trafficked. As if that is the focus, the purpose, of the people involved with 1740. Would you agree?"

"Yes," Conor said. He glanced at Tom. "Tell him."

"Uncle Mike, there is the same setup on a boat called *Psyche*. Everything about it is familiar to me. The Coast Guard is always on patrol for human traffickers. And we find them, even right here in Rhode Island. Harbors where you would least expect it. On boats you'd never guess."

Mike put his head in his hands for a few seconds, then looked up.

"Some detective I am. Our little group failed completely," he said, and Conor knew he was referring to the Old Detectives—himself, Anne, Nola, Edward, and Leo.

"Don't worry about that now," Conor said.

"Rhode Island has a task force to combat human trafficking," Mike said. "Federal, state, and local law enforcement officers. They all work together to investigate the crimes and bring justice to the victims."

"That's good," Tom said.

"Guess who is on the task force advisory committee? Representing the legal community?" Mike asked.

Conor just stared at him.

"Leo Kennedy," Mike said. "And Randall Flook is the federal court judge who hears many of the cases. He is responsible for issuing—or not issuing—warrants. As much as I admire him, he's known for being a stickler in terms of giving warrants to search or make arrests when it comes to trafficking. He gives the suspects the benefit of the doubt more than the prosecutors wish he would."

"You mean he's got his thumb on the scale in favor of the traffickers?" Conor asked.

"That's not what I would have said until now. You know that I am very strict when it comes to the Fourth Amendment . . ."

"Search and seizure," Tom said.

"Yes. The government has all the power, so I always want to make sure the police follow the rules and don't take shortcuts. In general, I might be more conservative in granting warrants than Randall. But right now, hearing all this, I have to wonder about him. Before I go off on this, tell me—specifically what makes you think they are involved?"

"I don't know about Judge Flook," Conor said. "But the name of Leo's boat is *Rosebud*."

"So what?" Mike asked, frowning.

"Roses are a theme from *Beauty and the Beast*," Conor said. "These boats have names connected with it. Just like the sailboat, *Psyche*. Kate told me that the inspiration for the fairy tale is the myth of Cupid and Psyche. And there's a boat tied up at Maynard-King called *Zémire*."

"What the hell is that?"

"Kate told me it's from an opera, the same story—a guy stops at a castle garden to pick a rose for his daughter, and he winds up having to sacrifice her to the owner."

"A rose," Mike said, sounding stunned. "*Rosebud.*"

He fell silent, obviously shaken by the explanation. Conor stared at him, getting even more restless. None of this was getting them closer to finding Kate. Tom's phone buzzed. He glanced at Conor, then answered the call and put it on speaker.

"Sir, this is IS Texiera. You wanted a report on the Hatteras, *Rosebud*," the voice said, and Conor knew that IS stood for intelligence specialist.

"*Rosebud* is not off Block Island," IS Texiera continued. "She's currently at a dock in Narragansett. I'm texting you the coordinates now."

As soon as Conor heard "Narragansett," he didn't even have to ask where the GPS latitude and longitude would place Leo's boat. Tom disconnected and turned back to Conor and Mike, just as Anne and the Aldriches came up the hotel stairs from the beach.

"Conor, we've got to go," Tom said.

"To Maynard-King?" Conor asked.

"Yes. *Rosebud* is at their dock."

"I'm going with you," Mike said.

"Wait, what is this about?" Anne asked, sounding alarmed.

"Kate is missing," Mike said, standing and putting his arm around his wife. "And she could very well be aboard Leo's boat." Conor could see that Anne was clearly distressed.

"What about that other girl, Kate's assistant? I thought *she* was missing . . ." Anne said.

"It's an epidemic," Edward Aldrich said, with a smile, as if he'd said something hilarious. Conor wanted to ram the smile right down his throat, but Tom caught his brother's arm.

"Leave it," Tom said.

"Edward, shut up," Nola said sharply.

"Sorry," Edward said, looking sheepish. "Really, I didn't mean it."

Mike kissed Anne goodbye, and he hurried across the verandah with Tom and Conor. They walked down the curved front steps of the Ocean House. The valets had kept Tom's truck in the top lot, and Dermot handed him the keys.

As Tom drove them east toward Route 1, Conor thought about what had just happened. When he had mentioned *Rosebud* to the group, Mike—clearly upset—had said that Kate might be aboard. Why had Edward made that joke instead of asking what Kate, whom he had just learned was missing, could be doing aboard a boat owned by his friend Leo Kennedy?

Did Edward know something about Leo's involvement?

Tuesday, July 6; 4:15 p.m.

Jennifer drove the ATV down the dirt road for half a mile or so, then cut through a stretch of manicured grass. The white hospital building was visible across the lawn, and Sam felt nervous. They were exposed, and anyone looking out the window could see them. Panic seized her—maybe Jennifer was going to hand her over to the group.

But then Jennifer sped straight toward the woods and drove along the property line. Now, they were at least partially hidden by shadows. Sam stared at the trail, just beyond the white fence, the one she had taken on her way from Enchanted Petals. Jennifer slowed the vehicle when she approached a break in the fence.

"Why are we stopping?" Sam asked.

"I have to think," Jennifer said. "Of the best place to go. They assume that you are here—or on your way here."

"How would they know that?"

"Because Maeve called to report it. She said that Lincoln let it slip to you that the properties were side by side. It's obvious that you would come here, because it's familiar to you. She said you'd try to hide until Conor brought the cops."

"You know Maeve?" Sam asked, wanting to bolt. "When we came here that time, and she was with us, you acted as if you'd never seen her before."

"I do know her, Sam. I know her very well. And I know Lincoln too," Jennifer said.

Sam scrambled off the vehicle and started to run. She didn't know where to go. She would start by losing herself in the woods, getting a head start on Jennifer.

"Don't go, Sam. I hate them!" Jennifer called.

The words thudded out, and when Sam turned around, she could see despair in Jennifer's eyes.

"I was used by them, but I was never one of them," Jennifer said. "They wanted me to be, they wanted me to help them with the new girls, but I'll die before I do that."

Sam took a few steps toward her. "But that first time, when we met you at the grave, you asked me, 'Are you one of us?' I remember that so clearly. We all assumed that you meant a patient here—not part of 1740. You sounded as if you practically worshipped Dr. Tyler. How much people admired him, how he did so much for his patients . . ."

"I was a patient, and I will tell you everything. But right now, I have to figure out where to hide you," Jennifer said.

"You know what's down that path?" Sam asked, pointing at the woods.

"Yes, Enchanted Petals. We can't go there. The members are all part of 1740."

"Members of what? It's a garden center."

Jennifer shook her head. "No, it only looks that way. It's a front for the group."

Sam nodded. That made sense—no wonder the phone number from the Yellow Pages ad still belonged to them, still rang at a place where 1740 gathered.

"But you know," Sam said. "It might be the perfect place to hide—I was just there, and they'd never think I would go back."

Jennifer half smiled and nodded, as if impressed by Sam's idea.

"That could work," Jennifer said.

"So let's go," Sam said.

"Not on that trail," Jennifer said. "It's too narrow for the ATV. We'll take the old logging road. It's never used, but it's a lot wider."

Sam wondered if the logging road was the trail Lincoln told her about. It felt dangerous to her, thinking that he might look for her there.

"Let's just walk through the woods," Sam said. "The path is more hidden. Just leave the ATV here."

Jennifer shook her head and patted the locked storage compartment. Then she opened it. Sam leaned over to look. She saw a pile of earrings, bracelets, charms, locks of hair, gauze bandages, and some photographs. There was a stack of cards held together with a ribbon.

"I've saved everything," Jennifer said. "People left offerings at the grave. And not just former patients—even some of the 1740 members. It's evidence, Sam."

"It is," Sam said.

"That's why I can't just leave the ATV behind. They'll find everything and destroy it before the police can get it."

"We need a phone," Sam said. "I'll call Conor."

Jennifer reached into her pocket and removed an iPhone. "I'd let you use mine, but it's a hospital phone, and there will be a record. They can even look at it in real time, and they'll see who I'm calling."

"Conor might get here before they figure it out," Sam said.

"And he might not. Let's take your idea and go to Enchanted Petals. You cut through the fence here, and I'll meet you at the access road. Even if they see me on camera, they won't suspect anything. They'll think I'm patrolling, looking for you." Jennifer pointed to the right.

"Just circle behind the pine trees and keep going straight until you see a clearing. That's where your path will intersect the road. I'll get there first. You'll see me."

Sam nodded. She set off toward the woods and heard Jennifer driving away. Sam's blood was pounding in her head. She could follow Jennifer's directions to the access road, or she could run in the opposite direction and try to escape on her own. It was a matter of whether she trusted Jennifer or not. This could all be an act, to get Sam to a place where she could be captured.

She headed toward the pine trees. Her instincts told her that Jennifer was telling the truth. That Jennifer wanted to help Sam. Something had happened to Jennifer, here at the hospital, that had turned her from a follower into someone who hated the people here. So much, that she wanted to give her evidence to the police and bring 1740 crashing down.

39

Tuesday, July 6; 4:15 p.m.

Maeve drove the Range Rover past the guard at Maynard-King, and Kate noticed how they exchanged friendly greetings. It had been very different when they had entered the grounds just two days ago, when Kate had still believed that Maeve cared about her and Conor. She stared at the back of her head, feeling shaken to her core.

When they approached the main hospital building, Kate wondered if she would be taken inside. Adrenaline was pumping through her veins; it had been since that morning, at Fernando's studio. But instead of pulling up to the front door, Maeve drove around the building to the little white house with green shutters.

"You're taking me to the business office?" Kate asked, remembering how Conor had knocked on the door, looking for Darla Vandeveer and information about Leprince de Beaumont Associates: LP de BA.

Nobody answered her. When Maeve stopped the car, Crispin got out and opened the back door for Suzanne. They both walked away without a word. Kate watched them go up the hospital stairs and disappear inside. She glanced at Caroline and raised her eyebrows, asking if she knew what they were doing. Caroline mouthed the word *Wait*.

That silent communication reminded Kate of seeing Maeve on the Ocean House security footage.

"You went to a lot of trouble," Kate said to Maeve, still in the driver's seat. "To lay the groundwork for whatever this is. Saying 'help' to the camera?"

"Let's not, Kate," Maeve said. "It wasn't personal."

"You dropped this," Kate said, reaching into her pocket and pulling out the gold chain.

"Thank you," Maeve said, reaching between the front seats to take it from Kate. But Kate's hand closed around it, and she pulled it back.

"What do you mean, 'it wasn't personal'?" Kate asked. "Of course it was. You worked in my gallery, helped me plan my wedding. Had you known all along that it wouldn't happen, that it would be ruined?"

Maeve stared at Kate in the rearview mirror.

"You must have known," Kate said. "I've heard all about how Belinda tricked Garrett into inviting her. And since it turns out you and Belinda knew each other, I'm sure you both had fun planning it. Hiring Suzanne to write out the place cards. And was it you who slipped that little 'mistake' into the wedding program?"

Kate pictured the program. She had looked at it just last night and caught the word that hadn't been in the text she had originally given Maeve to send to the printer:

KATE **W**OODWARD **& C**ONOR **R**EID

SATURDAY, **J**ULY **3**

CEREMONY **6:30** P.M.

WATCH **H**ILL **C**HAPEL

BELLES WILL RING!

DINNER AND **D**ANCING TO **F**OLLOW

OCEAN **H**OUSE

"'Belles will ring,'" Kate said. "You put that in for Belinda, didn't you?"

But Maeve didn't reply.

Maeve got out, then held the back door for Caroline and Kate. Kate slid across the seat slowly. When she stepped out of the car, Maeve put one handcuff on her left wrist and snapped the other on Caroline's right wrist, securing them together.

The links rattled when Kate and Caroline began to walk. Kate couldn't stop feeling that with every inch, she was getting farther away from Conor. She and Caroline followed Maeve to the front door. A woman answered, and Kate recognized her as Gabrielle, from the last visit.

Gabrielle led them into what looked like a professor's office, if the office was in Versailles. The pale gray-blue wall panels were decorated with ornate gold-leafed carvings of birds, vines, and leaves. There was a cream-colored Louis XV–style writing desk, similar to one that Kate had bid on at auction a few years before. A stack of books sat on the desk's surface. The gold-bordered green leather blotter was piled high with file folders.

There were two sitting areas at either end of the room, with formal blue silk-upholstered French furniture. The chairs had tapered legs with fluted columns, the gold-leafed arms adorned with carved rosettes and laurel leaves. Kate took in the atmosphere, feeling sick. The designer had tried to make this space romantic—half boudoir, half classroom.

Above the door was a carved sign with a blue background and gold letters that spelled:

THE FINISHING SCHOOL

Behind the desk was a blackboard with sticks of white chalk in the tray. A pointer leaned against the wall. Written on the blackboard were a series of phrases: *How may I please you? I'm ready to obey. Thank you for guiding me. I submit to your will. I will keep your secrets. I love you and I know you love me.*

A side table held a pile of drawing pads, small bottles of India ink, and crow quill pens, just like the one Suzanne had used to write the place cards. Kate glanced down and saw that someone had been practicing calligraphy, copying the disturbing lines that were written on the blackboard. She noticed that there were inkblots and cross outs, as if the writer couldn't bring herself to complete the assignment.

"You can sit there," Gabrielle said to Kate and Caroline, pointing at one of the sofas.

"Can you uncuff us?" Kate asked.

"Not right now," Gabrielle said. "Darla will take care of that when she gets here."

The elusive Darla. Apparently, she really did exist. Kate sat down next to Caroline. She gazed at the young woman's hands, folded in her lap. The long sleeves of her white dress hid her arms and wrists, but Kate could see red marks under the cuffs of her sleeves. They were too old to have been made today, and she pictured the restraints she had seen on *Psyche*.

"Are you okay?" Kate asked Caroline quietly.

"It's better you don't talk," Caroline whispered, her voice shaking. "You'll get in trouble."

"How much more trouble can I be in?" Kate asked.

Caroline's uneasy silence let Kate know that there was plenty more.

Kate stared at Caroline's wrists. She wanted to help her—get her salves, bandages, have her checked by a doctor to see if the wounds were infected. Kate had been an older sister, and although she didn't have children of her own, loving and raising her niece had made her protective of any younger person. Caroline looked terrified.

"How old are you?" Kate asked.

"Twenty-one."

"Were you on *Psyche*?" Kate asked, pointing at the raw, red circle around her wrist.

"How do you know about that?" Caroline asked.

"Because I saw the boat. I know that women were held there. They kept you there?"

"The boat is not long term. It is just a way-spot."

"A way-spot?"

"They call it that. A stopping place to see if we're worthy for the next step. They test us, determine which of us is a fighter . . ."

"And the fighters don't make it to the next step?"

"No, the opposite. They get rid of the meek ones, the ones who just give in."

"What do they do with them?" Kate asked.

"They disappear," Caroline said. "We don't see them again."

"How many of you are there?"

"No more than two or three at a time. Girl #1, Girl #2 . . . Once they get to Girl #3, they start over. I am the most recent #3. They call us girls, never women. But there are lots of 'graduates.' Girls—women—who came before us."

"What do they graduate from?" Kate asked.

"The Finishing School," Caroline said.

"And what happens when you graduate?"

"You have the honor of becoming the latest Belle," Caroline said, her voice breaking. She looked over at Kate with red-rimmed eyes. "Why are you here?"

"I'm trying to figure that out myself," Kate said.

"It's just that, most of the women they bring to the boat, and the houses, are younger than you. Around my age. They get us at the hospital. Were you a patient at Maynard-King, is that where they found you?" Caroline asked.

"No," Kate said. "Is that where they found you?"

"Yes," Caroline said. "I was very sick when I first got to the hospital. My fiancé died in a terrible accident at sea. I was really broken by it, and I didn't want to live anymore."

Kate was shocked and immediately filled with compassion. She wanted to hug Caroline, to comfort her.

"I'm so sorry, Caroline," Kate said. "What was his name?"

"William. He was the best man in the world," Caroline said, staring down. Kate saw tears drop onto the white fabric covering her knees.

"And somehow you wound up with these people?"

"Yes. I was targeted from the start. The older guy who was in the car with us just now—Crispin. William sailed with him, in the Bermuda Race. Before he left, he told me he thought Crispin was fixated on me."

"How bizarre," Kate said. "How did he know you?"

"I studied art history, and he knew one of my professors. He's interested in art."

"Yes, he is," Kate said, thinking of the many hours she had spent talking about American Impressionism with him, listening to him talk about his collection and the paintings that he wished to add to it.

"I guess he spotted me in one of my classes," Caroline said. "I never saw him, but he singled me out and got to know William."

"Why did he want to know William?"

Tears welled in Caroline's eyes, and she couldn't hold back the sobs. It was so hard for Kate to not be able to hug her, let her cry for as long as she needed.

"They say it was an accident," Caroline said, when she could talk again. "But I've stayed awake so many nights, running through the possibilities. William was in the Coast Guard. He knew boats better than anyone. Supposedly he was knocked out by the boom, in a big gust of wind, but I don't believe it—it just doesn't feel right to me."

"That is so awful," Kate said. "Are you saying you think Crispin killed him?"

"I didn't think that at the time. All I knew was that William wasn't coming home. I got so depressed, I stopped being able to eat or get out of bed. Crispin said he felt responsible for my breakdown, because William had died on his boat, and he insisted on getting me in here—Maynard-King, one of the best psychiatric hospitals in the East. And he made sure I was assigned to a woman he said was the 'best therapist' on staff."

"Was she?" Kate asked.

"She has a PhD in psychology. She is very respected in the field. She's written papers, been interviewed about her research, is quite well known. But she's evil, Kate," Caroline said. "Just like Crispin."

"In what way?"

"She works at another institution, and she has a private practice," Caroline said. "She convinces the women she treats to come here. She is a big believer in recovered memories. One of her tricks is to manipulate her patients into thinking they were sexually abused—that that is the root of their trauma. Of course, it sometimes is. And that is tragic. But other times, she found ways to warp people's minds into remembering horrible things that never really happened."

"Why?" Kate asked.

"To isolate them. Have them turn against their families for not protecting them. Have them hate their fathers or brothers or whomever. To get them to talk about sex. One of the worst parts is that it diminishes the women who really *were* abused in that way. But she doesn't care. All she wants is to beat us all down so far that we'll forget who we really are."

"You haven't forgotten who you really are," Kate said. "I can tell."

"Thank you," Caroline said. "I think she knows that too. It's one reason she gave me back my name—letting me be Caroline again, instead of Girl #3. She said I was ready to start training the others."

"Training them?" Kate asked.

"Look," Caroline said, gesturing. "Those sayings on the board? We have to memorize them. She makes us write them down, with pen and ink, and our handwriting has to be beautiful and perfect."

Kate stared at the subservient phrases on the board in the front of the room. More grooming, Kate thought. It was the way abusers indoctrinated their victims, the lead-up to what's to come. Teach them to please, to go along, to keep it all secret.

"Who are the sayings for? Who are you supposed to please?" Kate asked.

"Men," Caroline said. "The members."

"The members of 1740?" Kate asked.

"Yes. One at a time, we become Belle. And the men—whichever man whose turn it is—is the Beast. The owner of the castle."

"And the psychologist is the teacher?"

"She is the main teacher," Caroline said. "But sometimes she chooses one of us, once we've been here for a while, to start passing on our knowledge. We're like training teachers, junior professors. I've just been moved up, into that position." Her voice dropped. "But there is no way. I'd rather go through . . . what they do to me . . . than have to pass this on to other girls. I will never do that to them."

"What will happen to you if you don't?" Kate asked.

Caroline didn't speak for a moment. She turned her head and looked Kate straight in the eye. "I have a plan," she said. "I can't tell you right now. I don't want to lose my nerve. But if they keep you here for a while, you'll see."

"Okay," Kate said.

"I just can't figure out why you're here. You're too wise, you've learned too much about life for them. They have a big thing about age, about girls when they're inexperienced. I'm already at the outer edge of what's acceptable. So why did they take you?"

"It began the night before my wedding day . . ." Kate said.

"You're married?"

"I was supposed to be. But someone ruined it—the original Belle."

"The 'original Belle'? Do you mean Belinda Tyler?"

"Yes."

"She was Dr. Tyler's widow . . . they used to worship her here almost as much as him. What did she do?"

"She showed me a baby picture and said that my fiancé was the father." Kate paused. "You said 'used to' worship her. So you know she's dead?"

Caroline nodded. "Yes, they told us. She was very important to them—one of the biggest recruiters. She was the best at psychological manipulation—she'd learned directly from Dr. Tyler. I didn't know her well at all, but she could twist things around, make me believe that what I was feeling wasn't real, that I was misinterpreting what she'd said, that I wasn't seeing things that were right in front of my eyes."

"Making you doubt yourself," Kate asked.

"Yes," Caroline said.

"That's unforgivable," Kate said.

"It's what they do here," Caroline said. "People think Maynard-King is a place to be treated and regain mental health, but it's the opposite. Once you come here, if you're a young woman, it's a place to be driven crazy. Sometimes I feel I'm insane."

"It sounds like that's what they wanted," Kate said. "But you're not insane."

"I know," Caroline said. "I'm holding on. I keep thinking of William, how I have to get out of here for him."

"That's good, Caroline," Kate said, and she thought of Conor, how she needed to get back to him. "Do it for yourself, not just William. Fight with everything you have."

They heard a commotion in the hallway. Kate was dying to ask Caroline more questions, to see if she knew who the father of Belinda's daughter was. But the footsteps in the hall got closer, so she stopped talking. She sat straight up, turning to face the door to see who would enter.

Someone Kate had never seen before stepped in. The woman was looking at a notebook she held in her hand.

"Is that her?" Kate whispered. "The woman who trains you?"

But before Caroline could answer, the woman smiled and spoke.

"Hello, ladies. Good to see you, Caroline. And you must be Kate," she said. "I'm Darla Vandeveer. I'm so pleased to meet you."

Tuesday, July 6; 4:30 p.m.

Conor thought they should drive to Maynard-King, but Tom argued that since their focus was on the two vessels currently tied to the hospital's dock, *Zémire* and *Rosebud*, being aboard a boat made more sense, in case a water chase became necessary. Conor had to admit that made sense. Also, if they drove, they would alert the security guard right away.

The three Reid men boarded Tom's boat, *Meteor*. It was a thirty-two-foot custom Paul James lobster boat. People seeing it out on the water expected it to be puttering through coves, the engine idling while Tom took his time pulling pots; but instead, it was a sleeper, tricked out with an 800-horsepower 550 Chevy engine.

And now, Conor was very glad for his brother's fast boat. It wasn't a high-performance powerboat like a Donzi, but it could really move. It surprised boaters, seeing what they assumed was a sleepy work boat go flying through Block Island Sound. Tom was at the wheel in the cockpit, with the throttle open. Conor stood, bracing himself against the console, and Mike was seated.

"Boys, I hope this is a fool's errand," Mike said. "Confronting Leo Kennedy and Randall Flook about sex trafficking!"

"We'll find out if they're involved," Conor said.

"Good lord," Mike said. "They're my friends."

"Uncle Mike, I understand that. Maybe you shouldn't have come," Conor said. "This is going to put you in an awkward position."

"Well, that's for sure," Mike said. "But if they do have anything to do with Kate being missing, you'll need me with you."

"Yeah?" Tom asked.

"Yeah. Because I'll book them and arraign them and remand them all at the same time," Mike said. "I'm the only one on this boat with the power to do that, right?"

"Uncle Mike, I'm not sure that even you have that power," Conor said, "but I one hundred percent appreciate the spirit."

There was heavy boat traffic in lower Narragansett Bay. Many people took vacations the week of July 4, and Rhode Island was a favorite spot for people who loved being on the water. There were superyachts, small craft, tour boats, and the *Iver Prosperity*—a red-hulled oil tanker on its way up the bay to offload its cargo in Providence.

Approaching Maynard-King, Tom drove closer to shore and entered a no-wake zone. He slowed down. Other boaters ignored the rule, continuing to go so fast that their white wakes rocked kayaks and small sailboats, sent waves splashing into docks and beaches. Conor could feel Tom itching to pull them over and cite them for excessive speed but was grateful that his brother ignored them for now, focused on Kate.

Conor lifted the Steiner XP 7x50 binoculars to his eyes and gazed at the boats at the Maynard-King dock. Although he had been told to expect to see *Rosebud*, it still shocked him to spot it tied up just ahead of *Zémire*. It proved, if nothing else, that Leo had lied about going fishing off Block Island. There was no way that Leo could have gone out to Block and gotten back here in the time since they had spoken earlier that day.

Now Conor scanned the whole Maynard-King landscape. The large white hospital crested the rocky shoreline. Clusters of tall trees dotted the property, and Conor could see other buildings in clearings between the groves. He spotted the guardhouse, the cemetery, the gazebo, and the small house where Leprince de Beaumont Associates had their offices, where he had knocked on the door in search of Darla Vandeveer.

The storm that had threatened earlier had passed mainly to the north, with no more than a few showers. But a new front was coming through, with the sky darkening in the west. Conor heard some distant rumbles of thunder. The bay had been calm, but whitecaps were kicking up. He swept the glasses over the Maynard-King grounds and saw that people were still strolling around, sitting on benches near the tennis court.

Now he turned his attention back to the dock. At first, he didn't see any action on the decks of either of the boats, but then he noticed someone climbing out of the cockpit on *Rosebud*. The person walked down the dock to the freshwater connection and grabbed the end of a hose. He hopped back on the boat and began hosing down the deck.

Conor knew how fastidious boat owners could be, but if *Rosebud* had just left its marina that morning and hadn't been out on a fishing trip, did it really need cleaning? Conor thought of evidence being flushed into the bay.

"Who's that?" Tom asked, watching the person holding the hose.

"Can't tell," Conor said, adjusting the binoculars' focus. "Doesn't look like Leo."

"And too small to be Randall," Mike said. "Randy is a portly fellow, to put it mildly."

"Let's find out who it is," Tom said, steering toward the dock. He brought *Meteor* broadside and cut the engine.

Conor jumped onto the dock and secured the bowline, and Tom took care of the stern. Mike was agile for being nearly eighty, and he climbed off without any help. The three Reids walked over to *Rosebud*—sixty feet of gleaming fiberglass and stainless steel, rising to a massive tuna tower, perfect for spotting fish from a distance.

"Looks like a fast boat," Conor said as they approached.

"She's got twin Caterpillar diesel engines," Tom said. "But she still couldn't beat *Meteor* in a lobster boat race."

"She's not a lobster boat," Conor said.

"Details," Tom said.

The person they had seen washing off the deck must have gone below. A moment later, Conor saw someone wearing a yellow slicker and a Red Sox cap emerge from the cabin with a bucket, a scrub brush, and a bottle of Clorox bleach.

"Hey, there," Tom said, flashing his Coast Guard badge. "Can you step off the vessel, please?"

The person looked up but didn't move.

"Miranda?" Conor asked, startled.

"Hi," Miranda Forrest said. She didn't look surprised to see him, but she glanced down instead of meeting his eyes, and her greeting was subdued.

"Where's Leo?" Conor asked.

"Oh," she said. "I don't know. He got a text and said he had to leave."

"Who else is aboard?" Tom asked.

"No one. Just me," Miranda said.

"When did Leo leave?" Conor asked.

"Maybe twenty minutes ago?" Miranda asked.

Conor stared at her. Her right cheek was bruised and swollen. "What happened to you?" he asked.

"Nothing," she said, touching her cheek. "We hit a wave, and I crashed into the wall."

Conor recognized that excuse as the nautical version of walking into a door, the lie that victims of domestic violence were so often pressed into telling, to protect whomever had beaten them.

"Is Randall Flook aboard?" Tom asked.

"No, I told you. No one is. They left," she said.

"And you stayed behind to scrub the deck?" Conor asked.

"Yes," she said.

"Where did they go?" Tom asked.

"I don't know," she said. As she spoke, her gaze went to Conor's uncle. She looked at Mike for a moment, then away. Conor glanced at his uncle, wanting to see his reaction. Mike's face was bright red.

Conor's guard was up. He didn't know what it meant, but the interaction between Miranda and Uncle Mike wasn't casual. As they stood there, Miranda turned away and began to uncap the Clorox bottle.

"Stop that," Tom said. "Put the bottle down, and I'll say it again—step off the vessel."

"I have to clean up a mess," she said. "Before it stains the deck."

"You can do that later," Tom said. Conor caught his glance. "Call Joe," Tom said.

"Why are you acting this way?" Miranda asked. "We're all friends, aren't we? I didn't do anything . . ."

"We didn't say you did, Miranda," Conor said. "But can I ask you a couple of questions?"

"Okay," she said.

"You were Belinda's best friend, right?"

"Well, her cousin, actually. But yes, we were best friends. I already told Kate this. I feel horrible about playing along with Belinda. I didn't know what she planned to do at your rehearsal dinner! I would have stopped her . . ."

"Forget the rehearsal dinner," Conor said.

"You're not mad?"

Conor ignored that. "Tell me how you know Leo. He wasn't at the rehearsal dinner; he didn't even show up in Watch Hill until after Belinda was murdered and my uncle thought I needed a lawyer. You're not from Rhode Island, are you?"

"No," she said.

"So how would you have known Leo before? How do you know him well enough for him to take you out on his boat and make you clean the decks?"

"It's complicated," Miranda said. "We met when . . ."

"Don't say anything more," Mike barked.

"Uncle Mike!" Tom said. "What the hell?"

"She needs an attorney," Mike said. "Obviously Leo's out of the question. Miranda, don't say another word."

Conor and his uncle stared at each other.

"She's going to answer one question," Conor said. "And if you try to stop her, I swear I'll throw you off the dock."

Mike squinted at Conor, like an Irish boxer waiting for the punch.

"Miranda, where's Kate?" Conor asked.

"I swear I don't know," Miranda said.

"But you know they have her somewhere? Is it here, at Maynard-King?" Conor asked.

"I think so," Miranda said, looking straight at Conor. "Either here or at Enchanted Petals."

"Miranda!" Mike snapped, a sharp warning.

Both Conor and Tom stared at their uncle, and quickly and at the same time, took a step toward him.

40

Tuesday, July 6; 5:00 p.m.

Sam's teeth were rattled after fifteen minutes on Jennifer's ATV, bouncing over ruts and fallen branches on the logging road. The two women ducked to pass beneath low-hanging boughs as Jennifer steered around the last bend and pulled behind the red barn.

They both climbed off the ATV and leaned around the corner to see if there were any cars parked in front of the Victorian house. Sam didn't see any.

"Are there other places to park?" Sam asked in a low voice.

"No," Jennifer said. "I don't think anyone is here, but we should still be careful. These people are all about secrets and hiding."

Sam nodded. She stood very still, listening for voices and looking for any movement in the house's windows. If anyone would be expected to know about the people involved with the hospital and garden center, it would be Jennifer.

But Sam trusted her instincts, that Lincoln and the others would assume that she had run for her life and would never come back. So she inched around the corner of the barn, made sure the coast was clear, and bolted straight up the porch steps to the front door of the house. Jennifer was right behind her.

Sam tried the knob, but it was locked. She thought back to how Lincoln had called his father because he couldn't get in.

"Here," Jennifer said, and Sam turned around to see her holding up a single key. "I have the master."

"To the garden center?" Sam asked.

"To both properties," Jennifer said.

Sam watched her insert the key into the front door of Enchanted Petals and wondered how a low-level person at Maynard-King would gain access to the entire domain. Again, she felt a stab of doubt. Could Jennifer be leading her into a trap? She stayed back when Jennifer stepped into the house.

"What's the matter?" Jennifer asked, holding the door open.

"Why do you have a master key?" Sam asked.

"I stole it," Jennifer said.

"From where?"

"The guardhouse. See, Sam, you're not the only one who has to hide. Once they figure out the key is missing and check the security footage, they'll be after me too. So we're in this together, okay?"

"I just can't figure out why you decided to help me," Sam said. "To put yourself at risk this way."

"It's not just for you," Jennifer said. "I wanted to save myself and get the hell away from there. Like I told you, I'll die before I help them with the new girls. I'll die before I become one of them. Are you going to trust me or not?"

"I will," Sam said after a few seconds. "It's not every day I feel like I've got a target on my back. It makes me nervous, Jennifer. Sorry."

"I get it," Jennifer said.

"I'm assuming there's a phone," Sam said, thinking of how the number of the Yellow Pages ad had rung here.

"Yes, but it's connected to the hospital line. If we use it, they'll know."

They walked inside and shut the door behind them. Sam looked around and saw that the house was decorated more like a private men's club than a garden center. The foyer was paneled with dark wood, with rustic balusters on stairs leading to the second floor, a chandelier made of interlocking deer antlers, and landscape paintings in gold frames with discreet bronze lights highlighting the art.

"Are you sure they sell flowers here?" Sam asked.

"In the shop next door. I told you—this is where 1740 meets. It's their clubhouse," Jennifer said.

The floors were covered with Oriental rugs in muted colors. As they walked through the rooms, Sam saw reading nooks, window seats, Tiffany lamps on Craftsman-style tables beside burgundy leather armchairs, and more art. Sam recognized several of the paintings; she had seen them at her aunt's art gallery, and she knew that Crispin Adams had bought them.

There were antlers everywhere and other objects that made Sam shiver: one entire wall covered with animal skulls, each displayed on its own shelf; a corner cupboard filled with tiny fetishes of animals, all carved from stone; another cupboard filled with archaeological statues and artifacts; and a small dollhouse filled with dolls holding knives.

Sam crouched in front of the dollhouse, looking through the windows.

"Nice, right?" Jennifer asked.

"This looks real, I mean as if a child actually played with it," Sam said. "Someone made curtains for the windows and braided rugs for the floors. Look at the little coloring book . . . there are crayon marks on the open page."

"Take it out," Jennifer said. "Someone signed her initials on the back."

Sam didn't reach inside; she didn't want to touch anything. She peered more carefully at the tiny knives and saw that they were cutout pieces of cardboard, the hilts colored with brown crayon, the blades colored silver.

"How do you know someone signed her initials?" Sam asked. "Have you spent a lot of time in this house?"

"I've been here before," Jennifer said. "We all have, for the parties. But that's not how I know about the signature. Go ahead, look."

Sam wasn't sure why she felt so reluctant to put her hand inside the dollhouse. It felt as if she was reaching into something evil. When she took the tiny coloring book out, she turned it over and saw the crudely written letters.

"JS," Sam read out loud.

"Jennifer Stewart," Jennifer said. "That's me. I wrote those initials when I made the coloring book. I cut tiny squares of paper and sewed them together—like a real book binding."

"When did you make it, Jennifer?" Sam asked.

"When I was six," Jennifer said, staring at the book.

"Was this your dollhouse?" Sam asked.

"Yes. They let me bring it with me to the hospital," Jennifer said.

Sam stared at her. "Have you been at Maynard-King since you were six?"

"Not continuously," Jennifer said. "I've been in and out."

"So even though you're working there now, are you still a patient?" Sam asked.

"They want me to be," Jennifer said. "They would keep me sick forever if they had their way."

"Why?" Sam asked. "Is it for the money?"

"No, it's one therapist in particular. When I was fourteen, I was assigned to her. She used to tell me stories about her family, and she made it sound so perfect, like the family I wish I'd had. I couldn't wait until it was time to see her each day. And I'd go into her office, and she had postcards of mountains on a bulletin board. She told me she had climbed every one of them."

Sam listened; as Jennifer talked, she almost seemed to fall into a trance.

"I saw her all that year, and then the next, and the next. She made me feel as if I was part of her family. I loved her, just as if she were my mother, a good mother—and she told me she loved me, too, like a daughter. She made me feel safe. It got so I would rather be here, near her, than out in the world."

"Didn't you want to go home?" Sam asked.

"How do you define home?" Jennifer asked. "My mother killed my stepfather. It wasn't exactly a healthy environment."

"I'm so sorry," Sam said. "How old were you?"

"Six," Jennifer said. "That's when I came here. I saw my mother do it, but I couldn't remember the details. They got buried in my brain. To this day, I know more from what other people have told me than what's in my actual memory."

"That must be so traumatic. No wonder you had to go to a hospital."

"Yes, lucky me. Maynard-King. I really have that therapist to thank—the one I told you about. The thing is, she started off with my mother—evaluating her, after she was arrested. When she realized that my mother wasn't getting out of prison anytime soon, she found a way to help me—she took me out of the group home and brought me here."

"Do you still see her?" Sam asked.

"Sort of," Jennifer said. "But you know, it's not the same."

"Why?"

"All that I-love-you stopped when I wouldn't do what she wanted. She got angry instead. She would act cold to me, and it hurt a lot. I'd cry, and she'd reel me back, telling me she loved me again. And I'd go along with her for a while, and the pattern would go on and on."

"What did she want you to do?" Sam asked.

"She was grooming me," Jennifer said. "Raising me for 1740."

"That's horrible," Sam said.

"Yes, it is. She found a lot of troubled girls through working at the jail—either inmates or their daughters or victims. I was one of the youngest. She'd get us admitted to Maynard-King and then cull through us and decide which of us could be trained to make the men happy."

"The men?"

"Yes. Whoever can make it into the club."

"This club?" Sam asked. "Here?"

Jennifer nodded. "Where do you think the name came from? Enchanted Petals? It's because we are all flowers, and we're supposed to open our petals to the men. Let our petals just drop to the floor."

"Like dead roses," Sam said.

"Oh, they wouldn't like that," Jennifer said. "They actually think they're romantic. That we like what they're doing. We're supposed to pretend."

"Jennifer, I think I understand why you put all these knives in the dollhouse," Sam asked, feeling sick from what she was hearing.

"So that the dolls could protect themselves," Jennifer said. "And each other. So when bad people came after them, they could fight back."

Sam nodded, feeling sad for a little girl who had to think that way, in terms of weapons and attack, defense and protection.

"How long has 1740 been here?" Sam asked. "Did it start at the hospital or here at this house?"

"It goes back to the Civil War," Jennifer said. "Crispin Adams's family owned all of this property—hundreds of acres. Trafficking women has been around forever. His ancestors were doing it back when this house was built—when Abraham Lincoln was president. Crispin is very proud of that fact. Apparently, the supply of women in this part of Rhode Island wasn't enough for the demand, so a few generations later, Cantwell Adams—head of the family at the time—split the land and endowed an asylum. That's what they called it back then."

"Maynard-King," Sam said.

"Yes."

"Are there Maynards and Kings in the family tree?" Sam asked.

"Nope. 'Maynard' was the last name of Cantwell's favorite girl. Dorothy Maynard. She was just a young woman who worked here. Somewhere along the line she was taught to read, and her favorite story was *Beauty and the Beast*."

"That's how 1740 started?" Sam said. "Because of Dorothy loving the book?"

"Yes."

"And the name King?"

"Legend has it that Cantwell was incredibly ugly. But Dorothy's love—which is what they all call what they make us do—made him feel like a king. He wanted that for all his friends. So all the crazy girls who came to the hospital were turned into flowers who lost their petals. And Cantwell became so obsessed with *Beauty and the Beast*, he named his club for the year it was written."

"What happened to Dorothy?" Sam asked.

"The same thing that happens to all flowers," Jennifer said. "They wilt, then die, then get thrown away."

41

Conor stood on the dock next to *Rosebud*, restraining his uncle by grasping one of his arms while Tom held the other. Mike tried to wrench himself free, then gave up and stood still, stone faced. Miranda could have run away, but she moved close to Mike and looked up at the Reid brothers, from one to the other.

"It's not Mike's fault," she said. "You don't get it."

"Don't say another word, Miranda," Mike said loudly, even though she was just inches away from him.

"Mike, stop it. I want to tell them everything," she said. "This is ridiculous, them holding you this way." She turned from Mike to the brothers. "Let him go!"

"Um, no," Tom said. "Uncle Mike, what the hell?"

At first, Conor was too furious to say anything. They all stood there, breathing hard, as if they had just been in a sprint. Conor stared into Mike's eyes and saw how his uncle stared back without flinching.

"Tell us," Conor said. "We're in the middle of a murder investigation, and Miranda here called me to say Kate was the next to be taken, and you're keeping some kind of big crazy secret? Like, how you know this woman? And now you're advising her not to say anything to us?"

"You don't understand," Miranda said. "You need to hear this, but I won't tell you anything until you take your hands off him."

Tom looked at Conor, and Conor nodded. Tom released Mike's arm, but the two brothers stayed vigilant. Conor couldn't begin to figure out what was going on—how his father's brother could be embroiled in the pursuit that had led them back to the Maynard-King dock.

"Go ahead, Uncle Mike," Conor said. "Tell us how you know Miranda."

"That could be privileged information," Mike said. He was tall and stooped, and a shock of his thick white hair fell into his eyes. He looked every bit of seventy-eight, but his voice and the glare in his blue eyes were defiant.

"You're saying you're her lawyer?" Tom asked. "You're a judge."

"I'm an officer of the court," Mike said. "So yes, for the moment, I am her legal counsel."

"Look," Conor said. "With Kate missing, I don't care about privilege or you acting as her legal counsel. I don't even care about how you know her." He turned to Miranda. "Where is Kate?"

"I don't know . . ." Miranda began.

"Conor," Mike said. "This is the situation. Miranda doesn't have information about Kate's whereabouts. If she did, she would tell you. I would insist on it. But for her to say more would be to incriminate herself, and I have to advise her against that."

"If she knows anything—I don't care what it is," Conor said, his voice rising. "I need to hear it. Because any information will help me find Kate. And if I don't get it, I don't care whether you're my uncle or just some asshole defense attorney protecting your client . . . she is going to tell me where they took Kate."

They all stood there in a silent quadrangle, an atomic level of emotional energy building. Up among the four of them. Conor glanced over and caught Tom's expression. The sharp look was warning him to cool off, to quit pushing. Conor exhaled. As a detective, he had always been able to remain calm and objective. But this was about Kate. So he registered Tom's warning but didn't take it to heart.

"You're going to tell me, Uncle Mike," Conor said, grasping his uncle by the throat. "I swear to god . . . if you are part of 1740, and you know where Kate is, I will kill you."

Mike reached up and smashed Conor's arm away, landing a chop that cut to the bone and made Conor flinch.

"You back off," Mike shouted, nearly toppling over as he stumbled back. "You are my nephew, and I love you. But how dare you accuse me of this? I have spent my whole career working for good, and I love Kate as if she was my own daughter."

"Then what are you doing with *her*?" Conor asked, pointing at Miranda. "She just got off Leo's boat . . . He's involved, isn't he? He's part of it all, right? And so is she."

Miranda stepped forward, trying to get between Conor and Mike. "Mike, I am telling them. It's my choice, okay?"

Mike looked fierce, shrugged with defeat.

"Yes, Leo is part of it," she said, looking straight at Conor. "And so is Judge Flook. But I am not."

"Then why were you on Leo's boat?" Tom asked.

"Come aboard and see," Miranda said, sweeping her arm as if to invite everyone to board *Rosebud*.

"Miranda," Mike said, stepping in front of the gangway to prevent anyone going onto the boat. "Stop right there."

"Why should she stop right there?" Conor asked.

"Because she has rights," Mike said. "If you want to make a case against Leo that will hold, that will permit an effective prosecution, you have to do this correctly. Conor, if you go aboard without a warrant, you know what will happen—anything you find will get thrown out by the trial judge. And you can put Miranda in jeopardy. Do this right, Conor. Call Joe Harrington or Garrett Milne or any other Rhode Island law enforcement officer that you want. But respect criminal procedure. Don't mess this up."

"Uncle Mike," Conor said with steely calm. "Right now, I don't care about criminal procedure. Or a case. Or a prosecution. I only care about Kate, you know that. So let me go by." He pushed past his uncle and stepped aboard *Rosebud*'s deck.

The cop in Conor knew he should put on the brakes. But thinking of Kate, he stormed down the steps into the cabin.

The interior was very spare, not like that of *Psyche*—the opposite of *Psyche*'s old-world charm. The cabin contained electronics for navigation and entertainment, a well-equipped galley with storage and a stainless steel sink and stove, and seating on banquettes and swivel chairs.

The banquettes had white vinyl cushions. Conor sensed Miranda behind him.

"You're in the right place," she said.

"What am I looking for?" Conor asked.

Miranda pointed at a seam in the banquette cushion. There was a long, thin brownish line, with streaks, as if someone had tried to clean a stain.

"Some blood seeped in there," she said. "And Leo tried to clean it. He got most of it, but some soaked into that seam, and he couldn't get it out."

"Whose blood?" Conor asked, afraid to hear.

"The last girl's," Miranda said. "The one you found dead off Point Judith."

Now Uncle Mike and Tom had come down into the cabin, too, making it very crowded. "What's her name?" Conor asked.

"I just know her as Girl #2," Miranda said. "That's what they do, take away their names and give them a number."

"When you say 'they' . . ." Conor began.

"1740."

There was a metallic, rancid smell to the cabin. Blood sometimes smelled like copper; because the boat was a sportfishing vessel, Conor would have assumed it would be from the large fish Leo hauled in on his excursions. But this was different. There was human sweat—fear—mixed in, and it reminded him of the odor he'd noticed on *Psyche*.

"How did she die?" Conor asked.

Miranda was silent.

"Were you here when it happened?" Conor asked.

"Conor," Mike said. "Let me speak with Miranda privately, and then she might be able to tell you what you want to know."

"Up on deck," Conor said, gesturing for everyone to leave the cabin. He exchanged a glance with Tom. His brother went up to keep an eye on Miranda and their uncle, and Conor stood still in the main salon. He used his iPhone to take photos of the bloodstain and the area around the settee. He saw that a pink object—maybe a stone—had skidded under the table, but when he crouched down, he realized it was a broken fingernail. He remembered the hands of the young woman he'd seen in Galilee, of how she was missing a nail. He took photos of it but left it where it was.

Tom had gotten Uncle Mike and Miranda off the boat, which was now clearly a crime scene. Conor looked around. As far as he could tell, they had not attracted the attention of anyone at the hospital. The grounds looked quiet. A few people strolled the paths up the hill, by the main hospital building, but there was no sign of security.

"Where is Leo now?" Conor asked.

"Before we get to that," Mike said, "I want to explain something to you. It's important."

"Will it help me find Kate?"

"Conor, that's what this is all about."

"That would be a start," Conor said. "Because it seems to me you are in the middle of all this."

"Can I tell that part of it?" Miranda asked, and Mike nodded.

"Belinda was my cousin," Miranda said. "She talked about you all the time, Conor. When we were young, it was just like a girl with a crush. She kept it going, long after she moved away from New London. She stalked you, Conor. Got you to go away with her for the weekend. I think she wanted to get pregnant—she would do anything to have you in her life."

"That's insane," Conor said.

"I know. She was furious that you didn't want to see her after that. She had another relationship and did get pregnant."

"With the baby in the picture she showed Kate," Conor said.

"Yes. But they broke up, and she wound up here, at the hospital. She had a lot of problems, Conor—it was awful to see her that way. We had hope that she'd get well. She didn't."

"And she married the doctor."

Miranda nodded. "Yes, and it wasn't a happy marriage. Meanwhile, her daughter was living in the nightmare. Our family wanted to help, but Belinda was too sick—she shut us out. Anyway, last year, she got back in touch with me. She sounded better, happier. More stable."

Conor's chest was so tense, he felt like he was having a heart attack.

"What does this have to do with Kate?" he asked.

"Just listen," Miranda said. "Last winter, Belinda told me that you and she had started texting. Then that you decided to meet for dinner. She said you went away for the weekend and planned to be together, to get married."

"None of that ever happened," Conor said.

"Well, I didn't know that. I didn't know you, and Belinda had a way of sounding very convincing." Miranda took a breath. "Everything seemed fine until she found out that you were going to marry Kate—not her."

"How would she even know that?" Conor asked.

"She stalked you both," Miranda said. "Especially Kate. She put Maeve to work at the gallery, so she had an inside source."

"Put Maeve to work?" Conor asked. "How would she be able to do that?"

"Kate had advertised for a gallery assistant. And trust me, Belinda could get anyone to do what she wanted. She had BPD—borderline personality disorder. She was very manipulative."

"What if Kate hadn't hired Maeve?" Conor asked.

"Then Belinda would have sent Suzanne on an interview. Or any number of the others. But she didn't have to—Kate hired Maeve. And every wedding plan Kate made, Maeve was in on. Maeve reported everything to Belinda."

"And Lincoln was involved too?"

Miranda nodded.

"Conor," Mike said. "This is where I come in."

"You've known about this all along?" Conor asked.

"Yes and no," Mike said.

"What does that mean?"

"Years ago, I had this young lady in my courtroom," Mike said, gesturing at Miranda. "Her father was doing a play in Waterford, Connecticut, and Miranda had come to Rhode Island to see her cousin Belinda. The two of them were at a club in Providence, and Miranda was arrested for possession of drugs. I think you know that I've always taken an interest in young offenders, tried to get them into a mentorship program that would help them stay straight."

"He got me a lawyer," Miranda said. "Leo Kennedy."

"As you know, I admire—admired—Leo as an attorney and as a human being," Mike said. "I thought he would be a good influence, help Miranda. That was the end of my involvement—until today."

"Leo was good to me at first," Miranda said. "He was wonderful to talk to. He'd listen, let me go on for hours. The opposite of my dad. My father's an actor, and he always acts like he's onstage—it's always about him. And even though Leo's a big-time lawyer and does important cases, gets up in front of a courtroom and talks to the jury, he would rather hear about other people's lives than talk about his own. Such a good, caring person."

"But he's obviously involved with 1740 if he knows it's coming apart. So how good can he be?" Conor asked.

"He hid that from me," Miranda said. "I introduced him to Belinda. Or I *thought* I did. She was already a widow—she had been forced to grow up very fast. She just wanted to cut loose—have fun, party, go to clubs. At first, I thought Leo was helping her the way he was helping me."

"But it was quite different," Mike said solemnly.

"Yes," Miranda said. "I was still living in New York in the winter, Connecticut in the summer, and I only came to Rhode Island once or twice a year. Belinda was living here at the hospital—they had a special cottage for her and her daughter, and they let them stay—she was special to everyone at Maynard-King, considering how much they all loved her husband. Her daughter was growing up, everyone seemed happy and healthy."

"But she wasn't," Mike said. "Was she?"

"No. Everything Jonathan did wrong convinced Belinda that Conor could do it better. He could make her happier, take better care of her and her daughter . . ."

Conor took all that in, feeling overwhelmed by all that Miranda was telling him about Belinda. How was it possible that she had carried those feelings for him all this time? They had been destructive not only to Belinda and her daughter, but ultimately—disastrously—to Kate.

"After Jonathan's death, Belinda began acting out even worse. 1740 was already in action—there were plenty of members—Leo was one of them."

"I thought you said you introduced Belinda to Leo," Conor said.

"I thought that too. But Belinda had her reasons for hiding the truth from me, that they had known each other a long time."

Conor looked at Mike, to see how he was taking this, to gauge whether he was involved. But he saw disgust on Mike's face and a type of defeat.

"Today, Leo asked me to come on the boat with him and Randy," Miranda said. "With Belinda dead, Leo had lost his special way into 1740. Crispin and the others never really trusted him and his law friends."

"Crispin Adams," Conor said. "Lincoln's father."

"Yes. He's the president of the 1740 society," Miranda said. "Leo told me the group has been in existence for over a hundred and fifty years, and it started right here, on Maynard-King property. The land has always belonged to Crispin's family. It still does, even though Leo set up the Leprince de Beaumont Associates LLC to hide the true ownership."

"I thought Leo was one of the Old Detectives," Tom said. "Helping to uncover 1740."

"We thought so too," Mike said. "You know how much I trusted him? I asked him to represent you, Conor. I thought his character was impeccable. How wrong I was."

"Anyway," Miranda said. "Crispin and the rest of the group were afraid that Leo might have been setting them up—working with the police to infiltrate them so he could bring them down. They're afraid that 1740 is coming apart."

"If it has lasted a hundred years, why is it coming apart now?" Conor asked.

"Ever since Belinda's murder, everything has been toppling. You'd found *Psyche*, the mansion on the island, the note at Dr. Tyler's grave. The woman who trains the girls is getting nervous and wants to leave. It became a nightmare when they decided to lure Kate to Fernando Harris's studio. And as of today, Leo told me he wanted me to be his new Belinda."

"And do what?" Conor asked.

"Line up women for him—take over from the trainer. Find Belles he could dominate," Miranda said. "They had that poor girl on *Rosebud*. They made me look at her body, said that I was part of the murder now, and that if they were ever caught, I would be arrested. Leo said he would protect me, but only if I work with the organization."

"And what did you say?" Conor asked.

"I said yes, just to reassure them, so they wouldn't kill me too. And then, when they went out on deck to throw the body overboard, I picked up Leo's phone to look for Mike's number, so I could call him. But it was password protected."

"How did you get in?" Tom asked.

"I guessed the password. 1740," Miranda said.

"And that's when she called me," Mike said. "I should have told you right away."

"I'm sure you hoped to keep her from being involved in all this," Conor said. This was more of the Uncle Mike he knew. A great judge other than his soft heart, sometimes willing to bend the rules if he thought he could help someone in a less orthodox way.

"Yes," Mike said.

"Are we any closer to finding Kate?" Tom asked.

"I think she is somewhere on the property," Miranda said.

"Why do you think that?" Conor asked.

"I overheard Leo and Randy talking. They're angry that Kate was taken—it wasn't their idea."

"Why did they lure her to Fernando's studio, anyway? What good would that do?" Tom asked. "Why target Kate?"

Miranda hung her head for a moment, then looked up. "Someone blames her for the terrible life she had."

"This is crazy," Conor said. "Who?"

"We're dealing with a murderer," Tom said. "I'm assuming that person is Leo or Randy, since the woman was killed on Leo's boat."

"I didn't see the murder, so I am not sure," Miranda said. "I was only brought on after she was dead. But it's possible."

"Did one of them also kill Belinda?" Tom asked.

"Oh, no," Miranda said. "Not at all."

"Then who did?"

"The same person who killed Dr. Tyler," Miranda said. "Belinda's daughter."

Tuesday, July 6; 6:00 p.m.

Sam couldn't speak for a while. She sat there in silence, thinking of Dorothy, imagining how it had been for her. She thought about the start of 1740. She pictured Crispin, a man she had met through Kate and whom she had liked. And Lincoln—her friend—the latest descendant of Cantwell Adams. Sam glanced at Jennifer, wondering how she had lived through it all.

"You okay?" Jennifer asked.

"I'm not sure," Sam said. "Are you?"

"I've had more time to get used to this than you have."

Sam nodded. But she wasn't; she felt so shaken.

"What's our plan?" Jennifer asked after a few minutes. "It seems as if we're safe here for now, but we can't stay forever. One of the members is bound to show up at some point. Or the security guard will come through on patrol, looking for us."

"We should stay till dark," Sam said, looking out the window. "Then get out to the main road and find a phone." She remembered driving through farmland and open space on the way here with Lincoln. They had passed through a small town and gone by a shopping center, but how far away was it? "Are you sure we can't use the one here?" she asked.

"We could use it, but a button would light up at the hospital, and they'd come running," Jennifer said. She looked upset, the way Sam felt.

"Well, we might as well have something to eat," Jennifer said after a minute. "It's probably been a while since you had a meal, right?"

Sam shook her head. "I'm not hungry."

"Well, I'm going to feed you," Jennifer said, beckoning Sam and heading down a corridor.

Sam hung back, really not interested in food. But then she sighed and followed her down the hall. She noticed the walls were covered with framed photos that looked like headshots. There were also pictures of people at formal events.

"Who are they?" Sam asked, pointing.

"Oh," Jennifer said, stopping to see what she was looking at. "These photos are here to make the place seem more respectable. The hospital director, board members, donors, doctors."

"Are they all 1740?" Sam asked.

"Absolutely not," Jennifer said. "They have to mix it up with regular people, to make them seem legit."

Sam leaned closer to the wall so she could see faces in the photos. Right away, she recognized Crispin Adams at the helm of a big sailboat. There he was again, wearing black tie and holding a martini glass right here in the garden at Enchanted Petals. Lincoln and Maeve were also dressed in formal clothes, sitting with Suzanne; Sam's stomach dropped at the sight of them.

"Maeve really did lie," Sam said quietly, staring. "She told us she'd never met Suzanne before she hired her to do the calligraphy for Kate and Conor's wedding."

"They've known each other since childhood," Jennifer said. "They were always at the hospital."

"As patients?"

"Not all three of them. Lincoln was there because his family still owns this property. The Adamses would come to picnics and things like that. Lincoln would play with us kids, the ones who lived here. Some of the girls had crushes on him. And for a while, his father was interested in Belinda."

"Was Maeve in the hospital?" Sam asked.

"She was here," Jennifer said. "Best friends with Suzanne. We called them the 'BPD twins.'"

"Why?"

"They both have BPD—borderline personality disorder."

"What is that?" Sam asked.

"It's nasty," Jennifer said. "Fear of abandonment, extreme emotions, intense anger, doing anything to keep people from leaving them."

Sam thought of Belinda—the scene she had caused at the rehearsal dinner, stealing Kate's wedding dress, smashing the painting: the lengths she had gone to, to keep Conor from marrying Kate.

"Maybe Suzanne inherited BPD from Belinda," Sam said.

"How would that happen?" Jennifer asked, frowning.

"Because they're mother and daughter . . ." Sam began, but she gasped and forgot everything she was about to say. Sam stared at a photo of smiling people sitting on the Ocean House verandah: Mike and Anne Reid, Nola and Edward Aldrich, Leo Kennedy, and a woman Sam didn't recognize.

"Oh my god," Sam said.

"What's wrong?" Jennifer asked.

"It's impossible," Sam said. "They can't be involved . . . Why is their picture here?"

"I told you—a lot of these people are just donors or board members. Which photo?"

Sam's hand was shaking as she pointed at the photo of Uncle Mike and Aunt Anne, and the four others.

Jennifer laughed. "Oh, interesting."

"Why? Do you know them?"

"Of course," Jennifer said. "I'm always a server at the dinners for the board and the donors. That's Mr. and Mrs. Reid, Mr. and Mrs. Aldrich, Darla Vandeveer, and good old Leo."

"You know Leo Kennedy?" Sam asked.

Jennifer nodded. "Oh yes. He's not just a donor. He's a regular here. Pure 1740. Look at him, playing up to everyone with my therapist."

"Your therapist?"

"Yes, the one I told you about," Jennifer said. "The trainer, who teaches the girls to become Belles. Belles for 1740. That's her."

Sam stared at Darla Vandeveer, the only person in the photo whom she hadn't met; she tried to see evil in her face, but she couldn't. She saw an attractive woman with a big smile, who looked very happy to be at the Ocean House. And she tried to imagine how the people she cared about—the Old Detectives who were helping to find Belinda's murderer—had come to trust Leo Kennedy and Darla Vandeveer.

Jennifer had a walkie-talkie on her belt. It had been crackling now and then, since she and Sam had made their escape from Maynard-King, but now it squawked with a transmission so loud, they both jumped.

"The bride and Girl #3 are in the FS," the voice said. "Reception to follow."

"The bride?" Sam asked. The only person who had been about to be a bride was Kate.

"'Reception to follow' means they've got something planned for her," Jennifer said.

"What's the FS?"

"The Finishing School—it's a classroom in the second building, where most of the training takes place."

"If they have Kate there, we have to go back," Sam said, tugging on Jennifer's hand.

"That's crazy, Sam," Jennifer said. "They are already on high alert, looking for you. 'Reception' is a code word for a meeting. They're moving up their timetable with Caroline. If we go back, they'll get us too."

"Is Darla your therapist?" Sam asked.

"Of course. She's a huge part of it," Jennifer said.

"Let's go! I can't leave Kate to Darla," Sam said.

"What?" Jennifer asked. "What do you care about Darla?"

"Your psychologist, the one who was trying to groom you. The trainer!" Sam said. "Come on, we've got to get there!"

"You have it wrong," Jennifer said, but she ran with Sam to the ATV and began driving toward the access road, on the way to Maynard-King.

Tuesday, July 6; 6:00 p.m.

Kate sat beside Caroline, still tethered to the younger woman. Darla Vandeveer had gone in and out of the office several times, speaking in a low voice to someone just outside the door, then returning.

"The reception is about to start," Darla said, smiling at Kate and Caroline. "Are there any food allergies? Or particular dislikes? I'll take the liberty of ordering for you."

Kate was struck by the absurdity of the situation: sitting in an elegantly appointed room that felt more like a boudoir than a classroom, handcuffed to a terrified young woman she had just met, with a stranger taking her food order and seeming to be concerned about her food preferences. Kindness and normalcy met the cruel and surreal.

"I don't want anything," Kate said. "Except to be let go. Now."

Darla laughed. "But of course you must eat! We can't have you losing your strength. Kate, you pose the most challenging dilemma."

Kate gave her a defiant look. "I'm sure you'll tell me how."

"Just, what do we do with you?"

"You will let me go. And Caroline too."

The classroom door opened, and Suzanne walked in carrying a bottle of champagne and an ice bucket. She placed them on the desk in front of Darla, then went to a cabinet where she removed three champagne flutes. Kate watched as she presented the champagne bottle to Darla for her approval, then expertly opened and poured it.

"Very good, Suzanne," Darla said. "I remember the first time you opened champagne. The cork flew across the room, and the wine bubbled all over the table."

Suzanne laughed. "Give me a little credit. I was awfully young."

Kate watched Suzanne fill the glasses, wondering why Belinda hadn't protected her daughter more. The champagne was Taittinger Brut Rosé, and it fizzed with tiny pink stars in the late-afternoon light. Suzanne had pale skin, sharp cheekbones, and those blue eyes that had struck Kate when she had first seen them—they had reminded her of Conor.

"You're staring at me," Suzanne said, glancing at Kate.

"Yes," Kate said.

"You want to know if Conor is my father, right?" Suzanne asked.

"I know that Belinda planted that seed in your head," Kate said. "You were there at the rehearsal dinner when she caused that scene."

"Yes, I was there," Suzanne said. "So aren't you curious?"

"Not at all," Kate said. "I know it's not Conor. Belinda was a liar, a very troubled soul. She was just stirring things up."

"Don't say that about Belle," Suzanne said. She was gripping the neck of the champagne bottle tightly, and Kate flinched because she felt Suzanne wanting to swing it at her.

"Your mother, you mean?" Kate asked, and Suzanne laughed.

"Come now, ladies," Darla said. "Let's stop the squabbling and drink our champagne . . . We have things to discuss. Food is coming, along with a treat."

The door opened again, and Maeve walked in carrying a silver tray filled with canapés—foie gras on toast points, smoked salmon on brown bread, crabmeat-stuffed mushrooms, and a bowl overflowing with artistically arranged crudités.

"Very good, Maeve," Kate said. "Just like at my gallery. You were always so adept at planning receptions for exhibition openings. People always wanted to buy the paintings after you'd warmed them up with food and drink."

"I learned here, Kate. I was well trained," Maeve said.

"Did you hear what she said?" Suzanne asked Maeve. "She called Belle my mother."

"Enough of this," Darla said. "Kate, we have a surprise for you. Relax for a moment, and Maeve will get it."

"Oh, come on," Suzanne said, sounding exasperated.

"I've had enough surprises," Kate said. She stared at Maeve and felt an ache in her heart. She had really cared for—even loved—this young woman. She had considered herself Maeve's mentor, and she had felt an almost familiar bond with her. Now, looking into Maeve's eyes, she felt as if she had never known her at all.

"You look sad, Kate," Maeve said.

"I am," Kate said.

"About your wedding?"

"Right now, I'm sad about you," Kate said.

"Why?"

"Because you're someone I loved and thought I could trust," Kate said.

"Boo-hoo," Suzanne said. "Hear that, Maeve? She feels so sad for herself that you betrayed her."

"No, not for me. I'm sad for Maeve," Kate continued.

"Why?" Maeve asked.

But Kate just stared at her, saying nothing.

"Silent communication," Suzanne said. "How meaningful. This is getting a bit too fraught for me."

"Maeve, would you like to get the surprise for Kate?" Darla asked again.

Without another word, Maeve went to a closet across the room. Caroline was sitting very still beside Kate but lightly nudged one of Kate's feet with hers. Kate glanced down and saw that Caroline was very discreetly pointing toward the window.

The view from the classroom was of the long lawn sloping down toward Narragansett Bay. There were clusters of trees, but the blue water was visible through branches and leaves. As Kate gazed out the window, she saw Sam's head pop up. Their eyes met, and Kate caught her breath. She tried not to give anything away, terrified that Sam could get caught.

Maeve now turned from the closet, holding a large rectangular-shaped object covered with a sheet. Kate noticed that Maeve had an odd expression in her eyes—not quite triumph, not quite pride, but a combination of both. She stood in front of Kate.

"This is why we poured champagne," Darla said. "To celebrate Maeve being able to get this done so quickly. We're having a reception in honor of that—and other things."

Maeve unveiled the painting. It was *Foggy Night*, the oil by James Suydam, that Belinda had nearly destroyed. Kate leaned close to examine the work. The canvas had been expertly glued, and the frame had been repaired, gold paint dabbed onto the broken places. The ring around the moon that Kate had noticed at Fernando Harris's studio was still there.

"I wanted to take that circle—that ring—out of the painting for you," Maeve said softly. "But I was overruled. You get the symbolism, don't you?"

"The note made it clear," Kate said. She remembered it, word for word, and she would have recited it out loud, but Maeve reached into her pocket for the note and spread it on the desk.

A ring for a ring.

Miranda stole my mother's promise ring from Conor to give to you.

I am returning the favor, a ring around the moon, a circle in the sky.

Don't look up at the sky, Kate. Just turn around.

And there in Fernando's studio, Kate had turned around and come face-to-face with Maeve. She stared with sadness at Maeve now. She felt heartbroken by the betrayal.

"Whose ring?" Caroline asked.

"Belinda's," Kate said.

"Have you figured out who her daughter is?" Maeve asked.

Kate closed her eyes. She thought they were all Belinda's daughters, at least spiritually: the troubled girls of Maynard-King.

"It doesn't matter which one of you she gave birth to—Suzanne, you, some other girl here at Maynard-King. Maybe she made it all up," Kate said.

"She didn't make it up," Suzanne said, her face turning red.

"Belinda lived here and corrupted every young girl who came into her life," Kate said. "She brought you all into 1740—she obviously did that to her daughter too. Turned her into a monster just like herself."

"Don't say that," Suzanne said.

"Just look at Caroline," Kate said. "Girl #3. That's what Belinda's legacy is. Destruction, pain, robbing someone of her name and of her life."

Caroline was shaking, and when Kate glanced over at her, she saw tears running down her cheeks.

"And for what?" Kate asked. "To be raped by men who belong to 1740? I'm sorry if it happened to you, Maeve—but now you are just as bad as they are. Trauma doesn't excuse anyone from hurting someone else. I saw the handcuffs and the blood on *Psyche*."

"I didn't have anything to do with that! I'm not one of them!" Maeve said, so vehemently that it took Kate aback, made her almost believe she was telling the truth.

"No?" Kate asked, looking straight into Maeve's eyes. "Then what do you make of the fact that Caroline and I are handcuffed together, tied to the floor, so we can't get away?"

Maeve didn't reply. She looked nervously at Darla and inched closer to Kate.

"And you, Darla—what are you doing here?" Kate asked. "What role do you play in this nightmare?"

"I'm the business manager of Leprince de Beaumont Associates, LLC," Darla said.

"Part of doing business is keeping women restrained?" Kate asked, lifting her handcuffed wrist.

Suzanne noticed that Darla's champagne glass was empty, and she stepped forward to refill it. Darla nodded and thanked her. Suzanne leaned over to kiss her cheek. Kate barely saw any of it. She was staring out the window, hoping that Sam was safe: that she had seen Kate and run away to call the police. To call Conor, to tell him to come.

"Just go along with it for now, Kate," Maeve said in a low voice, with her back to Darla and Suzanne.

"What are you talking about?" Kate asked, startled.

"I'll help you escape," Maeve whispered urgently. "I promise. Just follow my lead. I've had enough."

Tuesday, July 6; 7:00 p.m.

"This is not good," Jennifer said, crouching beside Sam underneath the window of the classroom where Kate was being held.

"No kidding," Sam asked. "We have to get Kate out of there."

"You don't get it," Jennifer said. "They're serving pink champagne. Excuse me, rosé champagne. That always means someone important is about to show up. It means they're starting the party."

"What party?" Sam asked.

"1740 is gathering," Jennifer said.

Sam gripped the windowsill and peered inside to look at Kate again. She nearly shouted—Kate was sitting on a small sofa next to the young woman Sam had seen in the Range Rover earlier that afternoon, outside Enchanted Petals. Maeve was bent down in front of Kate, holding a painting.

It was _Foggy Night_, the wedding present that Kate had bought for Conor. It seemed cruel to show Kate the ruined artwork that had been meant to commemorate her marriage to Conor—was Maeve just rubbing it in her face? Sam wanted to storm into the building to save Kate, but she knew she had to hold herself back.

She and Jennifer hopped down from the planter and began to make their way around the house. It was surrounded by a border of rosebushes. Thorns snagged Sam's legs, but she kept going. The smell of the roses was strong in the heat of early evening, and along with worry for Kate, it made her feel sick.

"We don't have a plan," she said to Jennifer. "We need a way to call for help."

"That's not happening," Jennifer said. "There's no phone, Sam. We have to get inside and do this ourselves."

"You just said 1740 is gathering," Sam said. "How can we go up against all of them?"

Jennifer kept walking, as if she hadn't heard. The driveway curved behind the house, and Sam saw ten cars parked there. Did they all belong to staff, or had party guests already arrived? She spotted Crispin's Range Rover hidden behind a shed; Maeve's BMW was there too.

Both Sam and Jennifer ducked behind the hedge of roses when a large black Mercedes pulled into the lot. Sam heard one car door open and slam shut; she craned her neck to see who had gotten out, but her view was blocked by foliage. The person must have walked to the front door, because she heard muffled voices as people greeted each other.

Once the voices stopped, Jennifer ran to the back of the house. An air-conditioning unit hummed, masking the sound of hinges creaking as Jennifer pulled open a door that led into a flower room. It was like the one at Cloudlands, a room that existed solely for arranging bouquets of flowers picked from the grounds. Mounds of cut roses lay on the counter; discarded stems and fallen petals littered the floor.

The kitchen was next. Sam smelled something baking and saw trays of small tarts straight out of the oven. There were a tray of glasses and two bottles of champagne—freshly chilled and damp with dew—waiting to be served.

So far, the coast was clear. Sam's heart was pounding, because she knew that 1740 had convened somewhere in this building, and she had no idea how many there were. Kate was in that room she'd seen from outside, but Sam was convinced that she and Jennifer could get her out of there.

Jennifer walked over to the counter next to the large Viking gas stove and opened a drawer. She pulled out a knife and held it up. Was Jennifer equipping herself, as she had the dolls, to protect herself and Sam?

"I'm not going to stab anyone," Jennifer said. "But it will keep them back if they try to grab us."

Sam nodded. She followed Jennifer through a pantry and into a dimly lit hallway. It seemed as if it might have been the servants' passage, back when the house was built a century or more ago. They passed an open door that led into an empty dining room. As they crept along, the sound of voices grew louder. She heard both men and women, and she recognized Leo's laugh.

"They're in the classroom," Jennifer whispered.

"The one we saw Kate in?" Sam asked.

Jennifer nodded, and Sam closed her eyes for a moment, envisioning the room's layout. She pictured the door, the windows, the blackboard, the sofa where Kate was sitting with Caroline, and the spot where Maeve had rested the painting.

"I'll go in first," Jennifer whispered. "I'll distract them—tell them that I saw you on the grounds, near the cemetery. They'll follow me out the front door, and you can help Kate get away."

"But what if they know you're lying? They'll take you . . ."

"Don't worry, Sam," Jennifer said. "They'll never hurt me. I promise you that."

She gave Sam a quick hug and walked into the classroom. Sam held her breath, listening to Jennifer do exactly what she said she was going to do: tell everyone that she had spotted Samantha Lathrop and they could find her in the cemetery. Sam heard a flurry of voices and footsteps, and then it was silent.

She waited thirty seconds, then walked through the doorway of the classroom. Kate was sitting exactly where she had been before, and at the sight of her, Sam let out a cry and held out her arms to her.

Kate shouted, "Run, Sam!"

Sam lurched toward Kate but was stopped when someone grabbed her shoulder and yanked her back. She looked into Leo's face. His fingers squeezed her shoulder and made her wince. Behind him, she saw Darla, Suzanne, Maeve, Crispin, Lincoln, and another man. Jennifer was with them, and so was Nola Aldrich.

"Sorry, Sam," Jennifer said, smiling. "I had to bring you here. It was a fun little game, wasn't it?"

Sam shook herself away from Leo's grasp. She felt sick and couldn't bring herself to look at Jennifer. She thought of how she had said to Conor that Kate was too smart and careful to be taken, and look how it had just happened to both of them—Kate and Sam. Tricked by people they trusted.

"I loved that part at Enchanted Petals, when you looked at the photos on the wall. You were so upset, seeing the Old Detectives," Jennifer said. "And then I told you my psychologist was one of the people in the picture."

"I thought you meant Darla," Sam said.

"No," Jennifer said, putting her arms around Nola. "This is my therapist, the woman who was more my mother than my mother. She's the brilliant lady who trains us in the art of *Beauty and the Beast*. She sees the beauty in us and helps us tame the beasts."

The trainer, the bad therapist, Sam thought. Now she knew why the description had sounded so familiar; she remembered that day in the cabana, on the beach in front of the Ocean House, when Nola had said she was a behaviorist, a psychologist who worked with criminals and their victims.

"I thought you were trying to help us," Sam said to Nola. "Tracking down 1740, finding out who killed Belinda."

"I'm sorry, Sam," Nola said. "Truly. We wish you had stayed away."

"And besides, we already *know* who killed Belinda," Suzanne said.

"Her daughter did it," Jennifer said.

"You?" Sam asked, looking at Suzanne.

"No," Jennifer said, beaming as if she had just pulled off the best joke. "Me. I'm Belinda's daughter." She walked across the room to Leo. "And this is my dad."

Tuesday, July 6; 7:30 p.m.

Conor, Tom, and Mike walked up the path from the dock. Conor's gaze swept back and forth. Everything and nothing seemed to matter; Kate was here. Miranda had said it, and Conor felt it. When they got to the smaller of the two buildings, Mike stopped and looked at the cluster of cars parked out back.

"That's strange," Mike said. "That black Mercedes belongs to Edward and Nola."

"You sure it's theirs?" Conor asked.

"Yes, I see their yacht club sticker on the windshield."

"What's it doing here?" Tom asked.

"Nola is on an advisory board, to advocate for better mental health treatment for law enforcement officers. It came out of her work at the prison. Maybe they're meeting here tonight," Mike said.

"So far that's two of your friends who are connected with Maynard-King," Tom said. "Leo and Nola."

"Well, if you put it that way, Anne and I have a connection too. We all met at a conference on criminal justice in Aspen a few years ago, not long after I retired. Nola was leading a panel on the psychology of defendants who employ the insanity defense, and she asked Leo and me to join her. Anne and Edward were just along to keep us company."

"Nola's an expert in insanity defense?" Conor asked.

"She's a prison psychologist, as well as a very good profiler."

"And Leo?"

"He has used that defense very effectively for several clients—lack of culpability due to mental illness. I've presided over trials where it was argued. There were several staffers and board members, people from Maynard-King, in the audience. We had dinner with one of them."

"Who's that?" Conor asked.

"Her name is Darla Vandeveer," Mike said.

"What did she have to add to the panel?" Conor asked, remembering how he'd tried to find her his last time here. "I thought she was on the business side of this place."

"According to Nola, she has a master's in psychology. She admires Nola's work with victims of crimes, and she was there to observe. She talked about how many of the patients here have suffered trauma from one kind of assault or another and how she wanted to transition from business to clinical work."

"The trauma comes from being here," Conor said.

He walked into the parking area to have a closer look at the black Mercedes when he spotted a Range Rover hidden on the other side of a maintenance shed. His heart rate sped up at the sight of it.

"That's the Range Rover we saw on the video," Conor said. "The one Maeve got into. She's going to tell us where Kate is."

He ran to the driver's side and looked through the window. The vehicle was clean except for a paper on the floor in the back seat. Conor cupped his hands around his eyes and pressed close to the glass to get a better look.

It was a receipt on Fernando Harris's letterhead:

Restoration of *Foggy Night* by James Suydam
For Ms. Kate Woodward / Woodward-Lathrop Gallery

"Kate was in this Range Rover," Conor said, his heart starting to pound. "She left the receipt so I'd know. She's here."

He picked up a big rock and tested its weight. It would do. He walked over to his brother and uncle; Tom had just finished talking to Joe on his mobile and was looking at Conor to tell him what the next step in the plan was.

"You stay here," Conor said to them. "And see who comes out. I'll run inside and get Kate."

"You don't know she's in there," Tom said.

"Yeah, I do know," Conor said, holding the rock high above his head, then smashing it down on the windshield of the Range Rover. An earsplitting alarm began to screech. Tom and Mike ducked behind the shed, and Conor ran straight for the building. He figured that whoever would come out to investigate would exit by the back door, so he skirted around to the front.

He flew up the front steps and tried the door. It was locked. He jumped over the railing onto the ground and pulled himself up to look through the window. He was looking into a room full of people who were streaming to the other side of the building to see what had caused the alarm to go off.

Conor saw Kate, and he thought his heart would pound out of his chest. He had to hold himself back, just long enough to assess the situation, to not put her in greater danger. She was sitting on a couch, very close to a young woman Conor had never seen before. The young woman had bruises on her face and abrasions on her wrists. He had the immediate thought that she was one of the women held captive on *Psyche*.

They were whispering. Conor could see that they were handcuffed together. It drove him crazy, knowing that someone had touched Kate, put cuffs on her wrists, restrained her so she couldn't leave. Kate nodded, and then the two of them stood up with Sam; Maeve ran over with a key and undid the cuffs, and Sam grabbed Kate's hand and began pulling her toward the door. Then everything happened very fast.

Tuesday, July 6; 7:30 p.m.

A car alarm sounded from outside the building, and nearly everyone in the classroom ran to see what it was. Kate knew there was no point struggling against the bonds, so instead she leaned into Caroline.

"This is it," Kate said. "We're going to go for it, Caroline. We have to run hard and fast. We'll knock down anyone who gets in our way." They started to stand up, and Sam rushed over to them. She grabbed the handcuffs and rattled them, as if she could unlock them by force.

"Oh, Sam, why did you come?" Kate asked. "Now they're going to get you too!"

"No," Sam said. "We're in this together."

"Come on, let's go," Kate said. She started toward the front door with Caroline. Sam darted ahead. Maeve stood in their way, and at first, Kate thought she was going to stop them. But instead, she unlocked the handcuffs. Kate didn't know what had changed Maeve's attitude, but she had kept her promise to help.

"Hurry," Maeve said. "They'll be back in a minute. Lincoln's going to get the car, and he'll drive around front to pick us up. We've got to get out of here right away."

Kate stopped short, thinking how crazy it would be to get into a car with Maeve and Lincoln after what they had done—to put Sam and Caroline in danger by taking them with her. But what was the alternative?

"Where do you think you're going?" Jennifer asked, returning to the classroom, standing directly in front of Kate, looking straight into her eyes.

"We're leaving," Kate said calmly.

"I don't think so," Jennifer said, moving even closer. Kate had liked this young woman when she had met her at the cemetery. She had sensed a vulnerability had had bordered on emotional frailty, but just then she was speaking with force and authority. Kate knew that the power and coercion of 1740 had to be overwhelming, but she had to believe that a patient's innate goodness could override the evil.

"Jennifer," Kate said. "Come with us. We can all get away . . ."

"Don't you recognize me?" Jennifer asked.

"Yes," Kate said. "From the cemetery."

"Not just there. From my baby picture. The one my mother showed you. My blue eyes fooled you, didn't they?"

Kate stared at them, those blue eyes that Belinda had said were just like Conor's. But they were just like Leo's too. She remembered when she'd first met Leo, in the lobby of the Ocean House, she had noted how Irish he looked, how his eyes were the color of Galway Bay.

"I don't want to get away from this place," Jennifer said, glaring at Kate. "This is my home. I grew up here. And now it is really mine.

My stepfather's gone, my mother's gone, my father was never here, and my life is finally about to become mine. Fuck 1740, fuck every single person who messed with me. Especially you."

"Me?" Kate asked. She knew that Jennifer was delusional, and she didn't want to debate with her, but the statement shocked her.

"Do you know how much you ruled my existence?" Jennifer asked. "First, I had to hear about Conor all the time. How if he loved my mother, she would be so happy, we would have such a wonderful life. She said that all the time, even when she was married to Jonathan. He got sick of it. He was going to divorce her just to shut her up about Conor. So I killed him. If he'd divorced her, we'd have had nothing. They'd have kicked us out of here."

Kate looked into Jennifer's eyes and saw anguish and rage. "How old were you when you killed him?"

"Eleven. He didn't care about me. After he died, I saw all the 1740 men using my mother. Turning girls into an unending stream of Belles."

Kate saw Jennifer glancing at Caroline, then at Sam.

"You two would be next," Jennifer said. "That's how it goes here. Ask Maeve and Suzanne."

"Stop it, Jen," Maeve said. "It's over. Let them go."

"Oh, now you're on their side?" Jennifer asked. "You let my mother plant you in the art gallery. You hired Suzanne and sabotaged the wedding. And now you want to let them go waltzing out to tell everyone what you did?"

"I'm sick of it," Maeve said. "I hate what we've done. What you've done."

"Me?" Jennifer asked.

Maeve nodded. "If you hadn't killed her . . ."

"My mother?" Jennifer asked.

Kate watched Maeve and Jennifer sparring. Maeve shot her a glance that let her know that she was doing this to divert Jennifer, so Kate tapped Caroline's arm and began inching toward the door.

"Belle deserved it," Jennifer said. "It was bad enough that she spent the last year planning how to get invited to the wedding and how she had me make that little ring to resemble the one she claims Conor gave her when they were kids . . . It took up every minute of her life, her concentration. It was like I didn't exist other than to do things to perpetuate the fantasy. The ring. Stealing Kate's dress so she could try it on. Cutting up Kate's veil."

"What was the point of any of that?" Maeve asked. She was shifting her position so that Jennifer would have to pivot, leaving her back to Kate, Caroline, and Sam. Kate nudged Caroline, and they started moving faster toward the door.

"Her obsession was the point," Jennifer said. "And I'd had enough."

"I don't blame you," Maeve said. "All that, and you were just at the age for her to turn you into the new Belle."

"I hated her for that, and I hated you for making her go so crazy," Jennifer said, turning to face Kate. "Your marriage to Conor was going to finish her off."

Caroline caught her toe on the rug and stumbled. Kate stopped her from falling. Sam charged forward to the front door and slid the bolt. Kate heard the door open, and she heard Conor's voice: "Where's Kate?"

Jennifer must have heard it too. Or maybe Conor's presence didn't matter at all. Maybe she would have killed Kate no matter what, because when Kate looked over, she saw Jennifer holding a knife above her head, charging toward her. The knife blade flashed silver, and Jennifer gripped the handle so tightly, her fingers were white.

"Conor!" Kate called.

Hearing his name enraged Jennifer even more, and she let out a guttural scream. Kate tried to fight her off. She grabbed for the knife, felt searing pain as it slashed her palm. She stumbled and nearly lost her balance. She backed away from Jennifer, but Jennifer caught her, raised the knife overhead, and brought it down into Kate's chest, stabbing her over and over. Kate felt liquid running down her ribs. She looked at the floor and saw it covered with blood. She couldn't stand anymore, so she knelt in the blood, then lay down in it.

She heard Conor yelling, crying, saying her name. She felt him pick her up. She tried to keep her eyes open so she could look into his face. She saw agony in his eyes, and she wanted to tell him it was okay, she loved him. She loved him more than anything. They had had their time. She wouldn't have traded that for anything.

42

Conor sat beside Kate's bed in the intensive care unit at Rhode Island Hospital. She had been flown there by a medical transport helicopter two nights ago, had gone through multiple surgeries, and had been on life support ever since. Conor stared at her in the bright hospital light. She was hooked up to so many machines, with a breathing mask over her face, that by looking, he could barely tell it was Kate, but by his heart, he would know her no matter what.

Last night, her heart had stopped twice. The knife had barely missed it. Doctors determined that the thirteen stab wounds had caused extreme heart and lung failure. Her other organs began to fail, so they hooked her up to ECMO—an extracorporeal membrane oxygenation device.

It kept her heart and lungs going, doing all of the work for them. It kept her alive.

It was hard for Conor to remember everything that had happened back at Maynard-King. He had carried Kate outside after the stabbing, felt her hot blood soaking into his clothes, and laid her on the ground as gently as he could, kept his gaze fixed on her eyes as he held his hands over the gashes—so close to her heart. She had penetrating chest wounds, and he heard that telltale sucking sound as she struggled to breathe.

Tom had met them there on the lawn, and Joe showed up with a line of police cars, lights and sirens going. Conor pressed his hands into the knife wounds and tried to keep Kate's blood from pouring out of her body. Air hissed through the stab wound in her left lung.

"We need a helicopter," Tom shouted.

Conor was a first responder. He knew what to do—he had done it countless times. He saw Kate's life draining away, just as he had seen other victims of violent attacks losing their battles to stay alive. His muscle memory took over ministering to her injuries, while the rest of him tended to the part of Kate that was leaving this earth.

He couldn't communicate with words—he wasn't even sure she could hear them—so he did it with his soul. He talked to her. He felt her outside of her body, and he felt himself outside of his. There was energy that rose up from her heart, from his, it went up into the sky, and when he was up there with her, he could look down and see them both on the ground—her staring fiercely into his eyes as her blood spurted through his fingers.

He heard a voice saying *Don't go, don't leave me, I love you, I love you*, and even up in the sky he felt tears on his cheeks, and he knew the voice was his.

Her eyes had been open then. They stayed open even after the first EMTs arrived. They tried to push Conor aside so they could save her life. Conor had been in their shoes so often, had sternly ordered loved ones to step away from the accident or attack victim, to let the professionals do their jobs. Just then he didn't care—he didn't listen to the EMTs. He knelt beside Kate. He held her face between his hands, slick with her blood, and kept his eyes on hers.

As long as her eyes were open, she would be okay. She wouldn't go into cardiac arrest, she wouldn't have a stroke from blood loss, she wouldn't stop breathing because she couldn't get air. She needed him right there, she needed to see him looking at her, all of his love pouring from his eyes into hers. Eyes are the window of the soul, and they are the windows of the heart. His heart was giving her life. Her love was keeping him from dying right there on the ground next to her.

"Hey, Conor," Tom said, tugging his arm.

Conor shook him off. He moved his hands from Kate's face, because the EMTs were slipping an oxygen mask over her mouth, but he clutched her shoulders, as tightly as he could. Her eyes were still open. He was positive that she knew he was there. He was sure that she knew he would never let go of her.

There were words in his ears. *Pneumothorax, breathing tube, blood pressure falling, chest wall, shock.* And he heard her name being called over and over again. *Kate, Kate, Kate . . .*

Her eyes were still open.

Kate, Kate, Kate, how are you doing?

That time it wasn't him saying her name, asking that question. It was an EMT, trying to keep her alert. Conor heard the EMT speak louder, then stop because the rotors of the rescue helicopter were so deafening, coming from a distance, then almost overhead, and then when it landed on the open lawn.

The EMTs started shifting Kate onto a stretcher, but Conor wanted to stop them, they were being too rough, he wanted to carry her onto the helicopter himself. He shoved one of them out of the way, he heard that guy say *Hey, man!* And then he felt arms around him from behind. A strong grip, he fought against it, he was flailing his arms, he wanted to rip those arms off him. He heard his brother say his name, say they're helping her, let them take care of her. And then he heard himself say *Tom, I can't let her go.*

"You won't let her go," Tom said. "You're right there with her. She needs you. Get on the helicopter. That's it, Conor. Go with her . . ."

Tom gave him a shove, and Conor climbed onto the helicopter, behind the crew lifting the stretcher. He sat beside her as the helicopter took off straight into the wind, its nose pointed slightly downward, rotors roaring in his ears, on the way to the Level 1 trauma center at Rhode Island Hospital in Providence. Two flight nurses were wrapping blankets around Kate, taking vital signs, hooking her up to monitors. When they backed away, Conor looked down at her face. He tried to look into her beautiful eyes, but they weren't open anymore.

And now he was in the ICU with her. Her eyes hadn't opened even once since she had been lifted onto the helicopter. She was bandaged now. She had machines to circulate her blood, pump oxygen in and out of her lungs, send nutrients and antibiotics and morphine into her veins.

She had nurses checking on her every few minutes. They piled on blankets to keep her warm. One sensor monitored her heart rate and displayed it on a screen. Monitors revealed her rate of breathing and the level of oxygen in her body.

Her blood pressure was low. When it fell below a certain number, the machine beeped, and a nurse would come. They put her on pressors—medications to raise her blood pressure and increase cardiac function, to maintain blood flow to her organs.

Conor kept his eyes on Kate. The screens showed medical information, but they didn't tell him what he needed to know. He didn't even watch the rise and fall of her chest because that was determined by the respirator. He watched her eyes. He looked for the smallest flicker of her eyelids that told him she was dreaming.

Every time he saw that—a twitch, a tremble—he knew that she was working away, working so hard to get well. He knew that she was dreaming of the life she loved—the people she loved. She was dreaming of the sky—of flying above the sea in her plane, soaring over the islands, banking into the sun. She was dreaming of the ocean where she loved to swim, the beach where she loved to walk, the gallery she filled with paintings that stirred her soul and imagination.

And when he looked at her eyes closed tight, eyelashes resting on her cheeks, he saw how fiercely she was fighting. He knew that she was dreaming of coming back to him.

Conor was awake, but he was dreaming too. They were already married. They were living at Cloudlands. Everything was normal. They cooked dinner together, they watched movies, they sat outside and watched the sun set over Long Island Sound. Just ordinary things, daily things they didn't even have to think about. This was just their life.

The case against 1740 was coming together. It was strange to Conor, to think of Kate nearly being murdered and everything that had led up to it as a "case." He was a homicide detective. He knew how these things went. The people in the house had run to look outside when they heard the car alarm, but they had quickly returned to the room and saw Kate being stabbed. Every single one of them—no matter that they were part of 1740—would be a solid witness for the prosecution. And some of them were facing charges of their own.

Joe kept him informed. He had personally arrested Jennifer for attempted murder, and she was being held without bail. Conor heard this news as if it was coming through a telephone line running under the ocean. He knew that he might care about it someday, he knew that Jennifer deserved the stiffest punishment possible, but just then, he barely heard anything that Joe was telling him.

Nola, Crispin, and Leo were the first three to be charged with human trafficking, immediately remanded to jail. Maeve, Lincoln, and Suzanne were looking at a variety of charges, from trafficking to conspiracy to tampering with evidence. They weren't top-tier targets, and their ages and victim status complicated matters. Uncle Mike assured Conor that there would be many more arrests to follow. He would make sure that every single person involved would be prosecuted by both the office of the Rhode Island Attorney General and by the United States Attorney's Office of the District of Rhode Island.

Maynard-King had been shut down, and all patients had been transferred to other hospitals. A full investigation had already begun. The case was all over the news. The ICU staff were talking about it; the television in the waiting room blasted detail after detail. There were drone shots of the Maynard-King grounds, the Enchanted Petals property, and the hilltop mansion on Bellevigne Island. Reporters were scrambling to find *Psyche* and get the first photos of the horror chamber, but Tom had the vessel stored in a Coast Guard maintenance facility, behind a locked and well-guarded gate.

All of those things had happened. Tom, Joe, and Mike had made sure Conor knew how hard everyone was working on the case. How important it was to them to bring the criminals to justice. 1740 had been smashed. They told Conor that members were shaking in their boots, scared shitless that someone would make a plea deal—give up all their names in return for a lesser sentence.

Conor had lost track of time—time didn't really matter anymore. He existed on Kate's schedule in the ICU. A cardiac surgical resident called Conor away from Kate's bedside and asked if she had a living will. A Catholic priest came by and offered to give her last rites. Conor felt unreasonable rage and wanted to throw him out, but instead he closed his eyes and steadied himself while the priest prayed for Kate.

That night, after the priest had left, Conor listened to the beeping of the machines that kept Kate alive. The sounds were gentle; they meant that Kate was still here. After a while, Conor's eyelids got heavy, and he fell asleep in his chair.

He didn't know how long he was out, but all of a sudden, he woke with a start and looked at the watch on his wrist. Kate had given it to him last Christmas. The crystal was streaked with her blood. Conor hadn't cleaned it off, and he wouldn't. He could see the watch face clearly enough: It was 11:50 p.m. on July 8.

It was two days after she had been stabbed, five days after they were supposed to have been married.

It was ten minutes until midnight.

Why did the time matter to him? All of a sudden, it did, urgently. His heart sped up. He leaned forward, reaching over the guardrail on Kate's bed to take her hand. He suddenly had the strongest feeling that if she made it until midnight, she would make it one more day. Time would add up, minutes and hours would accumulate, and she would keep healing, and she would get well, she would be okay.

All she had to do was make it until midnight.

The machines kept her breathing, kept her blood flowing to her organs, and Conor held tightly to her hand. He didn't let go. He leaned over and kissed her. He whispered her name. He had things to say, and he needed for her to hear them.

Come on, Kate, he said. *One more day. Ten more minutes until midnight. Nine. Eight.*

One more day, Kate. Just make it until midnight . . . We're almost there. I love you, I love you, Kate. Will you marry me?

Seven, six.

Please live for another day.

Five, four.

Four minutes until midnight, Kate. Just make it until then, and we'll have forever.

Conor looked at his watch, at the second hand sweeping around the dial. The machines beeped. Kate's chest rose and fell, and Conor breathed in the same rhythm.

Three, two.

One.

Midnight.

43

Friday, December 24; 7:00 p.m.

This time, there was no tent.

Instead of bowers of hydrangeas, there would be laurel garlands and Christmas trees and fires in the fireplaces. There would be no calligraphed place cards, because at an almost-elopement, Kate knew exactly who everyone was and where she wanted them to sit. Besides, she wouldn't mind if she never saw calligraphed anything ever again.

There would definitely not be a rehearsal dinner.

At first, they really had planned to elope. No guests, just them. The talk had started on September 25.

Kate had stayed in the ICU for six weeks. She'd had cardiothoracic surgery, to repair a left ventricular tear and damage to blood vessels around the heart. She had needed other surgeries to repair lung and nerve damage and to address the other stab wounds. Just as she was about to move to a regular floor, a systemic infection set in. Sepsis razed through her body, causing her to spike a fever of 103 degrees. She needed another two weeks in the ICU with IV antibiotics to get the staph and strep infections under control.

She had been in a medically induced coma for part of her hospital stay, enough so that she remembered almost nothing of the first two months. Doctors told her that she had been close to death, flown by helicopter from Maynard-King to Rhode Island Hospital. They said that she had had surgery immediately upon arrival and several other operations in quick succession. They told her that she had been repeatedly stabbed and that she was very lucky that the knife had nicked her heart but missed a direct hit.

Visitors were limited in the ICU. She'd been told that Sam, Hadley, Tom, Jackie, Mike, Anne, and Tallulah had visited her; that even though CeCe was officially too young, she had been allowed one quick visit so she could leave Star with Kate. Star was the last fragment of CeCe's baby blanket, a four-inch square of threadbare flannel, and even though CeCe was now seven, she kept it close at all times—until tucking it into Kate's hand while Kate slept.

Kate remembered none of those visits from the people she loved so much.

Doctors told her that Conor had stayed with her almost twenty-four seven since she was admitted. They told her that he had taken indefinite leave from his detective job at the Connecticut State Police and been with her night and day.

The nurses told her that he had learned how to do many of the things they did: check her IVs, watch her O2 level and call them if he was alarmed, put salve on her bedsores and turn her body to relieve pressure on the worst ones, massage her legs to make sure she was getting good circulation, check her catheter and the color of urine flowing into the bag to make sure there wasn't blood in there.

Mostly he had just sat there, in a chair pulled close to Kate's bed, looking at her. He always had a book with him, but the nurses said he hardly ever seemed to read it. Sometimes he held Kate's hand. The nurses said that patients who stay in the hospital for a long time often get "helmet head"—where the hair gets so matted from having their head flat against the pillow. But Kate never did have that issue. Conor brushed her hair every day, and he made sure it never got tangled.

Even though Kate was in a coma and didn't remember her friends' and family's visits, she knew that Conor had been there every minute. She had felt him with her, as if he had been lying in the bed with her.

She remembered all the words he said to her—how much he loved her, how when she got better they would go to Baffin Island and see narwhals and the northern lights, how he would learn the guitar so he could write her songs, how they would elope.

Every single day, she heard him ask the same question: *Kate, will you marry me?*

And every single day, she answered: *Yes, Conor. I love you, I will marry you.*

The problem was, she was in a coma and couldn't form words or make her voice heard. But she believed that he knew what she was saying. Of course he did.

The day Kate woke up, she was completely disoriented. She could see that she was in a hospital room. When she'd been in the coma, she had traveled all kinds of places with Conor by her side—the Tower Suite at the Ocean House; the produce aisle in the Big Y; in her plane on the way to Block Island; in their bed at the Welcome Hotel in Villefranche-sur-Mer; in the Cocteau chapel, just down the quai.

Conor was the first to see her open her eyes. The funny thing was, she saw him open his too. When she first woke up, she saw him in a chair beside her bed. His eyes were closed, and he was asleep, making the little snoring sounds he always made when the sleep was deep. She stared at him for a long time. He must have felt it, because suddenly his eyes flew open and he stood up and leaned over her.

"Kate," he said. He grabbed her hand. He was both smiling and crying at the same time.

"Yes," Kate said. "I will."

For a moment, he looked confused.

She wondered whether he didn't know what she was talking about; that would be strange, because she was just answering the question he had been asking every day since she'd gotten here, during all their dream travels, during all the hushed hospital nights.

But then he knew exactly what she meant; she could tell because of the way his eyes softened.

"Can I ask you again, now that you're awake?" he asked.

She nodded.

"Will you marry me?"

And, for the second time since she'd opened her eyes, she said, "Yes. I will."

Then Kate said, "Why not do it here? We'll get the hospital chaplain to marry us. Our favorite nurses can be our witnesses."

Conor had been surprised and even a little leery that she was so ready to get married right away. After all they had gone through—the way their would-be summer wedding had been destroyed, how Kate's trust in him had been shattered, the hurt he'd felt when she'd turned against him, all the pangs of doubt about each other—he wasn't sure she would ever want to go through it again.

So, a few days after the hospital proposal, when the doctor had told her that getting out of bed was key to recovery, that walking a few steps each day was a goal, he asked her about it. They walked ten steps from the bed to the door of her room, where he had a wheelchair waiting.

Conor wheeled her to the family lounge at the end of the corridor. It had two separate seating areas. A group of grown children were clustered at one end of the room, speaking in low tones with a doctor while a talk show blared from a large TV. Conor pushed Kate's chair to the quieter part of the lounge.

"This is nice, getting out of the room," she said, taking in the surroundings—generic seascapes on the mint-green walls, a patterned sofa and matching chairs, and painted wooden signs with sayings like *Live Love Laugh; Life's a Beach; There is Always Hope.*

"I only take you to the best places," Conor said.

"You do, indeed," she said.

"You went through a nightmare," Conor said.

"Let's not talk about that," she said.

"We don't have to," he said. "But you really want to marry me, after everything?"

She looked into Conor's blue eyes, and her own vision clouded up with tears. Her stab wounds were covered with bandages—the doctors hadn't stitched them up, because that could trap bacteria inside and cause more infection. When she closed her eyes, she sometimes had visions of *them*—she didn't want to say their names or even think of them—the people of 1740, the girl who had stabbed her.

"I do," she said. "I want to marry you. And what about you? Do you still want to marry me, after what I did?"

"What did you do?" he asked, looking confused.

"I wrecked it the first time. I doubted you. I believed her just long enough . . ."

"Her?"

"I don't want to say her name," Kate said, shaking her head.

"Love means that you never have to," Conor said, and they both laughed.

Conor held her hand. The worried look had returned to his face. Their time in the family lounge had taken a lot out of Kate. He sensed that without her having to tell him, and he wheeled her back to her room and lifted her into bed.

Then it was October.

A few days before Halloween, Kate was well enough to leave the hospital but still not ready to go home, so Conor hired a private ambulance to drive her to a nursing facility in Westerly. Sam had gotten her room ready for her—with her favorite blanket, a pile of books, the kai body cream she loved, and some paintings from the gallery. The nursing home's halls were decorated with jack-o'-lanterns and cutouts of witches and ghosts. On Halloween, the residents gathered in the dining hall, and volunteers wearing costumes passed out SNICKERS bars and Reese's Cups.

Thanksgiving came. Conor had hoped to take Kate home for a big dinner with the family, but the doctors advised she give it another few weeks. She still needed wound care to make sure the infections didn't recur, and she needed more physical therapy to get her strong enough to move with more confidence and return to her regular activities.

Kate worked as hard as hell. She not only did PT, she also continued the exercises after the therapist left for the day. She stopped calling for help getting to the bathroom and did it all on her own—including showers. Instead of picking at the food, she ate full meals. She knew she needed to gain weight—she had lost twenty-five pounds when she was in the coma—so she concentrated on building up her muscle mass with healthy food and exercise.

Her mental health was precarious—she kept having nightmares, and for the first time in her life, she had panic attacks. She had almost died; her heart had stopped more than once. She hadn't felt pain at the moment of being stabbed—she'd felt numb. The pain came later; she'd felt it even when she was in the coma, writhing in her body, beneath the sea of morphine.

Conor protected her from the news the best he could. He wouldn't let anyone bring up what had happened. It was up to Kate, if and when she wanted to talk about it. Slowly, she began to ask him questions. Conor told her just as much as she could take at a time. And every time she absorbed a detail, she'd get incredibly tired and have to go to sleep.

And then she had a visitor.

The day after Thanksgiving, someone knocked on the door of her room. Conor was out for a few hours, and Kate had been dozing after a particularly grueling round of PT. But the knock woke her up, and when she opened her eyes, she saw Caroline standing by her bed.

"Hi," Caroline said. "Do you remember me?"

"Of course," Kate said. "How are you doing?"

"Oh god," Caroline said, shaking her head. "The real question is, how are *you* doing? Are you okay?"

"Yes," Kate said.

"After what she did to you? I . . . I thought you were going to die."

"I almost did," Kate said. "But they brought me back. Tell me about you."

"I got rescued that day," Caroline said. "I watched the police arrest them all. It felt so good, seeing *them* in handcuffs instead of us, taken away. I heard them screaming their excuses—telling the police they were making a mistake. Those rich, important people . . . now they're all locked up."

"That's good," Kate said. She still had pangs about Maeve, who had seemed to have a change of heart at the end, and about Lincoln, whom she had come to like. She thought of all the years Crispin had been her client, how many paintings she had helped him choose, how she had enjoyed their conversations, how deftly he had hidden the person he really was.

Conor walked into Kate's room and found Caroline there. At first, he wanted to usher her out, thinking that her presence would bring back too many bad memories. But Kate signaled that she was fine.

"I just hope 1740 eventually gets completely wiped out," Caroline said. "I'm sure a lot of it is underground, and members are everywhere. They've found ways to hide, until they can pop up in another location."

"Don't be too sure of that," Conor said. "They're finished."

Kate turned her head to look at him. He never talked about the case because she hadn't wanted to hear about it.

"They are?" Kate asked. "But how?"

"Yeah, how?" Caroline asked. "There are so many members. They protect each other. And they are so good at lying."

"That is true," Conor said. "But one of them is going to give it all up."

"What does that mean?" Kate asked.

"The ultimate insider has a black book with the names and numbers of every member of 1740, the dates of every meeting, every time they assaulted women," Conor said.

"Every time a Belle met a Beast," Caroline said softly.

"These are federal offenses because some of the victims were taken across state lines," Conor said. "And the Feds are negotiating a deal with the insider in return for cooperation in the trials. There will be *many* trials."

"Who is the ultimate insider?" Kate asked.

"Nola," Caroline said before Conor could answer.

"That's right," Conor said.

"Nola Aldrich," Kate said. She still couldn't believe it. Although she hadn't known Nola long, she had trusted her because they had been introduced by Conor's aunt and uncle. She knew that Mike and Anne were devastated by the fact that they had brought both Nola and Leo Kennedy into the Old Detectives family circle. And as much as Kate had tried to reassure them that she understood, they were still gutted.

"Nola knows everything," Caroline said. "She trained the women, and she knew all the men—friends from her social circle, and their friends too . . . She would get referrals, and as long as the men had the right pedigrees, they were in. And it was never for money. It wasn't like she was a society madam or anything."

"Then, what?" Kate asked.

"She liked the adulation. It made her feel important, in the eyes of Crispin and some of the others, to be able to fulfill fantasies."

"Not only that," Conor said, "but when Joe traced 1740 back to that old ad in the Yellow Pages, he found out that Nola's mother was involved with the original group. Passed down through the generations."

"They were proud of the lineage," Caroline said.

"You know, what you did aboard *Psyche* helped the Feds nail her," Conor said. "Their negotiating position wouldn't have been nearly as strong if you hadn't done that."

"What did you do?" Kate asked.

"I learned from one of the women who came before me," Caroline said.

"In what way?" Kate asked.

"I don't even know her name, but I saw the scratches she had made on the porthole on *Psyche*, and that gave me an idea. Nola told us all that the men wanted to think of us as princesses," Caroline said. "They gave us jewels and expected us to wear them. I had this gigantic diamond ring on my finger while I was chained down—it was probably the same one my predecessor wore before they killed her. I could just reach up to the porthole, and I scratched NOLAFS into the glass—for 'Nola Finishing School.'"

"Tom and I saw it, but we were looking from the wrong direction. We read it back to front, and some of the letters were backward. We thought it said SFALON. Or maybe the *S* was really a 5," Conor said. "Even though we didn't figure it out then, it will help the prosecution nail her—and all of them."

The conversation had almost finished Kate off. There was just so much she could handle hearing at one time. Her fists must have been clenched, because Conor reached for her hand; she relaxed it, and he kissed her palm.

"Thanks for the visit, Caroline," Conor said.

"I'd better say goodbye now," Kate said. "I'm getting a little tired."

"I understand," Caroline said. "But, Kate . . ." Caroline closed her eyes tight, and tears spilled down her cheeks. "I want to thank you. You kept me going that day. I don't think I could have survived whatever was going to happen next."

"You helped me too," Kate said.

"You gave me something so important," Caroline said. "You gave me William."

"How?"

"I think I told you that we were engaged. We were going to be married, when Crispin killed him and took me. I kept William with me, the best I could, while I was in that place. But I was faking it. I felt as if no love could survive that. No matter how good it had been, it was ruined. But then I met you and Conor."

Kate glanced at Conor, saw him staring, rapt, at Caroline.

"And I've learned what they put you through. What Belinda did and how Maeve and Suzanne helped her stop your wedding, how they tried to keep you from trusting and loving each other."

"They could never do that," Conor said. "It was tough, but we made it. We have each other."

"Just like I have William," Caroline said. "Knowing you has taken away the poison Crispin tried to pour on our love. I hope . . . you'll send me a wedding announcement. I want to know when it happens, and I'll celebrate you from wherever I am. I hope you'll have a big, wonderful wedding."

"Actually," Kate said, "we're going to elope. We're going to do it here."

She looked at Conor to affirm that, but he didn't. He didn't nod. He didn't say he agreed. He just smiled and thanked Caroline for coming. Caroline leaned over to kiss Kate's forehead, and she left.

Alone with each other, Conor gazed at Kate.

"Really?" he asked. "If that is truly what you want, to elope right here, I'll do it."

"It's not what you want?" Kate asked.

"No, it's not," Conor said.

"Then what?"

"I want to marry you at the Ocean House. I want us to stay in the Tower Suite. I want it to be in December, as close to the date when I proposed to you and you said yes," he said. "I want there to be music. I want to feed you wedding cake. I want to dance until midnight."

Kate closed her eyes. Thoughts and memories sped through her mind: the tent, the rehearsal dinner, the chapel, the hydrangeas, the dress. Every single memory hurt, but they also made her smile—because every detail had been decided with love. She and Conor loved the Ocean House more than anywhere in the world. It was where they had gotten engaged, and it held magic for them that they never found anywhere else.

"You're right," she said. "That's where we are getting married. The Ocean House."

"On Christmas Eve?" he asked.

"Yes," she said. "On Christmas Eve. Can we have snow?"

"Of course we can," Conor says.

Did he look a little nervous, making that promise? Kate smiled and kissed him. Not letting him off the hook for snow, but just because she wanted to kiss him.

And so, here they were.

It was Christmas Eve.

Outside the Ocean House, the verandah sparkled with white lights woven around evergreen garlands, wrapping the banisters, and up the stately white columns. A great, enormous wreath hung from the top of the portico, festive scarlet ribbons whipping in the ferocious winter wind. Snow blew sideways, straight off the Atlantic.

There was a nor'easter, and Conor swore to Kate that he hadn't planned it. He had proposed to her right here, in a suite upstairs, in a blizzard, at CeCe's party.

So, with that history, how could they not have CeCe as their flower girl? And Hadley, CeCe's aunt, as a bridesmaid? And Sam as Kate's maid of honor?

Tom, of course, was best man. His wife, Jackie, was a bridesmaid too. Actually, so was Aunt Anne.

Uncle Mike, in his capacity as a judge, would officiate.

Brian Goldrick was there to join them, and to serve Foggy Nights—the special cocktail he had created last summer, just for Kate and Conor's wedding.

The Watch Hill Chapel was the place Kate had dreamed of getting married, of walking down the aisle under curved beams reminiscent of the ribs of an old ship. She had always loved the messages beside the altar, especially:

THE CHURCH IS MANY

—AS THE WAVES—

BUT ONE AS THE SEA

But the chapel opened in June and closed in September, the lovely building suited only for the warmer weather, so Kate and Conor invited their guests to join them in the Tower Suite for their wedding. Frances, the fairy godmother of Ocean House weddings, made it perfect.

There was a fire in the hearth. No blue hydrangeas this time, and Kate had specifically requested no roses. Frances had offered to fill the suite with white ranunculus, bouvardia, calla lilies, anemone, and tulips, and at first Kate had said no, she didn't need a lot of flowers. Plus, flowers were such a big part of 1740: Enchanted Petals, the roses that opened and died and fell away.

But Sam had convinced Kate that she did need flowers.

"Auntie, the world went dark for a while, and nothing was in bloom. It was as if all the flowers died. I thought they'd never come back. But you're alive, you survived. I want you to have a whole garden. We all want that because we're so grateful you're here," Sam said, breaking down and hugging Kate so hard it hurt.

So Kate had said yes, and Frances had chosen the most beautiful flowers to be found anywhere, never mind in a blizzard. And Kate was so glad she did, because she had driven all those wicked associations away. She had given Kate a garden of love.

The Tower Suite was at the very top of the Ocean House. The suite had multiple levels. Kate got dressed in the bedroom; Conor and their wedding guests were one flight up. Faith, the harpist, was playing, but the roaring wind nearly drowned her out. Kate looked out the window and saw snow falling so hard it was impossible to see the ocean. The beam of Watch Hill Lighthouse was a mere flicker through the whiteout.

Kate's wounds had mostly healed, but the nerves were still raw, the muscles still strained. She didn't have a gown this time. She had a cream-colored long silk skirt that she'd worn in the past and a white cashmere cardigan that had belonged to her sister, Beth.

"Okay if I come in?" Conor asked through the closed bedroom door.

"Yes," Kate said.

He entered the room and walked over to where Kate stood by the bureau. Very carefully, he helped her step into her silk skirt, one leg at a time. He pulled it up, and she closed the button at her waist. He slid the sweater around her shoulders and gingerly helped her put each arm into a sleeve. She had to sit down on the edge of the bed from the exertion.

While she was sitting there, catching her breath, Conor brushed her hair. That gave her a chance to look at him. He was dressed the way he always was when they did something special: a blue blazer, white oxford shirt, striped tie, and gray pants.

Sam had offered to help Kate get dressed, but Kate had thanked her and said no. There was only one person she wanted to do this with her, and that was Conor. He had held her, fed her, loved her in ways she had never imagined possible. Even though it might have traditionally been the maid of honor's role to help the bride get ready, Kate knew she wanted only Conor.

"Are you okay?" he asked.

"I didn't think I was going to make it," she said, her voice shaking. "Back in the hospital—not the first night, maybe the second—I died, didn't I? I heard the nurses call a code, I felt the paddles on my chest. Or did I just dream that?"

"You didn't dream it," Conor said, taking her hand.

"You know how you hear stories about when people die, or almost die, they go toward the light?"

"Yes," he said.

"I didn't go toward the light," she said, swallowing hard. "I went toward you."

"Kate . . ."

"I felt myself dying," she said. "And all I could think about was, I want to see Conor again. I want him to have the most beautiful life, but when it's over, I want us to be together. I was seriously prepared to kick the bucket. And then, you know what?"

"What?"

"I was in that tunnel, and the white light at the end, and I said no way. So I turned around, and instead of going toward the light, I went toward you."

Conor put his arms around her. She felt his heart pounding through his chest. "Do you know when that was? What day?"

"I have no idea," she said.

"I think I know," he said. "There was one night when I was really afraid. You were on life support. Your heartbeat was so weak. Kate, I could feel you leaving me. And I held your hand and just kept saying—stay, stay with me. Just one more day. If you can make it until midnight, you're going to be okay. And you did—you made it until midnight, and then it was the next day, and the day after that, and now we're here."

Kate closed her eyes. She swore she could remember that night: hearing Conor begging her to stay with him, asking her to marry him. She was sure it was his voice, those words, that had made her decide it wasn't time to die, that she wanted to turn around and return to life. Return to Conor.

"Are you ready?" he asked after a minute.

"Not quite," she said.

"Is this too much?" he asked.

"Not at all," she said. She wrapped her arms around him, eased him down onto the bed so they were facing each other. She kissed him and wished the kiss could go on forever. They stayed there for a long time, holding each other.

Outside the Ocean House, the wind was howling. The snow fired off the Atlantic Ocean. It drifted on the long white sands of East Beach. It covered Bluff Avenue, obscured the view of the harbor down the hill. It tapped against the hotel windows. Kate and Conor lay together, looking into each other's eyes, and this time, she asked him:

"Are you ready?"

"I am," he said.

So they stood up and held hands. Upstairs, in the living room of the Tower Suite, their guests were waiting. Tom had offered to walk Kate up the stairs, give the bride away, but Kate had said no. There was only one person to do that.

Conor.

So the bride-to-be took the arm of her betrothed, and Kate Woodward and Conor Reid walked slowly up the stairs on their way to be married.

ACKNOWLEDGMENTS

Thank you to Jeff and Betsey Cooley of the Cooley Gallery in Old Lyme, Connecticut, for all our conversations about art, especially the Old Lyme Art Colony and the artists who stayed with Miss Florence during the early twentieth century (her house is now the Florence Griswold Museum). I so appreciated being able to talk with them about James Suydam (not an Old Lyme artist, and from an earlier period, but he did paint in Rhode Island, where this novel takes place) and the fictional painting that appears in these pages. Although, as far as I know, Suydam never did a painting called *Foggy Night*, his Luminist style inspired the imaginary work I wrote about. The painting does not exist in real life, but I hope you can see it in your mind, or if you ever visit East Beach in Watch Hill on a foggy, moonlit night.

I am grateful to Lieutenant Robert Derry—Connecticut State Police (retired) and Clinton, Connecticut, harbormaster—for the many years he has answered my questions about law enforcement. And to think our friendship began at Hubbard's Point, when he asked me to sign a book for his mom!

Matthew Cavaco USCG (retired) has been invaluable in helping me understand the investigative work Tom Reid does. (All mistakes are mine.) Matt has so much knowledge, so many experiences at sea, and I am always riveted to hear him talk about them. I very much appreciate him for that, and for his years of service in the United States Coast Guard.

Much gratitude to Patrick Carson for his friendship and support, and for being a wonderful social media manager.

Thank you to Ron Bernstein, my friend and film agent, for all our years together.

I send love to everyone at the Ocean House. You are the reason it is my home away from home. Thank you for everything!

Much gratitude to William Twigg Crawford for sharing his maritime knowledge and for telling all the old stories.

Thank you to my agent and dear friend, Andrea Cirillo, for being with me all through the years. I am grateful to everyone at JRA—the Jane Rotrosen Agency: Jane Berkey, Jessica Errera, Chris Prestia, Julianne Tinari, Meg Ruley, Christina Hogrebe, Amy Tannenbaum, Annelise Robey, Rebecca Scherer, Kathy Schneider, Danielle Marshall, Logan Harper, Casey Conniff, Celine Yarde, Allison Hufford, Kelly Olsen, Nancy Russo, John Achilla, Kristen Comeaux, Maria Burfield, Maria Mogavero, and, forever, Donald Cleary.

I am thankful to the wonderful Liz Pearsons of Thomas & Mercer. Thank you to Gracie Doyle for the amazing support. I am grateful to Charlotte Herscher and the rest of my publishing team, including Miranda Gardner, Ploy Siripant, Jarrod Taylor, Brittany Morris, Nicole Wagner, Davy Kent, Sarah Vostok, and Stephen Schul.

ABOUT THE AUTHOR

Photo © 2025 Noelle Wolcin

Luanne Rice is the *New York Times* bestselling author of thirty-nine novels, including *Last Night*, *The Shadow Box*, and *Last Day*. Several have been adapted for television: *Crazy in Love* for TNT, *Blue Moon* for CBS, *Follow the Stars Home* and *Silver Bells* for Hallmark Hall of Fame, and *Beach Girl* as a Lifetime miniseries. For more information, visit www.luannerice.com.